About the Authors

With the publication of *Temptation's Song* in July 2010, **Janice Sims** celebrates fourteen years as a romance writer. In fourteen years she's published seventeen novels and had nine stories included in anthologies. When asked why she writes romances, she smiles and says it's the only genre in which happily ever after is a foregone conclusion. Plus, where else are you going to find a perfect male?

Nina Singh lives just outside Boston, USA, with her husband, children, and a very rumbunctious Yorkie. After several years in the corporate world she finally followed the advice of family and friends to 'give the writing a go, already'. She's oh-so-happy she did. When not at her keyboard she likes to spend time on the tennis court or golf course. Or immersed in a good read.

Kate Hardy has been a bookworm since she was a toddler. When she isn't writing Kate enjoys reading, theatre, live music, ballet and the gym. She lives with her husband, student children and their spaniel in Norwich, England. You can contact her via her website: katehardy.com

D1388331

A Christmas Proposal

JANICE SIMS

NINA SINGH

KATE HARDY

MILLS & BOON

First Published in Great Britain 2022
By Mills & Boon, an imprint of HarperCollins*Publishers* Ltd
1 London Bridge Street, London, SE1 9GF
www.harpercollins.co.uk

HarperCollins*Publishers*
1st Floor, Watermarque Building,
Ringsend Road, Dublin 4, Ireland

A CHRISTMAS PROPOSAL © 2022 Harlequin Enterprises ULC

A Little Holiday Temptation © 2012 Janice Sims
Snowed in with the Reluctant Tycoon © 2017 Nilay Nina Singh
Christmas Bride for the Boss © 2017 Pamela Brooks

ISBN: 978-0-263-31790-9

MIX
Paper | Supporting
responsible forestry
FSC™ C007454

This book is produced from independently certified FSC™ paper
to ensure responsible forest management.

For more information visit: www.harpercollins.co.uk/green

Printed and Bound in Spain using 100% Renewable electricity
at CPI Black Print, Barcelona

A LITTLE HOLIDAY TEMPTATION

JANICE SIMS

Thanks to Glenda Howard for agreeing to publish this book when I asked her if it could be my next Kimani Romance book due to heightened reader interest. Also to Shannon Criss, whose editorial assistance was most appreciated. And, as always, thanks to my agent, Sha-Shana Crichton, for her kindness and encouragement.

Chapter 1

The cab pulled up to the midtown Manhattan restaurant whose large picture windows spilled forth a welcoming golden light. After paying the driver, Ana Corelli paused a moment with her hand on the door's handle. Nervousness caused her stomach muscles to clench painfully. Today she had made a decision that would change her life forever. If anyone would understand why she'd done it, Erik would.

With a determined grimace she opened the cab's door and stepped out. She shivered a little in the cold October night's air. "Thank you."

"My pleasure, Ms. Corelli," said the driver, craning his neck to smile at her.

Ana was no longer surprised when someone recognized her. Due to magazine covers, print ads, fashion shows and TV ads, her image was all over the world. She returned his smile. "You have a good evening," she said in parting, her Italian accent slight but present. She had grown up speaking both English and Italian. Her mother was an African-American opera singer who had married an Italian and moved to Milan. Ana, her brother, Dominic, and sister, Sophia, had been taught to revere both cultures.

After the cab sped away, she smoothed her leather jacket over her skirt and adjusted the bag on her shoulder before resolutely walking toward the restaurant's entrance. The hostess, an attractive African-American woman, smiled warmly as she approached her. "Good to see you again, Ms. Corelli, Mr. Whitaker is at the bar. We anticipate a twenty-minute wait for a table."

"Thank you," said Ana pleasantly. "I'll join Mr. Whitaker at the bar, then."

"Enjoy your evening," said the hostess, and returned to her post in time to greet a young couple entering the restaurant.

Ana stopped in her tracks when she spotted Erik sitting on a barstool at the cherrywood bar, a glass of lager sitting in front of him that looked like it hadn't been touched. She smiled. He wasn't a big drinker. Today, he was wearing a tailored dark blue suit with a white shirt and maroon-striped silk tie. It was Friday and he'd probably come straight here from the office. He rarely got out of there before seven.

She slid onto the stool beside him. He looked at her reflection in the mirror behind the bar, and smiled at her. Turning to her, his eyes swept over her face. "So, how does it feel to be back in the world of the living?"

She grinned, and leaned in to kiss his cheek. He smelled good, as if he'd taken the time to shave his five-o'clock shadow in his office bathroom before leaving to meet her. She placed her hand along his strong jaw. Erik looked at her in his enigmatic way. Those golden-hued eyes seemed to bore into her soul. "I finished the last painting only a few hours ago," she told him softly. "I slept for a couple hours then woke up, phoned you, and here I am. I've missed you."

"I've missed you, too," he murmured close to her ear. The sound of his voice, as always, made her warm inside.

She'd spent the last two weeks exiled in her Greenwich Village loft, completing paintings that would comprise her first show at a New York City gallery. Erik knew this. However he didn't know why she had asked to see him tonight.

She was about to blurt it out when a woman sat down on the other side of Erik and accidentally knocked her martini glass over, causing the drink to spill onto Erik's leg. Luckily, the woman had nearly finished the drink before sitting down so Erik only received a small stain on his pants' leg.

The woman grabbed a handful of napkins from the bar's top and began pressing the wadded up napkins on top of Erik's leg, apologizing all the while. "I'm so sorry," she said, screwing up her beautiful face in a pretty pout. "I'm such a klutz."

Erik laughed shortly, and held the woman's hand at bay. If she ran her hand any higher up on his leg, she would get entirely too personal for his comfort. "It's all right," he assured her. "It's an old suit."

The woman, who was dressed in designer clothes herself, obviously knew quality when she saw it. She was certainly looking at it. He was around six-one and in great shape. His clean-shaven, square-chinned face was handsome in a rugged, utterly masculine way. His eyes were so beautiful, she could drown in them, and if his voice were any sexier, she'd melt. She peered at his shoes, his watch, how perfectly his suit fit him, his skin, his teeth, his haircut, and realized that with him, money was no object. She wouldn't have conveniently spilled her drink on him if he had looked penniless.

"At least let me buy you a drink," she said. Her big brown eyes were very persuasive.

"That's sweet of you," said Erik, "but I already have a drink, and was just about to order one for my date." He indicated Ana with a nod in her direction.

The woman looked over at Ana who had watched the scene with an amused expression. She'd seen women use that "spilled drink" trick on more than one occasion. Erik was too much of a gentleman, however, to call the woman out on it.

"Oh," said the woman, her ample chest heaving with a sigh, "I see." Still not willing to give up entirely, she withdrew a card from her purse and placed it in Erik's palm. "Perhaps we can have that drink some other time," she said for his ears only.

She smoothly removed herself from the barstool, not giving him a chance to return her card, if he was of that mind. Looking at Ana, she said in parting, "Did anyone ever tell you you're a dead ringer for Ana Corelli?"

What nerve! Ana thought angrily. She sent mental daggers into the woman's retreating back. How desperate do you have to be to boldly accost a man who was obviously with another woman? She had to take several deep breaths before she trusted herself to return her attention to Erik who was watching her with a smile touching the corners of his generous mouth. "Where were we?" he asked, coaxing her back into their intimate circle.

For a moment, Ana couldn't form words. Heat flared in her face. Now she knew how being hot under the collar felt. For some reason that woman's behavior made her fiercely protective of Erik and ready to defend her territory. But Erik wasn't her territory. They were friends. In the beginning, he had told her he was attracted to her and wanted to date her, but at that time she had just gotten out of a disastrous relationship with an egotistical actor whose treatment of her had left her insecure. She'd told Erik that they could be friends, but she was giving up on dating for a while, but she hadn't dated anyone else since they had started hanging together. Come to think of it, neither had he that she knew of. Could he have a secret lover? Someone he hooked up with on occasion to satisfy his needs? He was a red-blooded male, after all. She had longings herself. It only stood to reason that he did, too.

Suddenly she was wondering if she were standing in his way of a real relationship. Someone he could get serious about, and consider marrying. Erik, married and no longer a major part of her life? The thought made her cringe inwardly. She could not imagine life without Erik.

"Ana?"

Ana realized Erik was waiting on her to tell him why she'd called. She cleared her throat. "I quit my day job," she announced.

Erik didn't look surprised. "You've been talking about it for a long time. Modeling doesn't make you happy, painting does. You should follow your heart."

"I still have to fulfill my cosmetics contract, plus my family's company is starting a new line of clothing for full-figured women. I'll be appearing in ads for it since I've put on a few pounds." She looked at him out of the corner of her eye to see if he'd respond to the mention of extra pounds. But there was no reaction whatsoever.

Erik only smiled. He had noticed. The added ten pounds or so made her look healthier and less angular. She'd filled out in all the right places, fuller breasts and hips, a rounder, less concave belly. He loved her new body. She had always been sexy to him. Now even sexier. He could tell she knew it, too. There was more jiggle in her walk, as if she were indeed feeling confident about her new body.

Of course, he couldn't say that out loud. They were supposed to be just friends. If she knew he coveted her body, often dreamed of making love to her, there was no telling how she would react. He remembered when he'd tried to date her in the beginning. She'd told him she'd given up on men. If he wanted to be a part of her life, he would have to be satisfied with her friendship, nothing else. It had been two long years. His frustration was coming to a head. He wanted, no, he *needed* more. Every time he resolved to tell her how he felt, however, he would talk himself out of it because having her in his life was preferable to not having her in his life at all. If she gave him any indication of feeling about him the way he felt about her, though, he would jump on the opportunity with both feet. All he needed was a sign.

The way she was looking at that woman who had come on to him could possibly be that sign. Could it be that she was possessive of him? The thought was intriguing.

The bartender took her drink order and once they were alone again, Ana regarded him with a contemplative expression on her face and said, "You and I have always been honest with each other, haven't we?"

A cautious man, Erik took a moment to wonder why she would ask that. "I've always thought so," he replied hesitantly.

Ana smiled warmly. Dimples appeared in both cheeks. Her deep brown eyes held his gaze. "Am I standing in the way of your future happiness?"

"What?" He looked genuinely puzzled. Then, he laughed. Looking down at the card lying on the bar the woman from earlier had given him, he said, "You mean that?" He met her gaze once more. "You know how I feel about you. I'm the man who's willing to wait, remember?" She detected no bitterness in his voice, which made her feel even worse.

She could let it drop but she had to get to the heart of the matter. "You don't feel as if I've been using you these past two years? I know you said you would wait until I was ready for a relationship. But maybe you've changed your mind and our being friends all this time has made you see me in a different light—as a friend. Not a lover."

Erik's brows raised in an incredulous expression. If anything, the time they'd spent together had made him fall for her even harder. They had met in Milan, on the opening night of *Temptation,* Ana's brother Dominic's modern opera, nearly two years ago. Initially, he had to admit, his attraction to her was physical. There was no denying she was gorgeous. Five ten and built for sin. Skin the color of toasted almonds. She had a heart-shaped face with big brown eyes, a well-shaped nose, full, sensually curved lips and a cleft in her chin, which gave her a distinctive look. Her naturally wavy black hair was long and usually falling down her back. Yes, all the physical parts fit together very nicely. But that was only part of why he loved Ana. To know her was to love her, and knowing her made him privy to her inner workings. For example, there was a great mind behind that beautiful face. She would rather be curled up with a good book than go to a social event where she would be the center of attention. Material posses-sions, though she could very well afford the best, were not of utmost importance to her. She gave generously of her time and money. And family meant more to her than anything else in the world.

"If you're asking if I'm no longer interested in you... romantically, then the answer is don't be ridiculous. Just give me the word and I'll throw you over my shoulder and take you to my place right now and make love to you all night long." His sensual perusal made her blush.

She demurely lowered her eyes and gave a contented sigh. So, he still wanted her. That was good to know. Now, what was she going to do about it? She raised her eyes to his. "Have you ever considered the idea of our being friends with benefits?"

Because she most certainly had—many, many times!

The bartender walked up and placed her chilled white wine in front of her, then promptly departed. She took a fortifying sip as she awaited Erik's answer. What was wrong with her tonight, she wondered. Was the fact that she had made one big decision psychologically urging her to make an even bigger one? She had been dragging her feet about their relationship because she was so content with Erik in her life. Why mess with perfection? Her last relationship had ended after she'd become intimate with the guy. It was as if getting her into bed was the ultimate goal and once that was accomplished she wasn't desirable to him anymore. And the guy before him had dropped her because she'd wanted to wait until she knew him better before going to bed with him. He had been conceited enough to tell her a requirement to being with him was sex, and lots of it. He'd called *her* a freak of nature! She was sure she was probably complicating her problem with men too much. She'd simply made bad choices in men. She was twenty-five and had had only one lover, and he'd turned out to be a bastard. Intellectually, she knew this. However, telling that to her broken heart was another thing, entirely.

Erik was so different from the others. He was solid and reliable. A brilliant businessman, he had taken his family's company to new heights. Of course, his father, John Whitaker, had given him a wonderful foundation to build upon but Erik was continuing the tradition of making the family name an honorable one in big business. Known for buying failing companies and turning them around, thereby saving the jobs of many Americans, Erik found satisfaction in a job well done.

His cognac-colored eyes held an amused expression when he answered her question, his tone seductive, "About twice a day, maybe four times a day on weekends."

Ana fanned her face. She'd flushed upon hearing him admit that. So, she wasn't the only one who had sex on the brain. "I've thought of it just as often," she admitted.

"But I'd never actually do it," said Erik, his expression turning serious. He sighed and sat up straighter on the barstool. Looking deep into her eyes, he said, "Ana, being friends with benefits means that you will somehow be able to detach yourself from your feelings while you're making love. I could never do that with you. When we make love it's going to be seriously emotional. I'm not going to hold anything back. Everything

I've wanted to express to you in a physical way over the last two years will be in every touch. So, if you want me, you'll have to take all of me, not just a part of me."

Ana was trying to calm her racing heart. The man was hot as hell. What would happen if she just let go and told him, "yes, let's go back to your place right now? It's time." Actually it was way past time to do something about the sexual tension building between them.

She was glad when the hostess approached and said their table was ready. Erik handed the bartender a tip and with it, the woman's card. "Would you mind disposing of that for me?"

He then escorted Ana to their table and helped her into her chair.

"Your waiter will be with you shortly," said the hostess, and left.

"You were saying?" Erik said, looking at Ana expectantly.

"You're right," Ana said a bit breathlessly. "We're well past the friends-with-benefits stage. I couldn't make love to you, and then return to being just friends the next day. I'm not made that way."

Erik grasped her hand. "I have to say I'm a little surprised by the suggestion. What brought this on?"

Suddenly Ana knew exactly why she hadn't given in to Erik until now. It wasn't just that she was afraid of messing up a good thing. The epiphany was a relief to her. But it also made her a little sad. Looking him straight in the eyes, Ana said, her voice awe filled, "I kept putting you off because…I didn't feel worthy of you."

"How could you have felt that way?" Erik asked. Surprise was evident in his tone.

Ana cut him off with, "I know it never crossed your mind. But listen, please. I grew up in a family of over-achievers. My mother was a world-renowned singer. My father has run the family business for decades with great success, and my sister is following in his foot-steps. Do I need to mention how beloved my brother, the maestro, is?" She paused to breathe. "Growing up, I didn't know what to do with myself. I loved to draw but in a country like Italy where so many of the great artists were born I felt more than a little intimidated. I hid my work for years, not wanting anyone to see what I'd created. Then, when I was a teenager and I just kept growing, five-ten at fifteen, someone told me I should be a model and I thought to myself, 'That's something I could be good at,' and to my utter surprise I was signed to an agency right away. But I never felt as if it were an accomplishment. After all, beauty is something you inherit from your parents. It's not something you earn."

"I think a lot of people who work hard on their physi-cal appearance would disagree with you," Erik pointed out.

"Yes, of course I have to eat right and exercise, but this face was a gift from God," Ana countered.

"Are you feeling guilty again because your image is used to make women feel insecure?" he asked softly. "So insecure that they'll buy the products your face helps to sell in order to aim for an impossibly high standard of beauty?"

"No, it isn't, Dr. Freud. It's about leaving behind something lasting when I'm dead," Ana insisted, smiling at his instant psychoanalysis. Although, she did, like several other models she knew, feel guilty about propagating an image of perfection that was, frankly, a lie. She had been honest in several interviews about the hours spent being made-up and then, if the subsequent photographs weren't up to par, being airbrushed to make them perfect.

"You're a man of substance, a man whose life means much more than the pursuit of self-gratification. To me, what you do is inspiring, saving peoples' jobs, keeping families together. Being a model doesn't compare to that."

"You have helped raise millions of dollars for New York City's homeless," Erik reminded her.

"Yes, as a result of modeling I've been able to help others. That's a plus. In my opinion, the only true benefit. It's not enough, though. You need a woman who is equal to you in every way."

Erik laughed softly. "You're already my equal in every way."

Ana took a sip of her wine and swallowed. "There's always room for improvement."

Erik raised her hand to his lips and kissed her fingers. "You do realize that this is your personal little quirk, and I wholeheartedly disagree with your assessment?"

"If that's business talk for you think I'm a little nuts to think this way, then, yeah, I do," Ana said, smiling.

Their waiter approached at that instance, and they ordered dinner. After the waiter left them alone, Ana changed the subject with, "So, are we going running in the park tomorrow morning?" They had a standing date on Saturday mornings to run in Central Park if both of them were in the city.

"No, I'm sorry, but tomorrow I'll be driving to Bridgeport for the weekend." Erik sighed. Some of the people he'd had to negotiate with over the years had made some strange stipulations before signing on the dotted line. However Leo Barone's invitation to spend the weekend with his family took the prize. Barone owned a shoe factory that Whitaker Enterprises was in the process of purchasing. Barone stated that he wanted to meet the head of Whitaker Enterprises in a social setting before signing over his company, and the people who worked for him, to him. The biggest hitch in the negotiations had been Barone's concern for his employees once he was no longer their boss.

According to Barone, lawyers were fine for ironing out the legalities. However nothing compared to spending time with a person to get a real feel for what kind of man he was. Erik relayed all of this to Ana after which she responded with a smile, "Do you think he'd mind another guest for the weekend?"

"Of course not," said Erik, smiling as if that was his plan all along. "I told him I would try to convince my lady friend to accompany me."

"Is that what I am—your lady friend?" Ana asked, her eyes sparkling with mischief.

"You're a lady and you're my friend," Erik replied, playing along.

"Could you drop the 'friend' part and refer to me as your lady from now on?" she asked, eyes sparkling with humor.

"As far as I'm concerned you've been my lady for quite some time now," Erik told her, looking into her eyes with sensual intensity. "I was just waiting for you to come to that conclusion."

"Then remember this date," Ana told him, "because the wait is over."

With that, she leaned in and kissed him. Because of where they were Ana held back, even though it took some strength to do so. Erik's mouth was one of the things she liked best about him. His lips were beautifully formed, and when he smiled, showing those even white teeth, she got all jittery inside. Each time she gave him a peck on the cheek she always entertained the notion of kissing him full on the lips. It had never happened before. Erik respected her wishes to keep things platonic. He'd not even "accidentally" missed her cheek, grazing her mouth—not once.

She glanced at his mouth now and made a vow: *this night will not end until I get my fill of those lips!*

Chapter 2

"Let me drive!" Ana exclaimed, running her hand along the driver's side of Erik's sleek, black Corvette the next morning. Erik couldn't hold back a laugh her face was so animated with pure delight.

She looked fresh and stylish in jeans, a cotton shirt open at the neck, a thick brown jacket to guard against the cold and brown suede boots. Her thick hair was pulled back in a ponytail. Erik also wore jeans, but had paired them with athletic shoes, an MIT T-shirt, and his favorite black leather jacket.

"I've barely had her out on the road myself since I bought her," he said, chuckling and holding the car keys high above his head out of her reach. Ana pressed her chest to his as she stretched on tiptoe, trying her best to snatch the keys from his grasp.

"Come on, I'll be good, I promise. No more than, five, ten miles over the speed limit."

"This is not Europe, and we don't have an autobahn," Erik reminded her as he handed over the keys. She had him at a disadvantage. Her close proximity—her breasts against his chest, the subtle erotic, utterly feminine scent she exuded—were causing an all too familiar physical reaction in him. Better to relent and let her drive.

Ana clutched the keys in her hand and let out a whoop. "You choose the music, and let's roll!"

Erik got in and buckled up. He watched as Ana slid into the driver's side, automatically adjusted the seat to her proportions, then fastened her seat belt.

She turned and smiled at him as she turned the key in the ignition. He could have sworn she got pleasure from the purring of the engine. He'd never known a woman who loved to drive as much as she did. He had to admit, she was a good driver. Yes, there was that one time when they got pulled over for speeding, but even the officer stated that she hadn't been driving recklessly, just over the speed limit. He had let her off with a warning.

Ana consulted the GPS and pulled into the early-morning Manhattan traffic. "Tell me more about the Barones."

Erik was riffling through the CDs. He selected a Howlin' Wolf album and put it in the CD player. "Well, the business was started by Leo's grandfather, Alphonse, in the early 1900s. He and his wife, Lucia, were from Salerno, Italy. Leo's father, Leo, Senior, took over in the sixties and left the business to Leo when he died in the eighties."

"Doesn't Leo have any children to leave the business to?" asked Ana. It made no sense to her that Leo would sell the family business, even if he were having financial troubles, when the tradition in the Barone family was for the children to inherit the business. The Corellis' clothing-manufacturing business was also an inherited family business.

"They had a son, but the boy was killed in a diving accident when he was nineteen."

"That's terrible," said Ana sympathetically.

"They still have a daughter. She's sixteen now."

"What a blessing. She doesn't show any interest in the business?"

"From what I'm told, she's more into soccer. Her team was the state champs last year."

"You seem to know a lot about them."

"I make it my business to know whom I'm dealing with," Erik said matter-of-factly. "Besides, Leo likes to talk about his family."

"What about his wife?"

"He met her in Rome when he visited the old country for the first time, is how he put it. It was love at first sight. He learned Italian in order to communicate with her."

"You mean he's Italian and didn't speak Italian?"

"Italian was the language his grandfather spoke, and

he never quite mastered. But when he met Teresa she refused to speak English so he had to learn it."

"Smart woman," said Ana laughing softly.

"Yes, he later found out she could speak English all along."

"Very smart woman," she added as she nodded her head to the beat of the music. "Who *is* that?"

"Howlin' Wolf," Erik told her. "He was known for classic Chicago blues. Like Muddy Waters."

He knew Ana was slowly working her way through American blues singers. She loved the gutbucket blues the best, the rough-and-ready singers who got under your skin with the emotion in their voices.

"He's got a gritty, sexy tone to his voice," she said. "I could listen to him all night."

Erik grinned, "Are you blushing?"

"No," she denied, eyes on the road. "Tell me more about him."

"He was a big guy," Erik said, "six-six and almost three hundred pounds."

"He *sounds* big," Ana said.

"He and Muddy Waters were rivals. I don't know why, exactly, but they reportedly didn't like each other much."

"Probably a professional rivalry," Ana suggested. "They competed for jobs, maybe record deals, maybe even women."

"They probably didn't have to compete for women. Women love musicians. There were undoubtedly enough to go around."

"Who knows, maybe they were in love with the same woman," Ana countered. "Men have feuded over women since the beginning of time. Remember Helen of Troy?"

Erik laughed. "The blues *is* usually about a broken romance," he said. "You could be right."

They talked about the blues and listened to it the entire trip. It was nearly noon when Ana turned onto the long driveway that led to the Barone house, a three-story Tudor-style mansion on the outskirts of Bridgeport. There were three other late-model cars parked on the circular drive.

Ana parked the Corvette and turned off the engine. Shy by nature, she was always a little apprehensive about meeting new people. "Here we are," she said to Erik hesitantly.

Before they could get out of the car, the Barones, looking relaxed in their casual weekend clothes and warm jackets, came out of the house, welcoming smiles on their faces.

"Oh my God, it *is* Ana Corelli!" Julianna Barone cried, sprinting to the driver's side and pulling open the door. "When Daddy said Mr. Whitaker was bringing his lady friend, Ana Corelli, I thought to myself, 'Not *the* Ana Corelli!' But it *is* you!"

Ana got out and was immediately enveloped in Julianna's arms. Ana hugged her back. Then they peered into each other's faces. "It's good to meet you…" Ana began.

"Julianna. I'm sorry. Where're my manners?" Juliana said.

"I was wondering that myself," said Teresa Barone. She was in her early fifties, five-six and curvy with tanned skin. Her dark brown hair was cut short and framed her lovely face nicely.

"This is my mom, Teresa," said Julianna.

"Welcome to our home," said Teresa in Italian, having noticed Ana's accent. "It's a pleasure to meet you, Ana."

Ana smiled, loving the way the language tripped off the other woman's tongue. It had been a while since anyone other than her family had spoken in Italian to her. She answered in Italian and soon the two of them were speaking rapidly in the language. Teresa took her by the arm and led her inside with Leo, Erik and Julianna following.

"Forgive her," said Leo to Erik, commenting on the fact that his wife had totally ignored him in favor of Ana. "It isn't often she meets someone who speaks her native tongue as fluently as she does. It goes to her head. How was your trip?"

Erik told him they'd had a pleasant drive. He looked around him, at the beautiful house and acres of greenery. "Is that a stable?" he asked about the outlying building east of the house.

"It is," Leo told him. He shaded his eyes with a hand as he looked across the field at the well-kept stables. "In good weather, Teresa and I ride every day. We're trying to interest Julianna."

"But I'm scared of horses," Julianna finished for her father. She smiled up at Erik. She was taller than her mother, but had the same chestnut hair. However hers was long and fell nearly to her waist in waves. Her complexion was also somewhere between her mother's dark skin and her father's fairer skin. She and her father were nearly the same height at around five-nine.

She and Leo stood aside as Erik retrieved his and Ana's luggage from the car's trunk.

"Yes, well, I've never gotten used to them myself," Erik told her. "My father raises horses. These days he calls himself a gentleman farmer, and horses are one of his obsessions."

"Finally," Julianna said, "someone else who doesn't think horses are the noble beasts my parents think they are. Those things are big! They've got hard hooves and they bite!"

"They don't bite," Leo said, chuckling. "Well, I've never been bitten by one, anyway."

"You've been lucky," his daughter said.

Leo suggested they put the luggage in the foyer closet until after lunch.

By the time they got into the kitchen where Teresa had led Ana, the two women were already putting lunch on the table while chattering away.

Teresa looked up at her husband when they came into the room. "Ana tells me that her mother is Natalie Davis-Corelli. Do you remember we saw her onstage in Rome over twenty-five years ago?"

"I do," said Leo. He regarded Ana with an amazed

look on his face. "I didn't care much for opera at that time. It was your mother who changed that for me. I'd never heard a voice so pure, so clear, or so emotional. Is she still singing?"

"She performs on special occasions," Ana told him, "but mostly she teaches voice lessons."

After years of singing, she gets a lot of joy out of helping other singers reach their full potential.

Leo, Erik and Julianna sat on stools around the granite-topped island in the middle of the large stylish kitchen while Teresa and Ana put the dishes Teresa had prepared earlier in the center of the island. The smells to Ana were reminiscent of home.

"You come from a family of musicians," Leo said to Ana. He smiled at his wife. "Being married to an opera expert, I've picked up a little knowledge over the years." He returned his attention to Ana. "If your mother is Natalie Davis-Corelli that means your grandmother was Renata Corelli."

"Yes," Ana said, pleased to know he knew of her grandmother who had died several years ago and was still sorely missed.

"I never saw her perform live," Leo said regrettably. "But I've seen her in films. She was amazing."

Ana couldn't think of her grandmother without getting a little choked up. She swallowed a lump in her throat, and softly said, "She was happiest when she was performing."

Leo continued, excitedly. "No wonder your brother is a composer, his mother and his grandmother—two world-renowned singers. It was in his blood. What about you, do you have musical talent?"

Ana laughed shortly. "Not a bit. Musical talent skipped me and my sister, Sophia. Neither of us can carry a tune. Or play an instrument with any proficiency. We went into fashion, like our father. Sophia works with him in his clothing business and I became a model."

"You sound so modest," Teresa said, smiling warmly. "You did more than just became a model. You're very successful at it."

"I've been lucky," Ana admitted.

"And very hard-working," Erik put in fondly.

"There's no substitution for hard work," Leo said. He gave his daughter a meaningful look. "That's what I've been trying to drive home with our soccer fanatic here. You have to burn the midnight oil to get anywhere."

"We were state champs this year," Julianna said a bit defensively.

"Yes, but a girl can't live by soccer alone," her father countered. "In order to get into a good college, you'll need more than just a good athletic record. You're too single minded. What about academics and other extracurricular activities? You have to be well-rounded."

"Ana was single-minded in her career," Julianna pointed out. "If she hadn't been focused on becoming the best model she could be, she wouldn't be where she is today."

"Ana?" Leo said, obviously looking for an ally in this argument. "Tell us, please, is that true?"

"My parents insisted I get a college degree," Ana told Julianna. "I have a bachelor's degree in business. And I've been taking art classes for years."

"See?" cried Teresa. "Beauty and brains!"

"That is so cool," said Julianna. "Don't take this the wrong way but I always thought of models as self-absorbed airheads."

"You can find self-absorbed airheads in any career," Ana said, to which everyone laughed.

They all sat down and soon were enjoying a lunch of Teresa's native southern Italian cuisine—a seafood soup with fresh tomatoes and savory herbs, hot crusty bread and peach gelato for dessert.

"You're a great cook," Ana said to Teresa. "This soup reminds me of my father's seafood soup."

"That's why I married her," Leo said cheerfully.

Teresa, who was sitting beside her husband, reached over and tousled his too-long dark hair. He was graying at the temples, which gave him a sexy, rugged appearance as far as she was concerned. She adored him and it was reflected in the way her eyes caressed his face. "One of the reasons, anyway," she said, then winked at him.

"Behave," their daughter said with a laugh. "We've got company." Then she turned to Erik and said, "Mr. Whitaker, Dad says you want to buy the family business. I searched your company on Google and found out you've bought several companies that were having problems."

"I don't think this is the time to discuss business,"

Leo said abruptly, obviously surprised by his daughter's comment.

"Dad, isn't that why you invited Mr. Whitaker and Ana here this weekend?"

"Please, call me Erik," said Erik with a smile.

"What I wanted to say," Julianna continued calmly, "is that if Dad is going to sell the family business, I hope it's to a company like yours. You're environmentally responsible. You have a good record when it comes to keeping the employees who're dependent on the companies you acquire to make a living." She regarded her father. "I know you're worried about that, Dad. That's why I decided to do a little research. Not that you haven't already done that, but I wanted to reassure myself. I know you think I don't have any interest in the business, but I do. I keep my ears and eyes open."

Leo looked at her with such pride that, seeing his expression, Teresa got emotional and had to wipe a tear away. "My baby," she said in a whisper.

"Dad, I'm sorry if it seems I'm being disrespectful, I don't mean to. But if you remember, I've tried to talk to you about the business for weeks now and you always tell me not to worry about it."

Leo didn't know what to say. He thought Julianna lived in her own world of soccer, her friends and the internet, in that order. That she had made an effort to find out what sort of company Whitaker Enterprises was made him wonder if perhaps he'd been too quick to call it a day where the company was concerned. Maybe there was a Barone who looked forward to running it one day. If he redoubled his efforts there was a possibility that with an infusion of new ideas, and investors, the Barone Shoe Company, whose slogan had always been Quality Italian Shoes Made in America, could remain in the family.

"I'm listening," he said to his daughter.

"Before you sell the family business," Julianna said, "I just want to make sure that's what you really want to do, or is it because Leo, Jr.'s in heaven and you don't think a woman could run the company after you retire?" She was all seriousness, her gaze unwavering. "Or maybe there's something you're not telling me— like you're sick and that's why you're selling the company and retiring at sixty."

Leo got up and pulled his daughter into his arms. "No, sweetheart, no to both of your questions," he said. "I know that if you put your mind to it, you're capable of anything. I just didn't know you were interested in working with me. And I'm as healthy as a horse!"

Julianna laughed. "You know I don't like horses."

"Okay, I'm as healthy as David Beckham," said Leo.

"That's better," said Julianna.

"Let's sit," said Leo. Once they were both seated, Leo turned to Erik. "It looks like we have a lot to talk about this weekend, after all. I was ready to sign, but now I'm having sudden misgivings."

Erik had been listening with interest. This wasn't the first time a deal had come this close to being finalized and had fallen through…if that's where this was going. He had learned to roll with the punches. "I'm sure we can work something out that will be agreeable to both of us. We're not in the business of trying to force anyone to sell. We only approached you because you had decided that selling might be an option out of your financial crunch. However we're willing to work with you. If you want to remain the company's CEO and train Julianna to eventually replace you with us as an investor, you can go that way. It's your decision. We like Barone Shoes and we think you can once again be a major competitor in the shoe market."

Leo regarded his wife. "Do you think we can postpone our months-long tour of Italy a few more years until Julianna's ready to assume control of the business?"

Teresa in turn regarded Julianna. "Baby, you're only sixteen. How can you be so sure you want to run the business one day?"

"Because it's my family," Julianna said firmly. "I'm a Barone. Like Grandpa and Dad before me. Plus, I feel a connection with Leo, Jr.—as if we'd be doing it together. I know I never knew him, but I love him anyway."

Teresa had tears in her eyes when she told her husband, "Okay, I can wait a few years. Give her a chance."

"Let's talk about taking you all on as investors," Leo said to Erik and offered him his hand across the table. Erik took it and firmly shook it.

"I'm sure we can work something out," Erik agreed.

After lunch, Erik and Leo, went into the family library and hammered out a deal that would give Whitaker Enterprises a quarter interest in Barone Shoes in exchange for a healthy loan. Erik felt confident that Whitaker Enterprises had made a good investment. And Leo felt he could trust Whitaker Enterprises to support them, but not interfere in the day-to-day running of Barone Shoes. However, Erik made one stipulation: Barone Shoes had to submit to Whitaker Enterprises' efficiency experts and accountants in order to insure that the company was being run in the black from now on. Whitaker Enterprises didn't invest in a losing proposition. They wouldn't be the powerhouse they were today if they did. Leo wholeheartedly agreed.

The two men stood and shook on it. "Since that's settled, Ana and I should be getting back on the road," Erik said.

"No, please stay the night," Leo said. He grinned. "We had planned a party for you tonight and invited some of the employees so they could meet you, the new owner. Now they can meet the new investor. Stay, won't you?"

Erik would like nothing better than to spend the rest of the day and the weekend with Ana. After last night, he was looking forward to some alone time with her. However, Ana had been promised a weekend in Connecticut and he hated disappointing her. Plus, it might be a good idea to meet some of Leo's employees. "All right," he said. "I'd like that."

Chapter 3

"Are you disappointed things didn't turn out as you thought they would?" Ana asked Erik when they were alone on the common balcony of the guestrooms Teresa had shown them to after Erik's talk with Leo. Earlier Teresa had discreetly asked Ana if she and Erik wanted to share a room and Ana had told her their relationship hadn't advanced that far yet, to which Teresa had smiled and said, "How refreshing."

"It's never wise to anticipate the outcome of a deal," Erik said, his smile denoting he wasn't that broken up about it. He closed the space between them and pulled her into his arms. Ana smiled up at him and said, "It's cold out here." She snuggled closer and breathed in the enticing male scent of him, which was like an aphrodisiac to her senses. Looking into his eyes, she said, "If

I've appeared a bit distant all day, it's because I can't forget that kiss last night."

He'd taken her home after dinner and had come in for coffee. Among the things they had in common was an addiction to caffeine. Neither was bothered by sleeplessness if they indulged before bed. Ana had gone into the kitchen of her loft to make the coffee and Erik, as he often did, followed her. While she was tiptoeing to reach the container of beans on the top shelf of the cabinet, he was admiring her backside. Ana turned around and caught him looking. "Is that something you do often or is it a new development?" she asked playfully.

"It's pretty much a habit," Erik confessed.

Ana set the container on the counter and faced him, her expression aghast. "You mean to tell me that for the last three years you've been looking at my bottom without my knowledge?"

"Oh, I think you knew," Erik said as he slipped his arm about her waist and pressed her to his muscular chest, smiling all the while. He lowered his head and inhaled her unique fragrance. She'd noticed that he liked doing that, as though the smell of her skin gave him sensual pleasure. It turned her on, too.

Her body immediately reacted to his. Her nipples grew hard, and she became moist between her legs. It was a heady, all-too-erotic sensation that was so delicious she let out a soft sigh. She looked at his lips. He was smiling and his white teeth, coupled with those juicy lips, looked so inviting that she threw her arms around his neck and kissed him. Erik didn't need any further provocation. Her lips were soft and her mouth so sweet that before he knew it he had lifted her body and her legs wrapped around him in a bid to get even closer. Their tongues danced gently at first and found the encounter so pleasing that the kiss deepened and soon they were both sounding as though they were consuming something extremely tasty as, no doubt, they were. Erik, as the one who had most of the physical strength between them, knew that he had to back off before things got out of hand. Ana wasn't ready for things to go any further than a kiss but it was their first real kiss and, heaven help him, if her kisses were this good, what would sex be like with her?

It was Ana who came up for air first and looked him in the eyes. She pressed her cheek to his. "Why haven't you kissed me before now?"

"I've been a fool," Erik said, and kissed her again.

Ana pulled his shirt out of his waistband so that she could run her hands over his hot skin. Another new experience since friends didn't routinely touch one another's naked bodies. Her feverish mind thought back. Yes, she'd seen Erik in a swimsuit on a couple occasions. Once when they had flown to Barbados for the weekend with his sister, Belana, and her husband, Nick, and another time when they'd taken a dip in the pool at his parents' house in Connecticut. He was in great shape. Cut from all the running and weightlifting he did on a daily basis. Ana was not nearly as disciplined. She liked running with Erik on Saturday mornings, but walking was more her taste. All this was going through her mind while the man of her dreams was kissing her, and she thought she must be neurotic to be thinking of anything other than the taste of his mouth and the warm, solid feel of his body touching hers. It was fear of change that stood in the way of her truly enjoying Erik.

What would she do if he made love to her and lost interest, just as that actor who would remain nameless had done? It would kill her—she realized at that instant in her kitchen, she adored this man. She loved him in a way she had never thought to love a man, completely. Until Erik she thought of men as enigmas whom women were doomed to never fully understand. However Erik had proved that theory a lie. She understood him. She knew, for example, that even though he denied it he had an abandonment issue with his mother. It's true that his mother had come back into his life briefly last year, but by that time the damage had been done. And she wasn't in his life long before she revealed she had a terminal illness. Only weeks later she had died with all her children holding her hands, the very children she had walked away from. No one came away from that without emotional scarring.

Erik had never let himself get close to anyone before Ana. He jokingly said it was because he'd just never found the right woman. Ana believed it was because he was afraid of being abandoned yet again by a woman he loved. This, Ana, thought last night in her kitchen, put a great deal of pressure on her. She would never dream of hurting him, but what if she did hurt him in spite of every effort not to? She was only human.

It was soon after this thought ran through her mind that Erik had tipped her chin toward him and said, "Let's not waste any more time than we already have. I love you, Ana. I believe I've loved you since the first time we met."

Tears instantly sprang to Ana's eyes. "I love you, too!" She hugged him tightly. "I love you so much that I'm afraid of my feelings for you."

He kissed her forehead. "Afraid? What do you mean?"

"What we have is perfect in a sense. You're my best friend, the person I confide in, aside from my own family. What if that changes? What if becoming lovers changes us?"

Erik laughed. "If anything it'll enhance how we already feel about each other." He became somber. "It's that actor, isn't it? The one who broke your heart after you'd slept with him? Ana, you're not guilty of doing anything to warrant his behavior. Some men are bastards and will always be bastards. He's one of them. I'm sure you're not the only woman he's treated that way."

"Maybe I'm not good in bed," Ana said miserably.

Erik held her by the shoulders and looked deeply in her eyes. "That's the most ludicrous statement I've ever heard." He smiled as he pulled her into his arms. "One day, my sweet Ana, you and I are going to make love, and you're going to know without a doubt that you are very, very good in bed and maybe the couch, the kitchen table and the shower, too."

Ana laughed and cried. "Someday? Why not this day, this night?"

"Because sex for the first time is an event," Erik said. "It'll be remembered forever and you don't want to mess with forever. We've waited this long, we can wait awhile longer."

Now, as they stood in each other's arms on the Barone's balcony, Ana gazed up at him and said, "It's just as well we didn't make love last night because I would want you again tonight and it would be awkward making love under the Barones' roof."

"We'd be very quiet," Erik joked.

"I doubt it," Ana countered.

Later, at the party, Erik spent most of the time fielding questions from Leo Barone's employees who wanted to know more about Whitaker Enterprises. It was apparent to him that they were grateful to be retaining their jobs in these hard economic times. So many people were out of jobs and finding it difficult to find another. They almost made him feel like some kind of hero for offering assistance to Barone Shoes, a feeling he fervently declined.

"I should be thanking you," he told them. "Leo has built a wonderful business and you've contributed to the quality of the product he produces. Without loyal, hardworking employees, no business would survive. Or be able to build a reputation investors like myself notice when we're looking to invest in someone."

Leo had stepped up and said, "That's a long way of

saying he wouldn't have been interested if we didn't make a quality product."

Everyone laughed, but Erik was happy he'd gotten his point across and from that moment on during the evening, business was not discussed. The topics stayed on golf and sports teams.

Meanwhile in another section of the great room, the women and children were gathered around Ana who was quickly making sketches of the children in charcoal. She didn't go anywhere without her sketch pad and the children were taking great delight in her swift manner of drawing their likenesses. Since it was only a few days from Halloween, Teresa had suggested that the children come in costumes and, now, Ana was drawing the image of a six-year-old African-American girl dressed as a fairy princess. The mother of the little girl stood behind Ana on one side, and Julianna stood on the other.

"You're very good," the mother said, smiling broadly. "You even captured the mischievous expression in Nikki's eyes."

Julianna laughed. "That's our Nikki to a T." She had babysat Nikki on occasion and knew the little girl was a handful.

Ana, sitting on a straight-backed chair directly in front of Nikki, smiled warmly. "She's adorable."

Finished with Nikki's portrait, she handed the finished product to Nikki's mother. Nikki climbed off her chair and spontaneously kissed Ana on the cheek. "Thank you," she said.

"Well," Ana said, laughing softly. "That's the first time I've ever been paid in kisses for my work. Thank you, Nikki."

With Nikki's portrait, Ana had drawn all four children who had attended the party with their parents. Not to be outdone, Teresa asked sweetly, "Would you draw my baby now?"

Julianna immediately took umbrage with being called a baby. "Mother, I'm not a baby!"

"You're my baby, and always will be. Get used to it," Teresa returned. "Now sit down and let Ana draw you. It's not every day that you get to have your picture drawn by an artist of her caliber." She smiled at Ana. "Don't you dare forget to phone and tell me when and where your show is going to take place."

"I won't," Ana promised. She met Julianna's gaze.

Julianna grinned and sat down. Then she crossed her eyes. "Will this do?"

Ana laughed. "Sure if that's how you want to be remembered."

Julianna uncrossed her eyes and gave Ana a genuine smile. "You're sneaky. I like that."

The men wandered over and stood admiring the sketch as it formed on Ana's pad. Leo joked, "Give her horns. I swear she's a little devil sometimes."

Teresa playfully hit Leo on the backside. "If anyone's a little devil in this family, it's you."

Erik stood back and watched Ana, how easily she was handling being the center of attention even though she insisted she was shy. Whether it was on the runway or in a room full of children, she always seemed comfortable in her own skin to him.

When Ana finished the portrait Julianna held it in her hands, admiring it. "You even managed to make me pretty," she said in awe.

"I just drew what I saw," Ana said truthfully.

Teresa took the drawing from Julianna. "This is going in a place of honor." She bent and kissed Ana on the cheek. "Thank you, Ana." She had to wipe away a tear.

Leo, feeling things were getting maudlin, bellowed, "The night's still young. Who's up for some virtual golf?"

The men were all for that, and once again the guests were divided by sex with the men heading downstairs to the finished basement where Leo's entertainment center was set up.

Teresa led the women to the kitchen where they indulged in coffee and delicious desserts the caterer had provided for the party. The children were in their own special heaven in the den playing video games.

Ana sat between two women in their thirties, one African-American, the other a blonde with dark roots who kept gazing at Ana as if she wanted to ask her something but couldn't muster up the nerve to do so. Ana smiled at her and said, "Your husband is the plant's manager, right?"

They'd all introduced themselves earlier. Ana recalled her husband—a tall, heavyset fellow with a ruddy complexion—was very tender with their son who looked about three.

"Yeah, Ben," said the woman. "And I'm Sasha."

"Your son's so sweet. I have a niece his age. She lives in Italy. I miss her so much."

"What's her name?"

"Ari...Ariana," said Ana. "Now she has a baby brother and she's having a hard time getting used to him. She told her mom to take him back to the hospital and trade him in for a puppy."

The other women who had been listening to their conversation laughed.

"Yes, older kids do sometimes take a while to get used to a new addition," Teresa said after swallowing a mouthful of pecan pie. "When Julianna was three months old Leo, Jr. once wrapped her in a blanket and left her on a neighbor's doorstep. Luckily we were living in a close-knit neighborhood at that time, and the neighbors saw him do it and immediately phoned me. He only got away with it because Leo was at work and I was in the shower. Of course when Leo, Jr. got older he absolutely loved his sister and doted on her. Or maybe it was guilt that made him so protective of her later on." She laughed, remembering her son fondly. "Julianna adored him from birth. She would follow him around like a lost puppy looking for a scrap of food."

Ana supposed the woman who went and pulled Teresa into her arms for a firm hug was an old friend. A sympathetic and knowing look passed between them and the woman said, "He adored her. You could see it every time you saw them together."

"Yes," another woman agreed.

Soon others were relating Leo, Jr. stories. It was obvious to Ana that the employees of Barone Shoes were more than employees to the Barones, they were old friends. It made her feel happy that Leo had decided not to sell the company after all.

On Sunday Ana and Erik got back to the city in the early afternoon. After dropping Ana off at her loft and making plans to meet for dinner later, Erik continued on to his apartment.

When Erik walked into this apartment, bags in hand, he dropped them in the foyer and walked back to the kitchen to get a bottle of water from the fridge. After drinking quickly he turned and went into the home office. The blinking light of the answering machine on the desk was like a beacon to him. Only his friends and family used his home phone number. Business calls went straight to his cell phone. He liked keeping them separate because on weekends, he ignored the office. He would never, however, ignore his friends and family.

He listened to the first message. It was his father, John. He began with a tired sigh, so Erik instinctively knew the message would be about his grandmother, Drusilla. No one could get under his father's skin quite like his grandmother. "Hey, son, your grandmother took another tumble today. She's so hardheaded. We keep telling her to use her cane but she insists she doesn't need it every day, just when, and these are her words, 'I'm feeling wobbly.'" John sighed heavily again. "It's Friday night and they're keeping her in the hospital overnight for observation. A fall can be dangerous for an eighty-two-year-old."

Let her be all right, Erik prayed as he continued listening.

"No need to come home, though," his father said. "She's fine. It's my nerves that are frayed." He laughed. "Thank God for Izzie. She remained calm and handled everything with her usual quiet efficiency." Izzie was Isobel, Erik's stepmother. She and his father had been married for three years and still behaved like newlyweds. Erik loved and admired her for how happy she'd made his father, who deserved a little happiness after all the heartache he'd experienced when Mari had left him for a French choreographer.

He dialed the house in New Haven, Connecticut and waited. Isobel answered with, "Hi, sweetie. I hope John's message didn't upset you. Dru's back home and is doing well. How're you?"

Erik smiled. Isobel rarely answered with hello. She anticipated your needs and got right into the conversation. "I'm fine, Mom, and how are you?" Both he and Belana referred to Isobel as "Mom." They'd known her for years before she and their father had fallen in love and gotten married. She was the mother of one of Belana's best friends, Elle, and consequently they were part of the same social circle. What's more, Isobel, as far as Belana and Erik were concerned, had earned the title of "Mom" since she loved them like her own even though they were not related by blood.

He could hear the smile in her voice when she said, "Just great. We're all sitting around the kitchen table having lunch. Would you like to speak with your father or Drusilla?"

"Put Her Majesty on, please."

When Drusilla got on the phone he could hear her clearing her throat. "Where are you that you can't come see about your poor old grandmother?"

"Who would that be?" Erik asked, "Because you are apparently as young and spry as ever! I'm told you don't think you need to use your cane anymore. Is that right?"

"It makes me look old and decrepit."

"You're too vain. What would you prefer? To look your age, or break a hip, or worse?" he asked, being careful not to raise his voice.

"I'd rather look good," was Drusilla's petulant reply. "What does it matter if I go out with a broken hip or not? The Grim Reaper has my number. I should have the right to choose how I live the rest of my life. After more than eighty years, I've earned it!"

Erik sighed. She had a point. Eighty-two years on earth should allow her certain privileges. He'd have to guilt her into behaving herself.

"Yes, you've earned the right to flip off the Grim Reaper if you want to. But, while you're tempting fate, what about the rest of us who would like to have you around a bit longer? What about Dad and Belana? What about those great-grandchildren you're always urging

Belana and me to have? And hurry up about it, too? Shouldn't they get the honor of having you as a cantankerous great-grandma? What do you say to that?"

"You should've been a lawyer," Drusilla groused. She laughed. "Okay, I'll use the damn cane from now on."

"Language!" Erik heard his dad admonish his grandmother before bursting into laughter himself. His dad must have taken the phone from his grandmother. "Okay, son, whatever you said seems to have worked. She looks dutifully repentant, *for now*."

Erik couldn't help laughing. Both he and his father knew it was only a matter of time before Drusilla found another outlet for her indefatigable spirit to get her into trouble.

"By the way, Dad, Ana and I are dating," Eric said after he'd gotten his laughter under control.

With his usual aplomb, John said without missing a beat, "Haven't you always been dating?"

"Technically, we were just friends."

"Seriously?" said John. "For two years you and Ana have been platonic friends?" He sounded so disbelieving that Erik started laughing again.

"Yes, seriously," he assured his father.

"I know you said you were just friends, but I never imagined that two young, healthy people like you and Ana were actually keeping your hands to yourselves. Son, I was just happy you had someone like Ana in your life. Mother, will you stop that!"

Drusilla said hastily, "It's about damn time!" Then she was gone.

John, sounding exasperated, said, "That's wonderful news. Now I've got to go, your grandmother's has had too much excitement for one day."

Erik hung up the phone and listened to the remaining messages on the machine. None were pressing, so he wandered into this bedroom and began changing his clothes. He felt restless and a long jog would go a long way in relaxing him and focusing his mind. His father's reaction to the news of him and Ana dating made him wonder if the rest of his family believed the two of them had been more than friends all the time.

Wasn't it possible for a man and a woman to be just friends? Surely he'd proven they could. Then again, even if his behavior had been above reproach, his thoughts definitely hadn't been. Not being able to express his feelings for Ana in a sexual way had made him very resourceful. Running helped, as did staying extremely busy. Now that they'd admitted their feelings for each other, and sex was sure to follow, he hoped he'd be able to make love to Ana without scaring the poor girl by howling like a beast or something else equally embarrassing. He was only a man.

Running clothes and shoes on, he grabbed the apartment key he kept in the foyer table on the way out the door. I hope Ana isn't overanalyzing everything like I am, he thought as he closed the door behind him.

Chapter 4

"I'm freaking out!" Ana cried, trying to control the panic in her voice. Her sister, Sophia, in Milan was half asleep. She usually slept in on Sunday and it was still quite early in her part of the world.

Ana was lying in bed with her back against the headboard and her long legs stretched out. Sophia was under the covers with her husband, Matteo, who was snugly pressed against her backside, gently snoring. It would take more than the shrill ringing of a phone to wake him.

Sophia yawned before replying, "Yes, I do detect a little freaking out on your part," she said. "But that's to be expected since you've let a guy as hot as Erik slip through your fingers for as long as you have. I was beginning to doubt your sanity."

That comment made Ana smile. Leave it to her practical sister to point out the obvious. "It's not like I'm jumping into bed with every man who shows interest," she said in her defense. "You know how inexperienced I am."

"I know your only experience was a negative one and you're not going to fully appreciate how truly bad it was until you have a good encounter with a man who knows what he's doing in bed. Then, what Jack Russo did to you will feel like a slight glitch in your very satisfying love life. Oh, sorry, we aren't supposed to be saying his name. Jack Russo, Jack Russo, Jack Russo. By saying his name you take some of the power out of it. You know the only reason he dropped you was because he had that actress waiting in the wings and she had more money and clout than you. I hate it when bastards like that just run over a woman's feelings. You know, if I had been anywhere in the vicinity he would be missing his most vital organ right now."

Ana giggled. "Matteo must be sleeping very hard not to react to that comment."

Sophia giggled, too. "Yeah, he's out. Your nephew had both of us up late last night."

"Oh, I'm sorry for interrupting your much needed rest. What was wrong with my nephew?"

"Teething," said Sophia. "Breast-feeding is becoming dangerous."

Ana sighed sympathetically. "Thinking of switching him to a bottle?"

"I'm going to have to," said Sophia. "Besides, according to his doctor he's gotten all the good nutrients from breast milk that he needs at six months."

Remembering the conversation about firstborns not accepting new sisters and brothers, Ana said, "How is Renata handling being a big sister?"

"She loves him, calls him her baby," said Sophia. She yawned again.

"Look, I'd better let you go," said Ana. "I just wanted to hear a calm voice."

"And you called *me?*" joked Sophia. "Mom is the only one with a calm voice in this family."

"Don't mention our conversation to them, okay? I'll tell them when the time's right."

"You *are* coming home for Christmas?" asked Sophia.

Ana always went home for Christmas, which was celebrated with all the trimmings by the Corellis.

"I don't know yet," Ana said truthfully. "With these new developments in my life I might want to go somewhere romantic with my man." The thought excited her. "I'll have to let you know."

"Now you sound like the idea of you and Erik as a couple is taking root," Sophia told her, pleased with the confidence in her sister's voice. "Okay, sis, talk to you later."

"Love you," said Ana.

"Love you!" Sophia replied.

Ana hung up the phone and got up. She glanced at the clock on the nightstand. It was nearly three. She and Erik were going to dinner at eight. She had plenty of time to work on a painting before getting dressed for their date.

She'd changed her clothes upon entering the loft and now she was in comfortable sweats and an oversize T-shirt. In thick white socks she padded over to her "studio"—a section of the loft next to two floor-to-ceiling windows, which let in a lot of natural light.

Although she had finished all of the paintings that were to be included in the upcoming show, she invariably had a work in progress on the easel. She removed the cloth and peered down at the half-finished portrait of Drusilla. She had sketched Drusilla so many times she knew every line and plane of her beloved face. Drusilla had never been a large woman. Not even five feet tall, she was also small boned. Because of her age, the skin on her face was thin and the bones were sharply delineated. Ana noticed things like that. Her artist's eye adored the bone structure of human beings. That's why she felt most comfortable painting portraits. She did some landscapes, too, but not many. Nothing was more beautiful to her than the human form. In Italy, when she first started taking lessons, her instructor had encouraged her to study anatomy. He gave her a battered copy of *Grey's Anatomy* and she had studied it from cover to cover, her teenaged mind becoming obsessed with the human body. Now when she looked at people she didn't just see their outward appearance, but their bone structure and consequently she saw beauty in every face she observed.

Two hours later, she was still constructing Drusilla's face on the canvas. Even though she'd been doing this for years it still amazed her, and felt somewhat miraculous, when from a blank slate an image emerged. She laughed, seeing that naughty expression in Drusilla's eyes, which captured her personality. She had to admit that she had begun thinking of Drusilla as her own grandmother. She missed her grandmother, Renata, so much and in many ways Drusilla reminded her of her. Not so much how they looked but their indomitable spirits. She supposed that with age came wisdom.

It was getting dark outside when she began cleaning up after herself, sealing the tubes of oil paint, washing the brushes and removing the drop cloth from the floor.

After a soak in the tub she dried off and rubbed lotion into her skin. Completely nude, she stood in front of the full-length mirror. Her brown skin was mostly unscarred except for an inch-long scar on her right knee from when she was seven and fell from a tree she'd climbed in spite of being told not to by her parents. Her best friend at that time had been a boy named Pietro and he had loved climbing trees. She might not have defied her parents if he hadn't accused her of being afraid of heights. She had to prove she wasn't. Unfortunately, she got dizzy after climbing thirty feet into the tree and wound up losing her balance. The lush lawn had cushioned her fall for the most part, except for the knee which sustained a deep gash.

She carefully regarded her body in the mirror. She

was neither obsessed with perfection nor too critical of herself. Her body was strong and healthy. That mattered most to her. Not that that attitude hadn't been hard won. She'd gone through a period when she was self-conscious about her body. Many models who were always being judged by how much they weighed, and were stripped naked in front of designers, dressers and myriad other people in the fashion business, had to distance themselves from rude comments. If you were smart you began to take all snide remarks for what they were: thoughtless and petty. Her brown, long-limbed, fit body with its pert breasts and nicely rounded bottom would pass muster.

Her cell phone rang a little after seven. Eric said, "Are you dressed yet?"

Ana knew what that meant: he was taking the Harley for a spin tonight. She looked down at her slinky red dress. "No, I'm still trying to decide what to wear."

"How would you like to go to Mario's in Queens tonight? We love the place and there's room to park the bike on the street."

"Sounds like a plan," Ana said cheerfully. She didn't feel much like wearing heels tonight anyway.

"See you in twenty," said Erik, his voice husky.

Ana hung up the phone and went to her walk-in closet and began putting together an outfit conducive to a bike ride through the city.

She emerged ten minutes later wearing black jeans, black leather boots, and a red cashmere sweater. Just because she was going to be on the back of a Harley didn't mean she couldn't feel girly.

She'd checked the weather forecast earlier and it was going to be in the forties tonight. She chose a jacket with a warm lining and a knit cap to go over her simple braid down her back. A spray of her favorite perfume, which she walked through while it was still a mist in the air finished her preparations for tonight.

Erik was there on time, and when she opened the door her breath caught in her throat. He looked good in a suit, but he absolutely made her melt when he wore leather. His muscular body was made for jeans and biker boots. His black leather jacket was open and she couldn't help running her hand inside it to caress his pectorals through his soft denim shirt. Erik grasped her hand, pulled her against him, their pelvises touching. He gently reached up to smooth her brow with the pad of his thumb, and then he kissed her upturned mouth. His scent, the warmth of his mouth, the hard muscles beneath his hot skin all became temptations that Ana could not resist. She gave herself over to his kiss, completely abandoning any thoughts of decorum and what impression she might be making. She was hungry for him and enjoyed every erotic thrust of his tongue as he slowly tasted her. She relished the feel of his firm lips as he turned this way and that, maximizing her pleasure.

She gazed dreamily at him when they parted. Momentarily weak with desire, she smiled up at him. "You can't imagine how much I've missed you since this afternoon."

Erik laughed softly. "Yes, I think I can."

Ana grinned from ear to ear when she felt his erection on her thigh. "I think you do."

There was definitely something to the term lovesick, Erik thought. Only hours since he'd seen Ana and he could hardly wait to see her again, touch her again, feel her lips on his. Love was a kind of madness you never wanted to be cured of.

He grabbed her hand. "Ready?"

Over dinner Erik told her about Drusilla's accident and that she was just fine, no need to worry. Then he told her he'd mentioned to his dad that they were dating.

"How did he react?" she asked cautiously. She knew his family liked her and she liked them, but still she wanted their blessing.

Erik's golden-brown eyes held amusement in their depths. "Dad thought we were already secret lovers and Drusilla is just happy we've finally made it official."

"Your dad thought we were sleeping together?" Ana said, laughing nervously. "That surprises me."

"Me, too," Erik told her, "but I shouldn't have been. He's my father. He knew how I felt about you and he was maintaining a positive attitude about our relationship. Hoping we were more than friends even when we weren't."

"When you put it that way, it was sweet of him to think we were lovers," Ana said.

"It's a sign of how much he likes you," Erik said, his tone gentle. "They all do."

"I love them," Ana said simply.

Erik grasped her hand across the tiny table for two. Mario's, an elegant family-owned restaurant, had been a mainstay in its Queens neighborhood for more than fifty years. Sunday night was popular for couples and the restaurant was fully booked.

Each time Erik brought Ana here he thought it would be the ideal place to propose. The idea ran through his mind tonight, too, but he stamped it down, way down. It was much too soon for that. But he enjoyed entertaining the idea.

Mario's menu consisted of dishes from southern Italy, rich red sauces, handmade pastas, crisp vegetables, all cooked with slow deliberation.

He watched as Ana ate a forkful of pasta dripping in tomato sauce. She took a sip of red wine afterward and mopped up the remaining sauce on her plate with a piece of crusty bread. Bringing the bread to her lips she ate it with something akin to ecstasy in her expression. Erik smiled. "Enjoying your pasta?"

Ana looked down at her clean plate, "Enjoyed it."

They ordered two desserts and shared them. Erik fed her some of his lemon tart. She plied him with tiramisu. They took a walk after leaving the restaurant. The night was quiet on this street. Other couples were out, too, holding hands, sitting on benches or frequenting the open shops. Erik and Ana stopped to check out the display in a bookstore window.

"They've got the new Walter Mosley," said Erik. "I

know you'd love to get your hands on that. Too bad they're closed."

Ana peered at the book a pout forming, "It's a Leonid McGill mystery, too. I love that character."

Erik took her hand as they resumed their walk they put their arms about each other's waists and Ana put her head on his shoulder.

"This is what I love about New York," Erik said. "Even if what you want is a quiet evening out with your girl, you can find it somewhere in the five boroughs."

"I like Queens," Ana agreed. "There's much more greenery here. Houses actually have gardens."

Erik smiled at her use of gardens. Not many people he knew called a yard a "garden."

But Ana had grown up in Europe where people said this even if they didn't grow flowers or vegetables.

"Gardens aren't unheard of in Manhattan," he said. "I've seen some elaborate rooftop gardens."

"Yes, I suppose if you have the money you can have a garden put on your roof or your terrace," she conceded. "But I like these gardens better."

Erik stopped in his tracks and peered down at her. "We could put a garden on the terrace of the penthouse. There's plenty of room for one."

Erik lived in the penthouse of the building that Whitaker Enterprises owned in Manhattan. His father used to live there but had taken up permanent residence in Connecticut since his retirement. "In fact, there are a couple of vacancies in the building. Why don't you move in?"

He wanted to take back what he'd said the moment the words were out of his mouth. Ana would think he was moving way too fast. He had to slow himself down. But his first instinct was to take their relationship to the level where it should rightly be by now: totally committed.

She laughed softly instead. "Your dad thought we were lovers just because we spent so much time together as friends. Imagine what our families would think if we lived in the same building?"

"I'm sorry. I'm getting ahead of myself. On the other hand, we're consenting adults. What does it matter what they think?"

"My dad's a devout Catholic. Believe me, I've had enough preaching about remaining pure from him and my grandmother when I was growing up. It's a wonder I'm capable of a normal sex life. He laid into Dominic when Dominic started living with Elle and told him to marry her if he loved her, and stop stringing her along. Now, if you don't want a visit from my father, we should live in separate buildings for a while longer."

Chuckling, Erik said, "Fine. But I'm still going to have a garden planted for you."

"It's nearly November. It's too cold for a garden," Ana said.

"A greenhouse, then," he said. "You can grow flowers year round."

She squeezed him affectionately. "That's so romantic."

Erik hugged her close and kissed her cheek. "I'm going to enjoy spoiling you."

One of the things Erik had missed when they weren't dating was not being able to give Ana romantic gifts. He'd tried to give her a diamond bracelet for her birthday last year and she'd handed it back to him with, "You're so good to me, Erik, but this is not the sort of gift a friend gives a friend." It had been yet another reminder for him to keep his distance. He couldn't help resenting the moment just a little bit.

On the ride back to her loft, Ana clung to Erik, the side of her face pressed to his solid back. She was giddy with anticipation. Would tonight be the night? She had tried not to make herself nervous with wondering exactly when they would make love. Erik had said it had to be an event. What constituted an event to him, she wondered. As far as she was concerned, tonight's date had been eventful enough. In fact, hadn't their confession of love for each other been one?

At her building they ran up the stairs to the top floor. She paused at the door after unlocking it. It was Sunday night and it would only be polite to ask him if he wanted to come in for coffee, not being too insistent about it. He had work in the morning, after all. She didn't want to seem too eager. Going through the niceties would offset that notion.

Looking into his eyes, her own expression innocent, she softly said, "I've got a new Kona blend I'd like you to try."

"I'm game," said Erik and reached out and turned

the doorknob. Ana smiled seductively, her confidence shooting up instantly, as she backed inside, pulling him with her. She closed and locked the door then took his coat and put it in the foyer closet along with hers. Gesturing to the comfortable sectional in the living room area of the loft, she said, "Relax," knowing that word was a foreign concept to Erik.

She went to the kitchen. Erik went over to the far wall where her entertainment system was shelved. He put Adele's latest CD in the player. Although Ana was lately into classic blues performers she also liked contemporary artists if their sound harkened back to yesteryear.

In the kitchen Ana heard Adele's soulful voice. She smiled as she measured coffee beans into the grinder. Maybe he *was* going to make this an eventful night. She was getting excited by the prospect.

Once she'd gotten the coffeemaker going, she went back to see what Erik was up to. She found him in her studio looking at the portrait of Drusilla.

Hearing her footsteps on the hardwood floor he smiled at her. "You really are talented." He gazed at her with a mixture of awe and admiration, his expression so intense that Ana had to lower her own. She looked at the portrait instead. In it Drusilla was sitting in the garden at the New Haven house. It was springtime and she was surrounded by flowering trees and plants in huge clay pots.

"Don't mention it to her. It's her birthday gift."

Erik went to stand beside her as he continued admiring the painting. "She's gonna love it. However, I have to say you made her much more angelic-looking than she is in real life."

"That's how I see her," Ana said. She laughed shortly. "I'm fully aware her behavior frustrates you sometimes. She's headstrong, and says whatever comes to her mind. In that way she reminds me of Grandma Renata. But she's been sweet to me from the first time we met."

"It's true," said Erik. "She only tries to control family members." *Wait until we're married,* he thought. *She'll be on your case every day asking when you're going to make her a great-grandmother.*

"What was that?" said Ana, "You had the funniest expression on your face." She gazed up at him, brows raised inquisitively. "What were you thinking?"

He couldn't dare tell her what he'd been thinking. So he said, "I was just thinking how nervous I am being here alone with you when we've been alone countless times before."

That was true. Now that the dynamics had changed and there was actually the possibility of their making love tonight, he was nervous. He worried that if he made a move on her she would have the image of Jack Russo in the back of her mind. *Was she entirely over that creep?*

"I know," Ana said. "I'm nervous too and I've been tormenting myself trying to figure out what exactly you think an event is."

Erik laughed shortly and took her in his arms. "I

wish I'd never said that. It took some of the spontaneity out of what's happening between us. But I wanted you to know that getting you into bed is not my main goal. Marriage is. And if you want to wait until we're married, I would be willing to do that."

"Are you asking me to marry you?" She stared at him with wide eyes and an even wider grin.

"Honestly, I would have married you two years ago," Erik said. So there, the secret was out.

Ana was waiting for him to say the words, *Will you marry me,* or something to that effect. She blinked. "You were saying?" she gently prodded him.

Erik gave her a puzzled look. Then, it dawned on him what she was asking him and he decided to go the old-fashioned route. He got down on one knee right there in her studio and grasped her hand in his. "Ana Maria Corelli, will you do me the honor of becoming my wife?"

Tears sprang to Ana's eyes. "Yes, Jonathan Erik Whitaker, it would make me very happy to become your wife!"

Erik rose, and Ana flew into his arms. Then they were kissing hungrily with words of love interspersed between the kisses.

"I love you so much," he breathed.

"It's always been you," she told him. "How could I have been so blind?"

"I should have had the ring before I asked you."

"The ring doesn't matter. Just that you love me."

"My darling, you *will* get a ring!" Erik promised.

"Make love to me," said Ana breathlessly, her beautiful brown eyes beseeching him. Erik could not deny her a thing when she looked at him that way. However, as his feverish mind soon realized, there was a problem. He was not the sort of man who carried a spare condom in his wallet thereby making that telltale indentation in the leather. He was now looking at *Ana* beseechingly. "I didn't bring any condoms."

From the expression on Ana's face, a look of utter disappointment, he could tell she didn't have any, either. "I could go to an all-night drugstore."

Ana knew her neighborhood better than he did. "The closest drugstore closed at midnight."

That took the edge off their excitement. They gazed into each other's eyes and burst out laughing. "Are we lame, or what?" Erik said between guffaws. "Both of us undoubtedly with sex on our minds but neither of us thought to buy condoms. Is there any hope for us?"

"Obviously, not tonight," Ana quipped, "Ah, well, I've waited this long for you. I can wait another twenty-four hours. But you will be mine tomorrow night, do you hear me?" she asked sternly, the smile wiped entirely off her face. "I've got some serious pent-up sexual tension in need of release."

"Damn it, I'll get on my bike and ride until I find an open drugstore," Erik said, turning to head to the foyer closet where his keys were in his jacket pocket.

Ana grasped his arm. "You are not going out into the night when you can be here cuddling with your fiancée."

Erik looked into her upturned face and sighed in frustration. "I will never be caught unprepared again," he vowed.

Chapter 5

Ana stayed busy on Monday. She had an appointment to meet with Damon Cohen at his gallery to discuss the upcoming show. Scheduled for the first week of December, Damon assured her that her work was in competent hands.

When she arrived at the gallery in Soho, Damon was with a client. His receptionist, a tall thin redhead, her hair tucked away in a smooth chignon, smiled up at her and said, "Mr. Cohen is expecting you, Ms. Corelli. He won't be long. May I offer you a coffee while you wait?"

Ana rarely refused coffee, but she was very discriminating about where her coffee came from. "What kind?"

"It's Jamaican," said the receptionist.

"I'd love some, thank you," Ana replied pleasantly

as she sat on the off-white leather couch and crossed her legs.

The receptionist was back in less than a minute with a steaming cup of coffee complete with saucer and spoon. "Black, two sugars," she said, letting Ana know she remembered how she took her coffee.

"How thoughtful," said Ana, as she accepted the coffee and took a sip. "Delicious."

The receptionist smiled her appreciation and returned to her desk.

Ana enjoyed her coffee in contemplative silence. She wondered what Erik was doing right now? He was probably in a meeting. He conducted meetings via computer with the officers of the company from all over the world. He liked being abreast of any new developments, no matter how minor. It amazed her that he was capable of mentally juggling everything with such ease. But he said it was a talent he'd learned from his father who was famous for multitasking. Sometimes she thought his penchant for business was hereditary. He didn't mind working long hours, actually thrived on it.

Ana remembered all of the social events she'd invited him to that Erik had to miss because of work. As his friend, she'd been magnanimous and not complained. She vowed to be just as understanding now that they were engaged. Engaged! She still hadn't been able to convince herself this was really happening. Smiling, she finished her coffee and set the cup and saucer on the table in front of her.

"Ana!"

She looked up into the dark brown eyes of Damon Cohen. He was moving toward her, hand outstretched, with a huge grin on his good-looking face. In his late thirties, Damon was about her height with a deep tan and curly black hair that he wore shorn close to his well-shaped head. He wore glasses with black frames, which gave him an intelligent, although somewhat myopic look.

She put her hand in his and he pulled her to her feet straight into his arms for a warm hug. "You look wonderful," he said effusively. He peered at her, noting the glowing skin with very little makeup and how bright her dark eyes were. "What's happened to you since I saw you last?" he asked suspiciously.

Ana laughed softly as they made their way to his office, "I don't know what you mean," she said coyly.

"I expected you to come in looking drained. Weeks in your studio, working like a madwoman. I'm used to artists who suffer for their work. You look like you just spent a week on the beach in the Mediterranean."

"Actually, I went to Connecticut for the weekend," she said.

"Ah, with Erik," he said knowingly. "No wonder you look so good."

She and Damon had been friends since they met at a party a male model friend of hers threw at his gallery. The party was to launch the model's new fragrance and Damon's gallery was chosen as the venue for its chic, modern style. Once Ana admitted to him that she painted, he insisted on seeing her work and after seeing it he had pestered her to let him introduce her to the New York City art world. It was finally happening.

Damon had also insisted, upon meeting Erik, that Erik was in love with her and she would be a fool not to act on it. Ana had laughed it off.

Now, she was pleased to be able to shock and delight him with, "Erik asked me to marry him."

Damon screamed like a little girl. The receptionist, who was the only other person in the gallery since his client had left, shot up from her desk and looked in their direction with her mouth open in astonishment. She undoubtedly had never heard her employer make that sound before. "Are you all right?" she asked.

Damon waved her off with, "Fine, fine, sorry about that—as you were."

He briskly pulled Ana into his glass-enclosed office and closed the door. He hugged her again, and Ana could tell it was all he could do to resist jumping up and down.

Holding her at arm's length, he beamed. "I couldn't be happier for you, darling. I knew it would happen sooner or later. When's the wedding?"

He gestured to the mocha-colored designer couch. After they were seated he turned to her, his eyes riveted on her. "Or have you had the chance to plan yet?"

"No plans," Ana told him. "It hasn't been twenty-four hours since he asked. I probably shouldn't even be talking about it, but it's hard to hold it in. Sophia phoned earlier and I blurted it out. After she stopped laughing, she said exactly what you just said. It was only a matter of time."

"What was she laughing about?" asked Damon. He always loved a good humorous story. But Ana couldn't divulge what Sophia had found so funny.

It did replay in her mind, though.

She was barely out of bed before the phone rang and her sister was on the other end. "Matty won't let me sleep anyway so I decided to call you and see how your date went last night," Sophia said, curiosity clearly evident in her tone. "I can't believe this is your first date with Erik!"

Ana told her about dinner and the walk, and riding on the back of Erik's Harley. How sensual the whole night had been, culminating in their expression of love for each other and…she gave a dramatic pause…then he'd proposed.

"Oh, my God!" Sophia had yelled into Ana's ear. "He proposed after one date? That man is not wasting time. I knew I liked him for a reason. Then, I suppose, you took him to bed. I'm not trying to be nosy or anything, you don't have to answer if it isn't something you want to talk about, but I'm curious. I mean it's been nearly two years that you two have known each other and have kept your hands to yourselves. There must have been a lot of…um…tension to get rid of."

"Well, yeah," Ana said. "There was…is…a lot of tension."

"Is?" asked Sophia. "You mean you didn't do anything?"

"Neither of us were equipped for sex last night," Ana admitted sheepishly.

"You mean you didn't have any condoms?" her big sister asked, giggling loudly.

"Not one," Ana confirmed.

"That's unbelievable," Sophia said, laughing even louder. "It's been so long since either of you made love that neither of you thought to buy condoms? Can I call Mom and tell her, can I, please?"

"You'd better not tell anyone," Ana warned fiercely.

"I've gotta tell someone," Sophia insisted. "Matty, did you hear how totally clueless your auntie and soon-to-be uncle are?"

Ana laughed in spite of being irritated with her sister. "Let Matty be the only person you tell!"

"Okay, okay," Sophia agreed. "Then tonight is the night?"

"Definitely," Ana said with a sigh.

"Are you ready?" her nosy sister wanted to know.

"More than ready," Ana said right away.

"Yeah, I'm sure you are. What I meant was are you ready for how it's going to change your relationship with Erik?"

"Why would our relationship change?"

"Sweetie, sex changes everything. Even the most enlightened male will become an alpha male on you. If he even detects some other guy sniffing after you, he becomes a beast. It's the pheromones or something. Sex changes everything, I'm telling you. So be prepared little sister."

Ana laughed, "Come on, Erik is the sweetest, most understanding man I've ever met. Sex isn't going to turn him into a Neanderthal."

"It's a physical thing," Sophia insisted. "Love combined with sex turns men into protective, possessive, obsessive beasts. I ought to know, I'm married to one. Just like our mother and our grandmother before her. Ask Mom, she'll tell you."

"I am not phoning Mom with a question like that," Ana adamantly refused.

"Okay, don't say I didn't warn you," Sophia said lightly. Lowering her voice, she added, "I can't believe your nephew has fallen asleep, as loud as I was talking. I'm gonna put him to bed. Good night, sis, have fun tonight."

It was already morning in New York City, but Ana said, "Goodnight, sis," anyway.

Now, Ana smiled at Damon and said, "It was just something I said that struck her as funny."

"Well, I'm seriously thrilled," said Damon. "I love weddings. I can give you the number of my wedding planner if you like."

Damon had married his long-time partner, Sidney, last year. Ana had been one of the bridesmaids. It had been a simple, tasteful affair at the Waldorf Astoria, if you can have a simple affair at the world-famous luxury hotel.

"I'd like that," Ana said thankfully. It was good she had friends who were happy to advise her. She was sure her mother also was going to want to be in on the planning. Natalie Corelli had taken great pains to give Sophia the wedding of her dreams when she had married Matteo. And that had been a rushed affair since Sophia was expecting before the wedding. Natalie warned her that even though she adored Matteo and their child-to-be, she would not ultimately be pleased with wedding photos of her with a huge belly.

Damon got up to find the wedding planner's number. When he located it on his computer, he scribbled the name and number for Ana on a notepad. He went back and sat down beside her, offering her the sheet of paper.

"I suppose we should talk business, even though I could spend a delightful morning talking weddings." He paused and breathed deeply. "The first thing I decide on when I'm introducing a new artist is the theme. You are a portrait painter. Your work is so realistic it's startling. When someone stands before your work, studying it, absorbing the emotions you convey they can't help feeling transported. They know they're not in Kansas anymore, so to speak. So your theme is going to be *The Wizard of Oz*. You do know that story, don't you? You grew up in Italy. You might not be familiar with it."

"Oh, yes, I've seen the movie several times," Ana told him. "I love it."

"Very good," said Damon. "Well, in the beginning the movie is in black and white. Then, when Dorothy is transported to Oz, the movie is in color. Your show will begin with your drawings in charcoal and will progress to your larger, more colorful works. In my opinion, even though you use real models in your work, finished results have a fantasy element to them."

Ana had been nodding in agreement. "I like the concept," she said.

"We will even have a yellow-brick road the night of the show," Damon said, smiling. "I know people in the theater who can make it happen. The patrons will walk the yellow-brick road while they get the full effect of your work."

Ana looked at him in amazement, "No wonder you're so successful," she exclaimed.

Damon smiled warmly. "I do know how to put on a show. But, darling, you're going to be the star."

Ana's phone rang while she was headed back home in a cab half an hour later. Seeing Erik's name and number in the display, she cooed, "Hello, how has your day been going?"

Erik sighed deeply. She could tell by the tone of that sigh that he missed her as much as she missed him. "I can't think of anything except seeing you again."

She laughed huskily. "I'm suffering, too."

"Where are you?"

She told him.

"Can you come to my office at noon?"

"Sure," she immediately said, excitement coursing through her.

"See you then," Erik said with a note of laughter in his voice.

They said goodbye, and she relaxed in the back of the cab.

Her mind was running ahead of her, wondering what he was planning. Surely not making love in his office? The door *did* have a lock on it. She laughed softly to herself, wondering when she'd started entertaining sexy thoughts like that.

When she got there Abigail Sinclair, Erik's long-time secretary, a petite African-American woman in her mid-fifties, smiled at her and said with warmth, "Ana, it's lovely to see you. How are you, dear?"

"Great, Abby, and you?" said Ana, returning her smile.

"I'm well, thank you. Go right in, Erik's waiting."

Abby was one of Ana's favorite people. Married, with two grown children, she loved her job and she and her schoolteacher husband, Harry, doted on one another. Ana had observed them at several Whitaker Enterprises social events such as their annual Christmas party. Abby was invariably impeccably dressed in business suits and two-inch-heeled pumps, her long auburn hair in a bun, glasses either perched on the end of her nose or hanging on a magnetic clip on her chest. Abby was always solicitous but there was an added excitement in her hazel eyes today.

After Ana had been ushered into Erik's office, she knew why. A representative from Tiffany's was in Erik's office. Two armed guards stood over by the window trying to look inconspicuous. But they all turned to look at Ana when she walked into the room.

The woman from Tiffany's was in her sixties with wavy white hair that she wore in a pixie cut. She had bright blue eyes and when she smiled she revealed slightly crooked but white teeth. To Ana the fact that she hadn't gone to the trouble of having her teeth made perfect-looking spoke to her belief that she didn't need artifice to feel beautiful about herself. Ana liked that.

Erik smiled and met her halfway. "Sweetheart, I hope you don't mind. With both of us pressured with business obligations I thought it would be more convenient if Tiffany's came to us." Taking her hand, he led her over to his desk where the Tiffany's representative had spread a black velvet cloth and placed several engagement rings in their boxes upon it.

Ana was sure her face reflected her surprise but could not for the life of her fix her facial muscles to look any other way. "They're all beautiful," she said, her gaze taking in all of the diamonds. The quality of the stones was irrefutable. White diamonds expertly cut and polished. All of them were five carats or higher. Her eyes were not drawn to the large stones, though, but the beauty of the cut and how well the stones caught the light.

"Darling, this is Carol Richards. Ms. Richards, my fiancée, Ana Corelli."

The two women shook hands and Carol said, "It's wonderful to meet you, Ms. Corelli."

"Likewise," Ana said, smiling. She looked up at Erik. He smiled, his love for her evident in his golden-brown depths. "I was going to choose one myself, but

I thought it would be best to get your input." He gestured to the rings. "What do you think? Does one strike your fancy?"

Once again, Ana perused the rings. Square-shaped, pear-shaped, they were all beautiful, but the one that she liked the most was a five-carat solitaire in a platinum setting. She pointed to it.

Carol picked up the ring and slipped it onto her finger. It fit perfectly. Ana gazed down at it, turning it this way and that, marveling at how the stone caught the light and the many colors that sparkled inside it.

"How did you know which size to get?" she asked Erik.

"I just described you to Carol," he said.

"After years of experience, I'm a good guesser," said Carol modestly.

"I don't believe I'm saying this," Erik joked, "but you chose the smallest ring. It's okay to choose something larger, sweetheart. I don't like to brag, but I can afford it."

"This is perfect," Ana said. She raised to her tiptoes and kissed his cheek. "Thank you. I assure you this is the one for me."

"Actually," said Carol authoritatively. "Ms. Corelli has a good eye for diamonds. The ring she chose might not be the largest, but it is the highest quality of them all. Pure white and although it's nearly impossible to find a diamond without any faults whatsoever because they are a product of nature this comes close."

Erik kissed Ana's cheek. "And I thought you were being thrifty."

Everyone laughed.

"Very well," Erik said to Carol. "We'll take this one."

Carol smiled, her eyes twinkling as she looked at Ana, then Erik. "Congratulations on your upcoming nuptials. I hope you two will be very happy."

She shook hands with Erik, then Ana, after which she began packing up the remaining diamonds while Erik pulled Ana aside and hugged her tightly. "Now, if you should change your mind, you can always take it back."

Ana looked at him as if he'd lost his mind. "Exchange it? No, never. This ring will not leave my finger, ever." Then, they kissed.

It took Carol clearing her throat to tear them apart. "If you'll sign here," she said to Erik. Erik went over and quickly signed the form. He glanced at the final sales price and didn't even flinch. "Thank you, Carol."

"It was my pleasure," said Carol who promptly signaled to the guards that it was time to depart. One of them opened the door for her and preceded her. The other followed.

When they were alone, Ana threw her arms around Erik's neck in excitement. "You're so sneaky. I thought you wanted me to come by for..."

"Love in the afternoon?" he guessed, his eyes alight with humor.

"Yes!" Ana admitted almost defiantly. At the time

it had sounded like a good idea to her. "Don't tell me it never crossed your mind."

Erik laughed softly and smoothed her brow with the pad of his thumb, a gesture he was fond of doing, Ana recalled, just before he kissed her, which he did, long and passionately. When they came up for air, he said, "I couldn't make love to you with Abby right outside my door. I'd never be able to look her in the eyes again."

Ana left Erik's office feeling as though she were floating on a cloud of happiness. And when she got home, she saw that someone had left a package at her door. Once she was inside she opened it. It was the Walter Mosley book she had admired in the bookstore window the night before.

Chapter 6

Etta James belted out lyrics to "I Just Wanna Make Love to You" as Ana danced around the living room area of the loft, supposedly cleaning. She wasn't the neatest person in the world. When they were teens her sister, Sophia, used to say her bedroom looked like a tornado had hit it. Once she was living on her own, however, Ana had learned to pick up after herself. Now her house looked shabby chic. At least that's how she liked to think of the juxtaposition of ultra-modern furnishings with antiques thrown in here and there. And the kitchen had recently had an upgrade. Now all the appliances were stainless steel, the countertops granite, and the floor Italian tile. Except for the two bathrooms, which had tile floors, the remainder of the loft had hardwood floors.

Ana warbled along with the CD.

She'd been listening to Etta ever since she'd returned from Erik's office. She would clean a little, dance a little and admire her ring—a lot. She couldn't stop smiling, sometimes laughing out loud. She was glad she was alone because anyone observing her would think she was certifiably insane. She wanted to talk with someone, but she had already tried to phone her mother and the message service had come on and she had not wanted to leave a mere message about this momentous occasion. This news had to be told live, not recorded. The same thing had happened when she'd phoned Sophia. She couldn't talk to anyone in Erik's family because he wanted to tell them about their engagement when they got together in New Haven for Thanksgiving. That was nearly a month away.

Finished dusting and straightening up in the living room, she moved on to the kitchen.

On the way home she'd stopped by the market and bought fresh salmon and salad fixings. She was making one of Erik's favorite meals tonight: grilled salmon with spicy red pepper sauce, a baked potato and garden salad. It was simple to prepare yet delicious and light. She didn't want anything weighing them down tonight. Nothing was going to go wrong when things started getting heated between them.

It had crossed her mind to go to a spa and get the works: hair, nails, facial, wax. But she was plucked and prodded enough in her work. Erik liked her natural. She liked her natural state, as well. Besides, doing all that bordered on the obsessive and she was already neurotic enough. She kept her legs and underarms shaved, took long baths, after which she moisturized. That was sufficient.

Erik was coming at eight. By seven, she had the salmon ready to put on the grill, the salad and the pepper sauce were prepared and the potatoes washed and ready to pop into the microwave and then afterward put on the grill a few minutes to make the skins crisp. A trick her dad had taught her via one of their Skype cooking lessons. He was the chef in the family. Her mother could cook but didn't really enjoy it. Carlo relished cooking all the recipes his mother, Renata, had taught him. Because Ana hadn't paid much attention when he'd tried to teach her to cook while she was growing up, she had persuaded him a couple years ago to teach her over the computer. So about once a month, they got together via Skype and he taught her another recipe from his ever-expanding handwritten cookbook. She was a quick learner and was becoming quite proficient in the kitchen.

She was just thinking she should start getting ready for her date when her cell phone rang. A quick glance at the display told her it was her mother phoning.

"Mom!" she answered with a huge grin. "Where have you been? I've been trying to get in touch."

"I know, I know, sweetie," said Natalie a bit breathlessly. "I saw all the missed calls. What's up? You sound good. You're not sick or anything?"

Ana laughed shortly. "No, I'm fine. Well, not fine,

exactly. I'm excited, a little scared, maybe. I mean this is such a huge step to take. It's something I only want to do once, like you and Daddy…"

"Ana Maria Corelli," Natalie interrupted her, her tone frustrated. "What are you talking about?"

Ana sighed, still grinning. "Erik asked me to marry him."

"Oh, my God. Carlo, get in here—your baby girl's engaged!" Natalie yelled, laughter bubbling up. Then, Ana could hear her mother talking to her father in the background.

"Erik finally popped the question! Okay, here, but I want to speak back with her when you're done," Natalie's voice trailed off as she handed the phone to Carlo.

Her father came on the line. "Is this true, *bambina?* You have accepted his proposal?"

"Yes," Ana told her father, her voice confident. "I love him, Daddy."

Carlo gave a resigned sigh. "Well, I suppose, your mother and I have a new son-in-law."

"You don't sound too happy about it," Ana said with a laugh to conceal the hurt. She had expected her father to sound as excited as her mother about her upcoming nuptials.

Her mother must have snatched the phone from her father's hand because hers was the next voice Ana heard, and she sounded miffed. "Honey, don't pay any attention to your father. You're the last daughter he has to walk down the aisle and he doesn't think there's a man alive who's good enough for you. Erik is a good man. I like him, and your father will learn to like him, or else."

Ana smiled, and said, "Give Dad a kiss for me and tell him I'm sorry but I had to grow up sometime. I'd better get ready for my date with your future son-in-law now. Love you both."

"We love you, too, sweetie," Natalie assured her. "Give our best to Erik."

A quarter after seven, she started counting down the minutes. A soak in the tub helped her to relax. Taking pains to smooth scented lotion over every inch of her body and making sure her nails were done kept her mind focused. Otherwise, she kept thinking about the last time she'd made love to Jack Russo and how she had thought of it as an act of love only to find out it had been a farewell performance. The next day she'd gotten a text saying, "Sorry, babe, this isn't working out. I wish you much happiness in your future endeavors. Truly, I do." It had been the longest text message she'd ever gotten from him. She immediately phoned him. He didn't answer, of course. She left a message that was brief, to the point and only two words. After she'd verbally given him the middle finger, she felt better, but the feeling didn't last long because she'd made the mistake of giving him her heart, one of the most worthless human beings to walk the planet. How could she have been so idiotic? She questioned her common sense. She questioned her ability to tell a decent human being from an indecent one. Most of all she questioned her taste in men.

Tonight is going to be so much different from that other night, long ago she thought confidently.

She had done her penance, suffered through the indignity of making a fool of herself over a man who wasn't worthy of her. She had earned the right to happiness.

When the doorbell rang, she was dressed in a short black dress that clung to her curves, and a pair of sexy, black Ferragamo sandals. Her wavy black hair was parted in the middle and fell down her back. Her lips were red and pouty, and her dark eyes were smoldering.

She opened the door and Erik stood there with deep red roses in one hand and a bottle of wine in the other. She heard his sharp intake of breath and enjoyed the deliberate, sensual perusal of her body. Her efforts had been rewarded. "Wow," was all he said before stepping into the loft.

Ana was likewise delighted by his appearance. She made that perfectly clear by relieving him of the roses and the wine and setting both on the foyer table, then grasping him by his jacket's lapels and pulling him down for a lingering kiss. One of Erik's muscular arms went around her waist and held her tightly while the other caressed her back and slipped further down to squeeze her behind. He was hard in seconds, and softly groaned with pleasure against her mouth.

Ana molded her body to his. She inhaled his heady scent, masculine and clean. His touch made her core melt. Her nipples grew erect and pressed against the fabric of her bra magnifying her arousal. Her sex throbbed. She was ready, so ready.

She tore her mouth from his. She smiled seductively. "I made dinner for you."

"Smells wonderful," Erik returned, devouring her with his eyes. It was apparent that food was the last thing on his mind right now. "It'll keep, won't it?"

"Oh, yeah," she breathed, and once again their lips were locked in a passionate embrace. Erik picked her up. Ana wrapped her legs around him and he carried her to the bedroom.

Anticipating an eventful night, Ana had readied the bed, folding the comforter down to the foot of the bed, and turning back the top sheet. Erik gently set her down and began undressing her. He slowly unzipped her dress and pulled it off her shoulders. Ana let the dress fall in folds to the floor. She stood in a skimpy teddy whose color nearly matched her brown skin. Erik bent and planted kisses along the curve of her neck, enjoying the warmth and fragrance of her skin. His nerve endings were on fire with pent-up desire. Touching her greatly enhanced his urgent need. He closed his eyes momentarily thinking that if he denied himself the sight of her it would ease the tension. He was wrong. Even if he were blind, her smell, the softness of her skin would drive him to distraction. Ana did not once think to close her eyes. She didn't want to miss a thing. She reveled in the fact that it was she he wanted so badly that…and she touched him to make sure…he was so hard he was about to burst! She felt the pulse in her neck where his lips were kissing right now throb with excitement. Her heart was racing.

Erik's hand gently squeezed her breast. She sighed with contentment. His hand slipped inside her bra and cupped her naked breast. That nearly made her scream with delight, but she muffled the exclamation and panted instead. Erik obviously took this as a sign to get a move on because after that he quickly dealt with the bra and pulled the teddy off her. She now stood before him in her bikini panties. Erik stared for a moment, unable to take his eyes off her. He had known she would be beautiful unclothed, that was a given, but anticipation paled in comparison to reality. Her breasts were firm, round and with nipples that looked so sweet, he had to taste them. When his tongue touched one of them he felt her tremble with pleasure, and a soft gasp escape from between her swollen lips.

He thought she might swoon. But he was wrong. She reached for his belt buckle. Her hand inadvertently touched his manhood and he steeled himself against coming too soon. He had to hastily back up, saying, "Let me." At this point he knew that their first time would not be slow and easy. They were both too excited for that.

While he got undressed, Ana peeled off her bikini panties with nary a blush in sight.

Now they were both naked and both got their fill of each other in all their glory. Ana's eyes rested on him and the smile on her lips told him she liked what she saw. Inspired by that smile, he reached for her and she went into his arms. Their mouths touched and he found himself kissing her almost shyly, feeling her out, then he felt her relent and give herself over to him. From that point on, their movements felt natural, as if this were not their first time at all, but one of many supremely intimate moments during which giving and taking of physical gratification was as natural as breathing.

He laid her on the bed and rained kisses all over her. His hands knew her every curve. With a great deal of joy he partook of her, her thighs wantonly spread open and with her writhing beneath him, until she moaned loudly and trembled in his arms. Then he got up and put on the condom. She watched him, could not take her eyes off him, and when he returned to the bed, she welcomed him inside of her and clung to him with renewed ardor. His thrusts were deep and satisfying to Ana. She held on to his butt, feeling the muscles contract with each push. After some time passed, she came. And it felt so good. At last, she knew what the difference was between making love to someone and just having sex. When you were in love the climax felt a hundred times better. It was sublime.

They lay looking in each other's eyes, smiling contentedly. Erik spoke first, "We're perfect together."

Ana, who felt full of emotions fighting for prominence inside of her, nodded. She hadn't known she would feel this way, full of joy that kept building in momentum until she feared she would burst into tears. She now wouldn't be plagued by her last encounter with

Jack Russo. Jack who? Sophia was right. Jack was a glitch in her sexual past. Erik was her future.

She reached up and gently touched his cheek. "How could it be anything less?"

"You really believe that?" Erik asked hopefully. She looked so beautiful to him, her hair wild and sexy, a faint layer of perspiration on her skin from making love. He could die a happy man right now. For so long he'd been in love with her, wishing that one day soon she would see that he was the man for her. Yes, she'd accepted his marriage proposal, but making love to her was an even bigger step in their relationship. It meant she trusted him with her heart. No matter what some guys say about their ability to make love to as many women as they can get in bed and walk away unaffected the next day, it was a lie. Oh, it affected you all right. Depending on your circumstances it either served to harden your heart or leave it vulnerable to being broken into pieces.

Peering deeply in his eyes, Ana smiled and softly said, "With all my heart. I can't regret how long it's taken us to get to this point, though, because the time we spent together as friends only strengthened my love and respect for you. I got to know the real you."

"Oh, yeah?" said Erik playfully, white teeth flashing in a grin. "Tell me three things you know about me, and I don't mean something simple like my favorite color is blue."

Ana pursed her lips, pretending this was an arduous task. "Hmm, let's see. When you were a boy of nine you stole your dad's car and went joyriding. This was in Connecticut. You probably would've gotten yourself killed in New York."

"Who told you that?" Erik asked genuinely surprised.

"Drusilla," Ana said, laughing. "She didn't swear me to secrecy so I think it's safe to divulge the name of my source."

"Okay, number two?"

"You have a copy of the *Sports Illustrated* that has me on the cover in your nightstand drawer."

"How long have you known that?" he asked, feeling not in the least guilty about being found out.

"Almost immediately after it hit the newsstands," she said. "I broke a nail while I was at your place and I couldn't find a nail clipper in your medicine cabinet so I figured you kept one in your nightstand drawer like I do."

"You didn't say anything," he said, his tone questioning.

"No, I didn't want to get into why you had it there. I knew we were attracted to each other. We have been from the beginning. But I was comfortable with what we had. I didn't want to risk losing it. You understand?"

"Of course," he said gently, and kissed her chin.

"Now that we can talk about it…you didn't do anything naughty with my *Sports Illustrated* cover, did you?"

Erik laughed shortly. "I take the fifth."

She giggled. "Don't be embarrassed. I had to invent ways of surviving without jumping you, too."

"Such as?" he asked, brows raised in an askance expression.

"The detachable showerhead in my shower got a work out," she admitted, blushing even if she *were* lying naked in bed with her lover.

"I'm shocked," Erik said, feigning horror. "Okay, on to number three."

"I know you never got over your mother leaving," Ana said seriously, which instantly killed the levity in the conversation.

For a moment Erik looked somewhat stricken. He was quiet for a full thirty seconds and those thirty seconds felt like hours to Ana who instinctively knew she had brought up an unwelcome subject.

Erik fought for the right words to say. He was not aware Ana had perceived how he felt about his mother. She had been there when Mari had suddenly reentered his and Belana's lives more than a year ago. Ana had held him after she had died. In fact, she had refused to let him spend the night alone and they had talked for hours before he'd fallen asleep, exhausted.

"I never said anything," he murmured, and sat up in bed. He busied himself by going into the bathroom and cleaning himself up.

Ana sat up in bed, too, and said, "You didn't have to say anything. It was written all over your face when you looked at her. I could feel waves of emotion coming off you whenever you talked about her before and after she died. Have you forgiven her?"

She could see into the bathroom from the bed. Erik thought about shutting the door to shut Ana out if only for a few moments. He needed privacy because he was not ready to discuss his mother. Or the impact her desertion had had on him, even if he claimed she had none at all.

Ana rose and went into the bathroom, too, which had a tub and a separate shower. "You don't have to answer that," she said, and went to turn on the hot water in the shower. "I'm going to take a quick shower. You're welcome to join me."

Erik relaxed and followed her into the stall, not saying a word. He didn't want their earlier rapport to end. He inwardly chided himself for his inability to be forthcoming about his mother. But then again he had no practice in the matter. For years he was stalwart and denied feeling anything about her. He thought the best defense was to pretend not to care. It was her loss if she didn't want anything to do with her son and daughter.

His father, the good man that he is, refused to badmouth Mari. He simply told Erik and Belana that Mari had made bad choices and someday she would realize her mistake.

Someday wound up being too late. By the time she had come to that conclusion she was dying of lung cancer. The few weeks she spent with him and Belana could never make up for years of neglect. Erik was a man, though, and saw to it that she had the best care possible.

And when she drew her last breath, he and Belana had been there to gently usher her out of this world. That's the least he thought he could do.

So why couldn't he talk about her with the woman he loved?

Ana ran her soapy hands across his broad shoulders as she stood in front of him in the shower. She didn't seem to mind getting her hair wet. It lay in ringlets about her lovely face. Her golden brown skin was beaded with drops of water. The contrast of her skin with those dark chocolate eyes killed him. He got weak with desire whenever she looked at him intently like she was now. He wanted to bare his soul, give her anything she wanted. "For a long time," he blurted out, "I thought I'd wind up just like my father—abandoned by the woman I loved. I know it makes no sense. I'm not my father. But children learn by example and my example was an extremely hardworking man who had been left by his beautiful wife for a poor man she lusted-after. I got the lusted after part from Drusilla when I got older and she stopped trying to hide the details from me. My mother, who was a ballet dancer, as you know, left my father for a handsome French dance instructor. She threw away her marriage and her two children for him."

Ana was afraid to interrupt. Sometimes you just had to be quiet and let the other person talk.

"Growing up I went through all kinds of emotions concerning Mari. Sometimes I hated her. Sometimes I missed her so much it hurt. Sometimes I prayed that she'd come back to us. When she did come back I felt cheated because she didn't have very much time left. Have I forgiven her? I realize that my forgiving her means nothing, she's gone, but, yeah, I guess I have forgiven her even though I sometimes still feel like that little lost boy inside. Because of her I was afraid of letting go and truly loving someone until you came along with your own neuroses." He smiled at her.

Ana laughed. "Yeah, me and my trust issues."

"You weren't the only one with issues. Loving you has freed me. I'm not afraid of being abandoned anymore."

"And I trust you," said Ana, smiling up at him.

"Good," said Erik, bending his head to claim her mouth in a searing kiss that left her weak in the knees. As he pulled her firmly against him Ana realized he'd recovered from their earlier session in bed and was ready to go again. She smiled against his hungry mouth. She fleetingly wondered if the shower floor were too slippery for them to make love right here. Erik's back was against the tiles. Now the shower's spray was hitting the back of Ana's body. She gazed up. "Do you think we could do it here?"

Erik shook his head in the negative. "No, baby, I'm not going to take a chance on you getting hurt."

Ana's stomach growled loud enough for both of them to hear.

"Besides, you're hungry," Erik said. "Come on, let's dry off. I'm a big boy, I can wait."

Ana looked pointedly at his erection, her expression doubtful. "Are you sure?"

"It'll calm down in a minute," Erik joked.

So they dried off, Ana put on her bathrobe, styled her damp hair in a hastily done braid down her back, and Erik slipped into his clothes of jeans and shirt. They went into the kitchen where Ana fired up the grill and put the prepared salmon and the potatoes on it while Erik set the table. They talked while they worked.

"Damon thinks the show is going to be a hit." She told him about her visit with Damon today. "I'm nervous."

"You have no need to be," Erik said with confidence. "You're brilliant."

"I'm an unknown entity," she said realistically. "The critics will tear me to shreds. A model trying to paint, they'll say? It's hilarious. That gossip show, I can't remember what it's called..."

"Anyway," Ana said as she adjusted the temperature on the grill, being mindful that fish cooked quickly, "they'll probably have people stationed outside the gallery getting opinions from people leaving the show and even if they like my work they'll have catty remarks for the viewing audience."

"You'll let it roll off your back," Erik said. "You've soldiered through bad reviews before."

"Yeah, but they didn't matter," Ana said. "I learned to detach my emotions from what people said about me."

"Same thing," Erik said. "You'll survive. We all have to take the knocks when we're doing something we love and are not going with the flow anymore. Independent thinkers are usually deemed nuts until everyone realizes they were on to something all along. At least you're doing what your heart desires. Imagine all the people out there who never took the risk. We could have had any number of inventors with wonderful ideas that never got off the launching pad. Writers who wrote great novels that never saw the light of day. Stick to your dreams."

"God, I love you!" Ana exclaimed, her eyes dancing with delight. She peeked at the salmon on the grill. "I think the fish is ready. But the potatoes need to stay on the grill a little longer so the skins will get crisp."

"She's beautiful and she cooks," said Erik.

"Well, she cooks some things," Ana said. "I'm slowly learning. I won't be writing a cookbook anytime soon."

"Then you'd say you're not a domestic goddess?" joked Erik.

"If it's a domestic goddess you want to marry, keep looking," Ana said truthfully. "I'm messy and, while I like to cook, I can prepare only around seven dishes with any hope of them turning out edible."

"Don't worry, darling, I can cook," Erik assured her.

"That's right, you can," said Ana as if the thought had just occurred to her. Erik had fed her numerous times. He wasn't a master chef, but he knew his way around a pasta dish and grilled a steak to perfection. And his pancakes were to die for. He'd learned his culinary skills from Drusilla whose belief was men needed to know how to feed themselves and not base their search for a mate on whether or not she could cook.

Women have to work nowadays just like men, Drusilla told him. And no matter how much money you have you should never have to depend on someone else preparing your meals.

"Your grandmother taught you well," she said. "I have to thank her next time I see her."

"Which will be on Thanksgiving," Erik reminded her.

"Yes, and I must remember not to wear my ring into the house because she'll spot it like a hawk on a mouse," Ana said, laughing.

"You've got that right," Erik agreed, imagining Drusilla's expression when they told her about the engagement. She would happily shout "Hallelujah!"

To be honest, he felt like shouting it himself.

Chapter 7

Like every holiday season, that period between Halloween and New Year's Eve, time seemed to speed up for Ana. The first week of November she had to fly to Tahiti to be filmed and photographed in a tropical setting for Dare's spring campaign. The perfume she represented in print and TV ads was selling quite well and there was talk of a whole line of complementary products to go with the perfume: shampoo, conditioner, skin lotion and bath salts. When she arrived for the shoot she thought someone would mention her weight gain but Josh Cannon, who worked for the cosmetics company and was coordinating the shoot, only said, "You look gorgeous, so full of life, what's your secret?"

Ana laughed and said, "I'm in love."

"That's better than cosmetic surgery," Josh avowed, laughing along with her.

Later that day Ana had cracked up when she was being poured into an ankle-length billowy white dress whose tight bodice produced prodigious cleavage and the wardrobe lady remarked, "Have you had a boob job since the last time I dressed you?"

"No, just a bit of happy weight," Ana told her.

Ana enjoyed the shoot. The weather was balmy compared to New York City's and she was spoiled between sessions with fresh fruit and spring water and the male model working with her had a repertoire of jokes that kept her laughing.

At the end of the shoot she got to see some of the film footage. Josh was right. She looked extremely happy and healthy. She and the male model appeared very much in love as they walked on the beach, shared a romantic dinner and stood wrapped in each other's arms as the breezes ruffled her dress and hair, the backdrop of the beach at night augmenting the sensual feel of the scene.

With the job done, she got the first flight back to New York. She arrived at JFK on a Saturday afternoon and was met at the terminal by Erik who picked her up in a bear hug as if he hadn't seen her in weeks instead of mere days.

Ana dropped her carry-on bags and hugged him tightly, breathing in his male essence as she did so, "I can't believe I've only been gone a few days. You were constantly on my mind."

Erik was too busy kissing her to answer her. And Ana forgot everything as they gave each other a proper hello. But they had to come up for air sometime and when they did, Erik said, "I think I must be addicted to you. No matter how busy I was I couldn't help remembering how you sound, how you smell, how you feel."

"You're so sweet," Ana said, reaching up to wipe the lipstick from his lower lip with the pad of her thumb. She was happy he'd missed her as much as she'd missed him. They picked up her bags and made their way across the terminal, talking all the way.

"How did it go?" he asked.

"It was great, everyone concentrated on their jobs. No drama. It was a dream shoot."

"Good," Erik said, his arm about her waist. Lucky for him Ana packed lightly for her frequent jaunts so he had a free arm to hug her with. The way she put it her employers provided her wardrobe, anyway. She needed to pack only the necessities.

"How was work for you?" she returned.

"Headaches," said Erik. "We're experiencing some suspicious losses at our dairy in Minnesota. I'm going to have to go check it out on Monday."

"Minnesota," Ana said glumly, "Where it's already probably below freezing this time of year?"

"You betcha," Erik joked with a passable Minnesotan accent.

Laughing, Ana said, "I'm not inviting myself along on this trip."

Erik squeezed her. "You mean you don't like biting

wind and snow? I was going to suggest a cabin in Aspen over the Christmas holidays."

"Just you and I?" asked Ana, her interest piqued.

"We don't need anyone else."

"That, I'm up for," Ana assured him.

"Then I'll reserve our cabin," Erik promised.

In the back of her mind Ana was thinking this would be the first time in years she hadn't gone home for Christmas. How would her parents take the news? She'd joked with Sophia about going someplace romantic with Erik, but that had only been wishful thinking.

They walked on in silence and when they got to the car Erik had hired so that he wouldn't have to go through the hassle of parking, he held the door open for her. Once the driver pulled away from the curb, he said, "Something on your mind?"

"I haven't missed Christmas in Milan since I moved here," she told him.

"Sweetheart, I'll understand if you want to go home for Christmas."

Ana looked deeply in his eyes. She saw only love and trust reflected back at her. Yes, he would make the sacrifice if it would make her happy.

"Would you go with me?"

"Sorry, I just couldn't spare the travel time," Erik said regrettably. "My work schedule won't allow it. Aspen I could do, but not Italy."

Yes, Ana thought sadly, going to Milan was not just a weekend getaway.

"I'll wait and go home in the New Year," she decided.

She would miss her family and all the accoutrements of Christmas with them provided. However, she and Erik were building a life together. Time and effort went into a good relationship.

He smiled. "I'm serious. I would understand."

"I know," she said softly. "But you work so hard. It would be great to get away for a couple days alone with you. Aspen, it is."

"All right," Erik conceded. However he still felt unsure about the situation.

On Monday after he'd boarded the company plane for Minnesota he put in a call to Abby. She answered in her usual efficient manner, "What can I do for you, Erik?"

"I have a dilemma," Erik said. "One that needs your special touch. Let me explain."

Five minutes later Erik could hear the smile in Abby's voice when she said, "I'd be happy to arrange everything. Consider it done."

"You're a godsend, Abby," said Erik with warmth. "I don't know what I'd do without you."

Abby had laughed softly. "Just make sure I get an invitation to the wedding."

"You and Harry will be there to dance the night away," Erik promised. "See you when I get back."

"Have a safe trip," Abby said and rang off.

Erik hung up the phone and relaxed in the plush leather seat. The flight attendant stopped next to him. "We're getting ready to take off, Mr. Whitaker. Please buckle your seat belt and turn off any electronic devices."

In Minneapolis, a hired car was waiting to take him to the nearby town where the plant manager and key members of his staff were waiting to meet with him. He enjoyed the scenery as the car sped toward the plant. Cows grazed in pastures. It was snowing but not heavily. He supposed it was still too early for one of Minnesota's snowstorms. But it was definitely cold outside at 28 degrees. And the wind was biting. He had checked the weather before the trip, though, so he was dressed warmly enough.

His cell phone rang and he took it out of his inside coat pocket and glanced at the display. It was his father, John. "Hey, Dad, what's up?"

"Just thought you should be advised that when I acquired the plant in Harris, Minnesota, the plant manager and the owner were at odds," he said. "I had both of them vetted and decided that if the owner sold, the manager could keep his job. Olsen is a good man. Hadn't had any trouble since then, till now. Harris is a small town and relatives of the former owner work at the plant. Maybe one of them holds a grudge."

"That's a possibility," said Erik. "We'll see." He already had a plan in the works.

Later, at the meeting, Jim Olsen, the plant manager appeared relieved to see Erik. He was a tall, heavyset man with blond hair and brows and a somewhat florid face. He introduced the other four persons seated around the conference room table. Then he and Erik sat down. "I'm sorry you had to come all this way," he began. "But the accountants were unable to pinpoint exactly why we've experienced losses in the last two quarters."

Jim had emailed Erik files with the most recent numbers. Erik noticed a ten percent drop in profits in the past nine months. His auditors found that the amount of stock ordered by stores remained high. However stores were reporting that they were not receiving the right amount of stock they had ordered. To Erik that meant someone was intercepting outgoing stock before it could be shipped to stores. In which case he had to discover who was doing it and get proof of their guilt. To that end, a week ago he had hired a local private detective to keep the loading dock under surveillance until further notice. He told this to the five people sitting at the conference table with him now. "I'm expecting the detective any minute," he informed them.

Erik wasn't sure his hunch was correct, but what his father had earlier told him made him somewhat confident that he was on the right track.

Jim Olsen's secretary stuck her head in the conference room. "Mr. Olsen, there is a Ms. Valerie Estes here to see you. She says she has important information for you."

His color turning even more florid, Jim hastily stood. "Show her in, Ms. Bern."

A tall brunette dressed in a dark pantsuit and a heavy coat entered the room carrying a black satchel. Erik noticed that when she set the bag on the conference table she did it with care. Jim made hasty introductions and once Erik had been identified, Ms. Estes gave him an almost imperceptible nod with a slight smile on her face. "I believe I have the information you requested, Mr. Whitaker," she said, her tone businesslike. From her satchel she retrieved a laptop, which she set on the conference table, opened and switched on. In only a couple of minutes she clicked on a file and opened it. "Please take a look at this," she said.

Everyone gathered around the laptop's screen and watched as a man approached the loading dock of the plant. It was early morning according to the time posted at the bottom of the screen. It was still dark out. He unlocked the loading-dock door and since it was the rolling kind, he pushed up on it and the mechanism did the rest. Then the viewing audience noticed a large van being backed up to the loading dock. Two other men got out and leaped onto the dock and followed the first man into the plant. Minutes later they returned with hand trucks loaded with boxes of the plant's dairy products.

"Do you recognize those men?" asked Erik of the five plant employees in the conference room. No one said a word, but Erik could tell they did. He sighed. It was time to clean house.

After a couple minutes, Jim spoke up. "I'm sorry to say one of them is my son, Jim, Jr. I don't know the names of the other two, although they look familiar."

"I do," said Bob Holstein, supervisor of the shipping department. "I hired them about a year ago." He looked regrettably at Jim. "Jim, Jr. recommended them."

Erik turned to Jim and placed a hand on his shoulder and squeezed reassuringly.

"Look, there is no easy way to do this, but I'll give you two options. You can fire Jim, Jr. and the other two men and have security cameras installed in the loading area. That was an oversight. Or we can let the police handle it. I'm truly sorry it turned out this way."

"So am I," Jim said with a hangdog expression. His fellow employees offered sympathy. Erik pulled the private detective aside. "Thank you for your assistance, Ms. Estes."

"Sometimes," she said with a glance in Jim Olsen's direction, "this job sucks."

Erik knew what she meant. He felt bad for Jim Olsen. However the situation had to be handled and the culprits punished.

When the conference room had been cleared of everyone except him and Jim Olsen, he looked at Jim with regret. "I realize at this point you don't think things can go back to how they were before this incident, but they can. My father tells me you're a good man, Jim. You run this plant well and you're fair with your employees. They obviously respect you. What's more, you seem to enjoy your job. Don't let this affect your satisfaction in it. I don't hold you responsible for what happened here." He held out his hand.

Jim gratefully shook it and said, "It's going to be hard. My wife will cry her heart out over the situation. Jim, Jr. has been in trouble before, and we thought he was trying to straighten his life out."

"I have every bit of confidence in you, Jim," Erik said sincerely.

Jim let go of his hand and walked over to the large window that looked down on the employee parking lot. "Twenty-five years in this job with a spotless record and it's come to this. I should have been watching him more closely when he moved back into the house. Of course, we couldn't let him be homeless. It really pisses me off that while I was sleeping he was stealing my keys to steal from the company." His eyes were tormented when he faced Erik again. "This is going to kill my wife. But I'm going to have to put him out, and let him fend for himself."

Erik didn't know what to say to that, not being a father himself. He had no sage advice to offer. Sometimes you had to make hard choices in life.

"That'll be tough," was all he said.

Jim nodded in agreement, then seemed to gather strength from someplace deep inside and said, "It has to be done."

Erik left the plant soon after that. The hired car drove him back to the airport in Minneapolis and the company plane was ready to take off within minutes. Erik had known the flight plan ahead of time and had made it back to the plane with minutes to spare.

As they winged their way back to New York, he slept, which is what he resorted to when he didn't want to think anymore. He honestly had not guessed that the culprit could have been someone so close to one of his employees. That kind of betrayal was difficult to get over. He wished Jim and his wife good luck.

He slept the entire flight and awakened only when the plane was touching down. It was dark in the city. The November air was chilly but nowhere near as cold as it had been in Minnesota.

He went directly to Ana's loft in Greenwich Village without having phoned ahead. It was around eight in the evening, and he wouldn't have been surprised if she were out. But he wanted desperately to see her.

He could use some comfort and when he needed comforting he automatically thought of Ana. The best part of his job was helping save people's jobs. The worst part was seeing someone emotionally devastated as Jim Olsen had been this afternoon.

She swung the door open and let out a scream of delight. She was in his arms in an instant and kissing him a second after that. She pulled him inside, her dark eyes shining. "You're just in time for dinner."

It snowed on Thanksgiving morning. The flurries were light, but by noon when Erik and Ana pulled onto the driveway of his parents' house in New Haven, there were two inches on the ground.

In the car, Ana removed her engagement ring and carefully placed it inside a zippered compartment in her handbag. She smiled at Erik who was behind the wheel of the SUV. "Here we go."

They got out and Erik firmly clasped her hand in his as they walked to the house. The door was opened by Isobel who looked smart in navy blue pants and a cream-colored, thick cable-knit sweater. Erik's step-mother hugged him first, then Ana. "We've been wondering when you two would get here."

Erik had noticed Nick and Belana's car in the drive-way, so he and Ana were the last of the out-of-town relatives to arrive. Isobel helped them out of their coats and put them in the foyer closet. "Everyone's in the den," she said. "Come on. Belana and Nick say they have news for us and wouldn't tell us until you got here."

The den was huge with a very high ceiling, crown moldings and furnished with lovely understated contemporary pieces. It was a room designed for the family's comfort and entertainment. A large-screen television was tucked away in a handsome cabinet alongside every other conceivable electronic gadget. Hundreds of DVDs and CDs were shelved next to it. Photos of the family lined the walls and sat atop the grand piano near French doors that led out to one of the gardens.

When Belana spotted Erik and Ana she sprang from her seat on a couch beside her husband, Nick. She hugged Ana. "I haven't seen you in ages, you look so happy!" she said for Ana's ears only.

She was five-four to Ana's five-ten and though Ana towered over her, Belana possessed a quiet strength that belied her size. Initially Belana had taken it upon herself to befriend Ana when Ana had moved to New York because she was her best friend Elle's sister-in-law. However, now, she loved her like a sister of her own.

"So do you," Ana whispered. She let go, so Erik could hug Belana.

The men in the room, John and Nick, stood and kissed Ana on the cheek and shook Erik's hand. Nick's mother, Yvonne and his teen daughter, Nona, were also there.

They also received hugs. Finally, when she could not stand being ignored any longer, Drusilla, who was sitting in a stately Queen Anne chair near the fireplace cleared her throat and tapped her cane on the hardwood floor. "Get over here and give your grandmother some sugar. You, too, Ana Banana!" she demanded.

Ana burst out laughing and hurried over to Drusilla. No one else called her that. She gently kissed Drusilla's soft cheek and let her cheek linger a moment on hers. She loved how Drusilla smelled, like peppermint and pine needles. It was probably something Drusilla rubbed in her joints to combat arthritis, but it reminded Ana of Grandma Renata, and she breathed in deeply. It was funny how smells took you back in time. "How are you, darling?" she asked Drusilla.

Drusilla, only five-one, was wearing one of her tailored suits with a frilly white blouse. She tended toward ultra-feminine attire and even wore gloves winter and summer. She said her hands got cold easily. Ana figured Drusilla didn't feel entirely dressed without them.

Drusilla planted a kiss on her cheek. "I'm fine now that you and Erik are here."

She was wearing her thick glasses today. She had a drawer full, which she chose from depending on how clearly she wanted to see when she got up in the morning. Her son warned her that she should only wear the last pair of glasses her optometrist had prescribed but she had claimed her eyesight changed from day to day. Why shouldn't her glasses? John had finally let it go. There was no winning an argument with his obstinate mother.

She peered closely at Ana's ring finger. There was a faint ring around it. She smiled to herself as Ana moved aside for Erik to hug his grandmother.

Drusilla moaned dramatically when Erik hugged her. She reached up and touched his cheek when he let go of her. Looking into his eyes, she said, "Love becomes you."

Erik was used to his grandmother's enigmatic sayings. This one was somewhat easier to understand than others had been in the past. Clearly she thought being in love suited him. "I couldn't agree more," he said softly.

He and Ana found seats on the couch closest to Drusilla, and Belana stood up, pulling Nick with her. "Happy Thanksgiving, everyone," she began. "I know you're wondering what Nick and I wanted to tell you. First of all, it's good news, not bad. We're not moving or anything. Nobody's sick. Well, I do feel a bit sick sometimes, but the doctor says it'll pass."

With that last sentence Drusilla cried, "Oh, my sweet Lord, are you going to have a baby?"

"Yes!" Belana exclaimed, unable to contain her excitement any longer. She was a dancer and in amazing shape, which was good because she began leaping with joy on those powerful legs and there wasn't much Nick could do to keep her from leaping to the ceiling.

He grabbed her and wrapped her in his arms. "As you can see," he said to everyone in the room. "We're pretty happy about it."

John and Isobel looked at each other and both had tears in their eyes. Elle and Dominic had given them two grandchildren but this would be the first for John's side of the family. They loved being grandparents and now would have a grandchild closer to them since Elle and Dominic lived in Italy.

More hugs and kisses all around.

Things had calmed down quite a bit by the time the housekeeper, Naomi, came into the room and announced that dinner was served.

Everyone rose to go into the dining room. But Drusilla remained seated. She loudly cleared her throat. "Wait I have a question for Erik and Ana before we sit down to eat."

Erik and Ana by eye contact and silent consensus had decided to wait until after dinner to announce their engagement thereby giving Belana and Nick time to savor the love they'd received from the family after their good news.

"What is it?" asked Erik. He stood next to Ana with her hand held in his.

"Was it an engagement ring that left that tan line on Ana's ring finger?" asked Drusilla pointblank.

"What?" asked Belana. She started dancing in place.

Erik and Ana looked at each other, stunned. "How did you spot that?" Erik said.

"I've got my good glasses on," Drusilla informed him. "I don't miss much in these babies."

"That's right, son, she can see through walls in those," said John, amused and curious as to how his son was going to reply to his grandmother's question. "Well, was it an engagement ring?"

Everyone waited impatiently.

Erik pulled Ana in the crook of his arm. "Yes, all right. We're engaged." He smiled at Belana and Nick. "We didn't want to steal your thunder."

"Don't be ridiculous!" his sister said, punching him playfully on the upper arm. "Happy news is always welcome." She grabbed him for a hug, whispering in his ear, "Didn't I tell you the key to her heart was through friendship?"

"Yes, but you didn't mention it would take two years," he returned, grinning.

"Where's the ring," Isobel wanted to know.

Ana removed it from her handbag and put it on. The women crowded around her, admiring it with exclamations of: "It's gorgeous!" and "How lovely."

Drusilla pronounced that it was in good taste. She hated huge ostentatious jewelry. She still was not satisfied, though. She looked suspiciously at Erik and Ana. "There isn't any more good news to share with us, is there?"

"What do you mean?" asked Erik, stumped this time by one of her questions.

She held her right hand out and touched Ana's flat belly. Ana couldn't help laughing.

"No, no, my darling grandmother-to-be," she said. "I'm not pregnant."

"Oh, really, Mother," John complained, his face a mass of smiles. "You are a greedy little woman. Your granddaughter just told you she's making you a great-grandmother and now you want to hurry Erik and Ana along. Be grateful for what you have."

"I'm just saying it would be good news if you were," Drusilla said to Ana. She took Ana's arm and they began walking toward the dining room. "Stranger things have happened," she continued. "I had given up hope of ever having a child when God sent me John…" she trailed off.

Chapter 8

The night of the show arrived before Ana knew it. She had been trying to mentally prepare herself for it but she had sadly failed. Nervousness trumped every other emotion as she and Erik were driven up to the gallery in a hired car.

Damon had warned her that the media would be out in force, and they were. She supposed even in a city as large as New York where celebrities were a dime a dozen, she was news. Three local news stations were represented as well as several online celebrity gossip sites.

She was dressed all in black. A fitted pantsuit that cinched her waist, underneath which was a crisp white shirt open at the collar to reveal a bit of cleavage and platform pumps. With the black overcoat flung across her shoulders she looked smart and stylish. Erik was handsome in a tailored black suit also with a white shirt underneath and dress shoes. He was not wearing a tie tonight, which Ana thought lent him a sexy, roguish air.

Their picture must have been taken dozens of times before they made it safely inside the gallery. Damon greeted them. Ana smiled. "You look wonderful tonight."

"So do you," Damon said, briefly kissing her on both cheeks.

He shook Erik's hand. "Delighted to see you, Erik," he said, his eyes darting around them. He grasped Ana by the hand too tightly. She winced. Something was definitely up with him.

"I have to warn you," he said regrettably, "that Russo is here." He looked behind him before returning his attention to Ana.

She followed his line of sight and saw Jack Russo, surrounded by his entourage, holding court in the back of the room. She noticed that members of his inner circle were effectively keeping the common man from getting too close to him.

She sighed. What the hell was he doing here? Was his career going down the drain so rapidly that he had to put in an appearance at his ex-girlfriend's art exhibit in order to keep the gossips buzzing? Any publicity was good publicity to people like him.

Ana had not voiced any of her thoughts so Damon wasn't sure of what she wanted him to do about Jack

Russo's attendance at the show. "What do you want me to do?" he asked plaintively.

Ana started to suggest he be *tossed out on his ass.* However that kind of behavior would feed the gossip mill more efficiently than a story in which everyone had conducted themselves like mature adults.

She looked to Erik for advice, her eyes somewhat panicked. Erik pulled her close to him reassuringly. "This is your night, sweetheart. Ignore the bastard."

"Then you agree that it would be worse if I made a scene?" Ana wanted his opinion clarified.

"Yes," he confirmed.

Ana hissed to Damon, "But don't sell him any of my work. Nothing, do you understand?"

"Gotcha," said Damon, relief softening his expression. "Let's do this, shall we?"

He stepped up to the podium that had been set up in the middle of the huge showroom. A path of what appeared to be yellow brick but what was in fact made of a hard slip-resistant plastic, made a path through the gallery. Ana smiled when she saw it: Damon's yellow-brick road from *The Wizard of Oz*.

"Ladies and gentlemen, may I present the very talented artist, Ms. Ana Corelli!"

The room was packed. Ana saw many faces she knew like the Barones from Bridgeport, Connecticut, and many friends she'd made in her career as a model. Jack Russo wasn't the only actor there. There were several New York City actors whom she knew from Broadway. More interesting to her were the people she did not know or who had no reason to be there except being lovers of art.

Damon had assured her that she would not have to answer questions, simply wave to the crowd and fade into the background while her work was being perused. After she had joined him at the podium and smiled at everyone and mouthed, *Thank you for coming,* she and Erik then joined the Barones.

Teresa and Julianna hugged Ana, and Erik and Leo shook hands. "I knew you were talented but this is out-rageous," Teresa said to Ana, gesturing to the general bedlam in the showroom. "We almost didn't get in."

"I have to have the painting of the elderly man in the tattered coat," Leo said. "Who is he? His face has such character."

"He's a homeless gentleman I met a few years ago," Ana told him. "Proceeds from the paintings are going to help fund several New York City organizations that help the homeless."

"Good cause," said Leo.

"Leo, if you want that painting, you need to go make an offer to that lovely man who introduced himself to us when we arrived," Teresa told him. "Otherwise some-one is going to beat you to it."

Leo looked concerned. "Yes, I'd better do that." He regarded Ana and Erik. "Excuse us."

The Barones went in search of Damon.

Ana and Erik weren't alone for long. From behind them came a well-modulated voice. "Ana, darling, aren't you going to say hello after I went to all the trouble of attending your first art show?"

Ana schooled her expression before turning to face Jack Russo. He was as she remembered him. Tall, dark and handsome, a Hollywood cliché expensively attired in a dark designer suit. His Italian ancestors had come from southern Italy so he was swarthy with dark, soulful eyes. His black hair was curly and he wore it overly long because he thought it looked sexy. Personally, she had always thought he should cut it and look more groomed.

With a flick of his wrist, he signaled his hangers-on to disperse, denoting he wanted to speak privately with Ana. The look he gave Ana after told her he expected her to do likewise with Erik.

Instead she smiled and said, "Jack Russo meet Erik Whitaker, my fiancé."

All his years of pretending to be someone else had not prepared Jack Russo for this. Erik and Ana had not made any public announcements of their engagement, only among family and friends, so Ana wasn't surprised he was shocked. Perhaps he expected her to still be alone, pining for him.

He laughed nervously. "I had no idea."

"You wouldn't expect me to send you a text message, would you?"

He did not miss her dig. "No, I wouldn't," he said. He regarded Erik and offered his hand. "Congratulations."

Erik firmly shook his hand and promptly let go of it. "Thank you."

Ana was done with niceties, although she vowed not to raise her voice. "What are you doing here?"

Jack gestured to one of her paintings. "I never knew you painted. When I read about the show I had to come see for myself. Little Ana whom we all thought was just a pretty face is also a talented artist. Good for you. I'm proud of you."

Ana was delighted to learn that his opinion meant nothing to her. In fact, peering closely at him, she wondered what she ever saw in him. Could it be she had been as shallow as he was? She had chosen to subject herself to him based solely on looks?

That had to be it. She could only conclude that she had grown over the years and he had remained the same. Because now all she saw was someone who had so little substance he had to rely on the elusive thing called fame in order to feel good about himself.

Here in this showroom, he was the center of attention. She saw the other patrons gawking at him, probably wondering what he was saying to her right now, his ex-girlfriend as some of them were undoubtedly well aware.

Suddenly, all of the hurt and anger that she had felt upon seeing him here dissipated. She no longer felt irritated by his presence.

She actually smiled at him and said, "Thank you, Jack, that's very sweet of you. Now, if you'll excuse us, we really should circulate."

She and Erik left him standing there. Of course he wasn't alone for long. His entourage again formed a protective circle around him and when he began talking, hung on his every word.

Erik pulled her close and kissed her cheek. "You're a class act."

Ana was about to say something to Erik when she noticed his parents coming through the door followed by Belana and Nick. "Our family's here," she said, and they made a beeline over to them.

Ana enjoyed herself from that moment on. Damon sold all of her paintings except the one of Drusilla in the garden, which was not for sale at any price.

He also told her that before Jack Russo had left the gallery he had offered a substantial amount for her self-portrait. Damon had claimed someone else had already purchased it. From the miffed expression on the handsome actor's face, Damon related, he had not believed him for a moment. That was when he had stormed out, followed by his lackeys.

Later, Erik took her home. Their footsteps made clicking sounds on the hardwood floor as they made their way back to the bedroom. Clothes were removed in the dark with only the streetlights lending little illumination through the slats in the blinds.

Erik pulled her warm body into his strong arms. Their kisses were tender, lingering and so intoxicating. She fell back onto the bed, pulling him on top of her. Her legs wrapped themselves around him as she guided him inside of her. Urgently the passion rose as his thrusts deepened, touching her very core. A sob tore from her throat as she reached the crescendo, and

Erik followed seconds later. They lay like that for a few minutes, his nose buried in the side of her neck. They trembled in ecstasy and soon found a more comfortable position but were not willing to let go too soon.

The next day Damon phoned her with good news. "I've gotten five requests from people who want you to paint them."

Ana was standing in the kitchen, stirring soft-scrambled eggs in a skillet. She reached over and turned off the flame under the skillet before replying, "You mean commissions?" She had heard of them but never considered that someone would want to hire her to paint them even though she knew that sort of thing came with the territory once word got around that you were talented.

"Who wants me to paint them?" she asked excitedly as she one-handedly slid the scrambled eggs onto a plate. Erik was in the shower. She had gotten up about an hour earlier and was already showered and dressed. It was a Sunday morning and they didn't have any commitments. They were planning on taking a leisurely walk around the city if it didn't snow today, perhaps do a little window shopping. December in New York was beautiful. And the closer to Christmas the more festive the displays in store windows became.

Damon named three people in the performing arts community in the city: two actors and a well-known soprano with the Metropolitan Opera, and the addition of two politicians.

"I don't know," Ana said. "I've never even thought of

doing something like that. *I* always choose my subjects. I don't even know if painting someone at their request would inspire me. It's not like a quick sketch that you can do in a matter of minutes. Painting a portrait takes days of effort and if I'm not feeling it I don't know if I can produce a decent portrait."

"Artists," Damon said. "The problem with artists today is none are starving anymore. When artists were starving they took commissions hand over fist because wanting to know where your next meal was coming from was inspiring. Think about it, darling. The more you earn, the more you can donate to the needy. Besides, I look at taking commissions as a way to build your reputation in the art community. If you later find you don't like doing it, you can always stop."

"I'll think about it," Ana agreed. "I've got to go. Thank you, Damon, for everything. Last night wasn't as frightening as I thought it would be."

Damon laughed. "I told you all you had to do was show up and be yourself. Your work would speak for itself."

Erik strode into the kitchen barefooted wearing jeans and a long-sleeve shirt. He came straight to Ana and began kissing her. She held the phone away from them but she was certain Damon could probably hear what was going on. Erik sounded like a starving man, moaning like crazy, eliciting the same response from her with his intensity. She managed to break off the kiss long enough to say into the receiver, "Gotta go!" She heard Damon laughing uproariously before she put the phone down on the counter and resumed kissing Erik.

"Good morning," said Erik, after he'd rendered her nearly breathless. His smile was electric. Ana loved seeing him like this: ready to take on the day, his attitude confident and infectious.

"Good morning," she said, her smile as wide as his. "How did you sleep?"

"Like the dead but, I swear, I could sense when you got out of bed."

Erik hadn't let go of her yet. And he obviously was not finished kissing her as his warm lips continued to leave a trail of kisses along the side of her neck. Ana was beginning to get the message. But the little Catholic girl in her was leery of where this might be headed, making love in the kitchen. She was enjoying their love life but there were still certain taboos she had no desire to break and making love on the kitchen counter or the kitchen table was one of them. Growing up she would have been traumatized if she had walked into the kitchen and found her parents making love on the table where they all sat down and had their meals.

She laughed nervously and turned out of his embrace. "Come on, let's eat. I made scrambled eggs and there's bread for toast, orange juice and, of course, coffee. I need to go shopping, the cupboard's nearly bare." Sometimes she talked too much when she was uneasy.

Picking up on her mood, Erik asked, "Is something the matter?"

She decided to tell him the truth. "I don't want to get overheated in the kitchen."

He laughed and reached down to smooth her brow the way he did when he's about to kiss her. Ana waited, then just as he was lowering his head to kiss her she twisted out of his embrace and Erik, off balance, stumbled and righted himself by pushing against the granite counter. By the time he turned around to face her, Ana was standing three feet away with her arms folded, giving him a stern look. "Don't play with me, Erik Whitaker. I told you—not in the kitchen."

With a determined expression, Erik went and picked her up and began walking in the direction of the bedroom. "All right, then, the bedroom it is."

"I'm hungry!" Ana protested, laughter evident in her tone.

"I'll take you out for breakfast afterward," Erik promised.

"We just got out of bed," she cried. "Aren't you ever satisfied?"

"Not when it comes to you," he said, pushing the bedroom door open.

They were both laughing by the time he put her down. "Look at you," she said as she unbuttoned his shirt, "showered and dressed and now you're going to get all funky again."

"Yes," he breathed lustily, apparently looking forward to being dirtied up by her and vice versa. That mischievous glint in his eye told her she was right.

"Oh, I know what this is," she said as he pulled her

sweater over her head and turned her around so that he could unfasten her bra. "I'm a fast learner. I might not know much about men and sex, but I do know you get horny in the mornings. I've noticed…things…but was too shy to talk about them with you."

Erik took her hand and put it on his hard member. "You mean this thing? You've noticed this thing in the mornings?"

Ana blushed but didn't try to remove her hand. "You're a corrupting influence," she lightly accused him. "If I stay with you much longer I'm going to know everything there is to know about pleasing a man."

"Well, this man, anyway," Erik said and bent to take one of her nipples, which he'd recently liberated from her bra into his mouth. Ana moaned and her bones seemed to turn to jelly. She fell backward onto the bed, which she hadn't yet had the chance to make this morning, and her fiancé made short work of removing her jeans and panties. This done, he gently spread her legs and touched her sex with the palm of his hand and moved it in small circles, enjoying the warmth and the feel of it. Her clitoris became aroused and as soon as he felt the wetness on his palm he used his index finger to further stimulate it while Ana writhed beneath him.

"Don't be afraid to express your sexual desires to me, Ana," he softly said as he continued his efforts. "You're safe with me. Let go of your inhibitions."

Ana sighed with pleasure as she tried to construct sentences in her head, sentences that he would understand. She liked sex as well as any other woman but the full enjoyment of sex, the letting go of her inhibitions seemed contrary to her Catholic upbringing. She remembered going to mass with her Grandma Renata and always being admonished to stay pure until marriage. That ship had definitely sailed. In these modern times women didn't save themselves for marriage as often as they used to. At least that's the general consensus she'd gotten from talking to other women of her generation. But if you were smart, you didn't sleep around, either. You tried to choose wisely. She hadn't chosen wisely until now.

She relaxed. Erik was right, she was safe with him. She could be herself and stop holding back, because that's what she had been doing. She looked him in the eyes, and said, "Aren't you forgetting something? I'm naked, splayed on the bed for your pleasure but you still have your pants on."

Erik rose and rectified the situation with rapidity. He stood before her without any clothes on. She got up and kissed him all the while backing him toward the bed. When he was in position, she placed her palm in the middle of his muscular chest and pushed him onto the bed. Climbing on top, she cooed, "Let me drive awhile."

Erik chuckled, remembering how much she liked to drive. It could prove interesting to see what she considered driving in the bedroom, little innocent girl that she was.

As he lay flat on his back Ana bent and licked him down the middle of his chest from his breastbone to his naval. His eyes never left her. Perhaps that was his

fatal mistake. He would try later to recall every move
Ana made.

"Mmm, you taste good," she said, her eyes looking directly into his. She held his attention like a cobra
holds a snake charmer's. Then she straddled him and
began rubbing her breasts until her nipples hardened.
This by itself was an erotic feast for Erik since he was
a breast man and hers were magnificent. But when she
bent and flicked her tongue out and licked her own nipples, first the right then the left, his member jumped of
its own accord.

That was only the beginning. After she had en-
ticed him with a demonstration of her flexibility, she
scooted backward and since he was fully engorged now
his penis stood straight up and she took what was offered. Her mouth below was almost his undoing. She
made him beg her to stop because he was afraid if she
didn't he'd come and he didn't want this lovemaking
session to end without Ana being satisfied. He always
made sure of that.

She smiled coyly at him as she got up to get a condom. Returning to him she rolled it onto him and straddled him. She was so wet by this time that when her
sex touched the tip of his penis all he wanted to do was
slide inside and experience the ultimate in pleasure.
But she worked her vaginal muscles so that she was
the one controlling how far he could enter her. She allowed him entrance inch by inch, squeezing him and
causing ripples of anticipatory sexual enjoyment to fan
out from his member to the rest of his body. God help

him, the girl was curling his toes. Where the hell had she learned that? Then, just as he had gained a little control and felt confident that he wouldn't embarrass himself by coming too soon, she pushed hard and impaled herself on him.

She cried out because he could tell he'd hit her sweet spot. He yelled because she'd caught him off guard and there was no turning back now. He came and he felt as if the tip of the condom wouldn't be able to hold it all. That's how good the release had felt.

She lay on top of him, her head on his chest. He felt her pulsating vaginal walls as she came down from the climax. She felt him throb inside of her. Their eyes met. "Where did you learn that?" he asked curiously.

"The *Kama Sutra*," she told him smiling. "I like to read, remember?"

Chapter 9

A few days before Christmas Ana phoned her parents to catch up. She had already told them she was staying in the States for Christmas, and they had expressed disappointment but said they understood she wanted to spend time with Erik. They were not the kind of parents who put added pressure on their children in the form of guilt. For that she was grateful.

"Is Dad preparing dinner this year, or will you go to one of my aunts' houses?" she asked her mother.

"Dominic and Elle invited us to Lake Como, so we'll be going there," Natalie told her. "Elle's going to prepare a traditional soul food meal for us. I'm supposed to get in the kitchen with her. We'll see how that works out. And I don't think your father can do without his panettone at Christmastime. He'll be baking at least a couple of loaves."

"Can't say that I blame him," Ana said with a smile. The traditional sweet loaf that originated in Milan was a family staple. Cupola-shaped and made with raisins, candied orange, citron and lemon zest, it was wrapped with care and put under the Christmas tree and enjoyed later in the evening with coffee or sweet wine.

"You sound kind of wistful," Natalie told her. "Is everything all right between you and Erik?"

Ana sighed happily. "Mom, I'm so in love with that man it feels unreal. I'm afraid I'm going to wake up one morning and find out it was all a dream."

Natalie laughed softly. "Baby, you're in the giddy stage of your relationship. Of course it feels dreamlike. You're so happy you think you might explode. He can do no wrong, you can do no wrong. And the sex…well the sex blows your mind. I've been there."

Ana was not embarrassed to discuss sex with her mother. It was her father with whom she never broached the subject.

"You're right," she confirmed. "I've never felt this way before."

"How could you?" asked Natalie reasonably. "You've never been in love before. Not really." She paused. "Yes, it's Ana, sweetheart."

Her father, Carlo, must have entered the room.

He came on the line. *"Buon Natale!"* he exclaimed in his deep, Italian-accented voice. "In case I don't get to speak with you on Christmas."

"Daddy, I don't care where I am in the world, I will find a way to speak with you on Christmas Day," Ana assured him. A tear rolled down her cheek, her father was so dear to her. She was the baby of the family and he had always made sure that she knew she was special and could depend on her old man, as he referred to himself, for anything.

She imagined his sweet face now: tanned skin, a full head of wavy dark brown hair with pieces of gray throughout, that Roman nose and a chin with a cleft in it. No wonder her mother had fallen in love with him on first sight.

She sniffed. "I'm coming home next Christmas, promise!"

Carlo laughed shortly. "Now, none of that or *Babbo Natale* will not visit you this Christmas. Stay cheerful, darling. We'll see you soon."

She smiled. She'd loved his *Babbo Natale*—Father Christmas—stories when she was a little girl. Point in fact: she *still* loved them.

"Okay," she said. He invariably ended their conversations with "We'll see you soon." As if she had only a short length of time to wait before she saw them again even though she knew that it would probably be months.

"Yes, see you soon, Dad," Ana said.

After she'd hung up the phone she got up from the couch where she'd been sitting in the living room and walked to the big picture window, which looked down on the busy street in front of her building. Pedestrians hurried to their destinations carrying shopping bags. It was dusk and lights were going on in windows of neighboring apartments. Christmas decorations predominated. She had framed her windows with tiny twinkling white lights and in the center of it was the huge fir tree strung with colorful lights.

She and Erik had decorated trees at her place and his. She was glad he enjoyed the custom as much as she did. She couldn't imagine Christmas without a tree.

Shrugging her shoulders as if she could shake off this melancholy feeling, she turned away from the window and walked to the kitchen where she got herself a bottle of water and thirstily drank half of it standing in front of the refrigerator. She had no reason to feel sad, yet the feeling persisted. Surely it wasn't because she wasn't going home for Christmas. She was an adult now and adults grew up, moved away from home, met someone and got married. From then on your first priority was your mate. Yes, you spent time with your extended family, but if you couldn't make it home for the holidays you didn't beat yourself up about it.

This is the first time, she reminded herself that was why she wasn't handling it so well.

Tomorrow she and Erik were flying to Aspen. They would spend December 23 through December 26 there. Then they would toast in the New Year here in New York with his family who would be coming to his penthouse for the annual Whitaker New Year's Eve party, an end of the year blowout where the family and employees of Whitaker Enterprises mingled. She had looked forward to the party every year. This year would be different because she wouldn't be coming as a guest, but as Erik's fiancée. She was even planning it this year, she had hired the caterer and the entertainment for the evening. They were going to dance the night away to the sounds of the best blues band in New York City. Then just before midnight they were going to tune in to the yearly broadcast of the ball dropping in Times Square on the big-screen TV.

Setting the bottle of water on the counter she went to her studio and pulled the drop cloth off her work in progress. It was a portrait of Erik in the nude. He was sitting in the classic pose of *The Thinker* by Auguste Rodin. There was nothing explicit about it. But the lines and planes of his body were very seductive. He didn't know she was painting it. She'd done it from memory. She knew his body intimately and loved it not only because she loved him but because of its symmetry. She didn't know how he would react to it. She had no intention of ever selling it or even allowing it to be shown at Damon's gallery. This was a gift for her. It would hang in her bedroom when it was complete.

She heard Erik's key in the lock. They had exchanged keys more than a year ago for safety purposes. If either of them were in trouble and couldn't answer their door the other would have a means of entry. They even knew each other's security codes. She smiled at the thought. That should have tipped her off that she and Erik were meant to be more than just friends. How implicitly they trusted each other.

"Babe, I'm home!"

She hastily covered the painting with the drop cloth before hurrying to him. Erik was already coming out of his overcoat when she got to the foyer. She helped him off with it and hung it up then went into his arms for a long kiss. It was during the kiss that her hands wandered to his head and she discovered his hair was damp. "Is it raining?"

"No, it's snowing," he said, grinning.

"What!" Ana ran to the window to look out. Sure enough snowflakes drifted down covering the city with a white mantle. She was delighted. Erik came up behind her and wrapped his arms around her. "We're gonna have a white Christmas, after all."

The weather service had been doubtful the last few days whenever they tuned in to the forecast.

"Looks like it," Ana said, smiling happily.

"You call this a cabin?" Ana asked Erik as the hired car pulled into the driveway leading up to what Ana thought looked more like a Swiss chalet than a cabin. It was dark out but she could see that the multilevel house was at least three stories and must have been five thousand square feet or more. Were those Christmas lights she saw in the windows? Snow was coming down pretty heavily but she didn't think her eyes were deceiving her. "Who decorated it?" she asked Erik, who was being suspiciously quiet all of a sudden. He'd chatted all the way from the airport.

The driver stopped the SUV fitted with snow tires in front of the chalet's awning. "Did you hire someone to prepare the house before we arrived?" Ana asked, looking at Erik. These vacation rentals sometimes had people who stocked the refrigerator for renters, cleaned and aired out the house and changed the bed linens. Why not decorate it for the holidays, too? "What's wrong, cat got your tongue?" Ana asked irritably. Something was up. She hated surprises and was learning, fast, that her fiancé loved surprising her. The way he'd sprung the ring on her had been hard enough on her heart. What girl picked out a ring from Tiffany's in her man's office?

She reached for the door's handle. The driver had already gotten out and was getting their luggage. Erik grabbed her hand before she could open the door. "Sweetheart, no matter what happens the next few minutes remember I love you." He looked at her gravely.

Frowning, Ana regarded him with a worried expression. "Now you're making me nervous. What have you done?"

"Let me get the door for you," was all he said before he got out and jogged around to her side of the SUV to open the door and help her out. He made sure she didn't slip on the snow as she stood on shaky legs. She hugged herself in her warm coat. The car had been warm but it was freezing out here. The driver was busy piling their luggage on the portico. Solar lights lit the path to the door. Erik rang the doorbell.

"Why are you ringing the doorbell?" asked Ana. "Don't you have the key?" Erik had handled the reservations for this trip. She assumed if he were renting a cabin the key would be sent to him prior to their departure from New York or someone representing the owner would meet them either at the airport or here with the key. Which hadn't happened, so where was the key?

"I don't need a key," he said cryptically.

Ana heard someone coming to the door. In fact it sounded like the rumble of several excited voices approaching.

The door was swung open and her mother and father stood there smiling at her. Elle, Dominic and Sophia and Matteo, each of them with a child, not far behind them. Ana screamed and launched herself at her parents whom she hugged together, with her in the middle and a parent on either side of her. She let them go and regarded them. Everyone was dressed casually. Her father had an apron on over his clothes. It's obvious who's been delegated to do the cooking, as usual, Ana thought with a smile. "I just spoke with you a few hours ago. You couldn't have come from Milan in that short time!"

Her mother helped her out of her coat and hung it on a nearby hall tree.

"No, baby, you phoned my cell number. We were here all along," Natalie said, smiling warmly. Natalie's rich brown skin glowed with good health and her dark brown eyes shone with happiness.

Ana hugged her brother, Dominic, her sister, Sophia, and their spouses as her mother continued, "Erik wanted to surprise you so we flew in yesterday. The house was all ready for us. Everything provided. We've just been enjoying ourselves getting ready for your arrival."

Ana kissed each niece and nephew, longing to hold the babies, but reluctant to take them out of the comfortable embrace of their parents' arms. Elle must have read her indecision on her face and thrust her four-month-old son, Dom, into his aunt's arms.

"Here, take him," she said. "Hold him close to your chest. He loves bosoms." She glanced at her husband, Dominic, when she said that and Ana laughed as she cradled her nephew in her arms. He grinned up at her looking for all the world like a miniature replica of her brother, dimples in his cheeks and curious glint in his light brown eyes as if he knew that life was a mystery he was going to have a ball solving.

She bent and kissed his chubby cheeks, "Hello, little Dominic, I'm your auntie Ana."

Her two nieces, Ariana and Renata, were both two but Ariana was a few months older than her cousin, Renata, suddenly felt the need to exert their claim on their aunt Ana since they had known her longer. They each latched on to one of Ana's legs and refused to budge. Then, sensing he was being left out of the fun, six month-old Matteo, in his father's arms, started crying and reaching for Ana.

Ana laughed happily. "It's good to be loved!" And holding little Dom to her chest she bent close and kissed Matty who stopped crying and stared at her, then looked at his mother.

"Oh, no, he's confused," laughed Sophia. She and Ana could never be mistaken for twins but, being sisters, they did closely resemble each other. They had the same golden brown skin, golden brown eyes and full lips. But Ana was taller and wore her hair in a wavy style while her sister preferred a braid, which hung nearly to her bottom.

Erik came into the house while all of this was going on after taking care of the driver's tip and bringing in the luggage. A smile of satisfaction tugged at the corners of his mouth. Ana was happy. He owed Abby a debt of thanks, which would be reflected in her bonus this year. He'd asked her to work a miracle, and she had.

Seeing that Erik had entered the house, Ana gingerly handed the baby back to Elle. As he closed the door, Ana came up behind him and as soon as he turned around she walked into his arms and kissed him with all the emotion she was feeling at that moment. That kiss left no doubt in his mind that she was grateful for his gesture.

Carlo loudly cleared his throat. Seeing his baby girl kiss a man like that was too much for a father to bear. Even though he knew, logically, that he would eventually have to let go of her, it wasn't that time yet. "Come, Ana, you and your old man are making the panettone together this year. Plus, there's dinner to get on the table."

Ana was so accustomed to helping her father prepare meals at home that the thought of slipping into the routine now was a very pleasant one.

Ana smiled up at Erik before turning to join her father, *"Ti amo,"* she said.

"I love you, too," Erik said, his love for her emanating from every cell of his body.

He was welcomed into the Corelli family's embrace while he watched his fiancée put her arm through her father's and accompany him to the kitchen.

When Ana and Carlo were out of earshot, Natalie helped Erik out of his coat and hung it next to Ana's then she gave Erik a hug and said, "Forgive Carlo, but in this family he wears the apron and he's not ready to cut the strings yet where Ana is concerned." She peered up at him. "But that doesn't mean he doesn't like you. He does. He just doesn't like it when you get too close to his daughter in his presence. It's primal. You'll understand when you're a father of a daughter."

Erik chuckled. "Thanks for the tip. I'll behave myself accordingly."

"See? I knew you were a smart man," said Sophia. She hugged him, too. Then she stepped aside for Elle to embrace him. Erik had considered Elle a sister ever since their parents were married. "Hello, sis," he murmured against her ear. "Motherhood definitely agrees with you." Elle had given birth to Dominic, Jr. a little over four months ago. Tonight she looked wonderful in a red long-sleeved wrap blouse over black slacks. She'd lost all the baby weight except for a little around her middle. She smiled up at him, "I have to agree with that." She glanced back at her husband. "If he had his way we'd have a house full."

Dominic shook Erik's hand. He couldn't help remembering that the first time he met Erik, he had pulled him aside to say that he had had a crush on Elle for years but she wouldn't give him the time of day because she was such good friends with Erik's sister, Belana, and hence considered him a brother. How time manipulated events. Now Erik was going to be his brother-in-law!

"Good to see you again," Dominic said. "I hope this will give us a chance to get to know each other better."

Sophia interrupted to introduce her husband, Matteo, whom Erik had not met before.

After shaking hands with Matteo and hearing his thick Italian accent Erik realized that there was quite a multicultural mix in this house tonight. He was African-American, as were Natalie and Elle. Carlo and Matteo were Italian and the offspring of Carlo and Natalie: Dominic, Sophia and Ana were half Italian and half African-American. To say nothing of the four children whom he hadn't been introduced to yet who also had a mixture of African and Italian blood.

Ariana and Renata regarded Erik with the assessment of little girls who although they don't yet understand it felt drawn to male beauty. They each took one of his hands and Erik smiled down at them respectively and said, "Hello, ladies."

"Meet Renata and Ariana," Natalie said, laughing softly at how easily her granddaughters had accepted Erik. "Come back to the entertainment room. We were in there watching a movie with the children when you rang the bell. While Carlo prepares dinner."

In the kitchen, Ana had washed her hands and put on an apron. Her father talked while he checked the pots on the stove and peeked at the roast in the oven. "So, how are you enjoying being an engaged woman?"

Ana was instantly on alert. Her father might have been asking an innocent enough question. On the other hand it could be a loaded one. How she answered would make all the difference in the world. "We were friends for a long time before we considered anything romantic. He knew he had to be patient with me."

"You're a little shy," said Carlo dismissively. "You've always been that way."

He had moved over to the center island, which had been cleared of everything except the ingredients he needed to make the panettone. Ana joined him and watched as he began sifting flour into a large bowl. "No, it was more than that, Daddy. I didn't trust my own judgment anymore. Erik knew that and didn't try to push me into a relationship even though, he told me later, he's been in love with me all along."

Her father set down the sifter and looked her in the eyes. He had known she had gotten her heart broken by that actor. He couldn't remember his name. As a rule he avoided gossip about his daughter like the plague. Gossip was insidious. Tabloids made up lies about celebrities. Terrible lies that any relative of the subject of such tales didn't want to hear.

"Has he behaved like a gentleman the whole time?" he asked.

"Yes, he did," Ana replied sincerely. "He's been my best friend for two years."

"And when did you know you loved him, as well?" her father wanted to know.

Ana hadn't even told Erik about the moment she realized she loved him. She began to recall the instant in which her emotions transformed from "like" to love for Erik. They were jogging in Central Park one Saturday morning in May of last year. She tripped and fell. She still didn't know what she had tripped over, just her own stupid feet she guessed. But she twisted her ankle and Erik had picked her up and carried her to a nearby cab and had taken her directly to the emergency room of the closest hospital. He had refused to leave her side for three hours while they waited. It seemed a twisted ankle did not warrant quick treatment. He had told her funny stories about his visits to the emergency room when he was a kid. He had not always been such a good athlete. When he was a boy he was clumsy, awkward, and constantly hurting himself. Once playing baseball he got hit in the face by a fly ball. Another time he and a neighborhood friend decided they were going to become Noble Prize–winning chemists. They mixed the wrong chemicals and nearly choked to death on billowing black smoke. They were lucky the mixture hadn't exploded in their faces. The smoke had stained the walls of his bedroom, though, and the entire room had to be repainted. His father banned him from using his chemistry set in the house after that. Lucky, too, because the next time he'd used it, he had indeed caused an explosion that resulted in the detached garage being burned to the ground.

"Your father had to have taken away your chemistry set then," she'd exclaimed in disbelief.

"No, but he did make me clean the debris out of the

garage so it could be rebuilt. It took me three weeks. I was the one who decided to give up the chemistry set and turn my attentions to something safer, like computers."

"He has a doctorate degree in computer science," Ana told her father now. Her expression grew wistful. "I couldn't help loving a man who had been such a geek growing up and had turned himself into such an accomplished person."

"You respect him," said Carlo.

"Yes," Ana said softly.

Carlo picked up the sifter again. "This is good," he said, "the fact that you respect him as well as love him. That will be good for your marriage because the intensity of romance you feel right now won't last. Sometimes you will feel such passion you will think that you'll die if you spend an hour apart. Then again sometimes you will wish you'd never met him." He chuckled. "I can see by your doubtful expression that you don't believe me. Take my word for it. Marriage is a lifelong commitment and it isn't something to be trifled with. When you say 'I do' to Erik you have to mean it. So many marriages end in divorce because the couple was not truly committed to each other before they tied the knot. Then they start living together and closeness breeds contempt. You will begin to find out personal things about him that you didn't know before you married him."

"What kind of things?" asked Ana, her tone light, matching her father's.

She figured he was trying to scare her into thinking twice before marrying Erik. She knew her father would be a hard sell no matter whom she decided to marry. No one, in his opinion, was good enough for her. He had felt the same way about Sophia's choice in a husband even though Sophia and Matteo had dated for over five years before Matteo proposed. Poor Sophia had assumed that Matteo was reluctant to propose because she was such a strong-willed woman, plus she earned more money than he did and probably always would. Matteo owned a landscaping business. He worked wonders in gardens. He was a sweet, caring man who fell in love with Sophia, and then found out she stood to inherit millions, a prospect that was quite daunting to a simple man like him. Sophia, however, would not let him go. She was of the mind that it was better to be loved by a man of modest means than to be used by a rich man. She didn't need her bank account bolstered. What she needed was a man who adored her, and she got him.

Carlo looked intently at his daughter. "That he farts in bed and talks with food in his mouth," he said jokingly, "Things that irritate feminine sensibilities. Men can be quite barbaric at times. At those times you have to remember that you love him and overlook the small things."

Ana laughed abruptly. "I was wrong. You're not trying to convince me to think twice before getting married, you're giving me advice."

Carlo put a hand over his heart. "You thought that

your old man would do such a despicable thing? I feel hurt!"

"I didn't expect you to be so accepting of Erik," Ana said truthfully. She could tell by the pent-up laughter in her father's eyes that he wasn't really upset by anything she'd said. "You made Sophia cry when you told her she shouldn't marry Matteo."

"I only said that because Matteo wasn't sure of himself," Carlo explained. "In order for a man to commit to a woman, he must first know his own heart. Matteo was afraid he wouldn't fit in Sophia's world. He doubted himself. Now he knows we love him for who he is, not for what he can bring to the table. Their marriage is solid. I didn't get that feeling from Erik. He knows what he wants. He was patient enough to wait for you. That says a lot about a man."

"Oh, Daddy, I'm so happy you feel that way!" Ana flung her arms around his waist and hugged him.

Carlo got misty-eyed. "Hey, we're wasting time here. Let's get this panettone ready for the oven. You know it has to be made a day in advance before it's ready to place under the tree. It's going to take longer than you think."

That was an understatement as Ana was to learn. The panettone took a total of fifteen hours to make from mixing bowl to oven. While they waited for the panettone to rise, the family caught up with each other's lives.

Chapter 10

Dinner was a savory meal of minestrone soup, roast beef, and crusty Italian bread. Afterward the couples with children gathered their little ones to prepare them for bed.

Carlo and Natalie with Ana and Erik made short work of clearing the table and cleaning the kitchen. While they worked, Natalie told Ana and Erik about the chores chart they had made upon arriving at the house yesterday. Erik had offered to hire someone to come in and cook and clean for them the three days they would be together, but the Corellis had graciously declined saying they were capable of taking care of themselves and that it would be fun to divide up the meals.

As Natalie dried dishes, she filled Ana in. "You and Erik have breakfast tomorrow morning at nine."

"No problem," said Ana, smiling at Erik. "Erik makes delicious pancakes and I'm a whiz at scrambled eggs and bacon."

"Sounds great," said Natalie.

With the dishes done, they all retired to the entertainment room. As soon as they sat down, Carlo asked, "Have you thought about where you want to get married?"

Ana, sitting close to Erik on a couch near the fireplace, smiled at him. "We've talked about it. But Erik says he doesn't care where we get married. He thinks I should have the wedding of my dreams and to just give him the time and date and he'll show up."

Carlo chuckled. "It would save time and money," he agreed. Ana hoped her mother had missed that surreptitious look her father had given her.

Natalie had not, and playfully elbowed her husband in the ribs. "Quit it. I was not that bossy about our wedding plans."

"Darling, you wanted things a certain way and when you didn't get your way you pouted," Carlo recalled. His eyebrows were raised as if to say, "Deny it."

Natalie laughed. "Okay, I was a bit…forceful about getting my way. But in my defense I did have your mother and your sisters to contend with and every last one of them had a vision of what our wedding should be like. I didn't think that was fair since it was our wedding!"

"I hear you, sweetheart," consoled Carlo. "Didn't I

not make it clear to them that it was our wedding not theirs?"

Natalie leaned her head on his shoulder. "You did, indeed."

"But I don't agree with Erik," Ana said, getting the conversation back on track. "I think the wedding should be his dream wedding, too."

"I've already got my dream girl. I'm satisfied," said Erik.

"Aren't they sweet?" Natalie cried wistfully.

"Aren't who sweet?" Sophia asked as she entered the room with Matteo.

"We were talking about our wedding plans," Ana told her.

Sophia and Matteo sat on the couch facing Ana and Erik. "You're coming home to get married, aren't you?" said Sophia expectantly. "Mom and Dad got married in the garden at the Lake Como villa, so did Dominic and Elle and Matteo and I. You're not going to stick to family tradition?"

"Lake Como *is* my first choice," Ana admitted. "But we haven't decided yet whether it would be more cost effective for my family to fly to the States or for my friends who live in the States plus Erik's family and friends to come all the way to Italy. Erik's parents have a very nice garden in Connecticut."

Erik could see how wedding negotiations could dissolve into an argument. Sophia's expression was none too friendly. She was looking at him now like he was the wedge that was keeping her family apart.

"You're not wearing a Corelli original, either?" Sophia asked as if Ana's not wearing a dress from her family's formal wear line would be the ultimate betrayal of familial loyalty.

"Yes, I'm wearing a Corelli original," Ana said. She had already been offered free wedding dresses by some of the best designers in the world. People whom she respected and who respected her. But she had declined. "I've already picked out my dress."

"Which one?" her father wanted to know. In his mind he kept a catalog of all his new merchandise. "Let me guess. The simple silk strapless empire-waist gown with pearl buttons down the back?"

"How did you know that?" asked Ana, amazed.

"I pictured you in that very dress," said Carlo, smiling.

Her father had an uncanny knack for choosing clothing that looked good on people.

"Well, I'll be campaigning for you to get married in Lake Como," Sophia said stubbornly.

"I'm sorry, sis, but you don't get a say in this," Ana said just as stubbornly. "Did I dictate to you how your wedding should be?"

"No," Sophia said, her voice now taking on a whiny tone, "but you're away from home all the time. I miss you! It would be nice if you, me, Mom, and the females in the family could get together and plan your wedding, that's all."

Elle and Dominic entered the room at that instance and Elle smiled and said, "Are we planning the wedding? When is it going to be? Where? Do I have time to finish losing weight so I can get in a decent dress?"

"Elle you look beautiful just the way you are," Ana told her sincerely. "And, yes, we're talking about the wedding, but no plans have been made."

Elle and Dominic sat down on the sofa with Carlo and Natalie. "Just tell us where it will be and we'll be there," said Dominic. "And take it from me, baby sister, keep it simple. Planning a wedding can tear a couple apart. Everybody wants to give you advice. It starts with the best of intentions, of course, but can turn ugly at the drop of a hat. I say, don't listen to anyone except Erik when it comes to how you two want to get married. Do it in a church. Do it on a boat. Do it at the courthouse, or on the beach. But do it your way."

"Yes," Elle said in agreement. "I was lucky. Our wedding was simple and elegant and everybody we loved was there."

"That's all that counted to us," said Dominic as he looked in Elle's direction and smiled.

"But you got married in your own garden," Sophia reminded him pointedly. "Where we've all gotten married, starting with Mom and Dad."

"Stop it," Matteo said. His arm was around Sophia's shoulders as he leaned down to smile at her. "Let it go, baby. This is not your decision to make."

"I know," Sophia said, sniffling. She gave Ana such a plaintive look that Ana also started crying.

Looking at his daughters, Carlo cried, "*Dio mio,* can we not have a conversation without emotions getting out of hand and tears flowing? We're blessed to be together at Christmas. Let's get some Christmas cheer in here!"

The sisters got up and hugged. "I'm sorry," said Sophia. "I guess I'm still a bit hormonal."

Ana hugged her sister tightly. It was just like her to make a joke out of it. There were no hard feelings. Sophia was outspoken, had always been, and Ana didn't believe that would ever change. However, it was her and Erik's wedding. They would have it as they saw fit.

"I'm not crying because you were rude, which you were. I was crying because I miss your being rude to me to my face instead of on the phone. I've missed you so much!"

"Now this is getting ridiculous," Carlo said. "Dominic and Elle, play something for us, please!"

Dominic and Elle got up and went to the grand piano sitting next to the huge picture window, which displayed the snowy night outside.

Before beginning they whispered something to each other and then Dominic sat down and started playing "Silent Night." Elle sang the operatic version. Her deep contralto tenderly caressed the words and sent them back out at the listeners in rich rounded tones.

Ana reached for Erik's hand as Elle sang and squeezed it reassuringly. His family was also given to emotional outbursts. His grandmother was incorrigible. But she would dub him a saint if he got through the next three days with his sanity intact. She was glad he had such a great sense of humor. Her family took some getting used to.

Erik must have been in tune with her because he leaned down and whispered, "They remind me of my family. I think this is a match made in heaven."

Ana grinned, then, and leaned her head on his shoulder for the rest of the performance. After "Silent Night," Dominic and Elle did a more contemporary song with "Please Come Home for Christmas." Elle belted it out as if she were a soul diva instead of an opera diva and had everyone clapping along. Carlo and Natalie were even inspired to get up and dance.

When she finished the song, Elle went and took Natalie by the hand. "Would you sing "What Child Is This?" I love the way you do it."

Natalie kissed her daughter-in-law on the cheek and said, "It would be my pleasure."

Elle went and sat down and Dominic and his mother took center stage. Natalie was a true soprano and her voice wreaked havoc on the listener's emotions with its sweetness. Although retired from the stage for the most part, she kept her voice in fine shape with daily exercises as was evident in the flawless rendition of the well-known Christmas song about the birth of Christ.

Carlo had tears in his eyes when his wife came back to reclaim her seat beside him. He hugged her, and said, "Thank you, my darling. That was one of Momma's favorites. You got me right here." His hand was over his heart.

Inspired by the other performances, Sophia suddenly grabbed Ana by the hand, saying, "Come on, sis, everyone else has sung a Christmas song. Let's do ours."

Ana looked stricken. "Our song?" she cried incredulously. "You and I don't sing, remember?"

"We did sing a Christmas song, once!" Sophia insisted.

The horror of it, Ana thought. She's talking about the song we did in a Christmas pageant in elementary school. "That song is the reason why *we don't* sing in public," Ana reminded her.

"I don't care," Sophia said. She pointed at Dominic as if to cue him. "'Jingle Bell Rock'!"

"I don't think I know that," Dominic said.

"You're a maestro," said his sister. "Wing it!" She hummed a little to give him the tune.

Laughing, Ana said, "All right, but in English. Last time we did it in Italian and I don't think it translated well."

Dominic winged it, and his sisters sang with gusto if not well. Caterwauling would be a better description of the sound coming out of their mouths. Like two cats fighting in an alley. However, not only did Ana remember the song, but the dance routine Sophia had come up with way back when. They pranced around the room. Their dancing was a whole lot more pleasing than their singing, especially to the men in their lives, because Sophia's choreography called for quite a bit of booty shaking. By the end, they had everyone laughing so hard tears were rolling down their faces. Theirs was the only act that got a standing ovation.

Later, Erik walked Ana to her room door. There was no question that they would not be sharing a room tonight. Ana had merely nodded when her mother had told her that their *rooms* were ready for them. "I hope we didn't wear you out tonight," Ana said almost apologetically as Erik's hand rested gently on her cheek. He bent and planted a kiss on her forehead. "Not at all," he said, "I have all kinds of energy in reserve." His gaze was blatantly sexual.

Ana laughed because she knew he had to be pulling her leg with that look. There was no way she was letting him anywhere near her until they were back in New York City.

"Surely you're kidding," she said, her gaze devouring him just as fervently. He had just set her pulse to racing. Two could play that game. She'd have him *running* to take a cold shower before she was done. "Although I wish I could undress you and tuck you into bed. You've been such a good boy today both with the surprise and keeping your hands to yourself. My parents may even be convinced that we're waiting until our wedding night to make love."

"I was that convincing, huh?" asked Erik. His cheek, which was bristly by this time of night, grazed hers but still the touch turned her on. She had only to turn her head a fraction of an inch and their mouths would meet in a longed-for kiss. She hadn't kissed him since they had arrived hours ago and that one had been interrupted by her dad.

"Oh, hell, I give up. Just kiss me and kiss me hard so I can go take a cold shower!" she said, frustrated. Erik grinned and went in for the kill. They had shared many kisses since their first kiss, but this one was special because it was somehow forbidden. He felt like a schoolboy stealing kisses and although this scenario should not be the least bit sensual to a grown man, it was.

The kiss deepened and, honestly, if not for the sound of footsteps on the hardwood floor behind them they would have continued for some time. However, the footsteps were followed by a deep voice with an Italian accent saying, *"Buona notte, Ana!"*

It was said with authority and finality. Unlike Erik, Ana knew that when her father said *"Buona notte,"* he only said it when the person he was speaking to was going directly to bed, no detours. That's all he had to say to them when they were children and they knew not to talk back.

"Buona notte, Papa," said Ana. *"Ti amo,"* she whispered to Erik.

"I love you," Erik whispered back.

Ana gave him one last glance and went into her room.

Erik turned to face Carlo. "Good night, sir."

Carlo laughed softly. "Good night? It's still early. There's something I'd like to talk with you about."

Concern was mirrored in Erik's eyes as he regarded Carlo. "Lead the way."

They went into the study, a masculine room with book-lined walls and leather furnishings. There was a bar in a corner of the room and Carlo went and poured them both shots of brandy.

"Only a little," Erik said. "I'm not much of a drinker."

Sometimes he hated admitting that because he knew that some men judged other men on their ability to hold their liquor. If he were to be judged on that basis, he'd fail miserably.

"Good for you," said Carlo. "I've seen the love of a drink ruin many a man."

He prepared them both perhaps half an inch in the tumblers. Handing Erik his drink, he said, "Please sit down."

Erik sat in a dark brown, tufted-leather armchair and Carlo sat in the matching chair opposite him. Carlo took a sip of his brandy before beginning. "What I know of you, I like, Erik. You've worked hard. You sincerely believe in what you do and from what I hear you love your family. But all of that is on the surface. A person is so much more than what shows on the surface. Human beings consist of many layers. Just because a man appears perfect, doesn't mean he is."

"None of us are perfect," Erik said. "I have my faults."

"I'm sure you do," said Carlo. "So have I. What I'm getting at is I don't want my daughter marrying a man who is interested only in what he sees. Ana's beautiful, that's a given. Her beauty, however, has been somewhat of a curse. Men are drawn to her because of it, but after a while learn that she's human, not some ideal, and they wind up breaking her heart. I want to make certain that you see more in Ana than what's on the surface. I see the way you look at her. I love my wife more than I did on our wedding day, so I know how you feel about Ana.

But will you love her when she's no longer young? Will you love her after she's given you children and can't lose the baby weight?

Because if the answer is no, I wish you would leave her now rather than later."

Erik started to say something and Carlo held up his hand. "I'm not finished. I wasn't going to say this. Earlier I told Ana I had no doubts about you and, truly, my gut tells me you're who you appear to be. But I wouldn't be a good father if I didn't get this off my chest. I've known too many rich men who married beautiful women and tossed them aside when a more beautiful woman came along."

Erik drank some of the brandy and grimaced. It was quality brandy, but it still burned going down. He simply had no tolerance for alcohol. He looked Carlo straight in the eye. "I don't make decisions lightly and I would never have proposed to Ana if I wasn't sure she's the woman I want to spend the rest of my life with."

He went on to tell Carlo about his mother and how he had been a grown man before he'd come to terms with her behavior toward his father and him and Belana. "I'm thirty-five, and Ana is the only woman I've ever loved because she is the only woman I ever trusted enough to allow to get close to me. And that wouldn't have happened if I hadn't followed the advice of my sister who told me to be Ana's friend, just her friend, for as long as she wanted me to be. It's true. I was smitten with Ana from the start. A fool in love, but spending time with her without having any romantic expectations gave me a good look into her soul. Yes, Mr. Corelli, I love Ana for much more than her appearance. I love that she's smart, she's kind to others. She adores her friends and family. And there's no truer friend than your daughter. Does that answer your question?"

Carlo smiled and nodded in the affirmative. "I'm satisfied," he said. He set his empty glass on the side table next to the lamp where he was sitting and got to his feet. Erik set his nearly untouched drink down, too, and stood. They shook hands, which felt like Carlo's seal of approval to Erik. "Welcome to the family, son," said Carlo. Then he hugged Erik briefly and added, *"Buono notte."* With that he turned and left the room.

Erik went to bed. When he got to his room he dialed Ana's cell phone number.

"Hello, darling," Ana said, her voice husky.

"I think I just had 'the talk' with your father," Erik said, laughter evident in his tone.

"It had to happen sooner or later," Ana told him. "He's a traditionalist. What did he say?"

"He just wanted to know that I'm sincere," Erik said, "and I assured him I was. Could we have all boys when we have children? I don't know if I can be a father to a girl. It's too complicated."

Ana laughed. "You'll have to talk to God about that."

"I'll do that when I say my prayers tonight. Right after I thank Him for you."

"Okay, darling, sleep well," Ana said, laughing softly. "I'll dream about you."

* * *

The following day was Christmas Eve, Ana and Erik were the first ones up since they had been designated to prepare breakfast. It was a bright day, the sunlight reflecting off the snowbanks outside. Per the rental agreement someone had come that morning to shovel the snow from the walkway in front of the house and the snow plow had been in the neighborhood as well, so the roads were clear. After breakfast the men went to buy a Christmas tree and the women, with the children, made the kitchen their gathering place as Elle and Natalie, along with help from Ana, began cooking Christmas dinner. Tomorrow no one planned to be slaving over a hot stove while they could be spending time with the family.

Sophia happily took charge of the children, keeping the girls entertained with games and coloring books and the babies were content to be in their carriers with cheerful sounds all around them.

Ana had to smile because her mother clearly deferred to Elle when it came to recipes. Elle listed items and Natalie followed orders as if she were Elle's sous chef and without attitude. She was not a diva in the kitchen.

The turkey and ham were in the oven. Elle was washing turnip greens in the sink and Natalie was stirring the macaroni and cheese in a pot on the stove top prior to putting it into the oven. Sophia had put on a CD of Christmas music to which they hummed.

"This reminds me of when my grandmother and I would cook together," Elle said, smiling at the thought.

"It was a lot of work but the end results were always worth it."

"I hope so," said Ana, struggling with the pecan pie she was making. She thought the mixture looked too watery but Elle assured her that the pie would firm up when it had finished baking. Ana went and put the pie in one of the double ovens. She peeked at the panettone while she had the oven door open. The dough had risen ten hours, after which Carlo had punched it down in its bowl and then transferred the dough to two baking pans and allowed the dough to rise five more hours. Her father had said the two loaves should cook for approximately forty-five minutes. No wonder most people in Milan buy their panettone from a reputable baker, Ana thought.

The conquering heroes got back around noon with the tree, an eight-foot fir. Famished, they were served hot soup and grilled cheese sandwiches for lunch. After which the women insisted they put the tree up so it could be decorated.

That night, after dinner, the family put the finishing touches on the tree and it took pride of place in front of the picture window in the entertainment room not far from the grand piano. Presents were put under the tree as well as the panettone which was carefully wrapped by Carlo. Ariana and Renata took particular delight in the tree-lighting ceremony. Ariana, with the help of her father, got to put the star at the top of the tree, and Renata with the help of *her* father got to switch on the lights.

The babies had been put to bed earlier in the evening. At around nine o'clock Carlo sternly told Ariana and Renata, "You must go to bed now, girls, or else *Babbo Natale* will not bring you any presents."

Ariana and Renata looked at each other with stretched eyes. They believed every word out of their grandfather's mouth. With urgency they began kissing everyone goodnight and hurried their parents along so they could be tucked into bed as quickly as possible and go fast asleep for fear of angering *Babbo Natale*.

Once the girls were off to bed and there was no chance of them hearing, Natalie exclaimed, "You get a kick out of scaring those sweet babies, don't you?"

Her husband laughed quietly. "That's half the fun, *cara mia.*"

On Christmas morning, Ana was awakened by the sound of her nieces' high-pitched screams of delight. *Babbo Natale* had apparently visited during the night and left them presents. She hurried into the nearby bathroom to wash her face and brush her teeth, then put on a bathrobe and slippers and joined her family around the Christmas tree.

Everyone was there, also in robes and slippers. The mothers held their sons and the fathers their daughters in their laps as the little girls tore the gift wrap off their presents. *"Buon Natale!"* Ana said, smiling.

"Buon Natale," chorused her family back at her.

The adults were not interested in exchanging gifts, only in seeing the joy on the children's faces. This to them was the true meaning of Christmas. After all, it was a child for whom the tradition was started.

Ana sat down beside Erik and he put his arms around her in a warm hug. She kissed his cheek. "Thank you again for doing this for me. I'm so happy!"

"Thank you for loving me," he said in her ear. "That's all the thanks I need."

The following day there were tearful goodbyes at the airport as Ana's family prepared to board the plane for New York City, after which they would take a connecting flight to Italy. She and Erik would also be flying to New York but her family's flight left earlier. She regretted that no one had had the foresight to try to book them all on the same flight.

She kissed them all at the terminal. Her father pulled her and Erik aside for a moment. "Oh, Ana, I forgot to tell you, Pietro Lanza is heading up the New York office. He's already in New York but is staying at a hotel until he can find more permanent accommodations. I gave him your number. He doesn't know anyone in the city."

"I didn't know Pietro had been promoted," said Ana. "Good for him."

"Yes," said her father. "He's earned it."

"It'll be nice to see your first love again, huh?" Sophia said, interrupting with a mischievous grin on her face. She looked at Erik. "Oh, she was wild about him."

Ana laughed. "We were twelve!"

"I don't care, you never forget your first love," Sophia teased.

It was announced that passengers could begin boarding the plane. Ana got in a few additional kisses, and she and Erik waved goodbye to her family.

Chapter 11

Natalie phoned Ana to let her know they had arrived home safely. Ana was snuggling in bed with Erik, his body pressed close to hers. He slept soundly while she talked.

The subject returned to wedding plans. "Your sister's heart was in the right place," Natalie said in her older daughter's defense. "You do need to start thinking seriously about what you want to do. Do you want a winter wedding or a spring wedding? Call me when you decide. As your mother, I do want to be involved."

"All right, Mom, I'll call you," Ana promised.

Natalie was unable to suppress a yawn. "I could sleep for a week. Your father's already snoring. I'd better go. Take care, sweetheart."

"You, too," said Ana. Ana hung up the phone and got comfortable in Erik's arms once more.

He stirred. "Your folks?"

"Yeah," she murmured. "Letting me know they're home. Are you awake or talking in your sleep?"

He kissed her naked shoulder. "I'm awake."

Ana felt him hardening. "Awake enough to discuss the wedding?"

"Okay," he said, sounding disappointed to her.

"You keep telling me to do what I like, but what about your schedule? Would work get in the way of a honeymoon if we were married during a certain time of year?"

"You're asking if I have a busy time of the year?" he asked.

"Well, yeah."

"I can arrange time off at any time you prefer," he told her.

"Really, Erik, you're too flexible."

He kissed the back of her neck. "I'll show you flexible."

She squirmed in his arms. "You're no help at all."

He cupped her left breast. "Let's get married in June. I hear June weddings are nice."

"Then you want to be married outdoors?"

"Yes, you choose the place."

"Your parents' garden in New Haven," she said. "I want Drusilla there and travel isn't easy on her, even though she'd deny it."

"I'm sure Mom and Dad and Grandma would love that," Erik said.

"Okay, that's settled," Ana said smiling, "How many guests?"

"Oh, a few hundred," Erik joked.

"Be serious. Family and close friends only," Ana said with a tired sigh. "The guest list is always longer in the end than when it starts out. Let's say a hundred, tops."

"That's fine," Erik said. "And I hope the paparazzi will leave you alone."

Ana hadn't thought about that. She didn't know why. She'd seen scenes where the paparazzi were camped out at wedding venues of celebrities hoping to get that money shot—that spectacular photo that would sell for an outrageous amount.

"We won't put the announcement in the papers," she suggested. "No one has to know except those who get invitations."

"And you expect everyone to keep our secret?" he asked skeptically.

"I know I'm being unrealistic, but we can try it," Ana returned.

Ana touched his cheek. He smiled. "Your eyes are the color of the sunset over the ocean in Tahiti," she said.

"You would know," he said.

"Yes," she said, grinning. She gently kissed his lips. "And your lips are soft as a feather from heaven."

"How poetic," he whispered with a naughty glint in

his eye. "Have you been in contact with many feathers from heaven lately?" His hands were squeezing her butt.

"I don't think you know your sexual appeal," she continued, ignoring for the moment the ache in her feminine core. "Women come on to you all the time and you don't even notice."

"I notice, I just don't care," Erik said truthfully. His penis was fully erect now. He rolled over and got a condom off the nightstand's top where he had tossed a couple a few hours ago. Handing it to Ana, he said, "Would you?"

Ana took it, tore it open and easily rolled the latex condom onto him. The wrapper was dropped onto the nightstand and she climbed on top of him. Her hair spilled down her back. Erik enjoyed the sight of her, full breasts with the nipples erect and pointing north. Her skin felt soft as silk beneath his fingers. He went deep inside her and felt her contract around his shaft. Felt the need building within her. She wasn't shy anymore.

She was now comfortable enough to tell him what she wanted, and bold enough to take it. Her breasts bounced up and down as they increased their efforts. She grasped his hands, their fingers entwined, soft pants issuing from her full lips. Sometimes they made love but sometimes they carried on like a pair of animals in the wild. This was one of those times. She closed her eyes and he knew she was about to scream when he felt her tremble inside. She screamed and fell on top of him. He came in a powerful rush, so turned on by her taking her pleasure that he could no longer hold on to his. As he collapsed back onto the bed she was smiling with satisfaction. He pushed the hair out of her eyes and wrapped his strong arms around her and then, worried she might catch a chill, he pulled the covers up over them.

Ana lay there thinking that if she had never gotten up the nerve to tell Erik how she really felt about him, she would be in this bed alone, except perhaps for a book by one of her favorite authors. Things had certainly changed.

To thank her for arranging the Aspen trip Ana sent Abby flowers and a gift certificate for the works at an exclusive spa. She knew from a past conversation with Abby that she longed for a day of pampering, however considered an expensive spa too much of a splurge. Her husband was a schoolteacher, after all. Ana got Erik to agree to give Abby the day off. Abby would have no feasible reason to refuse Ana's gift.

When Pietro Lanza phoned Ana a couple of days before New Year's Eve, she wasn't at all surprised. But she was a bit at a loss for words. She hadn't seen him or spoken to him since they were twelve and he and his widowed mother, Maria, moved to Rome. Ana's mother and Maria Lanza were friends and had stayed in touch, so when Pietro decided to work in the fashion industry he had been hired by Ana's father and moved back to Milan. Every now and then her father would mention that Pietro was doing well and swiftly climbing the corporate ladder. It was Sophia who had trained him and now Pietro had been given a position, which would have been hers if she had not wanted to remain in Milan. But she preferred raising her children in her hometown.

Ana didn't even recognize Pietro's voice, which was deep and sexy. They naturally lapsed into Italian as soon as he introduced himself and after ten minutes or so, Ana relaxed and remembered how comfortable she used to be around him. "You must come to the Whitaker's New Year's Eve party," she said. "I'd love to see you."

"I don't know," he hesitated. "I don't have a date."

"Come solo," Ana suggested. "You'll probably meet someone at the party."

"You always were an optimist," he said, laughter evident in his voice.

"Then you'll come?"

"Yes, I'll be there," he agreed.

The Whitaker's New Year's Eve party was an opportunity to dress to the nines and toast in the New Year with people you admired. Erik and Ana greeted guests as they began arriving at nine. She wore a short, sleeveless scoop-neck silver matte dress with black accessories. Erik wore a black tuxedo with a red bow tie and white cummerbund.

Music played softly in the background. The band wouldn't begin their first set until ten.

Guests mingled and partook of the feast at the buffet tables and imbibed spirits offered up by bars at either end of the room. The penthouse was huge with plenty of space to accommodate the expected one hundred-plus revelers.

The hardwood floors were ideal for dancing and the view of the New York City skyline was awe-inspiring in daylight but even more so at night.

Ana could not restrain herself when Abby arrived with her husband, Harry. She walked swiftly to the older woman and hugged her. "Wow, you look fantastic!"

Abby had abandoned her smooth chignon in favor of a wavy, chin length style that accentuated her high cheekbones and beautifully framed her heart-shaped face. She wore a sleeveless black dress with a square-shaped bodice and sparkly silver sandals with a matching clutch. Her fake fur sable coat was the same color as her hair, a warm auburn. Harry looked wonderful in a black tuxedo with white tie and white cummerbund. While his wife was petite, he was tall and lanky, his head completely bald. He reminded Ana of a young James Earl Jones, especially when he smiled and she saw a small gap between his teeth.

"I had a ball at the spa," Abby said, her eyes twinkling. She peered down at her feet and wiggled her toes. "Look, passionate pink."

"Fabulous!" Ana declared, admiring the color. They giggled together like little girls.

Meanwhile, Erik and Harry were shaking hands and murmuring masculine hellos. Harry glanced at Abby and Ana, a smile on his face. "How did we get so lucky?"

Erik laughed shortly. "Beats me," he said. Indeed,

both Ana and Abby were radiant tonight but it was not due to what they were wearing but to how content they seemed to be with their lives. Erik had always admired Harry and Abby for their devotion to one another. He wished for himself and Ana to enjoy such a long and happy marriage.

Abby came and grabbed Harry by the hand. "I'm starving."

Harry peered over his shoulder at Erik and Ana as he let himself be lead away by his wife. "She's been eating like a bird, afraid she wouldn't fit in that dress."

Ana and Erik smiled knowingly. A moment after Abby and Harry left in search of food the bell rang again and Ana opened the door to Pietro and his date, a curvy brunette in a little red dress. Ana recognized Pietro's dark brown, almost black eyes, at once. Those thick lashes were not easy to forget. Nor his darkly tanned skin, wavy black hair, square jaw and full-lipped mouth. He had been a beautiful boy and he was a gorgeous man.

"Ana!" he exclaimed and pulled her into his arms for a kiss on the mouth—a kiss that, in Erik's estimation, lasted far too long.

Ana was startled for two reasons: she hadn't expected to be kissed on the mouth by Pietro, on the cheek, yes; and she hadn't expected him to show up with a date, especially not a female date.

How had he put it thirteen years ago when she had confessed she liked him, her teenaged heart open and vulnerable? *I like you too, Ana. But, I'm sorry, not in that way. I don't like girls in that way.* His revelation had not been put eloquently but she had certainly understood. Pietro was gay.

"It's a secret," he'd told her in his innocence. "I haven't even told my parents." At the time his father was still living. But a short time after that his father had been killed in a construction accident, and he and his mother had moved to Rome to live with her family.

Ana pulled herself together and introduced Pietro to Erik. "Pietro this is my fiancé, Erik Whitaker. Erik, this is my childhood friend, Pietro Lanza."

The two men shook hands, Erik trying not to let his irritation show on his face.

If he did look irritated, Pietro didn't seem to notice. He enthusiastically pumped Erik's hand. "It's a pleasure to meet you, Erik." He gestured to his date. "I'd like you two to meet Hilary Eastbrook. Hilary is my assistant."

Ana shook Hilary's hand and smiled warmly. "How are you, Hilary?"

Hilary smiled back shyly. "Oh, it's a real treat to meet you, Ms. Corelli. I've followed your career forever!"

Ana continued to smile at the woman who appeared to be about her age, "How sweet," she said. "And, please, call me Ana." Her mind was racing. She knew she couldn't drag Pietro off and interrogate him. He'd just arrived. But she wanted to ask him what had happened to the lovely gay boy she had known thirteen years ago? Had he just been going through a phase? Was that even possible? Of her gay friends, and she had many, once they realized they were gay they didn't suddenly wake up to be heterosexual one morning.

"I happened to mention coming here tonight at the office," Pietro told Ana, "and Hilary started talking about her plans for tonight."

"Which consisted of microwave popcorn and a DVD," joked Hilary.

"So I asked her to join me," Pietro concluded. "Remember, I was reluctant to come without a date."

"I'm glad you asked Hilary," Ana said graciously. The bell rang announcing more guests. "Please, enjoy yourselves."

When Pietro and Hilary were out of earshot, Erik quipped, "He didn't tongue you, did he?"

"Absolutely not," said Ana as they walked to the door. "I wouldn't have let him. Frankly, I'm confused about his behavior."

"Well, I didn't like his behavior, either."

"I don't mean just the kiss," Ana said. She opened the door. Erik's parents and Drusilla had arrived. Pietro was forgotten as she and Erik welcomed them. A short time later, Belana and Nick showed up, looking wonderful in their evening clothes. They were the last of the guests on the list, so Erik and Ana went to stand in the middle of the dance floor to formally welcome everyone and introduce the band.

The local five-member blues band included a pianist, two guitar players, a drummer and a trumpet player. Their vocalist, who simply called herself Maybelline, was an attractive full-figured African-American woman with a powerful voice. She went right into an upbeat set that got the guests onto the dance floor. Erik and Ana set the example by being the first couple on the floor, followed by Belana and Nick.

Maybelline sang, "Something's Got a Hold on Me," with verve. It was lively enough to lend itself to a swing dance which is what Erik and Ana wound up doing to the delight of the guests. Not to be outdone Belana and Nick displayed their talent for the intricate twists and turns in that style of dance. At one point the couples' movements brought them close enough to converse on the dance floor and Ana called to Belana. "It's not fair. You're a professional."

"All's fair in love and dance," Belana joked, and allowed Nick to lift her in the air.

"I hope you don't want to try that," Erik said, laughing.

"And break my neck?" Ana replied, admiring Belana and Nick's skill. "No, thank you," she joked.

After two more songs, which were designed to get the party started, Maybelline slowed things down a bit with "This Magic Moment." Ana felt a gentle tap on her shoulder. She turned around to find Drusilla standing behind her. "May I have this dance with my grandson?"

Ana relinquished her dance partner after kissing Drusilla's cheek, and saying, "Don't wear him out."

"I can't make any promises," was Drusilla's cheeky response.

Because Drusilla was so short, Erik had to bend down a bit to dance with his grandmother. He felt like picking her up and setting her on the tops of his feet like he'd seen some fathers do with their little girls at weddings.

Drusilla gazed up at him through her thick glasses. "You're devilishly handsome tonight. You remind me of your grandfather when we first got married. We used to dance the night away at the Savoy in Harlem."

Ana was not without a dance partner for long. Pietro claimed her. She took the opportunity to catch up on as much as they could of the last thirteen years as they danced.

"Why didn't you answer any of my letters?" she asked, peering into his eyes.

"We were still grieving when we left Milan. Everything had changed overnight, it seemed. My mother cried all the time. I thankfully read your letters but didn't know how to respond. I had told you something I'd never shared with anyone else. I was scared I had done the wrong thing. And months later after I'd also told my mother, I knew I had to stop telling people about my true feelings. I thought it best to sever ties with anyone who knew the truth."

"She didn't take it well?" asked Ana, concerned.

"Not at all," Pietro confirmed. His expression was sad as he continued, "Her husband was dead and now her son was gay? She told me she had a heart condition and I shouldn't be joking about something that outrageous. I followed her cue and told her I'd been teasing and never brought it up again."

"Does she really have a heart condition?"

"I've never seen any medical records, but I doubt it."

"So you keep your private life private," Ana deduced.

"Unfortunately, yes," he said softly, smiling at her. "In all fairness I could have made things clear to her years ago, but even today it's easier to be considered hetero than it is to be outwardly gay. It isn't easy leading a double life. Women take it I'm an Italian stallion because of the way I look. And any serious relationship I attempt with a man ends badly because I won't declare to the world that I want to be with him. So I don't have anyone special in my life."

His explanation had the ring of truth to Ana. The recent glut of news stories about bullying and young gay people committing suicide because of continual mistreatment proved that it was still not safe to be yourself in today's society.

She hugged him. "You're still so young. You'll find someone. In the meantime, your secret's safe with me."

He sighed with relief. "I'm glad you're the same old Ana, the one I could always talk to."

They once again regained the proper distance and continued the dance. When the song ended, Pietro asked Hilary to dance, and Ana returned to Erik's arms.

"You looked kind of cozy with Pietro," Erik commented dryly.

"We were just talking," Ana said nonchalantly. "He's had a hard time finding someone he can relate to. We always found it easy to talk to each other." She moved closer to him and laid her head on his shoulder. "Don't worry, sweetie, I'm not his type."

"I'm not worried," Erik denied.

"You sounded a little put out."

"I get antsy when another man touches my girl."

She smiled up at him. "Rest assured, your girl would not allow anyone to touch her inappropriately. Italians are bit more demonstrative than Americans, that's all. When we see friends and family we kiss, we hug, we feed them." She ended with a laugh.

"You could also be describing African-Americans," Erik said with a grin. He gestured to the buffet table in the distance where Abby was feeding Harry a jumbo shrimp.

It was nearing the midnight hour when Ana went into the store room to retrieve the party hats and noisemakers. Everyone helped themselves from the huge box and then Erik directed their attention to the big screen TV that had been installed on the wall above the fireplace in the great room.

Champagne glasses were filled and then everyone was ready for the countdown. Couples put their arms around one another. When the ball dropped in Times Square everyone at the Whitaker's New Year's Eve party shouted, "Happy New Year!"

Erik and Ana kissed as did every other couple in the room. The band struck up "Auld Lang Syne" and those who remembered the words sang along. Laughter abounded, but some tears were shed, too.

"This year will be the best ever," Erik whispered in Ana's ear, "Because I'm marrying you."

Ana just smiled and kissed him again.

Chapter 12

"Eat, eat," Pietro encouraged Ana, stuffing pizza into his own mouth.

Laughing, Ana purposely put down the pizza slice in her hand. "What? Do you have orders to fatten me up or something?"

"You're representing a line of clothing designed for full-figured women and you're too skinny," Pietro complained good-naturedly.

"I'm not one of those size-zero models. I'm a size eight, I'm not skinny. Anyway, that's why you're using models of all sizes in the ads, so no woman will feel left out." She picked up the pizza again. "Now, let me eat in peace!"

They dined at a pizzeria not far from the studio of Ivan Ivanovich, the world-renowned photographer,

where Ana had posed for him in the new line of clothes.
The shoot had lasted for ten hours. Ana was worn out
and not very hungry but she'd agreed to a pizza with
Pietro after the shoot because Erik was out of town. She
was used to his frequent business trips and had vowed
not to become a nagging fiancée. Though she missed
him terribly.

It was now the last week in January and she and Pietro had been working hard to put the finishing touches
on the spring campaign for Voluptuous Woman, Corelli
Fashions' full-figured line.

She was enjoying getting to know Pietro all over
again. The boy she had loved was still in there. He was
sweet, and kind and funny. She found herself wanting
to find a guy for him. Matchmaking wasn't something
she usually considered, believing that sticking your nose
in someone else's love life rarely ended well. In spite
of her misgivings, though, whenever she ran into male
gay friends she made it a point to ask if they were pres-
ently involved with anyone.

She looked at Pietro now, "Are you still seeing Hilary?"

"We're friends," he said, but she could tell by his reluctance to meet her gaze he wasn't being completely
truthful. Pietro was a bad liar.

"Does she know that?"

"Nothing's going to happen between us," he said,
raising his gaze to hers. "I never get intimate with
women. I break up with them before it gets to that
stage."

"Isn't it going to be difficult to break up with Hilary since she's your assistant?" Ana asked pointedly. She hated to see him squirm but someone had to ask him the hard questions.

He sighed. "You're right. I should tell her we can't date anymore."

"Good luck with that," Ana said. "She's already half in love with you."

He shook his head. "She just has a little crush."

"Have you ever seen yourself in a mirror? You're better looking than most male models. You can't casually date women. One of these days you're going to run into a nut who won't take no for an answer."

"Been there," he admitted. "I've been stalked a few times."

"See? It's not nice to play with women's emotions," Ana said, reaching over to grasp his hand. She met his gaze, her expression serious. "How do you know your mother doesn't already know and accept your sexuality? Many of my gay friends have said that when they told their parents they already were aware they were gay. Kind of a letdown, isn't it? I mean you get all prepared for an emotional scene and your mom looks at you and says, 'Yeah, I've known that for a long time now.' Of course *you'll* never find out unless you talk to her."

"I know, I know," said Pietro, his eyes downcast.

"That's the end of my speech," said Ana. "I won't bring it up again, ever. I just hate to see you so unhappy."

"I'm getting there," Pietro said. "One day soon I'm going to tell her, and let it hit the fan."

Ana didn't comment. She felt she had harangued him enough. It was his life, therefore it was his decision.

"What I'd rather be talking about is how you and Ivan were looking at each other," she teased lightly. "He's available, you know. His longtime boyfriend was killed in a car accident about two years ago and he's been taking things slowly when it comes to romance. It's hard when you lose someone you love like that. But he recently told me he's thinking of dating again. If you're interested I could put in a good word for you."

Pietro colored. Ana smiled because she had obviously judged Ivan and Pietro's encounter correctly—Pietro was interested in the sexy photographer.

"He wouldn't be interested in me," Pietro said. "He's famous. I'm just a worker bee."

"You're the head of the New York office of an international company," Ana said enthusiastically. "I'm not gonna let you down-rate yourself."

Pietro scrunched up his face. "Do you really think he's interested? He's gorgeous. He reminds me of that guy who's in that vampire show on HBO."

"Alexander Skarsgard." Ana supplied the name of the handsome actor.

"Yeah, him," Pietro murmured wistfully. "I don't know, Ana."

"Faint heart never won fair…um, guy," Ana said encouragingly.

"I'll think about it," Pietro said noncommittally.

"Okay, cool," Ana relented. "But don't think too long. A guy like Ivan won't be on the market forever."

They finished the pizza, and when they left the restaurant it was nearly eleven. The wind was fierce and the temperature in the thirties. Nonetheless the streets were crowded in this part of town. Ana momentarily gazed up at the night sky. There were too many tall buildings obscuring her view of the heavens to tell if there were any stars out. When they were in Aspen one of the things she'd liked most was walking out at night and seeing the sky lit up with stars twinkling like diamonds.

"I'll take you home," said Pietro, putting her arm through his in a gentlemanly fashion.

"You live farther away than I do," Ana said reasonably. "I can get home on my own."

"I insist."

"All right," Ana relented, touched by his gesture.

Half an hour later they were walking into her loft. Ana shut and locked the door behind them, then turned to Pietro and said, "Look, why don't you just stay here tonight? I've plenty of room. It's Friday, you don't have to be at the office in the morning."

"You had to remind me," said Pietro as he walked into the living room and picked up the TV's remote and switched it on. "Friday night, and I don't have a date."

"I'm sure Hilary would have gone out with you if you hadn't had to work late," Ana said teasingly.

"I mean a real date."

Ana pulled off her jacket revealing jeans and a long-sleeve black pullover sweater. "So I take it that you're staying. Hand me your coat."

Pietro pulled off his zippered black leather coat and handed it to Ana. "You convinced me. What sort of movies do you have? Got any popcorn?"

Chuckling, Ana put their coats in the foyer closet and joined him in the living room. "Let's see, I just got *Ninja Assassin*, have you seen it?" She knew of Pietro's predilection for martial arts movies. Or, at least, he used to like them. They used to argue about who the best martial arts actor was. She liked Jackie Chan because he was also funny. Pietro preferred Jet Li because, in Pietro's words, he was such a badass.

"Seen it?" he said, his eyes lighting up. "About ten times. Put it on."

Ana did so, and then she went to the kitchen to microwave some popcorn. When she returned with the bowl of popcorn and two sodas, Pietro was fast-forwarding through the previews on the DVD.

"Hold on, I like watching those," she protested. "I might see something I'm interested in seeing."

Pietro laughed. "I knew people like you existed, but I just had never met one before. You actually have the patience to watch the previews and not want to get right to the movie?"

Ana set the bowl of popcorn on the coffee table in front of them and handed him a Coke. Her eyes were on the TV's screen. "Another *Nightmare on Elm Street* movie," she said. "Glad I missed that one. Freddy Krueger never dies."

She sat down beside him on the couch. Finally the movie's selection screen came on, and Ana grimaced. "This already looks like it's going to be bloody." The photo was of Rain, the star of the film, dressed in black leather with a chain whipped across his body a deadly blade at its tip, cuts over all of him and his mouth open in what looked like a war cry.

Pietro smiled. "It's not so bad." He pressed play.

The first ten minutes was a bloodbath. Ana watched only through slits of her eyelids. "Oh, my God, tell me when it's over!"

But then Naomie Harris came onto the screen portraying an investigator for Europol trying to prove that Ninjas existed and were hired assassins and the movie became more enjoyable.

Because she was exhausted Ana wound up going to sleep halfway through. Pietro finished watching the movie, then got up to go to the bathroom. When he returned to the living room, Erik was entering into the loft having used his key.

The expression on Erik's face froze Pietro in his footsteps. The muscles worked in Erik's strong jaw. His eyes narrowed. "I had no idea you would be here," he said coldly.

Erik had not yet seen Ana asleep on the couch because the couch's back was to the front door of the loft. He would've had to enter the living room to see her laying there.

"Ana and I worked late, I saw her home, and since I live quite a distance away she suggested I stay the night on the couch," Pietro told him in a low voice. Adding the couch part had seemed like a prudent choice. "I'm sorry but Ana didn't tell me she was expecting you."

"I was going to surprise her," Erik said. *And what's it to you?* "Where *is* Ana?" He knew he shouldn't be allowing his mind to take him to this dark place but seeing Pietro there at this late of an hour had brought out the jealous fool in him. And why was Pietro whispering?

Pietro gestured to the couch. Erik walked around and saw Ana. She was sleeping peacefully. He looked around the room. An empty bowl with a few popcorn kernels in it was on the coffee table, two soda cans beside it. Ana was fully clothed. So was Pietro. There was no evidence that anything of a sexual nature had happened here and, yet, he felt like he had walked in on Ana and Pietro and caught them red-handed.

He had to get hold of himself. He turned and began walking toward the door. He couldn't let Ana see him this way. Pietro started to say something but when he saw the tightly wound tension in Erik's face he thought better of it. "I'm going," Erik said to Pietro. "Don't tell Ana I was here."

Pietro let him go, but as soon as the door closed behind Erik, he hastily typed out a text message to Ana, explaining that he'd decided to go home after all. He grabbed his coat from the foyer closet, put it on and left.

He caught up with Erik out on the street. "Erik, wait!"

Erik stopped walking, but his face was still a mask

of anger when he turned toward Pietro. Pietro couldn't tell if the anger was directed at him or perhaps was the result of Erik waging a war within himself. It didn't matter. He needed to talk to Erik now.

However, before he could say a word, Erik said, "Don't try to tell me you don't love Ana because I've seen the way you look at her!"

"I've known Ana longer than I've known anyone else in this world besides my mother," Pietro began. "We played together as babies. We lost touch but now that I've found her, I don't ever want to let that happen again. I hope you and I can be friends. But if that's asking too much, I understand. Just know this, I do love her but not in the way you must imagine I do. I love her like a sister."

Erik laughed mockingly. "A man cannot love Ana like a sister unless he is her brother and you're not related to her by blood."

"Ana tells me you two were friends before you fell in love," Pietro said hopefully.

"Ana didn't tell you the whole truth. We were attracted to each other from the beginning. We used restraint."

"You think I'm biding my time until Ana realizes it's me she loves and she leaves you for me?" Pietro asked. He couldn't hide the disbelief in his voice.

"Look," said Erik. "I trust Ana. I know she wouldn't cheat on me. But I don't know you. Therefore, I don't trust you."

"Would you believe me if I told you that Ana isn't even my type?"

"No," said Erik flatly.

"Then I suppose I should save my breath," said Pietro. He sighed heavily. "It's obvious nothing's going to be resolved tonight. I'm going home. I suggest you go back upstairs and surprise Ana. She misses you. I sent her a text message telling her I went home. But if you want to bite off your nose to spite your face, go right ahead."

Pietro walked off. Damn Erik Whitaker! The lucky bastard had one of the best women in the world and he was going to mess it up with his jealous nature. Sure, he realized he could clear things up in seconds by telling Erik he was gay, but why should he? If Erik didn't trust Ana to stay faithful to him, he didn't deserve her! He wished he had someone in his life who loved *him* as much as Ana loved Erik.

Erik stood a moment on the sidewalk, indecision eating at him. He wanted to go back upstairs to Ana but he was still in a rotten mood. He didn't want to subject her to what might spill forth from his mouth while he was fighting to subdue his baser nature. He was only a man, a man with unresolved abandonment issues, if he wasn't mistaken about the gut-wrenching emotion that filled him when he walked in the door and found Pietro standing there.

He was afraid of losing Ana. That was the reason he had left. If she found out that for one split second he had thought her capable of cheating on him she would conclude that maybe they'd gotten engaged too quickly and would call the wedding off. He needed time to cool off.

So he went home.

A persistent beeping woke Ana. She raised herself on her elbow enough to reach her cell phone atop the coffee table. It was a message from Pietro. She sat up more and looked around her. "Pietro?" No answer. She read the message then knew that she was alone in the loft. He must have had something important to do at his place she surmised. She got up, collected the bowl and the empty drink cans and took them into the kitchen.

Once she'd washed the popcorn bowl and put the cans in the recycling bin, she glanced up at the clock. It was nearly two-thirty. She thought of Erik, alone in his hotel room in San Francisco. Should she phone him? What time was it out there? Three hours earlier, right? That made it only eleven thirty.

She went and got her cell phone and dialed his number. Curiously, it went straight to message. "Sweetie, I just wanted to hear your voice before going to bed. Pietro and I worked late on the spring campaign and then he insisted on seeing that I got home safely. He's such a gentleman. I told him to just stay over, it was so late. We started watching a movie and I fell asleep and when I woke up he was gone. I guess I snored." She ended with a laugh. "I love you! Call me when you get this. I don't care how late it is." Shortly after leaving the message, Ana drifted off to sleep again.

She woke up the next morning refreshed and ready

to take on her day. She had no plans to work with Pietro on the campaign today but first she had an appointment with a well-known actress whose portrait she had agreed to paint. That wasn't until eleven. It was now 8:28. She got up and showered.

Her cell phone rang as she was pouring herself a cup of coffee twenty minutes later. She grinned when she saw that it was Erik. "Good morning, my love," she said, her tone husky. "I hope you're home."

"I'm home," Erik confirmed. She could hear the smile in his voice. "I can't wait to see you."

"Then come on over."

"All right, I will."

He abruptly disconnected.

That was rude, Ana thought, and then she heard his key in the door. All thoughts of his being rude were abandoned as she fairly flew to meet him.

Erik felt like a heel for behaving the way he had last night. He'd spent most of the night lying awake going over and over in his head the reason why he'd reacted that way to Pietro's presence. The thing to do was to tell Ana what had happened with Pietro last night. That's all he could do because he knew now that his reaction had been visceral—he'd had no way of controlling it. It was just there like a physical reaction to being hit in the face, violent and painful.

Now as Ana rained kisses on him, he took her by the arms and set her away from him. "Ana, I've got something to say and I should say it quickly or else I might change my mind."

Ana's big brown eyes were concerned. She stood still and gave him her undivided attention. "What is it? Has something happened? You look sad."

"Let's sit down," he said and walked over to the couch he'd found her sleeping on last night and sat down. Ana joined him, sitting apart from him because she sensed he needed space this morning.

She was still in her bathrobe. He was wearing his running togs and a zippered jacket which was lined for warmth. His coppery eyes looked into hers. "I came by early this morning at around two and ran into Pietro. I was upset seeing him here. So I left, I didn't want you to see me that way. He followed me out and we argued a bit."

Shock registered on Ana's face but she didn't say anything. He knew her mind was making connections, though. Putting two and two together, probably deducing that Erik was the reason Pietro had gone home. But why hadn't *he* stayed?

He laid it all out for her, telling her exactly how he'd felt—like kicking Pietro's ass. Then he told her how vulnerable he had felt at the thought of losing her. And how he thought he had worked through his abandonment issues only to find that he had not. He apologized for allowing such feelings to enter his heart let alone his mind.

Ana listened intently. Her first thought was that she had slept through it all. She hadn't sensed him or smelled his aftershave, nothing. She must have been truly tired. Her second thought was that Pietro had not told Erik he was gay and it therefore was impossible for him to be her lover. Though some gay men have admittedly married and had children, Pietro clearly was not the type to do that. But still it was understandable that Erik would be jealous of all the time she spent with Pietro. Any man would be jealous.

She'd made a promise to Pietro to keep his secret, and that had to be honored even if she *wanted* to tell Erik to ease his mind. She was in a quandary. Should her loyalty be to a friend who had told her something in confidence thirteen years ago? Or to the man she loved to help him feel secure?

She took Erik's hands in hers and maintained eye contact. "You had every right to feel the way you did. I would have been livid if I'd walked in and a beautiful woman was in your house. A woman you'd had a prior relationship with, even though it was a friendly relationship. But Pietro and I aren't even attracted to each other."

Erik slowly shook his head in the negative. "I have the feeling you're not being totally honest with me. It seems as though you're holding something back."

Ana lowered her gaze only for a second or two, but Erik caught the guilty expression in her eyes and that was all it took for him to declare, "Ana, I came here because I felt guilty for my accusatory reaction last night. I wanted to tell you how I felt and apologize for feeling that way. I even considered apologizing to Pietro because, frankly, I think I scared the guy last night. Now I'm sensing some kind of subterfuge."

Ana's guilty conscience made her defensive. "Why can't you just trust that I'm not going to be unfaithful to you? Shouldn't that be enough? I trust *you!*"

"And I trust you," Erik returned evenly. Although as he stood, his jaw set stubbornly, and looked down at her. Ana could swear he didn't even like her very much at that moment, let alone trust her. "I have to go. It was a mistake coming back here so soon. I'm still angry and I don't want to say something I'll regret."

Ana stood, too, pulling her bathrobe tightly around her as if she didn't want to reveal too much of herself to Erik Whitaker. She felt wounded. His words cut like a knife. "Yes, you'd better go," she said, hurt. "I have nothing more to say. You either trust me or you don't. And you don't."

Erik simply looked at her, a frown knitting his brows together. What he wanted to say to her at that moment left a bitter taste in his mouth so he thought it wise not to voice the words. Why was she putting a childhood friend before him? He felt betrayed.

Ana met his gaze. She'd already looked away once and he'd taken that as a sign of guilt. She realized that she was nervously twisting the engagement ring around and around on her finger. Should she give it back to him? No, she thought. This was only the first argument they'd ever had. Surely this was not the end of them.

Erik broke eye contact with her and walked out, leaving her to close the door.

She stood with her back pressed against the closed door, willing herself not to cry. This was nothing. It would blow over as soon as Erik found out Pietro posed no threat to him. But then, it occurred to her that Pietro was not really the problem here. The problem was… Erik didn't trust her.

Chapter 13

Business kept Erik from stewing in his own juices the next few days. He thought about Ana, but he didn't have time to obsess over the situation. Like many businesses Whitaker Enterprises had taken a financial hit in the past three years but now the economy appeared to be rebounding, and since most of Whitaker Enterprises' interests were in the service industry demand was putting pressure on them to supply enough products to satisfy customers. The first quarter of the year promised to be a very good one. However he did take time to speak with his father about his and Ana's dispute and his father was his usual calm, and reasonable self. "Son, if you'd spent more time dating instead of working you would have known not to say everything that comes to your mind when dealing with women. You might have felt jealous and threatened by Ana's friendship with Pietro but you should have chosen your words more carefully," his father offered.

"Are you saying I shouldn't be completely honest with Ana?"

"No, that's not what I'm saying. I'm saying in any relationship you pick and choose your battles. Was it worth it to put your emotions out there and tell Ana you don't trust her?"

"That's not what I said!"

"When you told her you felt there was something she wasn't telling you," said John, "you were saying you thought she was withholding information and to withhold information is to lie. And if you think she's lying to you, it means you don't think you can trust her."

Erik had sighed over the phone. "That's not what I was trying to get across."

"That's the problem with communicating with the opposite sex. You say one thing, she thinks another. You have to be clear. Don't assume she can read your mind, because she can't. And you can't read hers. Don't leave anything to guesswork."

"It's been a week since we spoke. She won't even return my calls."

"A week, huh?" said his father. "That's not good. At any rate, you shouldn't see her until you're sure you won't project your insecurities onto her. That's what you did, son. I'm sorry to say that your parents weren't the best role models for you. Mari was selfish and I was a workaholic who didn't have one solid relationship with a woman in your formative years. If I hadn't let my hurt force me into an emotional cocoon, you would be better equipped to handle certain situations."

"That's no excuse," Erik insisted. "I'm a man. I should have more control over my behavior."

"Solving a problem takes constant vigilance," his father said. "You've been given your first test. You failed. The next time you'll pass with flying colors."

Erik cringed at the thought of a next time. But he knew there would be one. The way he felt about Ana, fiercely possessive and protective, there would certainly be another time when he would feel threatened and the beast would want to come out and growl at somebody.

"I'll apologize right away," he told his father. "I'll grovel if I have to."

"Oh, now, son, no groveling," said his father jokingly. "Whitaker men don't grovel."

Ana was staying busy, as well. Sometimes she painted until dawn broke. She relished the pleasure good honest work gave her. She had completed the portrait of the actress and since then had accepted a commission to paint the mayor. Also, the publicity person at Corelli Fashions had booked her on several area talk shows to reveal the spring line—she enjoyed doing that. Often the hosts would also mention the fact that she painted and show photos of her work. Subsequently, Damon had been selling her paintings as quickly as she could supply them.

She was a happy girl. Except that she was miserable without Erik. Her mother phoned her late one night when she was painting. She welcomed the interruption because while she was painting the mayor's visage, all she could think about was Erik.

"Darling, something's been on my mind and I'm just going to say it," Natalie said without preamble. "When you told me about Erik being jealous of you and Pietro and how Pietro hurried outside to speak with Erik before he left, I couldn't help wondering why Pietro didn't tell Erik he's gay. That would've diffused the situation in no time."

Ana was momentarily speechless. How did her mother know Pietro was gay?

"You know?" she cried, relief flooding her. If her mother knew there could be only one explanation for her knowledge...Maria Lanza had spoken to her mom about Pietro.

"I've known for years. I never talked about it because Maria says he's still in the closet. She said it seems to her that he started to mention it once when he was a teenager, but he couldn't get it out. Ever since then she's been waiting for him to be a man and come right out and tell her. But he hasn't. You knew?"

"Yeah, he told me when we were kids. He said he did tell her not long after they moved to Rome, but she said she had a heart problem and didn't want to hear something so awful. He didn't want to give her a heart attack so he never brought it up again."

Natalie laughed. "In all the years I've known her Maria has never mentioned having a heart problem. Somebody's not telling the truth. I can see why you wouldn't tell Erik, thinking that you were keeping a secret for a friend. But seeing the trouble he'd inadvertently caused, Pietro should have said something."

Ana didn't want to immediately put the blame on Pietro. "He's been hiding for years. It probably never occurred to him to tell Erik who's basically a stranger to him."

"That's not the point. You're his friend. As far as I know, his oldest friend since Maria and I had play dates for you two practically from birth. He should have done it for *you*."

Ana understood her mother's point of view. A mother fought for her child's happiness. But to allude that Pietro might have had an ulterior motive behind keeping silent was unfair. "No, Mom, the problem isn't Pietro. Erik doesn't trust me."

"Did I ever tell you about the time your father punched a guy in the nose?" Natalie paused. "He and I were dating at the time and the musical director I was working with was a big flirt. The guy made the mistake of commenting on my caboose when we were out to dinner with him and several other people. He'd had too much to drink and said I had the nicest ass he'd ever seen. Your father punched his lights out right at the dinner table. The waiter had to revive him by throwing a pitcher of water in his face. You're lucky Erik is not a violent man, like your father! And your father's attitude had nothing to do with not trusting me. He simply acted on impulse. It's not that Erik doesn't trust you. It's his possessiveness he has to curb."

"He never acted possessive before we got engaged," Ana pointed out.

"You never gave him reason to behave that way," her mother also pointed out. "Did you?"

"No," Ana admitted softly.

"Stop pouting and answer his calls," her mother advised.

"I will," Ana said. However, she had another idea. Implementing that idea would solve two problems at once. That is if, indeed, her mother was right about Pietro's behaving selfishly.

She ran the idea by her mother, who said, "Go for it!"

Ana put the first part of her plan in action the very next day. It was a Monday and she was scheduled to go over the final photographs Ivan had taken with Pietro in his office.

She arrived five minutes early for their nine o'clock appointment. Hilary told her to go on into Pietro's office. When she walked in she found Pietro poring over the photographs which he'd spread out atop his big desk. She smiled. He looked so serious. She knew he was under pressure worrying about making a good impression on her father. The success of the campaign would go a long way in achieving that.

She cleared her throat and he looked up at her and grinned. *"Buon giorno."*

"Buon giorno," Ana returned. He looked cosmopolitan in a well-fitting dark gray suit, white shirt and even darker gray tie. His wavy hair fell over his eyes.

He brushed it back with a hand and said, "Ivan did an amazing job on these. Come, have a look."

Ana went to stand next to him and picked up a couple of the photos. "I agree," she said after a few minutes. "What I really like, though, is his emphasis on the contours of the full-figure models, not the ones who're size twelve and under. He truly knows how to bring out the beauty of all body shapes."

They talked for several more minutes about the photos, then chose their favorite shots of each item in the line. When they were done for the day, Ana said, "Have you thought about Ivan any since I brought up the possibility of you two getting together for coffee sometime?"

"Yes," Pietro said, smiling, "I've given it a lot of thought, and I'm interested."

Ana's heartbeat sped up. He'd taken the hook. Now to reel him in, "Good, because I have an idea."

"What sort of an idea?" Pietro asked warily.

"Leave that up to me," said Ana. "Just be at my place on Valentine's Day at 7:00 p.m. I'll do the rest. Won't it be fun, letting someone else plan a romantic date for you and Ivan? All you need to do is look fabulous!"

"I don't know," Pietro began.

Ana interrupted him with, "Don't you trust me?" She cringed inside when she asked him that because what could he say except yes? She felt manipulative.

"Yes, of course, I trust you," said Pietro. She noticed sweat had broken out on his forehead. Why was he so nervous?

"Okay, great," said Ana casually. She picked up

her shoulder bag and began heading for the door, then paused to look back at Pietro. "By the way, my mom told me your mother already knows you're gay."

"You told your mother?" he asked, visibly astonished she would break her promise.

"No, no," Ana assured him. "She told *me*."

"When was this?" he asked, his attention riveted on her.

Ana laughed shortly. "It's funny, really. Mom says your mother doesn't have a heart condition. She suggested somebody was lying. Either you made it up or your mother really told you that when you tried to tell her you're gay. At any rate, according to Mom, your mother is waiting for you to tell her point-blank. She's living in anticipation of that momentous day!"

"Okay, I made it up!" Pietro shouted. "I needed a good excuse as to why I never told her. I've been telling that lie ever since. I'm the one who's not ready. I can't bear seeing the disappointment on her face. She's done everything for me. She worked two jobs to put me through school. I owe her more than making her the proud mother of a gay son. I owe her a wife and children."

Even though Pietro was shouting, Ana calmly said, "She's your mother. All she wants is for you to be happy. Are you happy living a lie?"

"Everybody lives a lie in one way or another," Pietro declared more quietly. "I'm not so different from you, Ana. You were so content with your perfect fiancé. You thought everything was going to be heavenly from now on. Only to have your relationship bomb because he's jealous of the time you spend with me. He's not so perfect after all, is he?"

"Now I get it," Ana said, smiling with sudden enlightenment. "You didn't say anything to Erik because you're jealous of us."

"Give her a prize, she's finally figured it out!" said Pietro, his demeanor not gloating as Ana expected. "I'm a terrible friend. I thought of telling Erik I'm gay that night but then he pissed me off with his attitude. He had you, Ana, and he didn't even have to work for you. You just fell into his arms."

"I didn't just fall into his arms. I tormented the poor man for two years with my neuroses. I was a mess and he stuck by me," Ana said vehemently. Her eyes flashed. "And you have no right to judge him. No right at all. What's more, I'm hurt that you didn't think any better of me that you let your low opinion of Erik keep you from helping me out."

"I know now it should have been about you and me, not you, me, and Erik. Even if Erik loathed me, I should have been in your corner."

"That's what friends do," Ana said.

"I haven't had a close friend since you," Pietro told her, his eyes pleading with her not to give up on him.

"That's nobody's fault but yours," Ana said. "You never answered *any* of my letters."

She grinned and opened her arms to him. He gratefully hugged her close.

"Are we going to beat that dead horse again?" he

joked. Then, more seriously Pietro said, "I'm so sorry, Ana. Please say you'll forgive me."

Ana smiled, "I do," she told him. "Now, I have a favor to ask of you."

"Anything you want," Pietro promised, smiling broadly.

Part one of her plan had worked out quite well. Now for part two.

Abby knocked on Erik's door and hastened inside. She held up a heavy vellum envelope in soft beige. It was hand addressed and included a wax stamp on it with the letter *C* embossed on it. "Look, Erik, it's an invitation from Ana!" she cried, excited for him. He had been a changed man the past three weeks. He was still a kind, thoughtful boss, but he was not as gregarious as he normally was with everyone. When she had first sensed something was the matter and had asked him about it, he'd simply said, "Ana and I aren't seeing eye to eye." Well, that almost broke Abby's heart. She liked Ana, and although she adored her boss it wasn't like her to interfere with his personal life. She was too traditional for that. She could, however, take pleasure in his personal happiness and Ana made him happy.

Erik who'd been going over financial reports stood up and accepted the envelope. Abby wanted to wait and see what was in it, but forced herself to walk smartly from the room.

Erik looked down at the envelope. It was formal. She'd taken such care with it he was sure it held some-

thing life-altering. Perhaps something like a note saying she was breaking their engagement. Why hadn't he
gone over there as soon as possible as he'd promised his
father he would? He knew the answer to that. His manly
pride was wounded. For the past three weeks he had
been suffering without Ana. Let her suffer a bit longer
without him. Then, when he finally came around she
would appreciate him more he had foolishly thought.

He broke the wax seal and it crumbled in a red pile
onto his desk. Opening the envelope he retrieved the
note inside.

*You are cordially invited to dinner tomorrow
night at 7:00 p.m. at the home of Ana Corelli. The
pleasure of your company is highly anticipated.
Don't be late.* Then, she had simply signed, *Ana.*

With his nerves back to normal, Erik smiled. Okay,
she wasn't kicking him to the curb, yet. He still had a
chance of winning her back.

He pressed the intercom. Abby answered. "What can
I do for you, Erik?"

"Please phone Ana and tell her that her invitation is
accepted," he said, his tone decisive.

"Right away!" said Abby.

Somewhere in the city two other men were receiving similar hand-delivered invitations from Ana, although their invitations stated they were invited for
drinks, not dinner.

On Valentine's Day Ana prepared an intimate dinner for two. She made sure the wine was chilled well ahead of time. She took special care with her appearance, choosing a short red dress, in honor of the holiday, with strips of material that crisscrossed her back. Her hair fell down her back in soft waves, and the only jewelry she wore was diamond stud earrings and her engagement ring. She glided across the hardwood floor in her favorite pair of black sandals by Jimmy Choo. They were both comfortable and elegant.

Appetizers were put next to the wine on the living room coffee table at exactly seven. She didn't expect anyone to actually show up on time, but her doorbell rang at the appointed hour. She briefly wondered who had shown up first as she walked across the room to get the door.

She laughed softly when she saw that all three of her guests were at her door, every one of them bearing flowers. An 'O' of awe and wonder shaped her red lips and a smile caressed her big brown eyes. "How lucky can a girl get?" She stepped aside, "Three handsome gentlemen on Valentine's Day! Please, come in."

Erik, Pietro and Ivan strode into the loft with smiles on their faces, the epitome of refinement.

They were fakers, all of them. Five minutes earlier, they were at each others' throats of course unbeknownst to Ana. The universe had conspired to have them arrive in the lobby of Ana's building almost simultaneously. Erik walked through the door with Pietro on his heels and shortly afterward, Ivan entered the building and exclaimed, "Erik! I haven't seen you since you and Ana got engaged. Congratulations! How are you?"

Erik who, with Ana, had socialized with Ivan and his partner, Miko, on occasion offered Ivan his hand in greeting. Grinning and sincerely glad to see Ivan, Erik said, "I'm well, and how're you holding up?" Erik had liked Miko, a sushi chef who had owned a small but successful sushi restaurant.

Ivan's long blond hair combed away from his face, smiled wistfully. "Some days are better than others, but I'm slowly trying to get back out there. That's why I'm here. Ana invited me over for drinks. She said she had someone she wanted me to meet."

Erik's expression suddenly lost its friendliness. He glanced at Pietro who had been standing close by because he was an inveterate eavesdropper and he was the only one who had been fully apprised of why Ana had invited all of them there tonight. "I suppose Ana invited you tonight, too?" Erik asked him, his voice cold.

"Brrr," Pietro said tauntingly. "It's suddenly freezing in here. Yes, Erik. My dear, sweet friend, Ana, invited me, as well. Get over it."

Erik was in his face in an instant. "Listen, *Lanza,* I've had about enough of your attitude. Frankly, I don't see why Ana can't see through your smarmy charm. She usually has better taste in friends."

"I thought that, too, until I met you," Pietro returned.

Ivan stepped between them. "Gentlemen, might I interject a bit of logic? It is now three minutes till seven, and Ana said not to be late. I'm going upstairs whether you two follow or not."

The elevator arrived and Ivan stepped into the empty conveyance with Erik on one side of him and Pietro on the other. Not a word was said as the car ascended. On Ana's floor, Ivan stepped off the elevator and walked away, leaving Pietro and Erik to follow. As the two men walked side by side, Pietro said, "I don't know why you dislike me so much. I never did anything to you."

"You didn't deny you want Ana for yourself," Erik accused.

"I didn't say I did, either," Pietro reminded him. "In fact I told you she wasn't my type but you didn't want to hear that."

Ivan had rang the bell already so they picked up their pace. "And I still don't," Erik said, "Because no man who likes women could resist her."

"Say that again," Pietro said pointedly, looking at Erik with a smirk on his face.

Pietro got great satisfaction out of the flummoxed expression on Erik's face. Erik didn't have time to respond, though, because Ana opened the door and the only thing the three men could think to do upon seeing her was smile as if all was well with the world.

Ana hugged Ivan first and admired him in his beautifully cut dark blue suit. The color brought out the blue in his aquamarine eyes. "Thank you for coming. I know it probably wasn't easy for you to let me set you up on, for want of a better expression, a blind date."

Then she hugged Pietro. "I don't think I've ever seen you looking happier."

Pietro wanted to tell her it was due to throwing her fiancé a curveball a minute ago, but held his tongue.

Finally, she turned to Erik and shook his hand. "Good to see you, Mr. Whitaker. It's so kind of you to take time out of your busy schedule to accept my invitation."

She gestured to the couch in front of the coffee table. "Please, sit down."

They did as they were bid and she began filling four wineglasses. "I asked you here to kill two birds with one stone." She handed Erik his glass of wine. "My fiancé believes that something…unseemly is going on between Pietro and me."

"I never said that," Erik began in his defense. "I said I felt you were not telling me something."

Ana ignored him, and handed Pietro a glass of wine. "And my oldest friend has chosen this day to say…"

"I'm gay," Pietro provided the words.

Ivan laughed.

Erik drank his wine in one gulp.

Ana pulled Pietro to his feet and put her arms around him. She whispered in his ear, "You're free now."

There were tears in her eyes. When they rolled down onto her cheeks, Pietro wiped them away. "Good God, woman, I'm the one who's coming out." He set her away from him. "Now, dry your tears and go finish him off."

Ana walked over to Erik and reached for his hand.

He took it and rose with a sigh of resignation. "I've been a damned fool."

"True, so true," Ana said, gazing up at him. "But my dad once told me that men are prone to act like fools on occasion and I should just ignore them when they do, and keep on loving them. Which, I do...love you."

Erik hugged her so tightly, Ana could barely breathe. "So, that's what you weren't telling me."

"It wasn't my secret to tell," she said reasonably. "He had to be ready."

She twisted in Erik's arms to glance back at Pietro and Ivan who were definitely simpatico. They were laughing companionably at something one or the other had said, and from their body language she could tell they didn't mind sharing personal space with each other.

"I should have known that if you weren't completely honest with me you had a very good reason," Erik cajoled, stroking her back.

Ana gazed up at him, "That doesn't make up for the fact that you felt insecure about me," she said, "What's up with that?"

"It's something I'll have to work on every single day we're together," he said honestly. "I'm far from cured. I nearly jumped down his throat a few minutes ago. I regret how I handled the situation. I regret that I hurt you. But I'm not gonna lie and say I'll never have those feelings again. I will promise to react to them in a better manner, though."

"I'll take that promise," Ana told him. She kissed him slowly and deliberately, taking the time to remind him what he'd been missing. When she looked into his eyes afterward she knew that he had gotten her message. He was putty in her hands. However, there was one last detail she had to take care of before their evening could begin.

"Excuse me a moment," she said as she left Erik's close embrace.

"Guys," she said to Pietro and Ivan as she walked over to the foyer table, opened the drawer and withdrew an envelope. Returning to them, she handed Pietro the envelope. "Follow these instructions for the romantic night of your lives. Get going now because your reservation is for eight. That's why I asked that you not be late."

In the envelope were the location of the five-star restaurant where she had reserved them a table and the name of the club they were going dancing at after dinner. "My treat. All you have to do is mention my name," she added with a grin. "Have fun, you two."

She saw them to the door and received grateful kisses on her cheek. "Happy Valentine's Day!" they said in unison.

"Happy Valentine's Day," Ana happily replied.

Erik was standing behind her when she turned around after closing and locking the door. "As for you," she said, pointing an accusing finger at him. "You've been a bad boy." Her eyes were fierce. She poked him in the chest, causing him to back up. "I think you need to be punished."

Erik grinned sexily. "Do with me what you will."

"That's just what I plan to do," Ana told him, as she

grabbed his tie and moved in for the kill. Standing close she slid one long, shapely leg along the inside of his thigh until she reached his package. She felt the pulsating need from that quickly hardening part of him and smiled with satisfaction. "Yes, I think you missed me."

"You have no idea," Erik breathed.

Ana's fingers were busy unbuttoning his pants. He couldn't wait for her to unzip him. He reached down and did it himself. Her hand slipped inside and she rubbed him. He was hard and ready for action.

Erik pulled up her dress and cupped her behind. Ana knew that if she didn't move this to the bedroom soon her neighbors were going to get an eyeful. The big picture window that looked down on the street was stark with no window treatment at all. She kissed him, teasingly bit his lower lip, then took off running for the bedroom. "Work for it," she cried, laughing all the way.

In April, Erik surprised Ana with the rooftop garden he'd promised her. She moved out of her loft into the penthouse, although that bit of information was kept from the families.

Their wedding took place at Erik's parents' home in New Haven in mid June. The garden was in full bloom and the one hundred and twenty guests were pretty loyal about not leaking information to the media about the time and place of the nuptials. However photos of the wedding still found their way onto the internet. Ana and Erik refused to allow any magazine to feature it, though.

On the day of the wedding, Ana was getting dressed

in her bedroom when Drusilla paid her a visit. "Darlin'
you're looking a little tired. Is there anything you'd like
to tell me?" Drusilla's eyes looked huge behind her Coke
bottle glasses and her gaze was relentless.

Smiling at Drusilla's curiosity, "Getting ready for a
wedding is exhausting," was all Ana would say. Leave
it to Drusilla to intuitively know her secret. She regretted not confiding in Drusilla that she was, indeed, pregnant. However she and Erik had decided that bit of news
would be shared with the family at a later date. Her folks
were here from Milan and it wouldn't go over well at
the wedding if the soon to be father-in-law punched the
groom, she thought with a smile.

Ana was not allowing anything to ruin her happiness today. This day in June in New Haven turned out
to be picture-perfect: an azure sky, temperature in the
lower eighties with just a hint of a cool breeze. Her
dress, taken from the Corelli wedding line, was a simple
strapless white empire-waist gown with pearl buttons
down the back. In spite of Drusilla's pronouncement
that she looked a bit tired, she was glowing!

The garden boasted an explosion of fragrant and colorful flowers and plants and the guests were resplen-
dent in their wedding finery, the ladies in intricate hats
of various shapes and sizes in all the colors of spring.

Among the guests she spotted her family and Erik's,
but also Damon and his partner, Sidney. Pietro and Ivan
were there with Pietro's mother, Maria, sitting between
them. Leo, Teresa and Julianna Barone smiled warmly

at her as she walked down the aisle on her father's arm. And Abby and Harry Sinclair had tears in their eyes.

A baby began crying, which only made her smile all the more. Everyone she loved was here today. Then, she glanced up into Erik's smiling face and her heart knew complete contentment.

When Erik saw her walking down the aisle on her father's arm, his heart was full of joy. He glanced at her belly momentarily, thinking of the life growing beneath her own heart— their child and their future.

Was he nervous on this, the most important day of his life? Not in the least. He'd waited for this day for so long that there was nothing that could spoil his utter pleasure in it finally having arrived.

He felt like the most blessed man on earth.

Soon, they were standing in front of one another and gazing expectantly into each other's eyes. Erik gently took Ana's hand in his.

"Dearly beloved," began the minister in a deep, resonant voice...

* * * * *

SNOWED IN WITH
THE RELUCTANT
TYCOON

NINA SINGH

To my mother and father. For all their faith.

CHAPTER ONE

THE HOUSE WAS COLD.

Carli Tynan wasn't surprised. In fact, she'd never once entered this mansion and ever felt warm. Regardless of the season. And, despite the myriad of Christmas decorations currently adorning the foyer, nothing about the home felt particularly festive. Or even like a home. No, the Hammond estate felt more like a staid museum.

The eleven-foot-tall pine Christmas tree that nearly touched the ceiling notwithstanding.

Shaking the thin layer of snow off her wool coat, she peeled off her faux leather gloves, the bound portfolio tucked under her right arm. The darn portfolio was the only reason she was here, the reason her usual morning routine had been so handily disrupted. Carli was not a fan of disruptions. She'd already had to deal with way too many in her twenty-six years.

Her boss, Jackson Hammond, had asked her just this morning to drop off the file on her way in to work. Right after she'd gotten back from her early-morning run. It had barely given her time to shower, let alone to put herself together as well as she normally liked. As a result, her unruly curls were now a mess of tangles hastily secured in a haphazard bun on top of her head. She hadn't even had a chance to iron her remaining clean suit. The only other option was a stretch pencil dress that had recently shrunk after she'd accidently thrown it in the dryer. Comfortable, it was not.

But she had a day full of meetings in the office, and this was the best she could do. Not at all the way she would have preferred to start off her morning. Or any morning for that matter.

All because the prodigal son was returning home.

Justin Hammond, Jackson's second-born, had been the one to request the portfolio. And apparently, he needed it before he could make it into the office. Carli had to accommodate him. Why was he suddenly heading back into town anyway? Justin hadn't had anything to do with Hammond's Toys since she'd been employed there. Now, suddenly, he was interested. Carli stepped farther into the foyer and couldn't resist the urge to roll her eyes. No doubt Justin's sudden interest was due to his older brother James's recent distractions, so to speak. James had apparently met someone and was now taking a well-deserved break from the day-to-day business. Little brother must have concluded that this was an ideal time to strike.

Never mind that Carli should be the one next in line to take over any of the duties James may be ready to relinquish. She couldn't help but feel a little insulted.

And hurt. Well, she'd just have to get over it. Then she'd have to work even harder to ensure she got the position she deserved.

She walked up to the foot of the stairs and yelled up toward the second floor. "Mr. Hammond, I'm dropping off the file."

No answer.

Jackson's hearing wasn't what it used to be. She shrugged

off her coat and dropped it on the nearby black leather settee, then walked halfway up the grand spiral stairway.

"Mr. Hammond, where would you like the files?"

Again, nothing. Carli let out a huff of frustration. She certainly didn't want to risk having come out here only to have the portfolio overlooked because the Hammond men couldn't find it. She would have texted Jackson, but he was notorious for wanting to have nothing to do with technology. He probably didn't even look at his phone every day. Hence the request for a paper file. As for Justin Hammond, she barely knew a thing about him, let alone his cell phone number.

She walked all the way up to the hallway and toward Mr. Hammond's suite. The shower was running. Great. She would have to yell through the door at the top of her lungs, or he would never hear her.

Could this morning get any worse? She didn't think so.

Stepping into the master suite, she walked over to Mr. Hammond's antique mahogany desk and dropped the portfolio atop it. Then yelled as loud as she dared across the room toward the closed master bathroom door. "The portfolio is on your desk, Mr. Hammond."

A muffled acknowledgment sounded from the other side, and Carli breathed a sigh of relief. Now she could get out of here and finally start her day.

But the day had other plans. When she was midway down the stairs, the front door opened and a shadowy, tall figure stepped into the foyer. He dropped his suitcase to the floor and seemed to hesitate before entering any farther. Carli's step nearly faltered as she took in the sight of him. Tall and dark with a firm square jaw and jet-black hair. There was no mistaking who he was—Justin, the other Hammond heir. All three men shared the same rugged features, but the one standing before her had a different vibe altogether. An aura she would be hard-pressed to describe.

Regaining her balance, she managed to finally make her way down the stairs.

Justin finally looked up as she reached the foyer. He seemed to do a double take. Most men did when they first got a look at her. A fact she was quite aware of. And quite uncomfortable with.

"I'm sorry," he began, though he looked anything but. "I didn't realize anyone was here." He looked downright annoyed.

She tried to summon a polite smile, but her facial muscles seemed useless. Justin Hammond had eyes that a sorcerer would envy. The lightest shade of hazel littered with gold specks. What was wrong with her? She so wasn't the type to notice men's eyes, for heaven's sake.

"Um, your father's in the shower. I'm sure he'll be right out." In an awkward attempt to introduce herself, she extended her right hand. "I'm Car—"

But he stopped her midsentence. "Look, that's hardly necessary."

Carli blinked. Okay. No time for a quick introduction? Maybe he was just jet-lagged and tired from travel. Or perhaps he was just plain rude.

She cleared her throat. "Oh, I guess—" She looked to the side, unable to bear his gaze much longer given the awkwardness. "I guess I'll be on my way then."

He merely nodded, then stepped aside.

Carli tried not to flinch. She'd just effectively been shown the door! By the man who threatened the job she'd been working so hard for, no less.

Straightening to her full height, Carli stepped around

him and went to grab her coat from the settee. Then did the only thing she could. She left.

Her words about the morning not getting any worse mocked her.

Justin watched as the woman walked out and firmly shut the door behind her. Perhaps he'd been on the slim side of rude just now, but he so hadn't been expecting a stunning bombshell to come down the stairs as he entered his boyhood home. Not that he'd really been expecting anything in particular after having been gone over two decades.

Looked like his father's womanizing ways hadn't changed.

He glanced out the side palladium window as the woman walked down the driveway toward the parked car outside. *Ravishing.* It was the only word that came to mind. She had curves that would stop a monk in his tracks. The dress she wore hugged those curves in all the right ways. His father apparently liked them much younger these days; she had to be barely in her late twenties.

Well, it was no business of his. He was only here for a few days to analyze some numbers his father wanted him to look at. Though why the old man suddenly requested his younger son's help after all these years was a mystery, one Justin had no interest in investigating. He'd been ready to turn down the request and tell his father where he could go, but his mother had insisted he do Jackson Hammond's bidding. The old man still held the purse strings after all. And his mother had always been all about the Hammond purse strings.

Even after she'd fled this house and his father all those years ago, taking their younger son, him, along with her. He'd been the lucky one to get whisked away in the middle of the night once his mother finally decided she'd had enough.

He hadn't been back since. Until today.

Justin tried to get his bearings as he examined the foyer he hadn't walked through since he'd been a small child. Everything appeared smaller. The traditional Christmas decorations were as spectacular as he remembered. The tall pine by the stairs glittered with gold and silver ornaments. Sparkling lights adorned the stairs and banisters, a line of poinsettias graced the walls. So festive. In a nauseating and annoying way. All that was missing was a background track of loud Christmas music.

Bah, humbug.

What was he doing here? He should have refused his parents' requests and the hell with the consequences. Who did they think he was? Who did his father think *he* was? This was the same man who had ignored him until his older and rightful heir had decided last month that he'd needed some time off to go do…whatever he was doing. Justin had no idea, but it probably involved a woman. Maybe his brother had fallen in love.

Yeah, right, Justin thought as he made his way toward the living room. He sincerely doubted it. The Hammond genes weren't really conducive to such things. Love wasn't in their DNA.

More Christmas decorations greeted him in the living room, which had been updated with new furniture in addition to a slightly less dark shade of green painted on the walls. Or perhaps that had been the same color all along. He'd been gone from home a long time. Not that it ever really felt like a home to begin with.

Overall, reentering his childhood house so far felt somewhat surreal. Like he'd stepped into a previous life.

The sound of footsteps coming down the stairs pulled

him out of his musings. Steeling himself against the anger barely contained under the surface, Justin turned to face Jackson Hammond—the man who had watched a young Justin being yanked out that front door all those years ago without lifting a finger to stop it.

Past history, Justin thought as he turned to greet his father. Or more accurately, the man who had sired him.

To his surprise, Jackson hadn't changed all that much. The graying at his temples had spread through to most of his thick, wavy hair. A few more wrinkles framed the area around his mouth. Other than that, Justin felt as if he could be looking at the same face he had last seen all those years ago.

"Thank you for coming, son," his father said, and extended a hand. It was the most awkward handshake Justin had ever performed.

"You're welcome."

"I know what a busy man you are, so I really appreciate it."

Justin merely nodded. No need for Jackson to know that if it weren't for his mother's insistence, Justin would still be on the other side of the country.

"Given your global reputation as a management consultant, I figured it was about time you did a full assessment of the company you're part heir to," his father added, then shook his head as if in disbelief. "Something I should have requested long ago."

"I suppose that makes sense," Justin offered.

"You've accomplished quite a lot for such a young age," Jackson added. "That consulting firm of yours is known all over the world." Was that a look of pride on his face? If so, it was too little, and much too late.

"Business has been good."

"So I've read. As well as reading about your fast rise in the industry."

Justin processed his father's words. Words that would have meant the world to him when he was a teenager, or even a college student. How many school events or sporting events had he desperately searched the audience on some small glimmer of hope that Jackson might have shown up? How many times had the phone rang on his birthday with none of the calls being from his father?

No. Justin had long ago stopped pining for any acknowledgment from the man standing before him. "Why don't I get started then?" he prompted, changing the subject.

What had Jackson expected? If his father had any notion that this visit was to be a touching reunion between long-lost father and son, he was in for a disappointment.

Carli found herself becoming more and more annoyed as she drove away from the Hammond mansion. Of all the nerve! She'd never been dismissed by anyone in such a fashion—and she'd grown up in a houseful of siblings. Undivided attention wasn't exactly something she was used to. But the way Justin Hammond had just practically ejected her had been downright insulting. To make matters worse, she'd done nothing but stood there like a stunned doe. How pathetic.

She took the curve around the next bend a little too fast and realized she was letting her anger get the best of her. Deep breaths. So what if her new boss was a rude, insensitive clod? She could handle it.

He would not get to her. She'd worked too hard and overcome too much to get to where she was in her career. Her job with Hammond's Toys meant everything. And she was good at it, damn it!

Why did Justin Hammond have to show up and put all

of it in jeopardy? But there was an even bigger question, she had to admit. Why hadn't she stood up for herself? It was like she'd looked into his eyes and gone totally mute. Recalling his gaze just now had her drawing in a deep breath. Heavens, those caramel-hued eyes were the devil's tool for distraction. And there was something behind them, a distant, haunted look if she'd ever seen one.

She hmmphed. Now she was just getting fanciful. He was just her new boss. And she had to deal with him, that's all.

The honk of a horn behind her startled her out of her thoughts. She'd stopped at a red light and hadn't even noticed it had turned. Time to get a grip.

Justin Hammond had already taken way too much of her time, and she had things to do.

That reminder became all too evident when she made her way into her office. Her assistant was already there at the desk, with a file of papers waiting for Carli's signature or attention. The latest cost-cutting initiative was becoming quite the project—one she'd been given the primary responsibility for. Until Justin was called in, that was.

"Hey, Jocelyn. Sorry I'm late."

The petite brunette gave her a friendly smile. "Don't sweat it. You're not that late."

"Well, it's late for me."

"Please tell me it's because you had a hot, steamy date last night that turned into a wild night. And that he wouldn't let you get up out of bed this morning."

"Last night was a Tuesday."

Jocelyn gave her a blank look. "What's your point?"

Why did she bother? "Never mind. Are those the latest data points?"

Her assistant nodded and handed her the thick pile of

folders. "I printed them like you requested. The electronic file is in your inbox."

"Thanks. You know where I'll be for most of the morning. These numbers are going to take a while to get through. And I'm already behind." *Due to an unexpected project I was just given this morning*, she added to herself. A project for the sole purpose of getting Justin Hammond up to speed on the latest business figures.

"Well, you can't be working on them all morning."

Carli lifted an eyebrow. "Why's that?"

"Mr. Hammond just called and asked me to schedule yet one more meeting. We have an unexpected guest coming in."

Oh, no. Carli could venture to guess who it might be. "Please tell me it's not Justin Hammond."

Jocelyn gave her a curious smile. "I could do that. But I'd be lying to you."

Great. Just great. Was the man sent here just to vex her at every turn? Apparently, she was supposed to jump whenever Justin Hammond needed anything.

Jocelyn studied her, the amused smile still on her face. "Something wrong?"

Carli tried to shake off the frustration. "I just have a lot to do. And he happens to be the reason I'm late to begin with."

"Aha! So I was right."

"Right about what?"

"You were indeed late because of a sexy man."

Jocelyn just didn't know when to let up. "Only because I had to prepare a report for him at the last minute and then deliver it before I got in today."

Her assistant waved her hand in dismissal. "Details."

"Honestly, Jocelyn. I barely met the man for a few scant moments."

"So tell me. Is he as handsome as he appears in all the photos?"

"I didn't notice."

That earned her a disbelieving look. "See. This is why I worry about you. Justin Hammond is one of the most eligible bachelors on the planet. He's on the celebrity sites weekly. Wealthy, successful and handsome. And you didn't even notice his looks?"

"Not really, no." She could fib quite well when she had to.

Jocelyn slammed her hands on her hips. "That's just disappointing. Most of the female staff around here are breathless with anticipation at his arrival. And you act like it's an ordinary day. You gotta give me something. Some small detail I can throw to them."

"That's just silly. He's just the other Hammond heir."

"Right. A mere handsome millionaire who not only has claim to half the largest retail toy company in North America but also made gobs of money on his own."

She did have a point there. Justin's life story so far was a bit on the exceptional side. She was about to begrudgingly admit to that when a small commotion outside her door drew both their attention. Looked like Jocelyn was about to find out firsthand what she was so curious about. Justin had arrived. And he was causing quite a stir, no doubt with most of the female staff. Carli heard "can I get you anything, Mr. Hammond" more than once.

Jocelyn jumped to the door. "Ooh, he's here." She gasped. "And he's heading right to your office."

A strange sensation spread through Carli's chest. Despite seeing several photos of him throughout the years, she had to admit he wasn't what she'd been expecting. All the pictures hadn't really done him justice. They hadn't captured the soft, tawny hue of his eyes. Or the way his hair fell sloppily over his forehead. She hadn't realized she'd noticed so much of him during those brief moments in the Hammond foyer earlier.

A quick knock on the door, and then Justin stepped into her office. He blinked in surprise when he saw her. "You?"

What was that supposed to mean? Did he want her out already? Genuine surprise registered on his face. Was he here to lay claim to her office, having expected her to vacate it for him already?

Too stunned to speak, Carli was relieved when Jocelyn stepped up to him. "Mr. Hammond, I'm Jocelyn Sumner. We weren't expecting you so early. The meeting isn't until nine thirty."

He hadn't taken his eyes off Carli. She resisted the urge to look away from the intense stare.

"I figured I'd get started," he answered Jocelyn. "I'm looking for the person who put this together." He held up the file of papers Carli dropped off less than an hour ago. "I was told this is their office."

Carli finally found her tongue. "It is."

He blinked at her. "Can you tell me where to find him now?"

Him. "You have," she answered, deliberately omitting further clarification. Let him hang in the wind a bit.

He lifted an eyebrow.

"I'm the one who put it together. I was dropping it off this morning when we…met." She added some emphasis on the last word.

Justin's eyes grew wide as understanding clearly dawned. Jocelyn stood between them, her gaze switching back and forth as if she were watching an exciting tennis game.

Justin cleared his throat. "You did this?" he asked, indicating the file in his hand. "It's, uh, very thorough. Very impressive."

Carli tried not to bristle at his surprised tone. How very insulting. This man didn't know a thing about her. But he'd made his initial judgment already. She wasn't surprised. Men like Justin always came to the most obvious conclusion when it came to her.

How disappointing that he was so typical.

CHAPTER TWO

GREAT, JUSTIN THOUGHT as the woman across the room shot daggers at him. He hadn't realized this morning that she worked for the company. He'd managed to offend one of Hammond's employees on his first day back in town. No, make that his first *hour* back.

She crossed her arms in front of her chest. "Well, you needn't look so surprised. I'm a project manager at Hammond. I can put together a business report."

"That's not what I meant." But what was she doing coming down from his father's suite at that hour? He couldn't be blamed for having jumped to the most obvious conclusion. And he still wasn't sure he was totally wrong. But clearly there was more to the circumstances. "I'm just surprised to see you here, that's all."

"This is my office. Of course, I'm here."

"Not here, in this room. Here at the company."

She merely quirked an eyebrow. A gesture that seemed to add a haughty quality to her features. Her almond-shaped eyes were a deep chocolate brown. Several tendrils of hair escaped her tight bun and framed an olive-shaped face.

Not classically beautiful, but she was striking in an unusual and rare way.

And her figure—he didn't even want to go there.

"Never mind," she declared, and stepped around her desk. "My name is Carli Tynan. I'm regional project manager for Hammond Retail. James hired me, but I work more closely with Jackson."

He reached his hand out to shake hers just as she said, "You, of course, need no introduction."

Her tone suggested she didn't mean that in a complimentary way. "Nice to meet you."

She pointed to the file he still held. "Is there anything you'd like to go over?" This woman was all business. Regardless of what she'd been doing at the mansion earlier, he had no doubt she was an efficient employee who clearly had things under control.

"I made a few notes, things that I wouldn't mind some further clarification on."

She indicated the chair in front of her desk. "Have a seat. We have some time before the meeting."

Justin hesitated. He wasn't used to being ordered around; the feeling made him uncomfortable. As did the incessant echo of Christmas music playing in the lobby.

"Would you mind if we closed the door?" he asked her, already walking to it.

"Any particular reason?"

"I can't focus with the cursed Christmas tunes playing in the background."

He shut the door and turned back to find her studying him with curious eyes. "You have something against Christmas music?"

"Christmas is one day. But for some reason the whole world is burdened with listening to those blasted tunes for weeks on end. That doesn't happen with any other holiday, now does it?"

"Christmas is hardly like any other holiday."

"Only because the whole world insists on dragging it

out. It's one day, yet we insist on calling it the holiday season."

"Some would argue it's at least twelve days," she countered.

Clever, she'd referenced another Christmas carol. "Don't tell me you're one of those types. The ones who make their shopping list in October. You pull out the tree and decorations as soon as the Thanksgiving turkey is consumed. Am I close?"

"And what would be so wrong about it if I was?"

He shrugged. He wasn't going to try to explain it. Christmastime around his house as a young boy had usually meant the start of weeks of arguments followed by loud, drunken fights. With his father working long hours and his mother growing more and more resentful at his absence. Of course, there were problems throughout the year, but the holiday season seemed to bring out the worst in his parents. An excuse to purge their anger and throw everything in the open. By the time Christmas morning rolled around, he and his brother were more than ready to have it all over with. Even the toys weren't enough to make up for the turmoil and chaos.

How had they even gotten into this conversation anyway? Justin wondered. All he'd asked was to shut the door so he didn't have to hear the music from the lobby. He didn't need to explain himself to a woman he'd just met.

Carli was still staring at him expectedly. She'd asked him a question that he'd left hanging. "Nothing. Never mind. Forget I said anything."

"Okay. But I feel I have to say just one more thing."

Why was he not surprised? "Go ahead."

"That you have to realize how—" she paused and glanced at the ceiling, as if scrambling for the correct word "—curious your perspective about Christmas is. Given who you are."

Of course he realized that. He was heir to one of the most successful retail toy operations in the Northern Hemisphere. A business that earned most of its profits in the weeks between Thanksgiving and Christmas Eve. Sure, it was true that as an adult he'd made his own way and had become a successful businessman in his own right. But he'd been granted worldly advantages at birth that most people could only dream of. He should be thanking his lucky stars for the gift of Christmas and the commercialism that surrounded it.

And to anyone on the outside, he probably sounded like an ungrateful, cranky Scrooge who didn't appreciate all the blessings he'd been granted.

Judging by Carli's expression, that's exactly what she was thinking.

Carli watched as Justin walked out of her office half an hour later, relieved to finally have some time to herself. What a strange morning it had been. It had taken all she had to remain cool and professional once he'd walked in here. She'd pulled it off, but barely. The whole while she was speaking with Justin regarding the business, her insides had felt like jelly. Thank heavens she hadn't eaten anything this morning. It probably wouldn't have stayed down.

The problem was, she wasn't sure what was causing all the turmoil. Sure, it had been upsetting when he'd so casually dismissed her as she was trying to introduce herself. And she'd known he was judging her by her appearance. But none of that was anything new for her.

People always underestimated her at first. She just made sure to prove herself, had been doing so her whole life.

Not to mention, she'd had to find ways to somehow differentiate herself from her four siblings. Right smack in the middle, she was oh-so-easy to overlook. Tammy was the wise oldest sister, happily married with a lovely little boy. Janie, the beautiful one. People in their town actually called her JB, short for Janie Beautiful. Janie had the sort of looks that made men stammer when they spoke to her. While Carli was curvy and voluptuous, her next older sister was gorgeous in an angelic and soft way that Carli could never compete with. She certainly hadn't been able to last year...

Don't even start with that.

And the twins...well, they were twins. That fact alone made them stand out.

Carli was just the middle sister. Nothing special there. Barely noticeable in the crowd. So she made sure to work harder than any of them. Years of study and long hours, first at business school and then at the office, she hadn't taken anything for granted.

And now the arrival of the other Hammond son might be threatening all of that. No wonder she felt so out of sorts when Justin was near. She had to do something to fix that, but what exactly?

Jocelyn tapped lightly on her door before she could answer her own question.

"Come in."

"Hey, how did it go? Were you even able to focus?"

Carli shrugged as she opened her email inbox. "Of course," she said, though it was a fib. "Why in the world wouldn't I?"

"I'm sure I wouldn't have been able to. Not with those deep dreamy eyes focused on me."

Carli resisted the urge to grunt. "Not this again." No way was she going to admit, not even to herself, that there might be a kernel of truth to Jocelyn's words, that in fact it *had* been pretty distracting every time she'd looked up and found herself under the intense focus of Justin's gaze.

"Jocelyn, you need a date."

Her assistant groaned with frustration. "Don't I know it."

"Are you bringing anyone to the party tonight?"

She answered with a sad shake of her head. "I'm really looking forward to it, still. You're very sweet to host one every year."

Being sweet really had nothing to do with it. Carli loved throwing that regular yearly party. She'd been planning and shopping for it since October.

"Well, in any case, you need to stop focusing on Justin Hammond's looks or his appeal," she admonished the younger woman, though part of her was addressing herself. "For all intents and purposes, the man is our boss."

Jocelyn pulled out the chair across from Carli's desk and plopped into it. "I know, I know. I'm just admiring him from afar. I wouldn't dream of going after the man who owns part of the company I work for."

"Good, I'm glad to hear it."

A mischievous smile formed on Jocelyn's lips. "Besides, he hardly glanced in my direction when he was here. He was much more focused on someone else."

Carli didn't like where she was going with this. "I want no part in where you're trying to take this conversation."

Jocelyn leaned forward in the chair, gave her a smile that could only be described as wicked. "Oh, come on! You had to notice."

"Notice what?"

"The way he was looking at you. Or more accurately, how he couldn't look away."

"All I noticed was how to make sure I gave him all

the information he needed to get himself situated. He just needed more info about how the company operates."

Jocelyn looked skeptical. "Right. Just admit it."

"I don't see the point." The last thing she wanted to talk about, in her office no less, was the way men looked at her. The way Justin had looked at her. Recalling the way his eyes had roamed over her sent a shiver down her spine even now.

"Does there have to be a point to everything?"

Carli couldn't help but smile. Had she ever been that lighthearted? She couldn't remember a time. Not even as a child. There was always too much to do. Always a mess to clean up or a sibling to look after.

"I'd just like to figure out why he's really here. After all these years," she said, trying to change the subject back to business.

Jocelyn shrugged slightly. "I thought it was just because James is going to be away for a while. And that Mr. Hammond, as both their father and CEO, decided it would be a good time to bring him on board with his older brother otherwise occupied."

Carli knew that's how things looked on the surface. But it still didn't explain Justin's sudden appearance. She was more than capable of holding down the fort while James Hammond was away. That wasn't self-aggrandizing or conceit. The eldest Mr. Hammond had expressed the notion in countless ways over the years.

"I'm glad he is here!" Jocelyn exclaimed. "Things were getting way too droll around this place. We needed some excitement."

"You just like looking at him."

"No doubt!" Jocelyn actually giggled. "I mean, what's not to like? He's downright dreamy. I've been watching him for years in all the tabloids. With one exotic model after another. Or that actress, what's her name. She was in that romantic comedy last year. I hear he's single now though."

"Uh-huh."

"Personally, I'm of the opinion that he should try to find someone with more substance. I mean, what are the chances he would ever fall for an everyday, average woman though, right? Men like that never do. He's way too glamourous and worldly for that. Wouldn't you agree?"

Carli's request to finally terminate this conversation died on her lips when she noticed someone had arrived at her open door. The blood left her brain when she realized who it was. Justin.

How long had he been standing there? And how much had he heard?

If the floorboards opened up and swallowed her whole, it wouldn't be enough to lessen her mortification.

This was just fabulous. On top of everything else, now he was going to see her as nothing but an office gossip.

His reputation preceded him yet again, Justin thought as he hesitated outside Carli's office door. He'd caught just enough of the women's conversation to realize it was absolutely about him. Also that it was mostly one-sided. Carli had barely spoken a word. In fact, she appeared ready to give her assistant a hard shake.

The other woman's back was turned to where he stood, but Carli had clearly seen him.

Damn.

This was awkward. Unable to come up with anything appropriate to say, he simply cleared his throat. Jocelyn, the assistant, actually jumped in her chair.

Carli didn't take her disapproving eyes off her when

she spoke. "Justin, something else I can do for you? Jocelyn was just leaving."

"Yes, yes, I was." Jocelyn bolted up and ran out of the room, making sure not to look Justin in the eye.

Carli motioned to the newly abandoned chair in front of her desk. "Please, have a seat." She glanced at her watch. "Though we don't have a lot of time before the staff meeting."

Her cheeks were flushed, and she wouldn't meet his eyes either. Still awkward.

"It's okay," he began, then sat. "This won't take long."

"What can I do for you?"

Justin swore under his breath. This was going to be even more uncomfortable after he'd walked in on the previous conversation. But it was too late to back out now. Besides, he owed her an apology. He took a deep breath. "Listen, I know we got off on the wrong foot. I mean this morning. At my father's house."

She quirked an eyebrow in surprise.

"I'm not usually so…"

"Rude?" she supplied as he trailed off.

"That's probably an accurate description. In my defense, I'd been traveling all night. Not that it's any kind of excuse."

"I agree. It's not any kind of excuse."

Wow. She was a tough one. He didn't need this; he was only trying to apologize. Albeit doing a terrible job at it. But instead of being annoyed by her directness, he found it somewhat intriguing. Refreshing in a way. Most people didn't bother to challenge him under any circumstances. Carli Tynan was clearly not like most people. Her gaze pinned him where he sat. He hadn't noticed before just how her eyes appeared to go from deep chocolate to hazel when the light hit her face a certain way. Or the fullness of her lips, even as tightly pursed as they were at the moment.

"You're right. I just wasn't expecting to see anyone in my father's house that early. Especially someone like you, coming down the stairs at that hour. My mistake."

Her eyes grew wide, and the color in her cheeks heightened to a deep shade of red. Her grip on the pen she held grew so tight that her knuckles turned pale. This did not bode well, he thought.

"What are you saying exactly, Mr. Hammond?" she asked through gritted teeth. Uh-oh. He'd just gone from being Justin to Mr. Hammond in the span of a few moments.

"Nothing. I mean, I'm simply trying to clear the air. To explain my reaction upon seeing you."

"Maybe you should do that. Explain exactly what your reaction was when you first saw me this morning."

She threw it out like a challenge. One he wasn't foolish enough to even attempt to accept. He'd begun this apology all wrong. But the conversation he'd overheard between Carli and her assistant had thrown him off. Heck, Carli herself kept throwing him off. It was like he didn't even know how to behave around her.

Where was it coming from?

"Never mind. It's not important," he said, hoping she would drop the whole matter.

Apparently, that was too much to hope for. He should have known better. She immediately shook her head. "No, please clarify. I'm very interested in what exactly it is you're trying to say."

The woman was relentless. "Look, it's not important. I simply wanted to offer an apology."

She studied him in a way that made him feel like a lab specimen under a microscope. Perhaps some sort of insect. If he wasn't so damn uncomfortable, he would have almost laughed at her scorn at him.

"Which you still haven't done," she said.

"What?"

"I've yet to hear an apology. Or a valid explanation, for that matter."

His mouth grew dry. Damn it, he was a successful executive, known for his cut-throat business style and ruthless negotiation skills. How was this woman cutting him off at the knees? And why was he almost enjoying it?

"Um? Explanation?"

She gave him a smirk of a smile, like he'd been caught. He supposed he had. "For why you behaved as you did. I was simply delivering a file at your father's request. And instead of introducing yourself, you dismissed me and practically shooed me out of the house."

Justin cringed at her description. He couldn't believe he'd been such a boor to her. Nor could he believe the way he was botching this apology now. Not only had be managed to insult a valuable Hammond employee, he couldn't even apologize for it in a sufficient manner. True to form, when it came to anything Hammond related, Justin was woefully lacking. He may have started his own wildly successful consulting firm and grown it from a one-man operation to a major international business. But when it came to being a Hammond, all he'd ever managed was failure. More proof that he didn't belong here back in Boston. Or at Hammond's Toys for that matter.

He had to pull himself together. Find a way to explain himself. But how? It's not like he could come out and admit to jumping to the worst conclusion—suspecting Carli to be his father's mistress. Though it was obvious she'd figured it out. If looks could kill and all that.

Nothing to do now but be completely straight. And

hope the damage could be repaired somehow. He and Carli would be working together for the next several days. She was clearly a major asset to this corporation, and he had managed to insult her in a major way. He had to fix this.

"The truth is there is no excuse or explanation for the way I behaved. Please believe that it had nothing to do with you personally and everything to do with my father."

She remained silent, not ready to give an inch.

"I can only say I'm sorry," he added. "And that I will somehow find a way to make it up to you."

She shrugged with derision, and though she didn't say the words, her response was clear: *as if you could.*

Maybe she was being petty, but Carli wasn't going to give him the benefit of a response. Justin Hammond had made a horribly insulting assumption about her and the older man she worked for. That's something she would not readily forget.

Still, she couldn't help but feel more than a little touched at his genuine apology. Even given how badly he'd botched it up. He really did seem to feel remorseful. If the circumstances were different, if he weren't the boss's son and instead they were somehow new friends, she might have explained to him that she'd been dealing with such impressions all her life.

But he *was* a Hammond. And they definitely were not friends.

She would do her best to help him while he was here and hope that his tenure at Hammond's Toys was a short one. The events of this morning proved that Justin was walking in blind. He'd had no clue who she was or just how much she was in charge of. She didn't have time to babysit the prodigal son on a long-term basis.

She stood up from her chair and walked around her

desk. "Well, I guess the prudent thing to do would be to move on and try our best to work together as productively as possible."

Justin stood, as well. He looked notably relieved. "I agree. And I appreciate it."

"We can start with this staff meeting. I asked Jocelyn earlier to forward you a copy of the agenda."

He nodded. "I got that. Thanks."

He followed her down the corridor to the meeting room where several employees had already gathered. After a brief round of introductions, Carli began the meeting with the first item on the agenda.

The first time she stammered, she chalked it up to feeling exhausted and due to the mishaps of the morning. By the third mistake, however, she had to admit that she was off her game. She also had to admit that it had everything to do with the new face sitting at the table.

Justin leaned forward, listening attentively and frequently jotting down note after note. He preferred old-fashioned paper and pen, which surprised her. Most of the executives she dealt with couldn't wait to purchase and show off the latest technology e-tablet or the sleekest new laptop.

Aside from an occasional question or request for clarification, he was mostly quiet. Still, his presence was jarring.

She wasn't the only one who seemed to think so. Several furtive glances were cast in Justin's direction. One of the younger new recruits from sales smiled at him demurely, not even pretending to pay attention to Carli's updates. Though annoyed, she could hardly blame the other women. Justin had a presence. Add to that the mystery surrounding his arrival, and people were having trouble feigning indifference.

Herself included.

At the conclusion of the meeting an hour later, she was more than ready to be done and to get out of there. A cup of coffee would be heaven right about now. She hadn't been able to get her usual cup due to her detour, and a dull ache was beginning to throb behind her eyes. No doubt the caffeine withdrawal had been at least partly responsible for her less than stellar performance.

"Well, if that's everything, I think we can wrap up."

Everyone stood except for a few stragglers who stuck around to discuss their next to-do or to make small talk. Eventually, even they slowly filed out of the room.

In fact, when she looked up, Carli found that everyone had left except for one lone holdout. Justin remained seated. He studied her with avid interest. He clearly had something to say.

Carli set her jaw. Looked like her caffeine hit was going to have to wait. "Was there something else, Justin?"

"Yes, as a matter of fact. If you have a few moments, I think there are some things we should probably discuss. Sooner rather than later."

Something in his tone made her stomach twist. She sat back down.

"Go on."

"I've been going over the numbers, and Hammond's profit margins are mostly impressive. But there are areas that are lagging."

"I'm aware of that."

"Then you also realize that a handful of the retail stores have seen steadily declining sales."

"I'm aware of that too. There are several ideas in the pipeline to address this. As I just mentioned."

He glanced down at the notes in his leather-bound notebook. "Yes, I heard. All well-thought-out ideas involving online expansion. The modifications to the website are particularly impressive."

"But?"

"My concern is that there's a need to remove some of the more sluggish units, so to speak. Hammond's should be making some cuts."

"What sort of cuts?" she asked, though she knew exactly where this was headed. The twist in her stomach turned a bit tighter.

"With your background and experience, I'm sure you've concluded which brick-and-mortar stores are just not pulling their weight. In fact, their only real profits register during the holidays."

"It's a very seasonal business."

"Nevertheless. Some of these stores just don't get enough foot traffic during the year to justify keeping them open." He glanced down at the file she had handed him just hours ago. "There's one in particular we need to seriously consider the future of. It hasn't seen any kind of significant sales for the past half decade."

Carli bit down on her lip. She knew exactly which store he was referring to. The one she'd started out in as a lowly retail clerk trying to save enough money for college. The same store that currently employed several people she'd grown up knowing and caring for. The one situated at the heart of Westerson, MA—a quaint, touristy spot along the inland coast of Cape Cod in Massachusetts. The same town she'd grown up in.

And Justin wanted to shut it down.

CHAPTER THREE

HER PARTY GUESTS were going to be here within the hour, and Carli was just now stepping out of the shower. So far, this day had been nothing but one big race against the clock. She should have started prepping as soon as she got home. Instead, she'd taken the time to go over the sales figures.

Not that there was any use, and Carli had known it. But she'd hoped for some small miracle that had somehow been missed. Something, anything she could use as leverage to argue that Justin should nix the idea of closing the doors of the Cape store for good.

Of all the retail stores in the Hammond chain, why did that have to be the one performing the worst? She'd practically grown up in that store. Mr. Freider, the manager going on twenty years, had always welcomed her with open arms. As a child, she'd go into that store by herself, just to pass the time in peace when things were just too noisy at home. During her teenage years, she'd spent countless hours in the Book Nook, the corner of the store dedicated to latest in children's and young adult books. She'd devoured a world of stories in that small area, Mr. Freider never complaining about her lack of purchases—purchases she couldn't afford. In fact, he'd been kind enough to bring hot chocolate on cold days and sweet lemon iced tea during summer.

That same kind man would very well lose his job if it were up to Justin.

There had to be something she could do. Perhaps she could go straight to Jackson. Plead her case. The only problem was, she didn't really have a professionally sound one. Essentially, that would amount to asking for a favor, as his protégé. As steep as the stakes were, she couldn't bring herself to do that. She'd never once approached Jackson Hammond as anything less than a professional and wouldn't start now. Not even under these circumstances.

Carli blinked away the thoughts. She had to get going already; no doubt some of the invitees would be straggling in early, ready to party on this cold December Boston evening without much else to do. She hadn't even towel dried her hair yet.

What had possessed her to plan a Christmas party on a Wednesday night anyway? And just her luck, it had happened to fall on the same day that Justin Hammond had blown into town and thrown her whole world into a spiral.

Now she was running late and dripping wet just as most of her colleagues were about to descend on her apartment for some yuletide Christmas cheer. A timer went off in the kitchen, a reminder to take the crab cakes out of the oven. Thank goodness she'd put out all the decorations weeks ago, the day after Thanksgiving. A tradition from her childhood. Exactly as Justin had guessed. The Tynan family may not have had much in the way of material things, but they made sure to celebrate their ceremonial traditions. Ceremonies that often got downright unruly and chaotic. She supposed that was to be expected in a family of five children.

By some Christmas miracle, she was ready when the

first guests arrived: Jocelyn and some of the account reps along with a couple of regional managers. Carli didn't even recognize two of the arrivals. That's what happened when you posted an open invite. She didn't mind. These people were her second family now, Hammond's Toys was her second home. She was lucky to have such an opportunity with such a wonderful company. Current situation with the boss's son notwithstanding.

In fact, an hour later when the party was in full swing and several champagne bottles had been corked, she found herself blessedly distracted and finally able to enjoy herself. Until one of the elderly secretaries walked in. She wasn't alone.

"I hope you don't mind," Miranda Sumpter said, her gray hair framing her maternal face. "I brought someone with me."

Carli tried to hide her surprise. Justin, to his credit, looked less than pleased to be there.

Miranda was staring at her expectedly. "I mean, it said open invitation on the company wide email. And Justin's definitely part of the company. You don't mind, do you?"

"Yes! No! I mean. Of course he's welcome." Now Justin just looked bemused. Carli gripped her glass flute in her hand tight enough that her fingers ached. Then she took a large swig.

Justin stepped toward her. "I didn't realize you'd be the host, Carli."

Well, how was she supposed to respond to that? Was the implication that he wouldn't have come if he'd known?

Miranda stood staring at the two of them as an awkward silence settled. Carli cleared her throat. "So, how do you two know each other?" she finally managed to ask.

Miranda gave Justin's arm an affectionate squeeze. "Oh, he and I go way back. I used to babysit this little hurricane when he was no more than a mischievous toddler. When I first started out in the Hammond secretarial pool and needed some extra cash."

She turned to Carli. "They were always looking for a sitter for this one. Couldn't handle him without a little help. He was constantly getting into trouble."

He still was, Carli thought. If the tabloids were to be believed.

"I just about fell over when I saw him in the hallway this afternoon," Miranda continued. "Almost didn't recognize him."

Justin gave her a playful wink. "I've changed just a bit, huh?"

"You still look plenty mischievous." The older woman laughed. "You should have seen some of the disasters he used to get himself into," Miranda said Carli. "Always in trouble. His parents were at their wits' end most days."

The tone was lighthearted, Miranda laughing merrily. But Carli couldn't help but notice Justin fidgeted as she spoke. He turned the watch on his wrist and pulled on the band. He was clearly uncomfortable. Probably regretted having come here now that he realized this was her party.

"I've since matured a bit," he offered.

"I would certainly hope so." Miranda laughed again. "You were quite the hellion."

"Yes, I recall my parents not being able to wait to rush out of the house as soon as you showed up."

Carli detected an undercurrent in his tone, a hardness. As the middle daughter in a family with five girls, she could certainly relate to growing up in a chaotic, messy household. But she couldn't remember her parents ever trying to "rush out" to get away from any of them. Lord knew, they'd given both Mom and Dad plenty of reasons to want to.

"At least I got to leave at the end of the night. Your parents were stuck with you, weren't they?" Miranda gave him a playful pinch on the cheek.

"I'm surprised you kept coming back."

"There were plenty of times I was tempted not to."

For such a playful conversation, Carli couldn't help but feel slightly uncomfortable. All she really knew about the Hammonds was that the parents had split while the boys were ten and twelve respectively. And for some unfathomable reason, one parent stayed with one son while the other took off with the other to live on the West Coast. She knew for a fact James hadn't seen his mother more than once or twice since the divorce. And she suspected the same of Justin and his father.

It was an incredibly sad scenario if one really thought about it. For all the turmoil and hassles of growing up with four siblings, Carli couldn't imagine years going by without seeing any one of them. Even after what had happened last year between her and her sister Janie.

She winced at that memory before realizing that Justin had just said something to her. Also, Miranda had excused herself and walked away.

"I'm sorry, I missed what you said."

"I was commenting on how festive your apartment is. You've obviously put a lot of effort into decorating for the holidays."

It was clearly an attempt to change the subject, but she couldn't help but feel a little flattered at the compliment.

She was about to give him a warm smile and answer that this decorative effect had taken weeks to achieve. But then she remembered what he wanted to do with the Cape Cod store.

"Thank you," she said with a curt nod. "Now, if you'll excuse me, I have other guests I should attend to."

* * *

Justin watched Carli walk away and grabbed a glass of wine off one of the trays sitting in the corner. It was hard not to appreciate the view as she made her way across the room. The woman was shaped like sin.

Looked like his apology hadn't quite cut it as it was clear she was still unhappy with him. He wasn't sure why that bothered him so much. It really shouldn't have. He'd only just met the woman this morning. They wouldn't even be working together for that long. He'd do what was asked of him by his father and return to the West Coast in a few days. Really, the opinion of some midlevel executive at Hammond's Toys should be the last thing on his mind.

Still, he had to admit he was vexed. His transgression toward her this morning wasn't that bad. Was it?

He bit out a silent curse as he thought about it. Yeah, he was fooling himself. It was bad. To assume she was his father's mistress. Simply based on the hour of the day and the way she looked. He couldn't blame her for still being upset.

Doubtful his older brother, James, would have ever been careless enough to make such a mistake. No, James probably always displayed the utmost professionalism and leadership. Usually, Justin wouldn't hesitate to describe himself the same way. Apparently not when he was here, however. In Boston and around Hammond Enterprises, Justin was out of his element to the point of near incompetence.

Clearly, Justin was a Hammond in name only.

The question was, what was he going to do about it as far as Carli was concerned?

Someone tapped on his shoulder as he tried to find Carli from the crowd of people in her apartment. He turned to find a petite, dark-haired woman smiling at him. It took him a minute to recognize her. Jocelyn, Carli's assistant.

She looked different without the professional ponytail she'd been wearing this morning.

"Well, hello," Jocelyn said, loud enough and with enough enthusiasm that two people turned to see who had spoken.

"Hello."

"I didn't expect to see you here."

He spread his arms and bowed slightly. "Here I am."

"Fantastic. We were sort of sad that James was going to miss it this year. And here you are in his place."

Justin tried not to snort with irony. As if there was any way he would ever be able to take his brother's place in any way, shape, or form. Not as far as Hammond's was concerned. And certainly not in his father's eyes.

He gave Jocelyn a neutral smile. "Glad I could make it."

"I'm glad Carli saw to it that you came," Jocelyn said, and took a sip of her ruby red wine.

He had no intention nor desire to correct her. Actually, he had no intention of staying around much longer. There was no feasible reason he hadn't left as soon as Carli walked away.

Other than some silly desire to see her again this evening. Funny how he'd never been a glutton for punishment until this very day. Carli didn't want anything to do with him.

He spotted her coming out of the kitchen with more drinks. Several people stopped her along the way; she gave one woman an affectionate air kiss. Several men approached her as well, one taking part of the load off her hands. They seemed friendly but not overly familiar. These men were all clearly just colleagues.

Not that it was any of his business. For all he knew she already had a steady boyfriend or partner. Women who looked like Carli and who had as much going for them weren't single for long.

Jocelyn waved a hand in front of his face. "Hello? Where'd you just drift off to?"

He smiled apologetically. "Sorry, I was just admiring all the Christmas decorations. Carli's got quite a talent for it."

"Really? Is that what you were admiring?"

Uh-oh. He had to be careful here. He couldn't be caught ogling his father's project manager. "What else?"

She gave him a knowing look but luckily dropped the matter. "Anyway, I'm glad two Hammond men will be at Carli's party after all."

Justin turned his full attention to her. "Excuse me?"

"You and your father. He never misses one of Carli's soirees."

Damn. The last thing Justin needed was to run into his father right now. Their brief meeting this morning had been awkward enough.

"I don't see him yet though," Jocelyn added. "He always seems to arrive much later. Likes to make an entrance."

That definitely sounded like the attention-craving father Justin remembered from his childhood. And from everything he'd been told or had read about the man.

He still had the chance to make his getaway before Jackson arrived. All the more reason to leave right now. So, what was stopping him?

He should have never come in the first place. He knew it had been a mistake. He never even went to these events at his own company. But seeing Miranda again after all these years, remembering how she'd always been so kind to him. Even as he'd been making her life miserable with one childish antic after another.

Still, he had every intention of gently turning Miranda down. But the woman had not taken no for an answer.

Someone turned up the volume on the sound system and "Holly Jolly Christmas" started pounding through the room. Great. Now he was going to have to put up with the damn Christmas carols again.

Jocelyn squealed as the song came on. He'd almost forgotten she was standing in front of him. Again. "I love this song!" she exclaimed. "Let's dance!"

Before he had a chance to protest, she pulled him into the center of the room where two other couples were already bouncing along to the tune. This wasn't the traditional version of the song he was used to. It was a bouncy, bassy remake of some sort. With a bit of urban rap lyrics thrown in between verses. As if the original song wasn't annoying enough. He was supposed to dance to this?

Pretty much a version of hell. Still, he knew what to do. Several years of mandated dance lessons thanks to his society-norm-conscious mother came in handy during moments like this. He matched Jocelyn's steps and earned a girly giggle when he dipped her.

By the time the song ended, Jocelyn was smiling from ear to ear. "You are quite a dancer, Mr. Justin Hammond."

"I am a man of many talents."

"Well, I don't want to hog you all to myself," she said, and before he knew it, she had somehow managed to steer them toward where Carli stood talking to a middle-aged man with a bad comb-over.

"You are the host of this party. You should be dancing too," Jocelyn admonished as she pulled Justin in front of her. "Justin is a terrific dancer. And he needs a partner." She turned to comb-over guy. "Tom, may I have the honor of this dance?"

Justin watched with both bemusement and dismay as Jocelyn and Tom walked onto the middle of the floor and started dancing.

"My assistant is not subtle," Carli said. "Obviously."

"Does that mean you're not interested in dancing with me?"

She tilted her head. "I'd never dream of making you dance. To a Christmas song, no less. I know how much you dislike them."

With that flippant comment, she tried to walk away. But he wasn't going to let her. It was about time they hashed out some stuff, he figured. Otherwise, he was just going to keep letting her get under his skin. That would not bode well for either of them. Even if he was only going to be around her for a few days.

"On the contrary, I'd love a dance," he said as he gently took her by the arm and led her to the makeshift dance floor.

The protest died on her lips as he spun her around toward him and started swaying with her to the music. He was close enough to sniff a hint of her perfume, a flowery subtle scent. Jasmine perhaps. It suited her.

As did the cocktail dress she wore, a silky, drippy number that hung on her curves in a tasteful, flattering way. He noticed she had whimsical snowman earrings dangling from her dainty lobes.

"See, I can dance to anything. Even annoying versions of Christmas songs."

She gave an exasperated huff. "How can you not like Christmas carols? There's got to be one that you're fond of."

He shook his head. "Can't think of one."

"Not even 'Jingle Bells'?"

"I find that one particularly grating."

The look she gave him was one mixed with both sympathy and bewilderment.

Justin sighed. She must think him the biggest Scrooge. "Christmas wasn't quite the jolly and wonderful time in the Hammond household as it was for most people," he admitted.

He twirled her around playfully as he said it.

"Makes no sense, I know," he added. "Given how we make our livelihood. In some ways it just made things worse."

"How so?"

"Well, for one thing, my father became even more obsessed with sales figures and profit projections. He'd go into the office early and come home late. Even more so than usual. His increased hours gave my parents yet one more excuse to argue."

He almost laughed at that. *Argue* was hardly an adequate word for the knockdown, soul-crushing fights his parents used to have.

"It made for less than a peaceful holiday," he added. Why was he telling her these things? This wasn't something he particularly liked to talk about with anyone. Let alone a woman he'd just met a few hours ago. A woman who'd made it painfully clear that she didn't seem to like him very much.

"That's so very sad. I can't imagine Christmas being a time of turmoil for a young child."

Well, now she felt sorry for him. "I wasn't looking for sympathy," he said, with a little more force in his voice than he'd intended. "Besides, it's not like I helped the situation. I was a bit of a frustrating child. As Miranda just pointed out."

"You were just a child."

"A rambunctious, unruly, very disobedient child."

She shook her head. "But still a child."

The look in her eyes was intense, he had the disquieting feeling she was looking deep into his soul in the most intimate way. What a silly notion that was. They were in the middle of an office holiday party, surrounded by people.

Before he could respond, the music changed. The upbeat, bouncy rhythm of "All I Want for Christmas" transitioned to the slow, rhythmic melody of "Baby, It's Cold Outside."

Carli immediately stopped. But he wasn't ready for this to end just yet. Whatever *this* was. Before he could give it too much thought and before she could turn to go, he stepped closer to her and took her by her waist. She felt warm and soft under the silky material of her dress. After a gentle nudge, she began to move with him to the slower tempo of the song.

Justin pulled her closer, until they were mere inches apart. Her eyes grew wide with shock but she didn't make any kind of move to pull away.

Good thing, he thought. Because he wasn't sure he'd be able to let her go.

CHAPTER FOUR

WHAT IN THE world was she doing?

Carli knew she should excuse herself and slip out of Justin's arms. Instead, she just stayed there, lulling herself into the cocoon of his embrace. Not even the fact that her guests were starting to stare could seem to make her pull away. And they weren't merely guests, she reminded herself. These were her colleagues. She'd never been anything less than professional and straitlaced in front of every single one of them. But for the life of her, she couldn't bring herself to end the dance.

Justin was indeed an ideal dance partner. He moved with fluid grace and coordination. It was hard not to enjoy being with him this way.

More than that, she couldn't stop thinking about the things he'd just confessed to her about his childhood. She'd heard rumors about the Hammonds' failed marriage, of course. Hammond's Toys was no different than any other company when it came to office gossip. But she'd never given the matter much thought. And certainly neither James nor Jackson had ever broached the topic.

She'd had no idea things had been that bad before the marriage ended.

"Let's talk about something else," Justin said quietly in

her ear. His proximity sent a shiver down her spine. "I'm bordering on party-pooper status here."

He'd just given her the perfect opportunity to bring up the disturbing topic that had been looming in her mind. The Cape Cod store. She could try to make a case for giving it another chance. The numbers weren't that bad, and surely they could be turned around. But she couldn't bring herself to answer with such a daunting subject. Not right now.

After all, was this really the time or place?

"What would you like to talk about?" she asked instead. She'd find some way to bring up the matter at some point. When the time was right.

And that decision had nothing to do with the way he was holding her right now.

"How about you? Tell me what your Christmases were like. You obviously have fonder memories related to the holiday than I do."

"What makes you say that?"

He laughed softly at the question. "It's rather obvious. One big clue is the sheer amount of decorations in here. You'd give the Hammond's Manhattan store a run for its money in comparison. The garland alone is impressively lavish."

"I have a confession to make," she admitted.

"What's that?"

"These are my regular Christmas decorations. Not just for the party."

His laughed once more, and Carli found herself smiling in return.

"This is what your place looks like under normal circumstances?"

"Only at Christmastime."

"And you did it all yourself?"

"Who else?"

He shrugged. "We always hired professional services to do our holiday decorating and to hang our lights. First at the house and then the various apartments my mom had us living in over the years."

Carli tried to imagine watching as strangers handled her delicate ornaments, or the tiny figurines that made up her Christmas village. She treasured every one of those items. Some she'd paid for with her own hard-earned funds, and others had been cherished gifts from friends or relatives. Every piece was a part of her in a tiny yet significant way. Each time she set one out, it triggered a special memory. Some of them even made her homesick. The idea of strangers handling such sentimental trophies made her shudder.

It occurred to her that Justin had most likely never experienced anything like that.

"I can't imagine having someone else do it."

"And I can't imagine even knowing where to put anything."

She could show him, was her first thought. An unbidden image flashed in her mind of the two of them standing in front of a brick fireplace with a roaring fire as they hung stockings above the mantel. She blinked it away. How utterly ridiculous of her.

She really had to get a grip. This man was the boss's son. Which essentially made him her boss. There was a chance he was going to usurp her duties while he was here. And there was an even greater chance that he was going to shut down the store that had meant the world to her growing up. She had zero business dreaming up idyllic, romantic fantasies of the two of them.

And anyway, he was absolutely not her type. Not that she even knew what her type was anymore. Not after the fiasco with Warren and his utter betrayal. In fact, she decided then and there that she no longer had a type. She'd sworn off men entirely. At least until she was fully established in her career.

Justin was invoking sensations she'd held dormant for too long, and this was not the way she wanted to reawaken them. With a man who was so outrageously out of her league in every single way.

Blessedly, the song ended and she moved to step away from his embrace.

But a commotion of noise and boisterous cheers distracted them both before she could excuse herself.

Jackson Hammond had just arrived.

Justin knew the exact moment his father walked in. He didn't have to see Jackson to know he was here. Even if other guests hadn't been calling out Jackson's name in greeting, Justin would have sensed his presence. The air changed whenever someone like his father entered a room.

The magic of dancing with Carli seemed to dissipate as the real world returned along with his father's arrival. He sighed slowly and let her go. Served him right. He'd forgotten for a brief moment that he wasn't one of those men who could dance carefree with a beautiful woman in her quaint, charming apartment full of holiday cheer.

Damn it. He should have left when he'd had the chance. What had he been thinking? Allowing himself to be distracted by Carli and her notions of perfect Christmases with happy memories. Now he had to make nice with the father he'd barely seen in several years who for some sudden, inexplicable reason had needed his expert financial advice.

He wasn't even curious as to why. He honestly didn't care. He just wanted to do what was asked of him and return to his life. There was nothing in Boston that endeared

it to him. Though he couldn't help but glance at Carli as
that thought flitted through his head. If only he'd met her
in a different time, under different circumstances.

And if only he'd been a completely different man.

"Looks like dear old Dad is here," he remarked.

Jackson made a beeline right to where they stood as
soon as he spotted them. Smiling, he placed a firm grip
on Justin's shoulder. "I didn't expect to see you here, son."

Justin winced inwardly at the last word. "Miranda can
be quite persuasive."

"She always did have a soft spot for you." He turned
to Carli and gave her a nod. "I see you've met the host of
this lovely get-together. She's also better known as my
right hand."

"Justin and I have gotten to know each other a bit over
the past few hours," Carli offered.

If his father had any kind of untoward feelings for his
young, beautiful project manager, he was doing an excellent job at hiding it. Maybe Jackson had indeed changed
and was no longer the notorious philanderer his mother
had frequently accused him of being. More likely, Carli
was the type of professional who would not abide that type
of attention from a man she worked for.

Justin hadn't known her for long, but he realized now
what a huge error in judgment it had been to even entertain the notion that Carli would be the type of employee
who would date her elderly boss.

"Yes, she's been very helpful. The report she prepared
and delivered held a wealth of useful information. Enough
that I was able to make some quick initial judgments."

Jackson studied him. Was that appreciation he detected
in the old man's eyes? Probably more for his protégé and
the file she'd prepared, Justin figured.

"Well, I don't like to get into business discussions at these events," Jackson said. "Let's go over everything tomorrow, the three of us, and you can tell me what you've concluded."

Justin was ready to agree when Carli surprised him by holding her hand up. "Wait. I'd like to say something about all this."

Both men turned to look at her. She appeared downright apprehensive. "Carli, do you have an issue with meeting tomorrow?" Jackson asked. "Is your schedule full?"

She shook her head, a tight firm line to her lips. "No, my schedule isn't the issue, Mr. Hammond."

"Then what is it?"

She turned to Justin. "I know what your first recommendation is going to be, Justin. And I'd urge you to reconsider."

"Reconsider?"

She swallowed. "Yes, I know you're going to argue that Hammond's should close the Cape store. And I realize you're the expert. But I think that would be a big mistake."

"I don't understand."

She inhaled on a deep breath. "If that's indeed your recommendation, I'm afraid I'll be fighting your decision."

Jackson at that point stepped slightly between them. "All right. Clearly we have some things to discuss. But I think we should save it for the office. This is not the time or place."

Carli looked ready to argue but then abruptly closed her mouth and looked away. "You're right, Mr. Hammond."

Justin nodded his agreement as an awkward silence descended. Finally, Justin excused himself and went to grab his coat hanging from the rack by the front door. He'd give his regrets to Miranda later about having left without saying goodbye. Right now, he had other things on his mind.

Looked like he and Carli Tynan were about to butt heads on yet another matter.

CHAPTER FIVE

SHE WAS EARLY; it had been impossible to sleep. Carli adjusted the collar of her business jacket and took a sip of her coffee. Jackson and Justin would be here in a few minutes. She was more than prepared to try to make her case, but the enormity of the task was not lost on her. The facts were definitely not on her side. How in the world was she supposed to convince a hard-nosed, by-the-numbers businessman that he should keep open a store that was seeing declining profits?

He'd appeared somewhat shocked last night at the party. She hadn't meant to blurt it out. But there was no way she could have kept quiet knowing where it was all leading.

Jackson's idea was that they sit together first thing this morning and hammer it all out.

Pulling out a chair at the long mahogany conference table, Carli took a deep breath and sat down. The whole floor was eerily quiet. No one else had come in yet. Traffic outside on Boylston Street had yet to pick up. The sun just now starting to burn through the crisp winter air.

The dinging of the elevator signaled the arrival of someone else. She glanced at her watch. Still another twenty minutes. So she was surprised when Justin appeared in the doorway. Dressed in a white shirt and silk navy tie, he looked every bit the successful tycoon.

Such a different image than the one he had projected last night at her party. Then he'd been casual, lighthearted. He'd danced with her, confided in her. He'd been friendly and open. Until the whole matter of the store.

He gave her a tight nod before entering the room. "Carli. Good morning."

"Justin."

"I see we're both early."

There was no hint of the genteel man who had swayed with her to hip-hop Christmas carols last night. The thought tugged at her heart. How she wished they could just sit down and discuss all this as just two friends who happened to work for the same company.

But Justin gave no indication that he was feeling at all friendly. The man was solidly in back-to-business mode. So be it. There was really only one objective here.

He glanced at his watch. They were both thinking the same thing: the sooner Jackson got here, the sooner they could get this all over with.

"There's coffee in the break room," she offered. For lack of anything else to say. The awkward silence was starting to rankle her.

"I've already had three cups this morning," he said dismissively.

"Oh."

"Thanks though," he said, his tone softer this time.

It was Carli's turn to check the time. She glanced at the classic wall clock behind Justin. Only five minutes had passed. What were the chances Jackson would be early for once in his life? Slim to none, she figured.

Clearing her throat, she made one more attempt at light conversation. "So, did you have fun last night? At the party?"

He looked up from his cell phone, his eyebrows lifted.

"Yes, I was having a great time." At his words, she realized how much fun she'd been having too. The way Justin had held her, how warm his arms had felt around her waist as they danced.

"Even with all the annoying Christmas music playing?"

He smiled at her. "Yes, even so."

Her mind automatically recalled the way it had felt to slow dance in his arms. The hammering of her pulse at the way he'd held her, pulled her closer to him on the dance floor. She'd felt his heartbeat against her chest, and it had served to accelerate her own.

It had been months since she'd even been out on a date, let alone been touched by a man. And to have that man be Justin Hammond of all people. She'd been thinking about it all night, when she wasn't fretting about this meeting.

Like a silly girl with a crush.

"I'm glad you came last night," she admitted, surprising herself. "I probably should not have brought up the matter of the store. It was really not the time nor place."

He merely shrugged.

"You're probably not used to being second-guessed. And I understand why that would make you frustrated," she began, and then cringed as the words left her mouth. The phrase was straight out of a management training handbook or seminar on dealing with difficult colleagues. She could tell by his expression that the same thought had occurred to him.

Carli hated this. This wasn't her. She was usually the articulate, straightforward professional who knew exactly what to say to get her point across. With Justin she just seemed to keep stumbling.

"That's not quite the word I would use."

She was trying to come up with an answer to that when he suddenly stood. "Perhaps I will go get a cup of coffee," he said, and moved to the door. "Would you mind texting me when Jackson comes in?"

He left the room before she could say yes.

Justin paced the hallway outside the break room and felt his phone vibrate with Carli's text. He'd had no intention of getting any coffee; the last thing he needed was more caffeine. He'd just had to get out of that conference room.

Carli Tynan affected him like no other woman he'd ever known. What had all that been about last night? He'd been about to give his father an overview of his observations on the retail operations when she'd cut him off like he was an errant child. Then she'd made some cryptic remark about how he was wrong on one major point, and she wanted a chance to explain.

Jackson had stepped in then and suggested they all meet this morning to get to the bottom of it all. Not that it would prove useful. Justin could guess what was happening. Carli must feel unsettled that he was here now. She'd been the one running the show alongside his brother and father. No doubt she felt threatened because of his presence.

He didn't even really blame her.

Well, now that his father was here, they could finally get to the bottom of it, once and for all.

He found Jackson at the head of the conference table when he arrived back in the meeting room. He nodded in greeting. Carli remained where she had been seated.

"Now, what's this all about, you two?" Jackson wasted no time.

Justin paused. Damned if he knew. He waited for Carli's answer.

She cleared her throat. "As you know, I prepared some figures and analysis for Justin like you requested."

"Thank you for getting that done so quickly," Jackson told her.

"You're welcome. It was just a matter of pulling together all the info."

"It was all very useful information," Justin added.

"So what's the problem, Carli?" his father asked.

She appeared visibly nervous. "I know Justin has come to some conclusions based on the information."

"That's correct," Justin jumped in. "Several issues can be addressed to increase profit margins. Some major, some minor."

"It's one of the more major ones that I have an issue with," Carli said. "Something Justin mentioned yesterday that he is considering."

Both men waited for her to continue.

"Justin is thinking of closing one of our stores. The one on the Cape. I have to stress that I think that would be a big mistake."

That's what this was all about? The closing of a store that was bleeding cash? If he recalled correctly, that particular location hadn't been in the red for about five years.

"I see," Jackson said, rubbing his chin.

Justin looked from one of them to the other. "I'm afraid I don't. The store is nothing but a drain. Frankly, I'm surprised no one's suggested shutting its doors before this."

"I'm very familiar with that store, Justin. I grew up in Westerson. Even worked there as a teen. It's how I ultimately came to work for Hammond's Toys corporate office. I'm personally aware of all it's potential."

Ah, so this was all about the human factor, even if Carli didn't want to admit it. Perhaps not even to herself. But as a businessman, every part of his being told him that something had to be done. The store just wasn't viable as a business unit.

"The fact of the matter is, that location cannot continue to run as a viable retail store. It's just not performing. That's my professional opinion."

Carli set down her pen. "But perhaps if we could just give it a chance to turn things around. I know the head manager. He's very hardworking. And flexible. He's been ill the past few years. But now that he's back on his feet, I think he'll be able to make the store profitable again now that he can devote all his time."

"I don't see how," Justin countered.

"There are several ways. For one, logistically the bulk of the town's children are getting older, so we'll need to invest more in things like video games and high end technology toys like drone flyers. Like I said, the store manager just hasn't been able to spend as much time on following the trends. But he's fine now."

"And if he gets sick again?" Justin knew it sounded like a cold and heartless question. The way she sucked in her breath and shot a surprised look at him said she thought so too. Something shifted in his chest at the thought that he'd disappointed her. He squelched it down.

He felt for Carli. He really did. But he'd been asked his professional opinion. He would have to be honest giving it. "I was asked to come here and offer my analysis based on experience. And to make suggestions. I'm only stating the facts. The brick-and-mortar stores are not where the sales are. Their expenses continue to grow as their sales slide more and more every year. This particular store is probably just the start."

Jackson raised a hand; he'd been surprisingly silent up until now. "I believe there's really only one way to approach this," he began.

Carli and Justin both looked at him expectedly. When he spoke again, it was with clear authority. "I'm going to have both of you go to the Cape for a few days. Look at the store, make some observations. See if there are indeed any opportunities to turn things around."

Carli's jaw dropped. Justin was taken a bit aback himself. What was there to see at the physical location that the file hadn't already told him?

"But Mr. Hammond—" Carli began before Jackson stood and stopped her with a curt nod.

"That's my final say." He pushed his chair in. "I'd like you both to spend at least a week. This is the ideal time to go. Right before Christmas. Go to the Cape. Make the decision together. We'll regroup once you get back."

A whole week? This was a disaster in the making. How was she supposed to spend a whole week with Justin? In her hometown, no less?

Carli shut her office door and leaned back against it. She had to somehow get her mind around this new development. All she'd wanted to do was make a case this morning to give the Cape store some more time to turn things around. Not in her wildest imaginings would she have guessed this would be the result.

This was so not the way she'd imagined returning home after everything that had happened last year. The truth was, she wasn't even sure if she was ready to go back. It was all too fresh. Sure, her family had come to visit her in Boston, even Janie. But she hadn't been able to make her way back to town. Not yet.

Now she was going to have to do it with Justin Hammond in tow.

A knock on her door startled her. She opened it to find Justin on the other side.

"I suppose we better discuss some of the logistics," he

said as she showed him in. She motioned for him to take a seat.

"We should probably leave within a day or so," she said with a sigh. "It's about a three-hour drive. Depending on traffic."

"I didn't bother to rent a car. I'll have to do that."

"Don't be ridiculous. I can drive you. It's my hometown." Not like she had a real choice. It would have been rude and unprofessional to not offer him a ride. Though no doubt it would be the longest ride of her life. "I'll pick you up from the house tomorrow morning."

"Can you recommend a place to stay?" he asked.

Carli nodded. "I'll have Jocelyn arrange it. There's a nice B and B near the beach. Within walking distance of the store."

"What about you?"

She shrugged. "I can stay with my parents. My childhood room is still empty, believe it or not."

"Won't that be a burden? On your mom and dad on such short notice?"

She blinked at him. A burden? On her own parents? The thought would never have occurred to her. Or her parents, for that matter. In fact, she was certain her parents would absolutely be thrilled that she was finally making her way back. "No. My parents are used to constant visitors at their house. I have a large family."

"How large?"

"I'm the middle child of five kids. All girls."

His eyes grew wide. "Wow."

"All my sisters still live in town. The younger ones are still in high school so still at home. My parents will hardly be fazed by another adult child visiting for a few days." They'd been gently pressuring her to do so for months. She didn't add that last part out loud.

He seemed to consider that like it was some sort of novel idea. Of course, he'd grown up with a single mom. Most likely in penthouses and palatial summer estates. Wait till he got a load of the small colonial house and rinky-dink town she'd grown up in.

"Maybe I'll get a chance to meet them all," Justin said, shocking her. She groaned inwardly. Introducing her worldly, sophisticated boss to the messy chaos that was her family was going to be another treat to this whole experience.

"I have no doubt," she told him. The Tynan clan wouldn't have it any other way. Once they found out she was in town with the other Hammond brother, all hell would break loose. Not just with her family either; the Westerson gossip mill would go into full swing.

"I'm sure my mom will want to feed you at some point. She's famous for her homemade lasagna."

He smiled at that. "That would be nice. I haven't had a home-cooked meal in I can't remember how long."

She couldn't tell if he was just being polite or if he really meant that. Probably the former, she decided. This man was used to dining in the finest restaurants all over the world, after all.

"Speaking of which, I should probably call her and let her know we're coming." She picked up her cell phone, already anticipating her mother's pleased excitement that she'd be returning after close to a year. Even if it was for business purposes.

Justin took the hint and stood to go. "Until tomorrow morning then."

CHAPTER SIX

By the time Carli arrived to pick him up the next morning, Justin was ruing his decision to ever come back to Boston in the first place. He should have never listened to his mother. He should have put his foot down and told them both, her and his father, that he wanted nothing to do with Hammond's Toys. When all this was over, he was going to return to the West Coast and try never to set foot in this state again.

This trip to the Cape was futile. It wasn't going to warrant any more information. In the end, he would have to be firm and reiterate the decision he'd already made. And upset Carli further. His final opinion wasn't going to be any different; he would just have to break Carli's heart.

He refused to let himself feel guilty about that. This was simply business. She had to understand that. He would expect no less if the shoe were on the other foot.

How many times had he been turned down by venture capitalists when trying to launch various projects? He'd been immensely disappointed too every time it had happened. But he'd moved on, found another way.

The Westerson store and its employees could do the same. And besides, the final decision wasn't his. He was merely there as an outside consultant. He had no intention of fabricating an untruth simply to tell people what they wanted to hear.

He just hated that he'd be the one delivering the lesson.

That was a completely new experience for him. Never before had he second-guessed himself about delivering a recommendation. But now, for some inexplicable reason, he hated that he'd be the messenger of bad news. It had everything to do with Carli.

She pulled up in front of the driveway and popped her trunk open. After tossing his bag in, he slid into the passenger seat.

"Thanks for the ride."

"You're welcome. We should be there way before after noon sometime. I can take you to the inn, and then we can talk about where to start. Mr. Freider is expecting us."

Justin recalled the name as the store's manager. "Sounds good."

"And I hope you haven't made any plans for dinner," she told him.

He laughed to himself. What kind of plans would he possibly have? He didn't know a single person in the town he was about to visit. He barely knew a soul in all of New England. Except for Carli.

"None whatsoever. Why?"

"I was right about my mom. She insists we have dinner with them this evening. Won't take no for an answer."

"That's very nice of her."

She signaled and looked over her shoulder as they merged onto the highway. A double-wide semi blew past them, barely slowing down. He'd only been here a few days and had already found Boston drivers deserved their nasty reputation.

"You may not think so once you get there," Carli warned. He couldn't even tell if she was serious.

"Come again?"

"It won't be a quiet affair. Dinner at my parents' house never is. All four of my sisters will be there. One of them with her husband. Along with my nephew. Who may actually bring a friend."

Justin pulled down the visor against the harsh morning glare. How many people were going to be at this dinner? "That does sound rather, um, busy."

"You mean chaotic, don't you?" Carli asked, not taking her eyes off the road. "Like I said, they don't take no for an answer. I tend to pick my battles when it comes to my parents."

The way she said the last few words held a wealth of emotion. He had to wonder what the story was there. Then he had to wonder what made him so damn curious about this woman. It was really none of his business why her voice grew wistful sometimes as it had just now. Just like it had the last time she'd spoken of her family.

"Sounds like you're all very close." That much at least was clear.

"Sometimes I think we may all be way too close."

He waited for her to elaborate, but she didn't expand on the comment. This was going to be a very long ride if he couldn't figure out a way to move the conversation forward. The last thing he wanted to do was bring up the closing of the store. That would just make the air too thick with tension. And how was he supposed to say anything relatable to her about her large family? He had only one sibling, and he'd rarely seen James over the years.

"You mentioned you have a young nephew?"

The tight line of her lips spread into a wide grin. "Yes, he's four. Quite a little dynamo." Her voice held genuine affection. Even a hint of awe.

"I have zero experience with children."

She gave him a quick side-eye. "Yeah, you don't really strike me as the babysitting type."

He chuckled. "Believe me, I'm not. I can't even keep a cactus plant alive."

"Well, don't let little Ray be a nuisance. He can be quite chatty. Just tell him to run along if he starts to bother you at dinner."

"How bad of a nuisance can he be?"

Carli's laugh was so deep and so sharp that he twisted in his seat to face her. "What?"

"You really haven't been around children, have you? And definitely not around four-year-olds."

"Never," he admitted.

"Well, you are in for a novel experience."

"I'm guessing you don't mean that in a good way?"

Her answer was another laugh.

"I'm starting to worry a bit," he admitted, only partially joking.

"Don't get me wrong. My nephew, Ray, is absolutely a little love. One of the biggest joys in my life. But he can resemble a tiny destructive tornado at times." She adjusted the heat setting on the dashboard, then continued, "It takes his two parents, all his aunties, a set of grandparents and practically most of the town to handle him. We take turns finding ways to channel all his considerable energy."

"It takes a village?"

"For Ray it certainly does." Despite her words, the love and affection she felt for her nephew were clear in the tone of her voice and the set of her jaw as she spoke about him.

Justin couldn't help but summon his own childhood memories. Carli was describing her nephew the same way he might have been characterized as a child. All he'd had were his mom and dad and slightly older brother. James was just a child, barely older than him. His father was gone most of the day. Various nannies and babysitters eventually just threw their hands up in utter defeat.

His mother was too busy trying to defeat her own demons to pay him any mind. The isolation had only grown worse when she'd finally left Jackson and James, taking only her younger son with her. They'd moved from one city to another, and she'd dated a string of men, never finding one who quite fit her needs.

His only paternal figures had been nannies who changed every time they moved. By the time he was a middle schooler, he'd known better than to develop any kind of affection for any of them.

Unlike Carli's nephew, Justin hadn't had anything resembling a village in his corner.

They were making good time until about halfway through the ride. Traffic suddenly slowed and then, much to Carli's dismay, became an annoying pattern of stop and go.

"Is there some sort of accident?" Justin asked.

Carli sighed and shook her head. "No. I'm afraid it's just impossible to time Cape traffic. You never know if you're going to hit a bottleneck."

"Sounds like California traffic," Justin commented.

"It's especially tricky this time of year, with the outlet mall along the way. Christmas shoppers looking for bargains."

"Another mark against the season."

Carli turned to look at him. How could he be such a downright Grinch? She gave her head an exasperated shake.

"What?"

"Nothing," Carli uttered as a mini-hatchback swerved and cut her off. "It's just that the irony of it all is almost too much. The second heir of Hammond's Toys, the biggest toy retailer in the Northern Hemisphere wants nothing to do with Christmas."

"Well, like I said at your party, we didn't celebrate like normal people. For us, it was mostly about the business. And things always got even more heated between my parents."

Carli felt a deep surge of sadness at his statement. He really had no clue what he'd missed out on. Or maybe he did. She couldn't decide which would be sadder.

"You don't have any good memories of that time of year? Not at all?"

"Not many." He seemed to hesitate. "There was maybe a…"

"What?"

"Nothing really. Just one time when I was about six. We were driving back from some store event, it was early evening. There was this drive-around with multiple light displays. The sign said Christmas Wonderland. I don't even remember what town it was."

He looked out the passenger side window. "Much to James's and my surprise, my father actually had the chauffeur drive through it. The displays and lights were magical. I thought so as a child anyway."

Carli felt a smile touch her lips. So he *was* human.

But then he added, "It was the first and last time we ever did anything like that."

How incredibly sad that as a child he hadn't been exposed to more such experiences during the holidays.

Then she realized what was up ahead, just off the next exit. It was almost too perfect. And since they were just sitting here stuck in traffic anyway.

"You happen to be in luck," she told him.

"Yeah? How so?"

"We happen to be very close to just such a setup. It's

not exactly a wonderland, so to speak. Just a town park to walk through. But every year they put up various Christmas displays and panoramas. Of course the lights won't be on this time of day, but we can go check out the decorations and everything else. I think we should stop in."

He laughed at the suggestion before turning to study her. "You're serious."

"Of course, I'm serious. It's just off the next exit. We can spend the time there waiting for the road to clear rather than sitting in stop-and-go traffic for an hour. It's not exactly as spectacular during the day, but it's better than watching rear taillights."

"Carli. It's really not necessary. It was just a useless childhood memory in answer to your question."

Useless. Why was he so stubborn? Did he ever allow himself to do anything just for fun or kicks? "Then do it for me. I could use the time to stretch my legs on a little walk. Not to mention, they have a stand that serves the tastiest hot spiced cider. And I'm feeling a little thirsty."

He sighed in defeat. "Then far be it from me to keep you from quenching your sudden thirst. Or depriving you of a good leg stretch."

"Thank you. It's the least you can do for your long-suffering driver."

"My empathy knows no bounds."

That made her laugh, and she was still chuckling several moments later as she turned her blinker on and got off the expressway at the next exit. Moments later they pulled into the parking lot of the town recreation area, which was now set up as a holiday bazaar. A large sign at the gate read Santa's Village in big bright letters. Several children ran past it shrieking and laughing as three harried moms followed close behind.

"This is it," she declared as they both got out of the car.

"Why exactly are we doing this again?" Justin asked. Judging by the hint of a smile on his face, he couldn't be too put out about it.

She ignored the question. "Let's start with the cider."

"Whatever you say."

"Follow me."

He did so but paused as they approached the barn where several children were feeding the livestock. "Are those reindeer?" His disbelief was audible.

"They are indeed."

She took him by the arm and continued their walk. "I don't recommend petting them before we get the cider."

"I had no intention of petting them at all."

In her haste and distraction, Carli didn't notice the patch of ice before planting her foot square in the center. Her leg slid out from under her, and then the other leg followed and gave way. Carli braced herself for the fall and prepared for the impact of falling hard on her bottom.

Until a strong arm suddenly grabbed her by the waist and pulled her up. Instead of on the ground, she found herself braced against Justin's hard length. Her heart did a jump in her chest.

"Nice reflexes." Her voice caught as she said it. There was that spicy, sandalwood scent again. She fought the urge to lean in closer to get a better whiff.

"Careful," Justin admonished. "I'd hate to present you to your family with any broken bones." He made no attempt to let her go, and heaven help her she didn't try at all to pull away. Her gaze dropped to his chin. He'd nipped himself slightly with the razor, the smallest of cuts near his ear. That observation led to an unbidden image of him shaving in the morning, shirtless.

Carli sucked in a breath and tried to regain some focus. What had he just said? Oh, yeah, something about her breaking a bone. "Thank you for saving me from such a terrible fate. That would certainly put a damper on the holidays."

He smiled at her, and she had to remind herself to breathe. Reluctantly, she pulled herself out of his grasp. "For that, the cider is on me." On wobbly legs, she resumed walking, making sure to watch where she was going this time. She didn't need Justin to have to catch her in his arms a second time. Though it was more tempting than she wanted to admit.

That thought made her visibly shudder.

Justin must have misread her reaction as a response to the temperature. He removed his scarf and held it out to her. "Here. You appear to be cold."

She wasn't about to explain what her shiver had really been about. "I can't take your scarf."

He ignored that and stopped her with a hand on her arm. "The only reason you're out here in the cold is because I foolishly revealed some long-lost memory that you're kind enough to help me try to relive. The least I can do is give you my scarf." Turning her to him, he wrapped the feather-light material around her neck.

It smelled of him. Carli sank into the sensation of the soft material against her skin as this time she allowed herself to breathe in Justin's scent.

Carli cast a furtive glance in his direction as they continued walking. Once again, she had to remind herself he was her boss. And there was way too much at stake for her to entertain any romantic illusions where he was concerned. Regardless of how handsome she found him. The last thing she needed at this point in her career was any gossip that she'd gotten ahead professionally by pursuing the boss's second son. She'd had enough of gossip to last her an entire lifetime after her last relationship. According to her oldest sister, the hometown folks were still talking about the details of her breakup a year later. Even if most of it was concern on her behalf, it wasn't the kind of attention she needed nor wanted. Something like that would be all the worse if it was happening to her in a professional capacity.

Not to mention, she had no intention of getting her heart broken again. The wounds were still too fresh. Justin had just told her to be careful. He had no idea how hard she was trying. But it was becoming more and more tempting to throw caution to the wind with each passing moment she spent in his company.

The scent of spice and cinnamon grew stronger the farther they walked. Along the way, they passed display after display of Christmas scenes with moving figurines and colorful backgrounds. Justin found himself actually laughing at some of the funnier ones—including one of a large mechanical dog scarfing down the plate of cookies that had been left out for Santa.

Finally, they approached a small shed with a small line in front. The spot was without a doubt where the delicious aroma had been coming from.

Carli ordered for both of them and handed him a steaming hot cup.

"Be careful," she warned him just as he took it from her. "It's even hotter than it looks."

She waited with expectation as he took a sip. "Well?" she asked. "Was it worth the stop?"

It was good. But Justin didn't say what he was thinking. He didn't tell her that the stop had been worth it simply because of the way she'd looked at him earlier when he'd caught her before she fell. And for the way her bright chocolate eyes were studying him with anticipation right at this moment, simply to gauge his reaction to tasting the cider.

Instead of trying to find the words, he lifted the cup toward his temple in a mock salute.

Carli gave a whoop. "I knew you'd like it!"

The enthusiasm this woman displayed, the sheer enjoyment of the simple pleasantries around her was an utterly new experience for him. She definitely worked hard; what he'd witnessed back in Boston and the level of her success left zero doubt about that. But clearly also appreciated the blessing she'd been given in life. To witness it was like a magnetic pull for someone like him.

Outside of his employees or clients, when had anyone ever really cared what his opinion was? Or if he was enjoying something as simple as a glass of juice outside on a cold December day?

When had anyone bothered to do anything like try to find a way for him to relive a silly childhood memory?

"It's like drinking an apple pie," he told her.

"That's exactly the way it is." She looked around at the various displays surrounding them. "We used to come here every year when we were young children. We don't so much anymore. But it used to be tradition."

He took another sip of his cider and studied her over the rim of the foam cup. "You and your family seem to have had a lot of those."

"Doesn't everyone?"

He shrugged. "I guess I wouldn't know. We didn't really. Unless you count lots of yelling and broken glass."

She reached out and placed a gentle hand on his arm. "You'll just have to start new ones then."

He hmmphed out an ironic laugh. Like what? All he ever wanted to do every Christmas Eve was watch an old baseball game on the DVR and enjoy a peaceful dinner alone. That was traditional enough for him. A picture popped into his head of someone with a startling resemblance to Carli Tynan sitting there at the table with him. He promptly shoved it out of his mind.

"What? It's never too late," she said softly next to him.

Justin didn't reply, just downed the rest of his beverage then tossed the cup into the trash can behind him. Carli hesitated for a moment before turning around. "Come on. Let's go say hello to Santa."

Surprisingly, an hour and half had gone by when they finally made it back to the car. Somehow, Carli had even persuaded him to pet the reindeer after all.

He studied her as they pulled back onto the expressway.

A little of the color had returned to her cheeks now that the car heater was fully on and blowing at them. Many of her wayward curls had escaped the tight band at the top of her head, and several dark tendrils framed her face. Why did she even bother putting her hair up? She'd been licking her lips and biting them after drinking the spiced cider. The abuse from her teeth turned them a pinkish red hue. He had an absurd urge to reach over and rub his fingers over her mouth to soothe them.

Damned if she hadn't been right. The little excursion had been a welcome respite from everything; he would even call it fun. That was the problem. It was way too easy to forget the world and just have fun with Carli Tynan.

He thought about what she'd said back there in the park. Her statement about starting new traditions. She was giving him way too much credit. He wouldn't even know where to start.

Her optimistic words just drove the truth home. They were too different. Trips to parks decorated with Christmas displays were all too common for someone like her. She had the kind of love and affection in her life that fully embodied everything that was good about Christmas. For him, Christmas was just another reminder of all he'd never had and never would.

CHAPTER SEVEN

"THIS IS IT," Carli said, and parked the car behind several others already in the driveway of a double structure colonial complete with a front porch and white picket fence. "Brace yourself," she warned. "Looks like everyone else is here too."

"Uh. Who would that be exactly?"

"Well, my two younger sisters live here. They're just teenagers. Marnie and Perri. Twins actually." She motioned with her chin to the white minivan. "Then there's my oldest sister, Tammy. That's her vehicle right there. Which means my nephew and brother-in-law must be here, as well. And that mini-coupe belongs to my other sister, Janie. She's about two years older than me. And I'm guessing her boyfriend came with her." The last statement held just a hint of tightness, lacking the soft quality he'd heard in her voice when referring to the other members of her family. He knew he hadn't imagined it. Something had happened between Carli and her next older sister.

Carli opened her door and stepped out of the vehicle. "And of course there's my mother and father."

He tried to count in his head all the names she'd just mentioned. How in the world was he going to keep track of all these people? Also, how did they all fit in that small structure?

"Come on. I'll make all the introductions inside," she told him, leaning back into the vehicle. "And you can get cleaned up. It's been a long ride, I know."

It had taken hours to get here. But Justin had to admit, it hadn't felt that way. In fact, he had to admit he was somewhat disappointed that his time alone with Carli in the car had come to an end. They'd decided to come straight to her home, as the delay of traffic made them even later. As much as he would have appreciated the time to stop by his room at the inn, he didn't want to risk being late and rude. Not an ideal first impression.

Though why he was so deeply concerned about Carli's family's perception of him was something of a mystery. He didn't plan on seeing any of these people again once this week was over.

Carli used her key and opened the front door. "Hello? We're here."

They stepped into a small but tidy living room. A large red sofa sat against the wall, covered with thick, plush cushions. A patterned throw rug sat atop the hardwood floor. Several toy trucks lay scattered throughout the area and down the hall. A Christmas tree without the lights turned on decorated the corner by the fireplace. It had to be the coziest looking room he'd ever stepped into.

"In the kitchen," someone called in response. Carli shook off her coat and indicated for him to do the same. She hung up both in a closet adjacent to the front door. He followed her farther inside. The aroma of rich seasonings and an appetizing mix of spices hung pleasantly in the air. He realized he was famished.

"Carli! You're here." A small woman with a broad smile approached them. Her apron had a cartoon picture of a large, red lobster wearing a Santa hat. It said Santa Claws in bold letters across the top.

Justin immediately saw the resemblance. Carli's mother had the same subtle features, the same deep brown colored eyes. She embraced her daughter in a tight hug.

"I'm so glad to have you home," the older woman said. Were those tears glistening in her eyes?

Carli cleared her throat and motion toward him. "Mom. This is Justin Hammond. He's uh…my boss."

Justin extended a hand. "Nice to meet you, Mrs. Tynan."

She ignored his outstretched hand and gave him a tight hug also. "Oh, you must call me Louise."

Justin awkwardly wrapped his arms around her shoulders. He tried to remember the last time he'd been bear-hugged by a middle-aged woman in a long apron, and couldn't recall a single time.

"Thank you for having me, Louise. Your home is lovely." In hindsight, he realized he should have brought some sort of house gift. How embarrassingly uncouth of him. He would have to pick something up in town. But visiting an employee's family in small-town Massachusetts was not his regular MO. He was a bit off his game here.

"Where are the others?" Carli asked, plucking a thick bread stick from a glass plate on the center of the table. She bit off the end and started chewing. Justin found himself momentarily distracted by the motion of her lips. He blinked and forced his attention back to her mother.

"Your father is out getting some groceries. Everyone else went for a quick walk," Louise answered. "Trying to wear out little Ray a bit. He wouldn't even take a nap this afternoon."

Carli smiled. "That sounds like our little Ray."

"He's very excited about his aunt Carli visiting. So it's partly your fault."

Carli laughed. "As if Ray needs an excuse to be over-excited."

"No, no, he doesn't." Louise turned to Justin. "Do you have any nieces or nephews?"

"No, ma'am. It's just me and my brother." Best to answer with a short and general response. No need to get into how Justin barely knew his own brother. Someone like Louise, with the family she had, would never understand the way he and James had grown up. On different sides of the coast. Hardly seeing each other, even on holidays or birthdays. It was the polar opposite of what Carli had grown up with.

"I've heard quite a bit from Carli about hers, though," he added, to turn the conversation spotlight elsewhere. "Can't wait to meet the little guy."

Though what he would say to a small child was beyond him.

Carli couldn't contain her laugh. As Justin's words left his mouth, a small blur in a puffy coat barreled through the kitchen and hurled itself into her.

"Aunt Carli! Aunt Carli! You're here. You're finally here!"

She kneeled down to Ray's height and wrapped her arms around her nephew. A swell of love and affection moved through her core. It never ceased to amaze her how much sheer emotion this child could invoke in her. Simply by the way he reacted whenever he saw her.

"Hey, little man." She tousled his hair. "I've missed you."

"I missed you too!" he said loudly.

Ray had no concept of an inside voice. Despite repeated attempts by all his elders to check him on it.

"You've grown," she observed and earned a huge smile.

"Momma says I'm a weed."

"You're growing like a weed. Let's see if I can even still

pick you up." She gave an exaggerated show of false effort as she lifted him. "Oh, you're so heavy! This is probably the last time I'll be able to lift you."

"Prolly," her nephew agreed.

With Ray still in her arms, she turned to Justin. "I'd like you to meet a friend of mine."

Justin appeared confused. He lifted his hand before dropping it right back down to his side. Then he lifted his other hand and gave a small wave. He was trying to determine the right protocol when it came to meeting a kid. Carli had to hide her amusement at the thought. Why was he always so serious?

"Who is dis?" Ray asked, his dark eyebrows lifted in his small face.

"Don't be rude, Ray," Carli admonished. "This is Justin Hammond. You should call him Mr. Hammond."

"Mr. Hammond," Ray repeated. Only his pronunciation and his missing teeth made it sound like ham bone. Carli couldn't decide whether to laugh or groan at that.

Justin stepped closer to the two of them. "Actually, I'd prefer it if you called me Justin. May I call you Ray?"

The child giggled. "Of course you can! It's my name!" he said with pride. Then to her horror, he added, "And your name is funny sounding."

"Ray…" Carli began but stopped when Justin laughed in response.

"My name is funny?"

Ray nodded. "Yup."

"What do you mean?" he asked with a curious smile.

Carli heard the other adults slowly make their way into the house as Ray wiggled in her arms.

"It's funny cause your last name has ham in it."

Justin lifted an eyebrow, seemingly deep in thought. "Hmm, that hadn't occurred to me. I suppose you're right."

Ray grinned. "Your first name is funny too."

Oh, sheesh. Now he was pushing it, Carli thought. Justin had zero experience with kids. He couldn't be expected to patiently listen to the silly ramblings of a four-year-old regarding the qualities of his name.

But he seemed to be playing along. "My first name too? How so?" he asked Ray.

"'Cause it sounds like something my mom says to me all the time."

"It does?"

"Yeah. Like she says 'Ray, it might be cold out. Put your coat on. Just in case.'"

Justin laughed out loud, and Carli couldn't help the humor that bubbled up from her throat either.

"Or she says 'There's your father. Just in time.'"

"Oh, Ray," Carli admonished, unable to keep the amusement out of her voice. "It isn't nice to make fun of people's names."

Ray turned to Justin. "I sowwy," he said, turning big chocolate-brown puppy dog eyes on him. Though he looked anything but. In fact, he looked plenty pleased with himself at the reaction he was getting.

To his credit, Justin turned serious in a very fake way. "Well, you've certainly given me something to think about," he said.

The others strolled into the kitchen just then. Carli made the proper introductions after receiving a welcoming hug from her oldest sister, Tammy.

Janie, on the other hand, seemed hesitant to approach her. As was she hesitant to approach Janie. Carli hated this. She hated the distance that now seemed so insurmountable between them. Up until a year ago, they'd grown up as close as two peas in a pod. The expression on her mother's face said she was displeased too.

She dared a glance at Justin. He'd noticed the tension in the air between her and her older sister. That much was clear.

And then Warren entered. Carli's chest tightened, and her pulse pounded in her veins. She gave Janie's current boyfriend as polite a smile as she could muster.

"Carli, nice to see you again," Warren said, then went to stand next to Janie. Seeing the two of them so close together still didn't feel right, and she had to look away.

But she was over it all, Carli reminded herself. She had to be.

"Warren. Hello."

She motioned to Justin. "I'd like you to meet Justin."

The two men shook hands just as Ray shouted out, "I think that's Aunt Carli's boyfriend!"

Carli tried not to gasp in shock and horror as she set her nephew down. She didn't dare look in Justin's direction.

"Oh, my God!" Tammy exclaimed, then addressed Justin. "I apologize for my son's behavior. We are working on manners."

"No need for apologies," Justin assured her. Then surprised her by saying, "He's actually quite entertaining."

Carli took a deep breath. "No, that's not right." She corrected the boy. "I just work with Justin."

Ray simply shrugged. "Okay. Wanna see my new truck?"

The innocence of the question immediately ebbed Carli's annoyance. "Sure," she said, and tousled his hair once more.

Ray turned to Justin. "You come too," he ordered with a mischievous smile. Carli was just about to remind him to say please when he impishly added, "Just in case you like trucks too!"

Carli certainly wasn't kidding when she said dinner at her parents' place would be chaotic. Everyone talked over each other; multiple hands reached for various dishes. As the guest, he was offered each dish first. After that, it seemed to be a free-for-all.

Everyone participated in the rapidly changing conversation, even little Ray to the extent that he could. No one shushed the child, no one told him he was a messy nuisance when he dropped half his salad on the floor. In fact, they all actually laughed at the mess he'd created at the base of his chair. One of the twin sisters simply cleaned it up, gave him a peck on his chubby cheek, then sat back down to her dinner.

It was the loudest dinner Justin had ever sat through. It was also the most enjoyable. So different from the silent meals he'd had to endure as a child. If his mother even deigned to join him, that was. And this certainly beat the stuffy business dinners he regularly had to sit through.

Whereas this one had to be the loudest meal he'd ever sat through, if anyone had asked him about that prospect a week ago, he would have said it sounded like a nightmare. So why in the world was he enjoying it so much?

"Justin, would you like another piece of lasagna?" Carli's mother asked.

He shook his head. "That would make it my third piece."

"So what's your point?" Carli's brother-in-law cracked from the other side of the table.

Her oldest sister poked the man in the ribs. "He's just saying that 'cause his average is about four servings each time Mom makes it."

Before Justin could answer, the twins started a mini tug-of-war in front of him with the last bread stick. It finally snapped in two, and for some reason they both thought that was the funniest thing and broke out in a peal of laughter.

Their little nephew joined in. Justin, in turn, couldn't help his own laughter. Apparently, a preschooler's giggles were highly contagious. Pretty soon, the whole table had broken out into laughter.

So this was what family meals normally looked like. A far cry from the silent dinners he and his brother shared around the television while their mom was up in her room wallowing in self-pity and their dad was still at the office. Back then, at least he hadn't been eating alone.

He hadn't even had that much after his mom had taken him away.

Carli watched as Justin laughed at something her brother-in-law told him by the hearth as they both sipped their after dinner coffee. Why was she not surprised that he had somehow fit so well in with her loud and boisterous family?

Sure, the Tynans had a way of making people feel welcome in their midst. But it was as if they'd all known him for years rather than having just met him. She'd daresay Justin seemed like he actually *belonged*.

She sighed. Probably just her imagination. Despite the circumstances, and despite the imminent danger he posed to the existence of her beloved store, Carli had to admit, deep down, he wasn't so bad. In fact, she might actually be growing quite fond of him.

Ray approached him right then and gave a tug on his pant leg. Justin immediately put down his cup and kneeled to hear what the boy had to say. The whole picture tugged at something within her chest, a longing she didn't want to examine in any way.

Carli made herself look away. What in the world was wrong with her? The man had simply had dinner with them. That's all that was happening here.

And a week from now, he'd be go back to being nothing more than a name on the company letterhead.

She turned to go back into the kitchen. As far as she could get from Justin and the picture he made in her family's living room.

Justin waited for Carli the next morning in the lobby of the Sailor's Inn Bed and Breakfast so that they could head over to the toy store. Overall the inn was a quaint, charming establishment unlike anything he would have encountered on the West Coast. The décor screamed New England, complete with a boat anchor hanging above a large hearth fireplace as well as the requisite ship in a glass bottle displayed in the center of the lobby.

Unbelievably, he was hungry. He didn't think he'd be able to eat for another week after the way Carli's parents had fed them last night. Louise had prepared enough food for an entire football team. Not that the numbers weren't damn near comparable. Carli had a large family.

As if reading his thoughts, or perhaps she'd heard his stomach grumbling, a matronly rotund woman appeared from the back holding a tray of steaming muffins.

"You weren't trying to sneak out without eating something first?" she asked.

She then smiled and set the tray next to a silver carafe on a side table against the wall. "I'm Betty Mills. My husband would have checked you in last night."

Justin shook her hand and introduced himself.

"Help yourself," she said, pointing to the tray from which drifted a delicious aroma of sweet sugary dough. "I've made vanilla almond and raspberry chocolate chip this morning. Plus, there's always the standard corn ones."

Justin's mouth actually watered. This certainly beat the dry granola bars he hastily grabbed on his way into work most mornings.

Betty laughed. "Or you can have one of each," she offered, clearly reading his mind once again.

The front door swung open behind them, and Carli walked through, bringing with her a gust of cold New England air.

Betty greeted her with a familiar smile. "Carli Tynan. So nice to see you back in town."

"Good morning, Betty. Justin." She glanced at the muffin tray. "I see you're taking good care of my friend here."

"I'd offer you some too, but I'm guessing Louise has handled that already?"

Carli patted her stomach and rolled her eyes. "She's been feeding me nonstop since I got here."

Justin couldn't take any more talk of food. He reached over and plucked one of the vanilla almond muffins, taking a big bite. A small burst of heaven exploded in his mouth.

He looked up to catch Carli watching him with a knowing smile.

"You're lucky to be here on vanilla almond day. Those are Betty's particular specialty. Though the cranberry comes in a close second."

"They go real well with a cup of coffee," Betty said, pouring him some of the chicory-colored brew. "How do you take it?"

"Black, please," Justin answered and took the beverage from her. The heat from the ceramic mug warmed his hands. He liked his Seattle brew just fine, but the smell of this coffee sparked his senses.

"And what brings Mr. Hammond into town?" Betty asked.

Justin looked to Carli, unsure how to answer. How much was she willing to share with the town about the trouble that had brought the two of them here? He'd been in Westerson less than twenty-four hours and could already tell what a tight, close-knit community it was. Hearing about the potential closing of one of their businesses would probably not sit well.

And it certainly wasn't how he wanted to introduce himself.

To his relief, Carli answered for him. "Justin is here to visit his family's store." She offered no further details.

Luckily, Betty didn't push.

Moments later, they were out on the street among scores of other pedestrians all bundled up against the harsh December air.

"Betty's quite the baker," Justin offered by way of conversation.

"Yes, quite." Carli seemed preoccupied. She had to be thinking about what he would say when after visiting the store. And how much credence his father would give it. He wished he could reassure her, he really did. But he'd been asked his professional opinion. He had an obligation to give it. Honestly and factually.

Even if it meant disappointing the woman next to him. Admittedly, that bothered him more than he cared for. Which made no sense. He had just met her a few days ago. This sense of familiarity and closeness that was developing within him had no basis in any kind of reality. Even so, he wanted badly to believe that it wasn't one-sided.

Several people waved and stopped them along the way to chat. Carli introduced him to everyone. At this rate, they would never get to Hammond's. She seemed to know every other person who walked by. Westerson wasn't the type of town where one could rush anywhere. Small talk and friendly conversation were a developed talent around here. A talent Carli had clearly perfected. She had kind words and a warm smile for everyone who approached.

Until one man in particular turned the corner. Carli's

step actually faltered at the sight of him. Justin immediately recognized who it was. He'd met him last night at dinner. Warren, her sister Janie's boyfriend.

All night, Justin had sensed a strange coldness between the two of them. As if they were both going out of their way to avoid each other. The sister seemed just as uncomfortable when she looked at them.

If he thought he was imagining it, the look on Carli's face right now reaffirmed any suspicion. Justin had no doubt that if it hadn't been so blatantly obvious that they'd spotted him, Carli would have ignored Warren and continued walking.

It was a strange dynamic for a family that otherwise seemed so devoted and close. Had Carli expressed some sort of objection to her sister's boyfriend?

Warren approached from the other direction. He offered a small wave. Carli merely nodded in his direction. To Justin's surprise they all kept right on walking. He'd been fully expecting to stop and say *something*, just as they had with so many others along the way so far. The whole thing made him wonder. Warren had seemed friendly enough last night. He was clearly good to the sister.

But there was no doubt. Whatever issues Carli had with the boyfriend, they seemed to run deep.

Carli had been enjoying the walk to the store. She really had. She'd missed this town. And strolling through the center of Westerson this time of year had always served to lift her spirits. It was doing so now.

Like every other year, the town council had spared no effort or expense with the decorations. Festive wreaths hung on each lamppost. The winterized bushes had been wrapped up like big presents or otherwise adorned with silvery tinsel and bright colorful ornaments. Her fellow townspeople knew how to do Christmas right, and she was glad to that was on display for Justin to see.

But her mood went south when Warren Mathews turned the corner and made a beeline right to them. It had been uncomfortable enough to have him there at dinner last night. For a split second, Carli thought about pretending she hadn't seen him. But he was directly in their line of sight. She had to acknowledge him in some way. So she did, just barely.

"It's just a bit farther, past this corner," she told Justin, more so to break the awkward silence than to give him an ETA update.

Justin remained wisely silent about the nonexchange with Warren just now. She gave him a side-eye glance. His hair was dotted with a slight layer of snow, his strong neck wrapped in a different cashmere scarf. The coat he wore fit him perfectly. Every inch of him looked the competent, successful tycoon that he was.

It was impossible not to notice the double takes that every woman who walked by gave them.

He definitely stuck out in this small town.

At that thought, Carli gave herself a mental kick. This was so not where her focus needed to be right now. Not when they were on their way to the store so that Justin could make observations about the way it was run. About its very existence.

A nervous flutter spun in her gut about what his reaction might be. Last night he'd been warm and friendly, fitting in with her family easily. But his reputation as a no-nonsense, numbers-oriented businessman preceded him. She couldn't let herself forget why they were even here in the first place.

It would be a mistake to take anything for granted when it came to Justin Hammond.

He held the door open for her when they arrived at the store. The heat hadn't quite kicked in yet for the day; a slight chill still hung to the air. It was still early. Yet the shelves were neat, and the displays were cheery and festive.

A tooting whistle sounded overhead. Carli looked up just as a model toy train went past above her head on a hanging track. That was new. Justin looked up too, but he didn't seem impressed. Probably making a mental note of how much constructing it must have cost the company.

"So this is it, huh?" Justin asked.

"Yes. Everything's organized by age group." She explained the layout as they walked. "The toddler toys line the aisles up front. As you move back, you start to get into the board games and such for the older children. Followed by video games."

"Makes sense."

"There's a corner that houses all the reading materials, the Book Nook. And a café that serves coffee, juice and some basic pastries. Shall we start there?"

"Sure."

"Mr. Freider is probably setting up in the café," she informed Justin. "It's in the back." She motioned for him to follow.

The aroma of hot chocolate and freshly baked croissants greeted them as they approached the café counter. Several customers were already in line for a quick breakfast. A young lady she didn't recognize waited on them with a cheery smile. Carli breathed a sigh of relief that Justin was witnessing the early-morning traffic in the store.

She turned to him. "I'd just like to point out that despite the early hour, the store has drawn several customers already."

"You'd like to point that out, huh?"

"Yes."

"The problem is we don't know yet how many of them will actually purchase an item before they leave. Notice there's no one at the registers."

She waved her hand in dismissal at that suggestion. "It's still early. Besides, a lot of people come to look around and help make their child's wish list to Santa."

"Which they may very well go purchase elsewhere. Most notably, online."

She was about to object to that comment when Mr. Freider stepped out of the kitchen area carrying a pitcher of creamer.

"Carli! I've been expecting you." He brightened when he saw them.

He set his load down and offered a hand to Justin. "Mr. Hammond."

"Call me Justin, please."

Carli realized she was holding her breath. Goodness, she was so nervous on Mr. Freider's behalf. The poor man had no idea of the reason behind their impromptu visit into town.

He took Carli gently by the arm. "I'm so glad you've decided to visit again, dear. It's been way too long."

"You sound like my parents, Mr. Freider," she teased.

"I'm just glad you're here. I was worried that scoundrel was going to keep you away for good."

Carli could feel the blood drain out of her face. Justin gave her a curious look. The last thing she wanted to talk about right now was Warren Mathews.

She frantically scrambled around in her brain for a way to head off the topic immediately. But Mr. Freider wasn't having it. He was old school and had no qualms whatsoever about speaking his mind.

"I don't care what anyone says about how these things

are meant to be." He shook his head with indignation and outrage on her behalf. "It's a disgrace the way Warren treated you."

Justin sat down next to Carli in the corner of the store she'd called the Book Nook. It was like being in a small book closet. The three surrounding walls were nothing but shelves of books. They were going through the several binders Mr. Freider had provided them about the store's numbers and operations. Dear heavens, the man hadn't even bothered to computerize any of the tracking data. How did he keep it all organized?

They'd started out in Freider's office, but there were just too many binders to go through and spread out. As a result, Justin felt ridiculous as all the chairs out here were clearly made for small children. Not to mention, customers were constantly stepping around them to peruse the books.

Still, Carli seemed to prefer being out here. And so far, they were both doing a remarkable job of conveniently ignoring Mr. Freider's cryptic comment earlier. It didn't mean Justin had stopped thinking about it, though.

A flash of anger surged through his chest. From what he knew of her so far, Carli was kind and soft hearted. Generous to boot. The thought of someone treating her badly or taking advantage of her made him want to crush something. Or to find the offender and personally make him answer for the transgression.

He gave his head a shake. How caveman of him. Again, none of this was really any of his business. His visit to Westerson would be a short one. He was only here to do a job.

To Carli's credit, she'd been right about the flow of traffic into the store. And he had to concede that people were actually purchasing items at a fairly steady rate at the registers. Maybe there was hope for the location after all. Or maybe he was just trying to come up with ways not to disappoint the lady sitting next to him.

"Well, isn't this a déjà vu!" Mr. Freider approached them, carrying a tray of scones and hot coffee. "Carli Tynan, sitting at the Book Nook. It's like all these years haven't gone by at all."

He set the tray amid the pile of files and binders. "Thought you both might like some refreshments."

"Thanks," both she and Justin said in unison as they both reached for the same scone. He could have sworn an electric current shot through his arm clear to his chest at the contact. Carli looked up at him in surprise. Had she felt it too?

"Please, go ahead." Justin nodded toward the tray, but he continued to let his fingers linger on hers. Heaven help him, she made no attempt to remove her hand either.

Mr. Freider hadn't moved. He stood staring at the two of them, a curious look on his face. "There's plenty more where that came from." He finally turned. "I'll let you two get back to work then."

Justin watched the older man walk away. "What did he mean exactly? About the whole déjà vu thing?"

Carli ducked her head slightly, didn't look up at him. "I spent a lot of time here as a kid. Guess I should admit that. Most of that time was spent right here in this very corner."

"I'm not surprised you were a big reader."

She turned to another page, her gaze still downward. "You have no idea. Sometimes it was the only escape."

He paused, wondering if he was being pushy. What exactly was the protocol under such circumstances? His curiosity won out. "How so?"

She gave a small shrug. "You've seen how loud and

busy living in that house can be. It's always been that way. Sometimes I just needed to be away from it all."

Justin thought about that. He hadn't known anything but solitude. And here she was telling him she'd actually sought that out.

"It's not like it was really noticed when I was gone," she added, shocking him. "As long as I returned home at a reasonable hour."

He waited in silence, giving her a chance to continue or stop. Though he was itching to know the truth behind that statement. He almost breathed a sigh of relief when she started speaking again.

"As you know, I was the middle child," she said, and highlighted an item on the page she was studying. "Sometimes, often, actually, that might be why I was easy to overlook."

"So you sought refuge here."

She nodded. "Books always gave me a whole other world to call my own. And even during the busy months, I always found it peaceful here." She finally looked up at him then. His breath caught at the depth of feeling shining in her eyes. "My sisters always had something that needed tending to. Tammy being the oldest was always on the brink of something new. The twins were so small, and they were double the work. And Janie...well, you've seen Janie." She blinked as if pushing away a thought. "My parents were always busy with one or all of them at once. I thought it best to just try to stay out of the way."

He didn't quite get her last point about her next older sister but didn't dare interrupt her.

"Me, I had my books at Hammond's Toys," she added.

Justin wanted to kick himself. He hadn't fully grasped her connection to this place. No wonder she was so invested in the success of the store. Still, he'd never, ever made a business decision based on anything but hard-core facts and data.

Logically, there was no reason to start doing anything differently now.

So why did he feel like such a lowly heel?

CHAPTER EIGHT

A CHILLY GUST of wind met Carli and Justin as they stepped outside later that afternoon. The light, barely noticeable flurries of earlier had turned into a steady snowfall.

Justin had tried really hard to focus on the plans for the store Mr. Freider had been discussing with them and on the figures he'd presented. But his usual sharp focus had failed him. He couldn't stop thinking about what the store manager had said to Carli. That Warren had somehow done Carli wrong. And then all the things Carli had revealed to him as they sat over the binders.

"Aunt Carli! Mr. Justin!" A child's voice rang out. Across the street, in what looked to be the town square, stood a short squat figure in a thick coat and a bright red hat. Ray. His mom sat reading on a bench a few feet away.

Justin felt an automatic and genuine smile. Carli immediately started walking to them, and he followed.

"Hey, little man," she said when she reached her nephew. "What are you up to?"

His mother stood and gave them a warm greeting.

"We got some hot chocolate and a doughnut. And then I wanted to build a snowman. There it is." He pointed to a bowling-ball-size pile of snow in the center of the square. "I just started."

"He wanted to enter the snowman contest. But he was

told he'd have to wait a few more years before being eligible," Tammy offered.

Ray's lip quivered. "It's not fair. Both Aunt Marnie and Aunt Perri are doin' it."

"They're quite a bit older than you." Carli looked up at her sister. "They've entered again, huh? Those two can't resist finding ways to compete with each other."

"Don't I know it."

Carli addressed Justin. "It never goes well. We'll just have to pray that neither one finals if the other doesn't."

Justin lifted an eyebrow in question. "Or?"

"Or you'll see fireworks in the middle of December."

Before he could comment, he felt a tug on his pant leg. "Wanna help me build a snowman, Mr. Justin?"

The question took Justin aback. He'd never actually built a snowman. Or a snow anything for that matter. Not even as a child. But how hard could it be? You just had to make three big balls of snow, then stack them.

He shrugged. "Sure, why not?"

Carli was staring at him with something akin to surprise on her face. "What?" he asked her. "Do you now doubt my snowman-making ability the same way you doubted my mechanical skills?" He wiggled his eyebrows at her in mock offense. That earned him a giggle from all three of his companions.

"Maybe we should hold our own little competition then?" he challenged.

"Yeah!" Ray chimed in, excitement ringing in his voice. "It'll be Aunt Carli and Mom against me and Mr. Justin. Boys against girls!"

"And who's going to judge?" Carli asked.

Ray looked over to the toy store. Mr. Freider stood by the window working on a Yuletide display. He gave them a friendly wave. "Mr. Freider will!"

Justin held his hands up. "Wait a minute. We need some kind of wager, or it's hardly worth it."

"Losers have to shovel Mom's walkway after the nor'easter," Tammy offered.

"Agreed." Justin gave Ray a fist bump. "Let's get started."

About thirty minutes later, he was definitely regretting his decision. The women had a medium-height structure that they'd clothed with Carli's scarf and decorated with various items from Tammy's handbag. It sported a trendy pair of sunglasses and a bright hair bow.

He and Ray had barely managed to form two balls of snow, and the one they tried to put above the other kept rolling off. Ray looked to be on the verge of tears. But to his credit, he was trying to keep it together.

Justin knelt to his height. "Don't worry. I have an idea. Trust me, okay?"

Ray gave him a brave nod.

They called Mr. Freider out to commence with the judging. He took one look at the males' creation and crossed his arms in front of his chest. "Is your snowman laying down?"

"That's a snow turtle!" Ray informed him.

Mr. Freider bent closer to look at the two uneven balls of snow that Ray and Justin had pushed together. Two black pebbles sat atop the smaller one.

"Those are his eyes," Justin added, trying very hard to keep a straight face.

"I see." Mr. Freider rubbed his chin, deeply considering. He turned to the ladies' snowman, then back to their "turtle."

Ray actually looked nervous. The poor kid was probably holding his breath, Justin thought.

"I have a decision," Mr. Freider declared. "Anyone can make a snowman. But a Christmas turtle? Now that's something special. The boys win!" he said with a dramatic bow in their direction. Ray squealed in delight and ran over to give him a high five.

Tammy and Carli protested with outrage. But Mr. Freider stood firm. "I have made my decision." He shook Ray's hand and then Justin's to congratulate their victory.

It was right then that Justin felt something cold and wet hit the back of his neck. Someone had just fired off a snowball! The culprit was no mystery. Carli had a distinctively smug look on her face. With no hint of guilt whatsoever.

Well, two could play at that game. He picked up a handful of snow and formed it into a tight ball, threw it right at her midsection. But she was too fast for him. She ducked to the side just in time. Then managed to pelt him with another snowball she'd prepared and had at the ready.

In moments, all five of them were ducking and launching snow at each other. Mr. Freider even joined in. Justin was marveling at the older man's accurate aim when Carli smacked him with yet another one. It landed on the side of his head that time. She clearly thought that was hilarious. Her laughter filled the air. Laughter at his expense!

That was it. Justin gave chase. He caught up to her by the side of the large gazebo that stood in the center of the square.

Grabbing her by the waist, he pulled her into his grasp from behind. She giggled and squirmed in his arms.

"You are not getting away. Sore loser."

"Let me go," she demanded, still laughing.

But then he turned her to face him. They stood nose to nose, his arms still wrapped around her middle. Her cheeks were rosy, eyes lit up with merriment. Her curly dark hair was in complete disarray, falling out of her wool knit cap.

She was the most stunning woman he'd ever laid eyes on. He knew he should let her go. Knew they were in the middle of a very public square. But even under her thick coat, he could feel the warmth of her skin. The faint scent of her fruity shampoo tickled his nose.

He was too far gone; there was no way he would be able to stop himself from kissing her.

So he didn't even try to resist.

Carli's laughter died on her lips as Justin leaned in. Before she knew it, somehow his lips were on hers. Her breath caught in her throat at the contact. A heady shiver ran down her spine, clear to her toes. His lips were firm and warm against mouth. Just as she'd imagined. And she had imagined it.

And now here he was, holding her. Kissing her.

This was insanity, complete foolishness. She was standing in the middle of Westerson town square in Justin Hammond's arms as they kissed. The taste of his mouth on hers felt like paradise. Every single cell along her skin tingled with desire. She'd been trying to fight it, but now there was no denying. She was attracted to him like she'd never been to any other man.

It scared her silly.

Justin was merely in New England for a business project. He had his own life, and his own business back on the West Coast. Oh, and there was also the small matter of him being heir to the company she worked for. She had to regain some sense.

With a sigh of regret, she made herself pull out of his grasp. Forcing herself to meet his eyes, she realized Justin looked just as shaken as she was.

A small hand tugged at the hem of her coat. "Hey. I thought you said he wasn't your boyfriend. Why you kissing him then?" Ray demanded.

Heavens, how in the world was she supposed to respond to the child? Not like she had any kind of real answer.

She looked away, desperate to come up with something she could say. Only to find her sister staring at her, eyes wide with shock. Great, just great. There was no way this little event wouldn't be shared with every member of her family.

Mr. Freider muttered something about having to return to the store and walked away. She was certain she'd seen a hint of a smile on the his face.

Correction, Carli thought. The bit of news about Carli kissing her boss would be shared with every member of the town, not just her immediate family. How could she have been so reckless?

She took a deep breath, fighting to regain some composure.

Thankfully, her sister saved her from having to answer Ray when she walked up and lifted the boy into her arms. "Hey, you're looking pretty wet. Let's get you home and cleaned up."

Carli mouthed a silent *thank you*. The look her sister returned left no question that they would be discussing the matter in due time. Carli suppressed a groan at that prospect. Nevertheless, Tammy had just saved her from what would have no doubt been a cringe-inducing conversation with her nephew. Now, if only someone would save her from what was sure to follow with Justin.

Justin looked down out his window at Main Street Westerson. The late-afternoon sun shone glaringly on the thin blanket of snow that covered the town. And word was there was more snow expected. The forecast predicted a powerful nor'easter that really just sounded to him like an overblown snowstorm. If he'd experienced any during his childhood, he couldn't recall. Not that he would. He'd perfected the art of burying his childhood memories over the years.

He was way more focused on the storm that had been brewing inside him. He'd managed to get in a few hours of work, but it had been like swimming against the current. The events of the morning kept playing through his head.

The walk with Carli when she'd reacted so strangely to Warren as they'd encountered him. Mr. Freider's words about whatever had happened between the two of them.

The snowball fight. And what it had somehow inexplicably led to. The way Carli had responded when he'd kissed her.

Justin rammed a frustrated hand through his hair. This was useless. He wasn't going to get anything done when his mind was a jumble of thoughts about Carli.

The digital clock on his nightstand read close to five o'clock. A bit earlier than he normally liked to eat but getting dinner would at least give him something mundane to do. He'd noticed a charming mom-and-pop pizza joint this morning on the way to the store. And the walk would do him good. Grabbing his coat, he took the stairs to the first floor.

Almost everyone he ran into on his way either offered a friendly nod or a smile. Several said a simple hello. This was so not Seattle. Or any other city he'd visited over the years. The townspeople of Westerson were beyond friendly straight to outgoing. It explained Carli's personality somewhat. She was a product of this town.

Maybe it was just the approach of Christmas that had all of them behaving in such a manner. This atmosphere couldn't be a permanent characteristic, could it? He wasn't going to be here long enough to find out.

Either way, he was enjoying it now, but he wasn't the

type who could really fit into a town like this. Everyone knew each other. He preferred the anonymity of the big city.

He made it to the pizza parlor where an early crowd of hungry customers had already gathered. The rich aroma of tangy tomato sauce and yeasty dough made his stomach growl. He'd intended to get a slice or two but decided a whole pie might be in order.

Someone tapped him on the back as he stood in line.

One of Carli's younger twin sisters. "I thought that was you," Perri told him with a smile.

"Fancy meeting you here."

Her eyes narrowed on him with confusion. What a fuddy-duddy thing to say to a teenager. "It must be pizza Sunday in Westerson, huh?" he asked, motioning to the growing crowd.

"Nah, it's always this packed at Diammatta's. Plus there's a hockey game on tonight. Pizza and hockey go great together."

"I suppose they do."

"You don't watch hockey?"

"No, not really. I'm more of a baseball fan."

She shrugged. "Anyway, I hope this doesn't take too long."

"You have plans?" What was there for a teen to do in a town this small?

"I wanna go work on my snowman. For the competition over at the tree farm next week. They decide the winner on Wednesday."

"I heard about that. You and your sister both entered"

Perri rolled her eyes. "Don't know why she bothers. As if she could beat me." There was no animosity or spite in the way she said it. Just a healthy dose of youthful confidence.

"Pretty sure you'll win, huh?" he asked, then thought about his pathetic attempt earlier with Ray. That only had him remembering the kiss he'd shared with Carli.

Damn.

The pizza line was barely moving despite several people taking orders behind the counter. Not that he was in a rush; the only thing waiting for him was an empty hotel room and a bottle of beer from the mini fridge.

"Marnie doesn't stand a chance," Perri declared. "She's been talking smack about it all week. I'll show her. Wait till you see my creation."

"I wasn't really planning on attending, actually."

She looked him up and down. "Well, why not?"

Justin shrugged. "I wasn't really invited."

"Well, consider yourself invited as of this very moment. By the likely contest winner, no less. Oh, and you should join us for dinner tonight too."

It struck Justin how poised this young lady was, how composed and confident. She'd met him two days ago. Yet she felt certain he would be accepted and welcome at her house for dinner, without having to run it by anyone else. Whatever Louise and her husband had done in raising their girls, they'd instilled in them a strong sense of self-worth. A rare thing these days.

The real question was, would Carli feel the same way about Perri's invitation? He had to admit, he really wanted to see her.

"Come on," Perri insisted. "Have pizza at our house."

He did owe the Tynan family a meal. They'd so graciously cooked for him his first night here. The least he could do was reciprocate with pizza tonight.

"I'd love to. On one condition."

"What's that?"

"The pizza is my treat."

She grinned. "I can't think of a reason to turn that down."

Maybe not. But Carli probably might. Would she be angry that Justin had found a way to see her? It was a chance he was willing to take.

It took close to an hour, but they were finally out the door with several steaming boxes of thick crusty pizza with various toppings. Perri made them rush back to the Tynan house to keep them as hot as possible. Between the steam from the boxes and the near run, Justin was in a sweat by the time they reached the front porch.

Carli was the one who answered the door. The shock on her face at seeing him on the other side had him questioning the spontaneous decision to come.

"Look who I found at Diammatta's!" Perri exclaimed as they made their way in. "He's treating us."

Carli's mom and dad were already in the kitchen, pulling out plates and cups. "How nice," both parents said in unison.

He noticed Carli didn't make eye contact as he moved past her to put down the pizzas. A whiff of her shampoo wafted to his nostrils, and his thoughts immediately went once again to the kiss they'd shared. It hadn't been his wisest move, but he'd hardly been thinking straight when he'd kissed her. Hell, he could barely think straight now with her just standing in the same room. He'd thought about that kiss all afternoon, had barely been able to focus on a conference call with his office assistant back home. The way she'd tasted, the way she'd felt in his arms. The way she'd responded.

He knew those things would haunt him for a good long while once he returned to Seattle. He was hardly likely to meet anyone else like Carli Tynan. That's why it made no sense that he was so damn attracted to her. Carli was nothing like the women he normally ran into. Most of the women he'd dated were practically carbon copies of each other. Wealthy, socialite types who could barely be bothered with much more than shopping for the next gala on their calendar.

He and Carli were from two different worlds. She had family, friends and a career she loved. Her Christmas party back in Boston showed she had the affection and respect of her colleagues.

Above all, she worked for his father, a man Justin wanted nothing to do with once this little project was over.

Yes, kissing her had been nothing less than foolish.

Finally, once slices were plated and drinks poured, Carli deigned to acknowledge him with a tight smile, albeit one that didn't quite reach her eyes. "You didn't have to spring for the pizza, Justin," she told him in a clipped voice.

"It was the least I could do after your family's been so gracious."

"It was really not necessary."

The exchange earned a shocked look from both her parents.

"That's just rude," Marnie admonished her, not holding back, like the younger sister that she was. "What she means to say is thank you."

Justin studied Carli's stern facial expression and the tight set of her jaw. Judging by her reaction since he'd first walked in, and the rigid set of her spine right now, she was far from thankful that he was here. In fact, she looked more than ready to toss him out on his behind.

Normally, Carli loved pizza from Diammatta's. Their pies were the best this side of the state. Tonight however, she could hardly taste any flavor. In fact, she may as well have been eating cardboard. No fault could be placed on the cook. It had nothing to do with the food but had everything to do with the man sitting across from her at her parent's kitchen table. She'd almost dropped in shock when she'd opened the door to find Perri standing there with him.

Her behavior bordered on being rude, she was well aware, barely having said more than a few words to him since he'd walked in. Luckily for her, both her younger sisters and parents were seasoned conversationalists.

But what was there for her to say? She could hardly make small talk, pretending that what had happened between them earlier today wasn't foremost in her mind. Justin was thinking about it too. She could tell by the way she caught him looking at her, how his gaze lingered on her lips whenever she took a bite. How in the world was she supposed to try to eat?

When all she could think about was if she would ever be kissed that way again.

Forget the fact that she worked for the company Justin was heir to. Men like him didn't fall for women like her. He was only in New England for a short-term project, one aspect of which she was desperately trying to get him to change his mind about. After that, he would be gone for good.

If she hadn't been able to maintain a relationship with someone she'd known for years and who had grown up in the same town, how could she dare hope to interest someone as worldly as Justin Hammond?

Blessedly, an hour later the dishes were finally cleared and the table wiped down. Carli was more than ready to show Justin the door. But then her father did the unthinkable. He invited Justin to stay to watch the hockey game.

Leaving her with no choice but to join them.

It would look suspicious to her parents to try to get out of it. She never missed watching a game with her father while in town. Her dad already had a roaring fire started in the fireplace when they all made it into sitting room. Normally, she would have grabbed one of the sofa cushions and plopped herself down in front of the flames as they cheered and shouted at the TV. But there was no way she was going to enjoy either the fire or any of the ice action tonight.

If any of her family members sensed her discomfort, they didn't show it.

At the end of the second period, she was more than ready to come up with an excuse and call it a night. But her father caught Justin staring at one of the framed sketches hanging on the wall.

Oh, no.

"Those make us proud of our girl's talent," her father boasted.

Justin raised an eyebrow in surprise. "One of your daughters drew that?"

Her father lifted his chin in a show of pride. "Sure did. That one sitting right there. The one who works for you."

Carli tried not to groan out loud. She did not want to talk about her portrait sketches with Justin Hammond. Especially not tonight. Then her father made it even worse when he added, "It's second-period intermission, Carli. Why don't you show him the others that are hanging around the house?"

Justin turned to her expectedly. She had no choice but to stand up. He followed her down the corridor.

"This one is of my two younger sisters," she said, pointing to a frame hanging near the kitchen hallway. It was a profile picture of Perri and Marnie about four years ago when they were thirteen or so.

She tried to move on, farther down the hallway where a

portrait she'd drawn of her mother hung. But Justin stopped her with a hand on her arm.

"Carli, wait."

She stopped in her tracks, but couldn't look him in the eye.

"First of all, these are amazing," he stated, motioning to the sketch on the wall. "I'm no expert but even to a novice it's clear you have a real talent."

She inhaled a deep breath, oddly touched by the compliment. It wasn't anything she hadn't heard before, but somehow coming from him… It just felt *more*.

"Thank you. It was just a hobby I had a while back."

"You had?"

She shrugged. "I haven't drawn in a while. I have my reasons." Reasons she had no intention of getting into with him of all people.

As far as she was concerned, the last sketch she'd started would be her last one. The only one she'd ever torn to shreds.

Justin looked as if he was ready to question her further but apparently changed his mind. Must have been her closed expression.

"Second," he began, "I know I should I apologize for what happened this morning. In the town square." He took a deep breath before continuing. "But I'd be lying if I said I was sorry."

Well, that was certainly a straightforward and honest statement. She had no idea what to make of it, however. What exactly did he mean? That mistakes happened? Did he even consider it a mistake?

"I think we should just move past it," she blurted out, too tired and too frazzled to analyze any of it further. The truth was, she would welcome his kiss even now. As ridiculous as it was, part of her wished he would take her in his arms right here in the hallway.

"Move past it?"

She nodded with emphasis, though not entirely certain exactly what she was arguing for. "It was a fluke, right? We were both having fun and then things just took an unexpected turn. Nothing more."

Justin stepped closer, so close she could see the hint of shadow that had appeared on his chin since this morning. The scent of his aftershave wafted to her nose, and she had to resist the urge to lean into him and take a deeper sniff.

"So you'd like to just forget it happened."

Carli's answer was interrupted when the front door swung open and Tammy walked in with Ray in tow.

"Aunt Carli. Mr. Justin," Ray squealed when he saw them and made a beeline to where they both stood.

"Aunt Marnie texted that there was pizza. I love pizza!"

Carli took the interruption as a chance to catch her breath, thankful for her clueless nephew's disruption. Things with Justin were getting just a tad too intense. She didn't think she'd be able to give him the same nonchalant response if he asked her about the kiss again.

"Did you guys save me any?" Ray asked with a hint of panic in his voice, as if it just occurred to him that there might not be any pizza left.

"Of course we did," Carli reassured him. "Your favorite, extra cheese. Let's go get you some."

She reached for her nephew's hand and started to lead him to the kitchen.

Justin cleared his throat. "I guess I should get going. I haven't answered any emails all day, and it's already eight o'clock."

Ray stopped in his tracks and turned to him, clear disappointment etched in his small face. "Do you really have to go, Mr. Justin?"

Carli felt a little taken aback. Ray was clearly developing a fondness for him. In the span of two short days, Justin had already made an impression on the little boy. Her heart sank. It was no wonder. Besides Carli's father and his own dad, Ray was surrounded mostly by women. Another man around was probably a real novelty for him. He was going to be heartbroken when Justin left. Add that to the list of casualties when Justin walked out of their lives for good in less than a week.

Justin leaned over to Ray's height. "I'm afraid so."

"Can you come over tomorrow? Aunt Carli and I are baking cookies."

Carli groaned inwardly. She'd promised Ray on the phone they would make a batch of Christmas cookies, then spend part of the day decorating them.

Why did her family keep inviting Justin to events? First Perri, now Ray.

She couldn't exactly rescind the invitation. Even if had just come from a four-year-old.

"I would," Justin answered, "but I'm not much of a cook."

"That's okay. I can show you what to do. Please?" He gave Justin a big, toothless grin. "Me and Aunt Carli could teach you how."

Justin looked up and met her eyes above her nephew's head. "I'd like that," he said. "I'd like that a lot."

CHAPTER NINE

CARLI TOSSED AND TURNED. Her bedside clock said it was 12:30 a.m. This was the same bed she'd slept in as a teenager. Right in this very room. She was never uncomfortable here. Not even during all those years of dramatic teenage anguish. But tonight was a different story. She couldn't find a comfortable position. And she couldn't seem to fall asleep.

Her thoughts kept returning to the man about three blocks away at the Sailor's Inn Bed and Breakfast. Was he fast asleep as was likely at this hour? Or was there a chance he was thinking about her?

He'd seemed genuinely interested in her artwork. But she wasn't quite ready to talk about that yet.

She needed sleep. But it was no use. Huffing out a breath, Carli got out of bed and put on her slippers. She walked over to the window and lifted the blind. She could see the rooftop of the B and B from where she stood. From there, her imagination took over. She thought of Justin in his bed, under the covers. A man like him probably slept with only pajama bottoms. Or nothing at all.

She sucked in a breath at that thought and tried to force the image out of her head.

This was the closest she'd ever come to fantasizing about a real actual man in her life. Not even with ex-boyfriends had she done such a thing. But here she was, in the dead of night, unable to get Justin Hammond out of her mind. A curse escaped her lips on a whisper. Damn him for kissing her the way he did. And damn her for responding. What a mistake. She should have never gotten playful with him in the first place. Why, oh, why hadn't she just said hello to her nephew and then walked away when she'd seen him in the town square? If only she could go back in time and stop herself from throwing that snowball.

It was such a ridiculous thing to wish for that she couldn't help but laugh. To think, an ill-timed snowball fight had led to such turmoil within her. She would have happily gone on with her life, admiring Justin from afar. But now there was no turning back from the line she had crossed. And that's exactly what she'd done—crossed a line.

Well, maybe there was no turning back time or rectifying the mistake she had made. But she could certainly vow to be more cautious in the future. From now on, for the week or so that she and Justin were in Westerson, she would be the utmost professional. She wasn't one of those women to wallow in her mistakes, but she certainly made sure to learn from them.

Starting tomorrow morning, Justin would see nothing but the serious and accomplished career woman that she was. She'd make sure to steer the conversation toward business matters and details surrounding the store and its operations.

She just had to figure out how to do that exactly, while baking Christmas cookies with the man all day. Right. Easy-peasy. Carli sighed and walked over to the bookcase in the corner of her room. Plucking out one of her childhood favorites, she settled back onto the bed and opened the well-worn pages to one of her preferred chapters.

May as well read, she thought. There was no way she was going to fall asleep anytime soon.

The smell of newly baked muffins and freshly brewed coffee hit Justin as soon as he left his room. Betty was already pouring a cup when he reached the small dining room.

She handed it to him. "I heard you coming down the stairs," she told him with a bright warm smile.

Justin blinked as he took the cup and uttered a heartfelt thanks. He couldn't remember a time someone had listened for him in the morning just to have a cup of coffee ready. No doubt Betty was simply being an attentive innkeeper. Still, he felt oddly touched by the gesture.

She handed him a napkin as he sat down at one of the small linen-covered tables.

"I also baked more of those vanilla almond muffins that you liked so much," she told him offhandedly.

Justin felt his mouth water at that bit of news. He was going to gain so much weight this week. "But I thought those were only made on Saturdays?"

"Normally. But you seemed to enjoy them so much. I wanted to make them for you again."

Justin felt an odd sensation at the base of his throat. Perhaps Betty really was simply responding to the tastes of a paying customer. But this was a novel experience for him. The large chains and glamorous hotels he usually stayed in offered the utmost in glitz and luxury. But no one had ever gone out of their way to specifically make something just because he'd liked it.

Hell, no one would have even noted such a thing, even in one of the establishments where he was a regular, highly regarded guest. The notion left him with an unexpected sense of familiarity. "I know you must be busy, Betty, but do you have a minute or two to join me?"

She didn't hesitate and pulled out a chair. "That would be lovely, thank you. It will give me an excuse to put off the myriad of items on my to-do list this morning."

"Glad to oblige," he said, and gave her a conspiratorial wink.

"And what are your plans for the day?" she asked him.

Justin grabbed one of the muffins and split it open. Aromatic steam arose from the center. "Unbelievably, I'll be baking Christmas cookies."

Her smile grew. "Why is that so unbelievable?"

He swallowed. "It's nothing I've ever done before. Nor ever expected to do."

Betty's eyebrows drew together. "You've never baked Christmas cookies? Not even as a child?"

He wasn't aware it was so unheard-of. The truth was, his mother hadn't been the baking type. Heck, she hadn't really been the *mother* type in any way. There were always baked goods and pastries laying around in the various kitchens he'd been in over the years, but he'd be hard-pressed to say where they'd come from.

"Well, I imagine the Hammonds had plenty of people on staff to bake for them. I guess it makes sense that you never did so yourself."

Justin wasn't going to get into the whole Christmas conversation and tell this kindly woman that cookies were the last thing on his mind whenever the holidays came around. And then when he and his mother had left New England, it had just become another day.

Christmas celebrations were a family affair for most of the world. He had a brother, but he may as well have been an only child. And even the parent he'd grown up with had barely been around. Very different than the way Carli had grown up, for instance.

"So how'd you get corralled into it then?" Betty asked.

"A very persuasive four-year-old," Justin answered, hardly believing it himself. It was difficult to say no to that little nephew of Carli's.

She laughed at his answer. "I should have known. Ray can be quite persuasive when he wants something," she said, echoing his thoughts.

"He certainly had my number."

He didn't tell her that there was more to it. Or about how he knew he'd be spending this Sunday alone otherwise. How he'd jumped at the chance to be able to spend it with Carli. Even doing something as mundane as baking cookies.

Betty somehow seemed to read his thoughts yet again. "Mmm-hmm. And tell me, was Ray the only reason you agreed to do this?"

He lifted an eyebrow in question, though he obviously knew what she was getting at. The woman was very perceptive, it appeared.

"I just thought I'd give it a try."

She wasn't falling for it. "I see. And it had nothing to do with the way you were looking at Carli Tynan yesterday morning, I suppose."

Wow. Was everybody in this town so direct? He bit down on another piece of muffin as he tried to scramble for a way to respond.

"I'm sorry," Betty began, sparing him. "It's just that I've known that girl since she was knee-high. One of the sweetest, purest souls you'll ever meet. She doesn't deserve to have her heart broken."

Again. Though unspoken, the word hung in the air as clear as day between them. Then the older woman suddenly stood up with a soft clap of her hands. "Oh, dear. I hadn't realized how late it was getting. I really should get to those chores. Please excuse me."

"Of course." Justin stood, but she'd already turned away and was walking to the front desk.

Leaving Justin with the succinct feeling that, sweet old lady or not, he'd just been issued a gentle yet clear warning.

Carli opened the door to him with a yawn, then stepped aside to let him in. She was dressed in baggy gray sweatpants, an oversize flannel shirt and thick fuzzy socks. Her hair was pulled back in a loose ponytail at the base of her neck but several tendrils had made a blatant escape and framed her face haphazardly.

She looked downright adorable.

What was wrong with him? Justin thought as she took his coat and hung it. He'd been less attracted to women wearing scanty lace panties than he was to her right now. None of it made any sense.

He glanced around the empty house. "Where is everyone?"

She stifled another yawn and shook her head. "Sundays are pretty busy around here."

"I see."

"My parents are out running errands after services, the twins had breakfast plans with friends. And Tammy's due to drop Ray off. But she's always late, usually because it can be a military level challenge getting a four-year-old out the door. Particularly on a Sunday when *The Squigglies* are on."

"*The Squigglies*?"

"Ray's favorite TV show."

He followed her to the kitchen. "Can I get you some more coffee? Though I'm guessing Betty has already filled you up to the brim."

People in this town really seemed to know each other well. "Correct call."

"Just as well. I might actually need the full pot for myself," she said through yet another yawn.

"Long night?"

She didn't look at him as she poured her coffee. "I didn't get much sleep. Sometimes I have trouble sleeping right before a big storm hits."

For some reason, her statement didn't quite ring true. "I've never heard of that. Weather-induced insomnia."

She glared at him over the rim of her coffee cup, so intensely that he had to stifle a laugh. So what was the real reason for her insomnia? What were the chances it had anything to do with him? He was most likely just flattering himself. But it was an intriguing notion. Lord knew he'd spent more than a few waking moments overnight remembering that kiss. The way she had felt in his arms, the warmth of her body up against his. The way she'd tasted.

He cleared his throat. "So tell me, just how bad is this storm supposed to be? When is it due even?"

She swallowed the gulp of coffee and sighed with pleasure as it went down. The whole image sent a surge of longing through his chest. He gripped the granite counter in front of him just to give his hands something to do.

"Well, it's a nor'easter. Set to bring several inches of snow with high, gusting winds. And of course, out here on the Cape there's always the real risk of flooding."

Justin recalled nasty storms from his childhood in Metro Boston. The way he'd hide under thick blankets as the wind rattled the windows. But not much else. He must have blocked it out. Too bad there was no real way to block out everything.

"And it's due to hit sometime tomorrow night." Carli answered the second part of his question.

"No one seems terribly nervous."

She shrugged. "Winter storms are a way of life around

here. Some things you just can't change." She gave him a pointed look.

Wasn't that the truth? If he could, he would change the way he was starting to feel. Carli had awakened a longing within him that he hadn't known existed. More than his attraction to her physically, it was her warmth, her humor, the way she interacted with her family and friends. The combination was like a gravitational pull that seemed to suck him into her orbit. It made no sense; he would have to get over it. Carli deserved someone with the same sense of belonging and roots that she'd known all her life. He was too far removed from being such a person.

He'd remember kissing her for the rest of his life; that tender, sweet moment would live with him from now on. A cherished memory of a woman who could never be his.

"I guess not," he answered. Such a simple response. It warranted no further conversation. Nothing more needed to be said. On the surface anyway.

If he could tell her everything, if he could bare his soul, he'd admit that right now he wanted nothing more than to repeat the mistake he had apologized for. He wanted to pull her up against him, right here in her parents' kitchen and taste her plump soft lips. He wanted to run his fingers through her hair and feel her warmth.

No, he couldn't come out and say all that. But there had to be a way to somehow convey how impressed he was of the woman Carli Tynan was. Or how fond he'd grown of her in such a short time, even though it couldn't lead to anything more.

He was trying to come up with the words when they were interrupted by the shuffle of small feet running through the house toward the kitchen.

Any further revelations would have to wait.

* * *

Justin Hammond had no idea how to separate an egg. Carli had to hold in her laughter as she watched him crack it open then stare blankly at it in his hands, clearly trying to figure out how to get the yoke apart from the rest.

When he reached for a spoon to do heaven knew what, she figured she'd better intervene in the interest of avoiding a food-borne illness.

"Here, let me help."

He looked so grateful that she had to suppress another laugh. Between Ray and Justin, she'd be hard-pressed to decide which one of them was less useful in the kitchen. So far, she might have to say it was Justin. As if to challenge that conclusion, her nephew chose that moment to knock over a bowl of sifted flour, making a colossal mess on the floor.

"Oops."

Carli sighed. Something told her they'd be heading to the bakery or they'd have to do without Christmas cookies this year. Her parents were both still out on their errands. Tammy had begged to run to the nail salon while they watched Ray. Maybe she should just call one of them now and have them pick up a box from Patty's Pastries on their way home.

She was debating whether to pull out a broom and dust pan or a vacuum when Justin somehow managed to drop both parts of the egg right into the pile of flour Ray had just spilled.

"Oops." This time, both males said it unison.

Carli didn't know whether to cry or just run out of the room screaming. Let someone else deal with all this.

Of course, that wasn't an option. She grabbed a large kitchen towel and threw it at Justin. "You work on the egg that got on the counter. While I try tackle the mountain of flour on the floor."

An hour later, they hadn't even managed to put anything into the oven. Yep, no doubt about it. Someone was going to have to make a bakery run.

The entire kitchen was a disaster area. She'd seen neater construction sites in Metro Boston. But just to go through the motions, for Ray's sake, she walked into the pantry where her mother kept the holiday themed cookie cutters. As if any of their creations would actually be viable enough to hold any kind of shape. Except for perhaps one mound of sugar cookie dough, they were batting zero.

A loud clanging sound followed by Ray's horrified scream had her dropping the cutters and running back out into the main area.

"What happened?"

Ray's lip quivered as he looked up at her. Justin seemed at a complete loss. Half the counter and part of the floor were covered in a shiny puddle of green.

"I don't really know," Justin began. "We were trying out the food coloring, trying to decide which color to use."

"I dropped the whole bottle," Ray wailed. Large fat tears began to roll down his cheeks.

Carli immediately ran to him.

"It was my fault," Justin said, ramming his hand into his hair. "I shouldn't have let him play with it."

Ray climbed off the counter stool he'd been standing on and ran straight into her arms. "I made a mess, Aunt Carli. And now we have no cookies."

Carli didn't doubt that the latter statement was the real cause of all the tears. She brushed them off his wet, ruddy cheeks.

"Oh, buddy. It's okay. It was just an accident."

Justin swiftly crouched next to them both. "Ray, it was my fault. I should have known better. Please don't cry."

For an insane moment, Carli had the thought that Justin might need comforting even more than the child. He seemed really shaken. He'd clearly never been around a crying child before. Heaven help them, he didn't realize they did it all the time.

Or was there something else behind his inflated response to the minor disaster?

Ray hiccupped on another sob.

"Hey, we'll still have some cookies," she reassured him. "This is no big deal." She spoke over his head, looking straight into Justin's eyes.

Her mother chose that moment to walk in. Taking in the scene, she blew out a deep breath. Then she went over to her grandson. Ray pulled away and ran to his grandmother as soon as he saw her.

"I ruined the cookies, Nana."

"Mmm-hmm. And the kitchen is a mess," she said in an even, soothing tone. "But it's nothing that can't be fixed. Okay?"

Ray sniffed and nodded.

"Let's go get you cleaned up," she said, and picked him up.

"Thanks, Mom!" Her mother could comfort Ray like no one else could.

"Don't thank me," Louise threw over her shoulder as she walked out with her grandson. "Just get that mess cleaned up. Both of you."

"Yes, ma'am."

Poor Justin looked like he'd just run through a minefield. "So that went well."

He blinked at her. "Where do we start?"

She pointed to the one ball of dough on the counter

that had somehow survived, albeit it was the color of a mossy lake. "I say we try to salvage that dough so that we can throw at least one batch in the oven. Then we start scrubbing."

"You still want to bake? Using that dough?"

"Sure. Why not?"

"For one thing, it's green. Very green."

She shrugged. "So, we'll have green cookies."

"Uh-huh."

"Are you okay?"

He ran a hand through his hair. "I'm not sure. The little guy was pretty upset."

"He's four. It doesn't take much. He'll forget about the whole fiasco by bedtime."

"He will?"

"Of course."

"If that's true, it will be thanks to you. And the way you handled it. Your mom too."

"How else would I have handled it?"

He gave her a blank, confused stare. "You were just so... I don't know...gentle. And understanding." He took a deep breath. "And your mother was the same. Even as she agreed that the cookies were ruined, she calmed and reassured him."

"That's what one does when it comes to children. They're just learning their way."

"I guess I wouldn't know."

Carli grabbed a roll of paper towels and tore off a good amount. The green was starting to settle into her mom's granite counters. She handed a few to Justin, who followed her lead and began wiping furiously. "Maybe not. But you were a child once."

He snorted. "Trust me when I tell you, I don't ever recall any adult behaving quite so evenly after a major mishap. Or even in general."

Carli's heart nearly burst in her chest. How could that be? "You don't?"

Justin shook his head. "No. When I did something wrong, which was often, I got a thorough lashing of the tongue. Followed by some form of punishment. Then my mother would make sure my dad heard about what I did and what an awful handful I was, usually the moment he got home. That always led to loud, long arguments with plenty of door slamming."

"Oh, my God." She stilled. "Justin, that sounds terribly unfair."

"It's how I remember. I suppose a lot of it was my fault. I should have tried harder."

"You can't be serious. You were a child."

"Still, I was aware enough to realize my behavior was causing strife."

"Like every other child."

He shook his head. "Not really. Not James. I can't ever recall him acting out. It was always me."

"I'm sure James had his moments. It's just that some children are more active than others."

"Maybe. My behavior had ramifications for him too. He'd always turn tail and hide in his room whenever it started. I knew he was angry with me for causing so much trouble."

Carli's heart sank. She wanted to cry for the little boy Justin must have been. She doubted he was anything more than an energetic and curious child like so many others. Apparently, his parents used that as an excuse to vent their own issues and anger. To make it all worse, the two brothers had apparently turned on each other as a result.

He took another deep breath before adding, "So I know

he must have blamed me for the destruction of our parents' marriage."

"How can that be?"

"On some level, he's right."

"Don't say that. A mere child can't cause the breakup of a marriage. There has to be underlying issues at play."

"You're right. But I caused the final fight that led to my mother reaching her last nerve, so to speak."

"What happened?"

Justin was wiping the counter, not looking at her as he spoke. The events he was recalling happened years ago, but they seemed to have left considerable if invisible scars.

"It was Christmas Eve. The big tree had been set up in the main foyer. I couldn't stop admiring it. It was so majestic. Bright lights and shiny ornaments. And it was so tall, I could barely see the top."

Oh, no. Carli could guess where this was going.

"I remember one particular ornament. Just out of my reach. A Red Sox catcher's mitt. It looked more like a toy. I just wanted to play with it for a bit. I was going to put it right back. But when I jumped up to grab it, the whole tree fell over. Almost all the ornaments broke."

"Oh, Justin. You must have been so scared."

"You have no idea. I came so close to running out the door in that moment. Thought maybe I could just keep running and never go back."

Carli noticed he'd bunched up the paper towels into a tight ball, gripping it in his fist.

"But my mother came rushing down the stairs. She kept yelling over and over how I'd been told so often to leave it alone. And why couldn't I just listen. She called my father and demanded he come home right then."

Carli's gasped in horror at the woman's reaction. To a simple accident that could have very well severely injured her son. She'd never wanted so badly to give another adult a reassuring hug. To hold him and tell him he'd done nothing wrong all those years ago. If anything, he'd been the one who'd been betrayed and disappointed. But though her arms itched to hold him, she clenched her muscles instead. It was doubtful Justin would want her sympathy. He seemed way too proud for that.

"What ensued when he arrived is not a pleasant memory," Justin continued.

"I'm sure it wasn't." She figured he didn't have too many pleasant memories based on what he was revealing to her right now.

"I was young, but I remember the expression on James's face. He'd turned white as a ghost. I'll never forget what he said later that night. We could hear our parents having it out upstairs. He just walked over to me and gave me a hard shove. I couldn't blame him. He was so angry."

Carli was afraid to guess and almost didn't want to ask. But she had to. "What did he say?"

"He said he hated me."

She couldn't help it. Walking over to where he stood, Carli rubbed a soothing hand along his arm. He'd gone tight and rigid.

"That was the last time I saw him until we were well into our teens. Simply coincidentally at some boating event on the Charles. And didn't see him again after that for years."

What a burden to bear as a child, Carli thought. Justin had been too young to understand that his parents' tumultuous relationship hadn't been his fault.

"You can't believe you were the real cause of their divorce."

"I know that now. But for years I kept replaying that day in my mind. If only I had just left the tree alone."

"You were a child." She wanted to just say it over and over again until it somehow sunk into his psyche.

"Maybe. But I was old enough to know better."

"You can't honestly believe that. Sooner or later something was going to happen that triggered the same result—your parents didn't want to be together."

He gave her an indulgent smile. "Interesting theory. I always wonder though."

"Wonder about what?"

"What would have happened if I hadn't been their son. After all, I seemed to be the cause of all the animosity. If it wasn't for me, they probably would have been the perfect family who had everything. But then I came along."

Carli could no longer stop herself. Her arms automatically went up and went around Justin's wide shoulders in a tight embrace. They stood that way silently for several lengthy moments. There didn't need to be any words between them. Right now she just wanted him to feel her understanding and her support, wishing with all her heart that someone had done the same years ago when he'd been a small boy.

A boy who thought his family hated him.

CHAPTER TEN

JUSTIN WANTED TO kick himself. He hadn't meant to get into the whole sordid story of his childhood and what had led to him and James growing up on opposite coasts. But he'd just been so struck and so touched at how she'd gently dealt with Ray just now. Plus, it was so easy to talk to her. He'd be hard-pressed to say why that was. Never before had he divulged so much of his past to anyone, let alone a woman who he'd essentially just met.

He was usually much more restrained, more in control. But what little of it he had snapped like a stretched rubber band when she wrapped her arms around him and held him against her. This felt right; *she* felt right. He could smell the perfumed scent of her soft, delicate skin. Mixed with the hint of sweetness in the air, it shook his senses.

He had to taste her again.

Lifting her chin, he watched as desire shaded her eyes. She had the longest lashes. Her lips were lush and beckoning. He knew what he was about to do wasn't wise. He was technically in this town as her boss on a project. He had no business kissing her. Even as that thought ran through his head, he reached down and took her lips with his own.

She tasted as good as he remembered. No, even better. Like honey and forbidden fruit. He thought he might lose his mind when she responded. With a soft sigh against his mouth, she molded herself tighter against the length of him.

Unlike in the square, this time they were alone. The knowledge brought a heady sense of excitement that he found difficult to clamp down on.

Placing his hands against the small of her back, he pulled her even closer. He wanted her to feel his full reaction. She had to know how attracted he was to her. More than he'd felt for any other woman. Inexplicable on every logical level, but there it was.

But it was more than a physical attraction. He'd just opened up to Carli Tynan like no one else before. Her response had been to try to comfort him, to reassure him with both her words and her touch.

Her hands went up to his shoulders and she gave him a small nudge back, and he pulled away from the kiss.

"We really shouldn't be…" she whispered against his mouth.

"I know." But he guided her with his body up against the counter and kissed her again, deeper. She gasped in shock but didn't try to stop him.

If anyone had told him last week he'd be standing in a rustic New England kitchen kissing a Hammond employee, he would have laughed in their face.

The wisest thing to do would be to pull away. On top of everything else, they were in her parents' kitchen for heaven's sake. That reality was driven home when they heard the water turn off upstairs just as someone walked in through the front door of the house.

Carli jumped back and jerked out of his arms. She ran around to the other side of the kitchen island, clearly putting distance between them. Rubbing her lips, she averted her eyes.

Justin ran a hand down his face. How had things between them gotten so heated, so out of control? He'd just barely delivered an apology for the first time he'd kissed her.

"I don't know how that happened," he began before Carli held up a hand to stop him.

Her sister Tammy entered the kitchen at that very moment. She stopped in her tracks as soon as she took in the scene. Justin tried not to groan out loud as Tammy's gaze traveled from her sister to him, then to the mess in the kitchen before landing back on Carli's bewildered face.

"You have some 'splainin' to do," she addressed her sister.

"Yes, she does," another voice chimed in as Carli's mother walked in. "Carli Tynan. That food coloring is going to leave permanent green stains on my counter. Why in the world have you two not cleaned it all up yet?" she demanded to know and then gave Justin a scolding glare for good measure. He squelched an urge to actually step back.

And now he was standing in that same style kitchen being reprimanded by the Hammond employee's mother. The whole scenario could be straight out of a sitcom.

Carli looked like she didn't know whether to laugh or cry. He felt pretty torn himself.

"This is all my fault."

Carli actually stomped her foot. "No, it's not. It just happened. Ray spilled the food coloring by accident. No one is at fault." She emphasized the last word.

Tammy gasped while Carli's mother tilted her head. "I must not have made myself clear," Louise said. "All I care about is that it gets cleaned up. Now."

"Yes, ma'am," they both said in unison. Tammy's sisterly smirk was undeniable as she followed her mother out of the room.

Carli let out a deep sigh as she watched the other two

women leave. Grabbing the paper towels off the counter, she tore off a bunch before throwing the roll to him without warning. He caught it as it landed on his chest.

"Justin?"

"Yes?"

"You are really bad at making cookies."

Forty-five minutes later, Carli pulled the final tray of cookies out of the oven and set them on a rack to cool. They were definitely the greenest sugar cookies she'd ever seen.

Justin leaned over and gave them a long look. "They don't look like sugar cookies."

She didn't care. She just wanted this whole afternoon to be over. Also, she wanted to stop dwelling on the way Justin kissed.

"They look more like mint cookies," Justin added. He was right.

"Or perhaps spinach," she said, and earned a snicker.

They'd worked mostly in silence as they'd baked and cleaned. Everyone else seemed to have left. Traitors. No one had wanted to stay and help clean the mess. Not that she could blame them. Her mother's counter and a good portion of her floor tiles still held a greenish hue.

"All that matters is how they taste," she told Justin, poking one of the star-shaped cookies. Though it was still hot, she gingerly picked it up and tasted a small piece. "See, they taste great." She held it up to him. "Try it."

Justin's reached to take it from her. The touch of his hand on hers triggered another fiery tingle along the edge of her skin. Dear heavens, she was a fool. She had to fight this crazy attraction. He would be gone from New England and out of her life within a week. She worked for his family business. What was she doing kissing the man and then fantasizing about it afterward?

She had to get out of here.

"We should head to the store," she blurted out.

"The store?"

"Yeah, Hammond's Cape store. The reason you're here in town."

He gave a quick nod. "Of course. I was hoping to stop in there a bit today."

"It's a good time to go. Sundays are crafts days. Mr. Freider always has some kind of activity set up for the kids. I think it's gingerbread houses this time."

"Sounds fun. As long as it doesn't involve any baking," he quipped, then frowned as if realizing the lameness of the joke.

"I know Ray's been looking forward to it. We'll bring him with us. He should be up from his nap soon."

And he'd also make for a useful buffer between her and Justin, she added silently. They'd been in way too close proximity for the past several hours.

"Great idea."

Carli was right. By the time they got to Hammond's with Ray, the little boy had completely forgotten about the epic baking disaster and was back to his regular bouncy self. The prospect of decorating a gingerbread house proved an effective distraction.

If only Carli could find a distraction for herself. She was all too aware of Justin still. And all too quick to recall his kisses. Subconsciously, she ran a hand over her lips.

Stop it.

"This is a great crowd—" she made sure to point out "—despite the prospect of a major snowstorm that usually keeps people indoors."

"Point taken," Justin acknowledged.

She smiled with satisfaction. At least she had that much

going for her, despite the circus that this visit was turning into.

Ray saw a little friend and immediately ran over to where the other child was setting up his craft area. He tugged Justin along with him.

"Hi, Josh," he said to the other boy, pronouncing the end of the name with a "th" sound. "This is my friend Justin," he added, and pointed up. "You know, like just in time."

Josh giggled and Ray looked pretty proud of himself. Justin crouched to both boys' level. He stuck out his hand.

"Nice to meet you, Josh. I'm a good friend of Ray here. You know, like ray of sunshine."

He said it with such a straight face that Carli had to laugh. Now both boys were giggling.

"Do another one," Ray demanded.

"Sure, ray-nee day."

The two boys collapsed on each other in a fit of giggles now.

"Your friend is funny," Josh proclaimed, and laughed some more. Justin was so naturally at ease with children. No wonder Ray had grown so fond of him in such a short time. Carli's eyes suddenly stung as she watched the three of them. It broke her heart that Justin had never been afforded the opportunity to be that carefree when he was little.

So different from the way she'd grown up. The Tynan girls had been pretty fortunate as children. Things were often crazy and hectic when you had four other siblings. It was a fact of life that things could get very competitive with five girls under one roof. Her younger twin sisters were constantly trying to better each other.

But she'd truly been blessed with a caring family unit and loving, doting parents. She couldn't deny that, no matter how betrayed she'd felt last year. Not only by Janie and

Warren, but by the way her family had reacted in response. Carli tried not to bristle at those thoughts. She loved every last one of her family members, she really did. With all her heart. But not a single one of them had shared in her outrage. Not even Tammy. Essentially, they'd all just expected her to accept it and move on. For the sake of family harmony, no doubt. No one bothered to try to put her feelings first. The betrayal still stung, even after all these months.

"Hello. Earth to Carli. Come in, Carli." She looked up to find Justin waving a hand in front of her face.

"Sorry, I was just admiring all the kids' handiwork."

He nodded, then glanced around the store as the boys continued. He had to be noticing the numerous people in the aisles and line leading up to the checkout area. He had to see how well the store was doing. She just had to make him realize that it had the potential to be this way throughout the year. She knew Mr. Freider could pull it off. Carli would do whatever she could to help.

She turned to Justin to tell him so, but just right then he leaned over Ray to help him mount the base of his gingerbread house. Her nephew's smile widened with appreciation. And she knew no matter Justin's thoughts on the store, she was glad he was here with them.

Ray's gingerbread house was a complete failure. Between that and the baking fiasco earlier, Justin had to admit that he didn't possess a creative cell in his whole body. It didn't help that Ray kept popping the candy corn and gum drops into his mouth rather than using them as decorations.

"Your parents are here," Carli said to Ray, then took him by a sticky hand toward where Tammy and her husband, Raymond, had just walked in. Tammy gave her sister a hug. Her brother-in-law did as well, then turned to shake Justin's hand.

"Thanks for taking care of the little tyke," he said to them both. "We saw the cookies at the house. Decided to make mint ones this year, huh?"

Tammy laughed out loud, and Carli gave her a useless punch on the arm.

"What did I say?" her brother-in-law asked.

"Nothing. Never mind."

He shrugged and picked up his son. "Guess we'll see you all tomorrow then. Unless this storm has everybody housebound, that is. Looks like a nasty one."

Justin watched as the three of them left the store. Tammy hooked her arm inside her husband's as he carried their son. It was such a touching domestic scene. So simple. So pure.

For an insane moment, Justin thought about himself as part of such a picture. An image of him and Carli walking arm in arm the same way sprang into his head. He shook it away.

Hammond men didn't do the whole family thing. Look at what a fiasco it had been when his parents had tried.

"We should get going," Carli said, interrupting his thoughts. He was reaching for his coat when Mr. Freider came rushing out to them. He held a framed photo in his hand.

"Wait. Justin, I have something for you." He held out the frame.

Justin reached for it, unsure what he was looking at. Then an unfamiliar sensation settled across his chest as he realized what it was.

"I don't understand."

"After you left yesterday, I remembered I had it. Thought you might want it as a memento."

"What is it?" Carli leaned over her arm to look.

"It's a newspaper clipping. Of a photo of me as a little boy." He held a toy truck in his hand, a big grin on his boyish face. He couldn't have been more than the age Ray was now.

Mr. Freider smiled. "That was the day of the store's grand opening. Your whole family came to cut the ribbon. This is from the write-up in the local paper."

Now that he studied the picture, Justin vaguely remembered the day. Even at that age, he could tell that his parents were simply going through the motions. But he and James had been excited nonetheless.

Unfortunately, the memory of it all had been overshadowed by the stinging fight that occurred within hours of them getting home. No wonder he'd blocked it out.

Until now. Justin found his mouth had gone dry. "I don't know what to say, Mr. Freider. This is such a thoughtful gesture."

"Nonsense. We picked up several copies of that issue all those years ago. Of course, the paper it's printed on has yellowed a bit. But not bad for twenty something years, huh?"

"No." Justin choked out the word over an achy lump that had formed in his throat. "It's not bad at all. I can't thank you enough."

Mr. Freider's smile grew wider. "Like I said, it wasn't that big a deal. Just thought it might recall some happy memories."

But it was a big deal. Bigger than Mr. Freider would ever know. He tucked the picture under his arm and went to shake the older man's hand.

But Mr. Freider had other ideas. He embraced Justin in a big bear hug. "You two have a good night now. That snow's about to come down at any minute. Much earlier than they said."

"You, too, Mr. Freider."

Out on the sidewalk, Justin couldn't help but glance at the picture once more.

"You were a very cute child," Carli said.

"Think so?"

She pointed to the frame. "No doubt about it. Look at those big round eyes, the thick wavy hair. Very cute."

It was childish, but her words pleased him to a ridiculous degree. "That was very nice of him."

"Mmm-hmm," Carli agreed. "He's one of a kind."

So are you. The words hovered on his tongue but he knew not to speak them out loud.

"No one's ever done anything like that for me before."

Carli looked up and studied the air. "He also seems to have been right about the snow." A big fat snowflake landed on her nose. He had to clench his fist to keep from brushing it off with his finger. Then kissing the spot where it had landed.

There were plenty more to follow. Suddenly, a flurry of white flakes blew like confetti all around them.

By the time they reached the inn, the snow was blinding. He couldn't believe the speed at which it fell, accompanied by a blinding cold wind he could feel down to his bones.

"Well, looks like you'll be snowed in at least for the night." Carli stopped in front of the glass door. "I'll call you later tomorrow. Make sure to charge your cell phone as soon as you get in. We're likely to lose power at some point." She turned to walk away. "I should be getting home."

He gently grabbed her by the arm. "There is no way I'm letting you walk back alone to your house." He could barely see her face in front of him for the white cloud of snow between them. "Not in this mess."

"I'll be fine," Carli assured him. But he wasn't buying it.

"No way," he insisted. "I'll come with you."

"And then what? You'd have to walk back here. And this is just going to get worse. Something tells me you won't be comfortable on my mom's lumpy couch all night if you get stranded there."

"I'll take my chances."

She looked ready to argue some more when Betty stepped outside. "What in the angel's name are you two doing out here? You'll both catch your death of a cold."

Without waiting for an answer, she physically ushered them both into the lobby. Carli looked ready to protest, but Betty stopped her with a no-nonsense look and thrust her hands on her hips.

"Carli Tynan. What kind of neighbor do you think I am? If I let you walk the rest of the way home in that?" She jutted her chin toward the window to indicate the snow.

"But Bet—"

"But nothing. I have plenty of extra rooms. You are staying here tonight. You can borrow something Leddy left here before heading away to college. And I don't want to hear another word about it. Now call your folks and let them know."

Another sleepless night. Despite all the homely comforts of the Sailor's Inn, Carli was getting no more rest tonight than she had the one before. The loud whooshing of the wind outside her window did not help the situation.

Sighing, she pulled off the covers and got out of bed. One more insomnia-laden night meant she was going to be a total wreck tomorrow. Warm milk. It had never worked for her before, but it was worth a try. Betty wouldn't mind if she checked the kitchen fridge and heated some for herself. Things were getting desperate here.

The well-placed outlet night-lights afforded just enough

illumination to make it downstairs without disrupting the other guests. There was at least one more couple staying at the inn. Within moments, she had a steamy hot cup of creamy milk in her hands. Not quite ready to go back upstairs, Carli made a detour through the lobby into the main sitting room. She'd always loved this room, even as a small child when her mother had come to visit Betty and dragged her girls along. Carli had spent hours sitting in front of the large fireplace with her book while her mother and Betty chatted over tea. She walked over to the hearth now. It was no longer a wood fireplace. The Mills had a newer, more convenient electronic model installed several years ago. But the rest of the room looked achingly familiar. Carli flipped the switch on the wall and a blue-tinged fire roared to life in front of her. She sighed with satisfaction as the heat spread over her skin.

"You can't sleep either, huh?"

Though he'd spoken softly, the unexpected sound of Justin's voice behind her made her jump. Warm milk sloshed over her cup and spilled onto her hand. She wiped it away on the side of her borrowed nightgown.

"Justin, you startled me."

"Sorry," he said, and made his way into the room. He came to stand next to her by the fire. "I thought I'd come down and watch the storm through the big bay window down here. It's something to behold. All this snow."

"We get at least one or two of these a year, and it never ceases to amaze me, the sheer magnitude of their power."

"It's beautiful, really. The entire town covered in sparkling white. Like an ivory blanket sprinkled with glitter."

She turned to look at him. "Wow. That was very poetic. We'll see how pretty you think it is when it's time to shovel tomorrow. And don't think my father won't ask you to. Guest or not."

He laughed, then surprised her by lowering himself to the floor and sitting cross-legged in front of the fire. "I have an electric fireplace too," he offered. "Back in my condo in Seattle."

Feeling awkward and rude at speaking down to him from her standing position, Carli felt no choice but to join him on the thick faux fur rug on the floor. "Yeah?"

"Yes. Funny though. It's not nearly as...cozy as this one is. It's designed to look like a pit. With fake charcoal and kindling. I like this one much better."

She wasn't sure what to say to that so she remained silent and took another sip of her milk. It wasn't doing a thing to make her sleepy, not that she had any hope of that with Justin sitting right next to her. He wore drawstring flannel pajama bottoms that somehow looked sexy on him. And a crisp white T-shirt that accented his solid chest and biceps. She could feel his warmth next to her along with the warmth of the fire in front of them, like a safe comfortable cocoon.

An empty yet easy silence settled between them. This was nice, Carli decided, allowing herself to relax into a peaceful lull. There were worse ways to sit through a storm than lounging in front of a fire watching the flames while listening to the sound of the wind.

So she wasn't prepared for what came next. When he spoke again, the next words out of Justin's mouth shocked her to her core.

"I need to ask you something. Are you in love with your sister's boyfriend?"

Justin hadn't meant to blurt it out that way. Subtle, it was not. Carli was clearly uncomfortable now, and he could have kicked himself for that. They'd been having such a pleasant and casual conversation. He'd just ruined the whole relaxed ambience with one question.

"Why do you ask?" She took a sip from her mug, not taking her eyes off the fire.

They were sitting so close together, his knee brushed against hers when he turned. Shadows from the flames fell across her face and highlighted the silky chocolate brown of her eyes. He fought the urge to pull her into his lap.

"Never mind. Forget I said anything."

"But you did."

"I shouldn't have. It's none of my business. I apologize."

Carli set the cup she'd been holding on the floor. "There's nothing between Warren and me," she said with a firm note of finality.

She was clearly uncomfortable talking about it. Which had to mean there was something there. A surge of emotion shot through his chest, a feeling he refused to acknowledge as jealousy. What he'd said earlier was true. It really was none of his business. In a few short days, he'd be back on the West Coast and likely not see Carli Tynan again for a good long time, if ever. There could never be anything real between them. Carli wasn't the type to have a casual fling, and there was no way he could give her anything more.

"He and I had a messy breakup about a year ago. I was angry and betrayed when he ended it."

Justin sucked in a breath. Hearing how much she'd cared for another man affected him way more than he would have liked, more than it should have.

"Because you were in love with him."

"I thought I was. But he fell for my sister. As I'm sure you surmised at dinner."

"I can't imagine that." He meant that with all his heart. How could any man prefer the quiet, albeit beautiful sister to the dynamic, intelligent woman who sat beside him now?

She looked off into the fire, the reflection of the flames dancing in her eyes.

"Why do I get the feeling there's more to the story?" Justin prodded.

She didn't look away from the fire when she answered. "Very perceptive, Mr. Hammond."

"So I'm right."

"Yes. But the summary is that I felt betrayed and deceived. The two of them were too afraid to tell me what was happening at first. Maybe for fear of hurting me, I don't know. But I just felt deceived. To make matters worse, I felt like my parents sided with Janie, at first."

"How so?"

She shrugged. "Little things. Warren was still always welcome at the house. I know that sounds petty. But I felt like he should have been made to feel at least a little out of place." Her chest heaved as she took a deep sigh. "Plus, Mom and Dad would make these quaint remarks about how things that are meant to be will happen. Or not. You know, que será, será."

He wasn't sure what to say to that. After witnessing how close the family was, he couldn't imagine what it must have felt like to think you were losing your place within it.

She wrapped her arms around herself, lost in her thoughts. Justin had never felt a stronger urge to comfort someone. He leaned closer to her, literally giving her a shoulder to lean on if she so wanted.

It thrilled him beyond words when she took him up on the offer and placed her head gently against him.

He could smell the sweet fruity scent of her shampoo. Her warmth settled over his skin. "I have to tell you something," he began.

"Hmm?"

"I think Warren is a fool."

Her first response was to snuggle in closer to him. "But you've seen my sister."

"So?"

He could feel her breathing; her hair tickled his chin. "So she's stunningly beautiful. Poor Warren can hardly be blamed."

He cupped her chin, turning her face to his. "I'll repeat. Warren is a fool."

Carli sucked in a breath, studied his face. She was so close, barely half an inch separated them. "Do you really think so?"

"Without a doubt. Janie's a pretty girl. But I never went for the frail, dainty type. I prefer women with unruly hair and inner strength. Like you."

She swallowed, and he couldn't resist leaning even closer. "You do?"

"Oh, yeah."

Justin didn't even know who moved first. He just thanked the heavens that suddenly her lips were on his. She tasted like sugar and cream, her mouth warm and soft against his. It was the slightest, gentlest of kisses.

But somehow he felt it through to his soul.

What time was it? Justin awoke disoriented and confused. The wind outside rattled the windows. There was a clear crisp chill in the air; the fireplace had gone out. The room was dark as hades. They must have lost power at some point, as Carli had predicted. But somehow he felt surprisingly warm. It took a moment for his eyes and senses to focus.

He realized with a shock why he wasn't cold. Carli was nuzzled against him, cradled along his length. Her back snug tight against his stomach.

They'd fallen asleep in front of the fireplace. Right there

on the faux fur rug. His traitorous body immediately reacted.

Control.

But it was no use. He was only human, and he'd been
wildly attracted to this woman from the moment he'd laid
eyes on her. His arousal hit fast and strong. She'd be horrified if she woke up and became aware of the current
state he was in.

"Carli, wake up."

Her response was to nuzzle her head against the bottom of his chin. The action did nothing to diminish his
arousal. He bit out a silent curse.

"Carli. Hon. It's the middle of the night."

That attempt didn't work either. She moaned softly and
shifted closer to him. Justin couldn't help but groan out
loud. This was torture. He dared a glance at her face. Thick
dark lashes framed her closed lids. She looked so peaceful, so content.

He couldn't do it. He couldn't force her awake. Just a
few more minutes. Let her get some rest, she'd been yawn-
ing all day yesterday. Clearly she needed the sleep.

He would just have to suffer it out for a while.

Justin found himself second-guessing that decision three
hours later when he heard footsteps approaching. Through
some miracle, he'd fallen asleep despite his inconvenient
reaction to having Carli in his arms. And now someone
was about to find them in a very compromising position.

There was nothing for it, nothing he could do to try to
rectify the situation. Way too late for that.

Making himself look up, Justin found Betty staring
down at them with clear shock on her face. But was there
also a ghost of a smile? She cleared her throat. Loudly.

Carli awoke with a start and jolted back in his arms.

A harsh flash of pain shot through his jaw as the top her head connected hard with his chin. He couldn't help his grunt in response.

"Good morning," Betty said, as if nothing was amiss.

Carli removed herself from his grasp. She opened her mouth to speak and then promptly shut it again. Clearly at a loss for words, she sat up.

"Hello, Betty," Justin managed to choke out. His jaw actually clicked. Just then the lights flickered and the power came back on. Something hummed back to life in the kitchen area, and the fireplace lit up.

"Well, thank goodness," Betty said, still staring at the two of them. She had to be referring to the lights coming back on, right?

"Mr. Freider has been trying to get a hold of you, dear." She addressed Carli. "I'm afraid he has some bad news."

Justin helped Carli to her feet and then stood himself, ignoring the aches and pains that came with sleeping on a hard floor all night.

"What's happened?" Carli asked, a little unsteady on her feet.

"It's the toy store. Apparently, the roof was too weak for the massive onslaught of snow in such a short period of time. It collapsed under the weight, snapping a water pipe as it came down." She took a breath. "I'm afraid the store has flooded."

Carli gasped. "Oh, no. How much damage?"

"I'm sorry, dear. That's all I know."

CHAPTER ELEVEN

IT WAS EVEN worse than she'd feared. The whole back corner of Hammond's Toys Cape store looked like a demolition zone. Carli bit back a cry of despair as she and Justin entered what was left of the store. Most of the damage had occurred in her favorite section, the Book Nook. Her heart broke when she saw the collapsed shelves, the scattered books with soaked and torn pages. A mountain of snow had piled up in the corner; thick icicles covered the shelves.

Mr. Freider was already there, trying to save anything that was salvageable. The poor man must have been freezing. Either that, or he was shaking from sheer sadness. Probably both.

"Oh, Mr. Freider." She walked over and gave him a gentle hug. "We'll find a way to fix all this." Though she couldn't imagine how. The store's very existence was already in jeopardy. Not that Mr. Freider had any idea. And now this.

He gave her a skeptical look. "Thank you for coming, dear."

"Would you like me to call the insurance company?"

For some reason, Mr. Freider's eyes started to tear up at the question. Then she understood. Technically, this would be considered flood damage. Something most insurance companies didn't cover.

This was devastating. What were the chances Justin would ever commit to keeping the store open now? It would take considerable cost and resources to repair all this and open up again.

"The alarm went off and alerted me at home around dawn," Mr. Freider told them. "I ran down as soon as I could to shut the water off. But by then…" He let the sentence trail off. "For it to happen this time of year."

Justin stepped over and placed a hand on the other man's back. "Why don't you take a break, Mr. Freider. Go home for a couple of hours. If you've been here since dawn, you're past due for some rest.

"Carli and I will take over for a while," Justin added when he hesitated. Finally he gave a reluctant nod and put down the book he'd been holding.

Carli watched him walk away and had an urge to hug Justin too—for the consideration and kindness he'd just shown. "That was very thoughtful of you."

Justin shrugged. "He looked ready to collapse. It was a no-brainer to send him home."

"Where do we start?"

"I'm going to find some boxes. He must have some empty shipping boxes somewhere."

"What for?"

"We can't do this out here. We'll freeze. It'll be easier and more effective if we work in batches. We'll carry a box or two at a time to his office and sort them out there."

"Great idea." Good thing one of them was thinking straight. "I'm sure there's some empty boxes in the storage area. Follow me."

Twenty minutes later, Justin had covered the exposed area with a heavy tarp he'd found in the storage room and the two of them were in the back office. They'd already made several piles, sorting through the various books and items depending on their level of damage.

Despite the unfortunate distraction with the flood, Carli couldn't stop thinking about what had happened this morning. Or last night. Justin had to be thinking about it too. How could he not? They'd spent the night in each other's arms. The fact that it had happened without knowledge or intent mattered little. He'd been the perfect gentleman; she had to let him know how much that meant to her.

"Thank you for helping me with this." Carli clutched the book she was holding against her chest like a shield. "And there's something else I should thank you for."

"What's that?"

"Last night. When you…uh…you know…didn't even try. I mean, all we did was sleep." She clutched the book tighter. Why was this so hard?

"Trust me, it wasn't for lack of wanting to." He blew out a breath. "If you only knew."

Electricity cackled between them. "You shouldn't say such things."

Justin visibly stiffened. "What exactly am I supposed to say to that?" He threw the question out like a challenge, a hard glint in his voice. Anger flashed in his eyes.

"Is something bothering you?"

"One of my family's retail locations has just incurred considerable damage."

She nodded, mustered a wealth of sarcasm into her voice. "Mmm-hmm. You've cared so much about the family business over the years, I can see how that would agitate you now."

She saw immediately that it was the wrong thing to say. He clearly didn't appreciate the sarcastic remark. Justin's mouth tightened into a thin line. But she wasn't buying that his sour mood was the result of the flood or the damage it had caused. So what else could it be?

"You know what's bothering me?"

A shiver ran through Carli at his tone and the tightness in his shoulders. But she decided to take the bait. "What?"

Suddenly, he'd moved in front of her. A mere breath separated them. Her heart pounded in her chest. She couldn't even tell if it was due to the proximity or because of the frustration blaring in his eyes.

"The way you're standing there thanking me for not touching you last night." With a finger, he lifted her chin. "When I make love to a woman, I can guarantee you it won't be when she's half asleep and tired after a restless night."

Her mouth went dry. She'd simply meant to thank him. "I didn't mean to imply otherwise." He had to know that.

"Right. I just have one question: Did you want me to?"

Well, he'd clearly gone and thrown the gauntlet down, hadn't he? She refused to lie. "I think you know the answer to that."

"Oh, no you don't. You're not getting off that easy. Answer the question. Did you want me to?"

Her breath caught in her throat. But she blurted out the only answer she could. "Yes."

She didn't know what she'd been expecting, but in the next instant, she found herself lifted up by the hips. Justin carried her the few steps to the desk behind them. Then he set her down and conquered her lips with a savage kiss.

Desire slammed through her as he ran his hands along her rib cage, then plunged them into her hair. She wanted him, all of him. The taste of him sent fire through her nerve endings, igniting wants and needs she could no longer hope to suppress. All that mattered was this moment and where it might lead to. She lay back on the desk surface, bringing him down with her. All the while, his hungry lips continued their sweet onslaught.

Something shifted under her weight and dug into the small of her back. The small nuisance was just distracting enough that Carli regained some semblance of sanity. On a regretful moan, she gave Justin a gentle push and he immediately pulled back. She straightened back to a sitting position.

"What the—" But Justin didn't finish. He appeared as shell-shocked as she felt.

Dear God, she'd nearly made love to him right there in the middle of the store office, on top of a metal desk. A man she hardly knew. What if someone had walked in? Or worse, what if one of her parents had come to the store to check on her? It was bad enough Betty had discovered them asleep in front of the fireplace this morning.

The thought of someone walking in on the two of them was too horrifying to further contemplate.

One thing she knew for certain. She'd become an unrecognizable version of herself since Justin Hammond had arrived in her life. She didn't like this incarnation of Carli. A woman who was too reckless and too unrestrained. It had to stop. All of it.

One way or another, they were going to have to resolve the question about the fate of the store. Then she was going to have to return to her previous life. And to her previous self.

Justin stepped away from Carli and rammed his hand through his hair. Damn it. What was it about her that made him lose control the way he did? He barely had a grasp on it now. She arranged her top and fixed the collar, breathing heavy all the while. Her lips were swollen from his kiss, her cheeks reddened from the stubble he had due to not having had time to shave this morning. He knew it was insane, but all he wanted to do was rub that stubble all over her soft, supple skin. Leave his mark on every inch of her body.

She may have done the sensible thing and pushed him away just now, but her eyes were clouded with passion and desire. For him. She wanted him as much as he wanted her.

But not here, not now.

The roar of a siren pulled them both out of a breathless stupor. The sound grew closer and within seconds could be heard right outside the wall. Damn it. He should have figured the fire marshal would want to come make sure the building was structurally sound.

"The fire department," he told Carli. Her clothes were in disarray, her hair a mess of tangles from the way he'd rammed his hands through her curls.

"I'll go greet them, if you want to…you know." He motioned to her.

"Yes, thank you. I'd like a minute or so."

Rubbing his chin in frustration and self-reproach, he left the office, the taste of her on his tongue still teasing his senses.

It took the fire marshal less than fifteen minutes to declare the building safe pending an electrician's assessment. Also, he told them that they'd been lucky to actually lose power as the flooding could have cause an electrical fire.

Justin saw the man off and went to tell Carli the news. His phone vibrated in his pocket before he got far. A text had arrived from Jackson. To call him as soon as he had a free moment.

Justin sighed. No time like the present.

He dialed the number and waited as Jackson answered.

"Mr. Freider called me," Jackson said. "How bad is the damage?"

"Pretty bad. It's going to take a huge amount of resources to restore and become operational again. My original conclusion makes even more sense now..." He paused, an idea suddenly occurring to him. "But if you're going to put money into restoration, it might be an opportunity to invest a bit more and take the unit into an expanded direction."

"I'd be very interested in hearing about that."

"I'll sum up the proposal and email it to you."

Justin ended the call and returned the cell phone to his pants pocket. He might have come up with a way to make the flood damage an opportunity in disguise.

Jackson sounded open to the idea. He had no doubt Carli would love it. He couldn't wait to tell her.

Justin had been gone for quite a while. Was the fire marshal taking that long to wrap things up?

Carli's curiosity got the better of her and she left the office to go find him. To her surprise, Justin was in the hallway speaking to someone on the phone. She immediately turned to give him some privacy until she heard a snippet of the conversation.

He was talking to Jackson.

"My original conclusion makes even more sense now..."

That was all Carli needed to hear. She felt like she had just taken a punch to the midsection.

Without her knowledge or her input, Justin was speaking to his father about the future of the store. And from the sound of it, he was making the argument that storm damage had only served to finalize his decision. He thought it should be shut down. She ran back into the office and slammed the door shut.

Justin had betrayed her.

He hadn't even bothered to mention anything to her before making his decision. He'd just gone straight to Jackson. Using the storm as an excuse to argue for what he'd originally planned all along.

Like a fool, she'd gone ahead and trusted yet another man she shouldn't have.

A knock sounded on the door. "Are you decent yet?" Justin asked from the other side.

With a huff of annoyance, Carli strode to the door and pulled it open to let him in.

Justin's smile faded from his lips when he saw the look on her face.

"Has the wrecking crew been called in then?" she demanded to know.

He blinked at her. "I beg your pardon."

"I suppose we'll need to auction or donate the remaining items."

"I'm afraid I still don't understand."

"You were talking to Jackson just now, weren't you?"

"Yes, I called him after—"

She cut him off with a dismissive wave of her hand. Her heart sank further. So Justin *had* been the one to initiate the phone call.

"I know why you called him. And you did it behind my back."

"What are you talking about?"

"You didn't have to courtesy to come to me first. Just went ahead and gave your decision to your father. I don't expect someone like you to understand just how wrong that was."

"Someone like me?"

"You've never felt a loyalty to anyone or anything, have you? That's why you don't give a damn about keeping this store open. You never felt the sense of belonging that a place like this affords to the people who love it. After all, you never really felt like you belonged or were a part of anything, did you? Not to a town. Not to a family. All you manage to do is ruin things for others."

"Wait just a minute—"

She didn't want to hear it. Not right now. She had no use for his explanation, which that would no doubt involve numbers and returns and all the factual things that men like him always cared so much about. She crossed her arms in front of her chest to quell the shaking that had suddenly gripped her and turned away. "Just go."

Justin had heard enough. Carli's anger was palpable. And why? All because he'd had the nerve to talk to Jackson without her knowledge. She didn't even care what the content of the conversation may have been. Her immediate assumption had been to think the worst.

You never really belonged...

Well, he had better things to do with his time than to try to explain himself to her.

He stepped closer to where she stood. Even now, with her anger directed straight at him, he couldn't help but long to pull her to him, to kiss her fury away until they both couldn't care less about some damn store and some ruined toys.

He clenched his fists at his side instead.

She paced around the desk, then turned to shoot him an accusatory look. A wealth of anger shone in her eyes. All directed at him.

Something snapped within his soul as he met her gaze. Somehow, some way, he'd done it again. He'd damaged something precious. Damned if he knew how or why. But it seemed to be a talent he had.

Served him right for ever thinking things could be any

different. And curse Carli Tynan for ever leading him toward that misconception in the first place.

Well, he'd heard enough. "I'm not sure why you're so worked up. But understand this—I don't need to run my intentions by you or anyone else."

She gasped, then lifted her chin. "You're absolutely right. I'm not sure why I thought you would have the decency to do so."

Justin didn't bother to reply to that. Without a word, he turned and stepped out of the office.

After all, what was there left to say?

Justin walked out of the rental agency and over to the late model SUV he'd just secured. He'd drive back to Boston, then arrange for a flight out of Logan. There was nothing left for him to do here.

In the interest of professionalism, he'd stop by Hammond's corporate office building and give his father a quick summary. Not that it mattered at this point.

Shame too. He actually may have figured out a way to save Carli's precious store and make some money for Hammond's in the process. Well, it was none of his concern now.

Getting into the rental vehicle, he started the ignition, then sighed and pounded the steering wheel with his fist. Damn it. None of this felt right.

Every inch of him wanted to delay leaving, despite what had just happened back at the store. Only one explanation for it.

There was no denying he had inexplicably, unwittingly developed deeply serious feelings for Carli Tynan.

Look where it had led. He didn't have it in him to have a healthy relationship. Certainly not with a woman like Carli who had a rich, fulfilling life. With family and friends who loved her.

Look how much havoc he'd caused her in the short time he'd known her.

Had it really been barely a week since he'd touched down at Logan Airport for the first time? It felt like years had gone by. The fact was, he'd be leaving a changed man. More so than he would have ever guessed.

He should have never come to New England. He'd known it was a bad idea from the beginning to come here, running to do Jackson's bidding like an eager errand boy. He should have known it wouldn't end well.

The conversation with Betty Mills had been awkward and uncomfortable when he'd gone to grab his belongings from the inn. She didn't buy the explanation that he had to leave early due to a pressing business matter back in his Seattle office. The woman was too perceptive by half. She'd told him to visit again as soon as he could. He assured her he would. A lie. Betty would most likely never see him again, as sad as that was.

He didn't have any business here in Westerson, regardless of how fond he'd grown of everyone he'd met during his short stay.

Now, sitting in the driver's seat of the rental, all he wanted to do was drive straight out of town and keep going until he reached Logan Airport.

Begrudgingly, he realized he couldn't do that. It would be a coward's way out. He had to at least talk to Carli like a man and tell her he was leaving. And somehow explain that he hadn't intended to mislead her in any way.

Not the easiest conversation.

He shifted into gear. Best to just get it over with. If he was lucky, Ray would be there at the house. He didn't want to leave without saying goodbye to the little guy. Justin realized with a start that he would genuinely miss him.

Carli was on the porch as he approached the driveway. Unfortunately, she wasn't alone.

Justin swore out loud. He just wanted to talk to her one-on-one, in private, to say all the things that needed to be said between them. For one final time. Unfortunately, it appeared that waiting for her to finish with whoever she was with was his only option. The last thing he wanted was a delay right now. He started to pull over across the street. After all, she wouldn't recognize the car.

But then he realized three of her sisters and her mother were surrounding her. They were all laughing, sharing snacks and a bottle of wine. The scene was the perfect picture of a close, tight-knit family. A family full of love and affection. It was a picture someone like him had no business interrupting. Or trying to be a part of. Not with his history.

Her angry words echoed in his head once more—*I don't expect someone like you to understand.*

An image of the Christmas tree crashing down in the Hammond foyer flashed across his vision. No, there was really no point in talking to Carli.

Justin drove on.

CHAPTER TWELVE

JUSTIN RODE UP the elevator to the top floor of the Hammond corporate office building. Still late afternoon. If he knew his father, the old man would still be at his desk.

He didn't intend to be here long. He wasn't going to leave Boston without personally notifying his father that as far as he was concerned, his responsibilities here were finished. Justin would email him the figures and ideas at a later time. Not that it mattered at this point. But the professional businessman in him wouldn't let it slide. Not even when it came to his father.

To his dismay, Jackson's office was empty. The lights turned off. Justin bit out a curse. He probably should have called first, but he'd been certain Jackson would still be at work.

"Justin? Can I help you?"

He turned to find Miranda, his old babysitter, in the hallway. "I was just looking for Jackson. Is he traveling?"

"No, dear. Believe it or not he's already gone for the day."

He had to admit he wasn't quite sure if he believed it. At his curious stare, Miranda gave a small shrug. "He's a different man these days. Ever since the Fryberg acquisition. Frankly, both your father and brother are behaving out of the norm."

Could nothing go his way today? He really didn't need to go back to that house. The Hammond mansion held no fond memories for him. "They have?"

She nodded. "No one can figure out why, but Jackson's been leaving earlier and earlier. Some days he calls to say he's working from home."

Justin didn't even know what to say to that. This was his father they were talking about, right? The same man he didn't see for days at times as a child because he came home late from work and left early the next day?

"Anyway, is there something I can help you with?" Miranda asked.

"No, thank you."

"Okay then." She turned to go, but Justin felt an uncharacteristic tug in his chest. He hadn't had a chance to say goodbye to anyone besides Betty back in Westerson.

And he had no idea if he would ever see Miranda again, for that matter. It surprised him that he cared. "Wait."

"Yes, dear?"

"I just want to say how glad I am that I got to see you again, after all these years. I'm leaving tonight. So I guess this will have to be goodbye." The words left his mouth in a swift torrent. He wasn't used to being so damn sentimental. What had Carli Tynan done to him? With some awkwardness, he extended his arm to shake Miranda's hand.

She ignored it and wrapped him in a big bear hug instead. He gingerly hugged her back. "Do you have to leave so soon?" she asked against when she finally let him go.

"I'm afraid so. I just need to wrap some things up with my father, and then I need to be on my way."

"I see. It's a shame James missed you entirely. I think it would have been good to have you two see each other again." She slammed a hand against her chest. "Silly me. Just look at me sticking my nose where it doesn't belong.

But it broke my heart to see you boys yanked apart all those years ago. I think about it a lot."

"You do?"

"Of course. It was wrong. So wrong. James just wasn't himself those first few years after."

"He wasn't?"

She studied him with wide eyes. "Of course not. I know you must have struggled too, dear. But I saw firsthand how hard it was for that little boy to have his mother and brother just disappear like that."

Justin had to admit, with no small amount of shame, that he hadn't really given James much thought over the years. After all, he'd been the son who'd gotten to stay home, able to grow up in the same house he was born in. He slept in the same bed, kept attending the same school.

Whereas Justin's whole life had been upended.

But of course, it couldn't have been easy for James either. Justin hadn't allowed himself to think about that. The reason was simple really: he knew James blamed him for all of it.

And he wasn't wrong to do so.

"I wondered a lot about how you were doing," Miranda added. "But I never doubted you'd grow to be a successful, decent young man."

Justin had to stifle a groan. A decent man would have tried harder to get Carli to understand. Instead he'd simply walked off. But she'd get over it, he was sure. Judging by what he'd seen on the porch, maybe she had already started to.

"I wish I could have watched you grow up," Miranda added, breaking into his thoughts. Tears shimmered in her bright blue eyes, which had grown dimmer and surrounded by more wrinkles over the years. This woman had genuinely cared for him. He'd been too much of a child to appreciate that at the time. The notion brought on a profound sadness. It might have made a difference all those years ago if he'd only known there was someone he could have turned to.

"Thank you. But I guess that ship sailed when my father made his choice."

"Your mother did the leaving, dear. She took you with her."

Justin had to laugh at that. Why was he getting into all this anyway? With a woman he barely remembered. Simply because she'd watched him a few evenings when he was a child. "Maybe so. But my father didn't exactly go out of his way to reach out me. No, he chose the son he wanted to keep with him just as much as my mother did."

Miranda patted his cheek. "But don't you see?"

"See what?"

"From where James stood, it was the exact same thing. As far as he was concerned, you were the favored one."

"I don't understand."

"Your mother chose you. And she never looked back. He was the one who was left behind."

With her words, Justin had to face a possibility he'd never let himself entertain before. His brother hadn't fared any better in the aftermath of their parents' breakup.

All these years, he and James had lived alternate versions of the same reality. Their lives were just flip sides of the same coin.

Where was Justin now? She hadn't heard from him, only knew that he'd left yesterday per Betty. Carli needed to get going too. This morning, the contractors had started reparations on the store. All that was left to do was to grab her bag and drive back to Boston. So why was she putting off the inevitable?

She glanced at her phone for the thousandth time, trying to decide whether to call him or not. He shouldn't have gone behind her back as he did. But throwing his lack of family in his face was clearly a low blow. Something she wasn't exactly proud of now upon reflection.

Carli swore out loud and threw her cell phone across her parents' living room. Luckily, it landed on the couch.

"Annoying spam?" A delicate voice startled her. She turned to see Janie standing in the doorway.

Carli squeezed her eyes in frustration. "I'm trying to decide if I should call Justin. I might owe him an apology."

"Oh?"

"Yeah… I may have said some things I shouldn't have."

"Then I think you should just bite the bullet and call. He might be waiting for you," Janie offered.

Carli blew out a puff of air in frustration. "More likely, he never wants to talk to me again. He couldn't wait to get out of town."

Janie nodded. "Yeah, Mom may have mentioned something about him leaving prematurely."

"Thanks to me."

"Wanna talk about it?"

The question caught Carli off guard. The truth was, Janie was the first person she'd always been able to talk to. That was part of the reason this whole past year had been so hellish. She'd lost a dear confidante when things had turned icy between them. All those times Carli had thought to reach out but had been too stubborn to do so. And for what? A relationship with a man who she'd never really believed would work out anyway.

"I made a huge mistake," Carli admitted on a low sob, not even certain if she was still referring to Justin or the wedge that had been sitting between her and Janie for the past year.

Janie rushed over to her. Soon they were both holding each other as the tears flowed like a sudden rain. "Me too, sis. Me too," Janie said, then handed her a tissue from the side table and grabbed one for herself.

"Are we okay?" Janie asked, dabbing her eyes. "Please say yes."

"We will be," Carli answered, realizing she'd known that all along. "But I just wish you'd told me. When it first started between you and Warren."

Janie nodded. "You're right. It was just so hard. Neither one of us wanted to hurt you. That was the only reason we kept it from you at the beginning. You have to believe that."

Carli gulped back a sob.

"I've missed you," Janie said, her voice a scratchy rasp from her crying.

"I've missed you too."

If only one of them had had the courage to admit that before so much time had passed. She wouldn't have had to do without her closest sister for all these months. Not to mention, maybe she would never have lashed out at Justin the way she had after the storm.

She'd felt let down and betrayed when he'd called his father. Just as she'd felt betrayed by Janie and Warren. And her response at the first sign of trouble had been to put the blame squarely on Justin's shoulders, exactly the way his parents had when he was just a mere child.

She had to make this right.

"I think you have a phone call to make," Janie stated. "I'll give you some privacy."

"Thanks, sis."

Janie gave her a tight hug and left the room.

Carli didn't give herself time to think. Grabbing her phone, she clicked on Justin's number. But his phone went straight to voice mail.

A lump formed at the base of her throat. With her luck, Justin might very well be on a plane back to Seattle.

She was probably too late.

Carli rubbed her thumb absentmindedly along the corner of her mother's granite counter where a stubborn green stain still marked it. In time it would fade. She hoped so anyway. There were a lot of things she was banking on having time fix.

Though none of the mountains of snow had melted, the late-morning sunshine brought with it a golden touch to the vast amount of white outside. Everyone had shoveled out for the most part. Life in town was back to normal. But it felt anything but for her. She felt like the world had somehow tilted on its axis. Nothing would ever be the same.

Her mother walked in carrying a load of freshly laundered kitchen towels. It occurred to Carli how content her mother was, how so very in tune with her existence. Louise had worked hard all her life to build a loving home and a strong family, foundations that Carli had depended on growing up.

Alas, it appeared very unlikely that Carli would ever be able to achieve the same for herself. Not at the rate she was going when it came to men.

Her mom did a bit of a double take when she saw her. "I thought you'd be on your way by now. I heard Justin already left."

"He did indeed."

Her mother put the towels down and studied her with concerned, motherly eyes.

"I'm surprised you haven't. You usually can't wait to scram out of here and head back to the big city after a couple of days of visiting."

That was Louise, her mother was always straight to the point.

"Are you trying to get rid of me, Mom?" Carli said with as much comical outrage as she could muster.

"Of course not." Louise came over and gave her small kiss on the top of her head. "But if you stick around, I'm very likely to put you to work. The pine needles that keep shedding off the Christmas tree and onto the floor need to be swept up. And heaven knows there's always more shoveling and deicing to do."

Carli held her hands up in mock surrender. "Okay. Okay. I was just leaving." But she didn't make a move out of her chair. "Can I just ask you something first?"

Louise's eyes narrowed; whatever she saw on Carli's face made her pull out a counter stool and sit across from her daughter.

"Shoot."

"It's about you and Dad."

Her mom lifted a finely shaped, dark eyebrow. "What about us?"

"You're just so, I don't know, strong together."

"I suppose. We've been together for over three decades."

"And then there's Tammy and Raymond. They're just so happy together with their new house and their son."

"They were high school sweethearts. They've known each other a long time too."

"I know." She sighed deeply before continuing. "And now Warren and Janie."

Her mother leaned over and gave her hand an affectionate pat.

"Janie and I just had a bit of a chat," Carli told her. "Finally."

"Are you okay?"

Surprisingly, she was. Despite the shattered mass that

now sat where her heart used to be, she genuinely felt no loss over Warren. Not anymore. "We are, Mom. I'm happy for them. I really am. I realize now they fit much better than Warren and I ever could."

"You may not have seen it at the time, but he wasn't right for you. You're too independent, too driven." She leaned closer before continuing. "He's the type who wants to stay in Westerson and plant more roots here. Just like Janie. You have to see now that those two belong together."

Carli sighed. "I do see that. Now. So do Tammy and Raymond. But you and Dad especially. I've seen you have arguments, but they never last. And you're both always so in tune." She took a deep breath; she had her mother's full attention now.

"Trust me when I tell you that wasn't always the case. None of you kids know this, but we almost broke off the engagement a month before the wedding."

Carli felt genuine surprise at that last comment. "You did? Why?"

"I was starting to get cold feet. And your father could tell. He didn't want to rush me into a commitment as serious as marriage if I wasn't totally ready for it."

"You? You were the one who got cold feet?"

"Believe it or not, there was a time I couldn't decide what I wanted or what path I needed to take in life to be happy. And your father was man enough not to put any pressure on me."

"Huh? I never knew."

"It's true. Now, every time I walk through this house, or hold my grandson—or even sit in the kitchen having a conversation with one of my girls—I know I made the right decision."

Carli felt the tears spring into her eyes. She was so lucky to be part of this family, to be this woman's daughter.

So what if her love life was in shambles. In a few years, she may even be able to get over the foolish way she'd fallen for a man who had turned and walked out of her life at the first sign of discord.

"Tell me," her mother began. "Do your questions have anything to do with Justin Hammond perhaps?"

Carli wasn't surprised by the question. Louise Tynan was very on top of things when it came to her children. It was one of the reasons she loved her parents so much.

"As well as the way you were looking at him?" her mother added when she didn't respond right away.

Carli bit down on a bitter chortle. "I guess. But it's over. Almost as soon as it began."

"What happened?"

"I let my guard down. I wasn't careful enough and didn't see the obvious. Kind of like with Warren." She gulped down on a low sob. "But this feels so much worse, Mom. This feels like the hurt might never end."

Her mother stood and gathered her in her arms. "You've fallen for him."

"I'm afraid so."

"And he's leaving?"

"Probably flying out at this very moment."

"I see." She rubbed Carli's cheek. "Do you know why Dad and I mostly stayed out of the whole situation between you, Warren and your sister?"

She sniffled. "Because you wanted us all to learn a valuable lesson on how thoroughly Carli could make a fool of herself?"

Louise gave her an affectionate smile. "Hardly. Because we knew you would figure out what was best for you. You've always been good at deciding what you want and going after it."

"I am?"

"Indeed." She gave her arm a tender squeeze. "From what I can see, you've determined what you want. Now are you going to go after it?"

Justin had decided to sleep in for the first time in his life. But whoever was calling his cell phone apparently had other plans. The screen read Hammond Ent, so he picked it up without delay fully expecting Carli to be on the other end.

Only it wasn't Carli calling.

A bolt of disappointment shot through him. Foolish, wishful thinking. Carli wanted nothing to do with him. He'd managed to earn her ire and scorn. Just as he'd earned his brother's all those years ago when his antics had finally pulled the family apart.

No, the deep baritone voice on the other end of the line belonged to his father. Looked like he had indeed blown his chance to rectify things with her. Justin sat up in bed and rubbed the sleep out of his eyes.

"Do you have a moment, son?"

Would he ever get used to hearing that word coming from Jackson? He glanced at the bedside clock on the bureau across his hotel room: 8:30 a.m. Much later than he usually slept, but he'd been restless and unable to fall asleep last night, reliving the events of the previous day repeatedly in his head.

"Sure." He just had to wake up fully first.

"I wanted to let you know I was very impressed with the initial plans you sent over. Once the repairs to the Cape store are completed, I'd like to begin implementing your ideas."

Justin sighed with relief. He'd been fully prepared to take matters into his own hands if he had to. "I'm glad to near it. I'm sure Carli will be more than anxious to get started on it all."

His father was silent a moment on the other end. "That's one of the things I'd like to discuss with you, in fact. I don't know what your plans are, but would you be able to come in later this morning to go over some of this?"

He couldn't mean what Justin was beginning to suspect he meant. Did he honestly have someone else besides Carli in mind to run the project? Rubbing his eyes, he answered, "I can be there within the hour."

"That's great, son. I'll see you then."

"Wait, Jackson."

"What is it?"

"I just want to be clear. All those ideas I proposed, I had Carli firmly in mind as the project manager to carry them through. I think she's the best qualified given how well she knows the store and the town."

He could hear his father's pride in Carli when he answered. "I couldn't agree with you more."

Then what was this all about?

Jackson gave him a jolt when he answered the unasked question. "I believe she may need some help. I wanted to talk to you about perhaps clearing your calendar for the next several months. Perhaps even permanently, depending on what you're comfortable with."

Now he was awake. "Never mind what I said earlier. I can be there in half an hour."

It took only twenty minutes.

His father was standing in front of his office window, staring down at the traffic bottleneck along Boylston Street when Justin knocked on his door.

Jackson motioned to the chair in front of his classic executive desk, and then waited for Justin to sit down before taking his own seat.

"Thank you for coming in so quickly, son."

"I had nothing else to do. What's this about?"

"To put it mildly, I'd like you to come back. Back to the Boston area, the Cape specifically. Back as a Hammond working for Hammond's Toys."

Mildly? Justin would not have called that mild. Bluntly sharp was more like it. "Just like that?"

"I realize what it would mean. You have a life back in Seattle, but we can talk about relocation incentives."

Justin was too shocked to speak.

"You're a rightful heir of this company. You need to be here at the helm, along with your brother."

A jarring thought occurred to him. "Are you dying?"

Jackson's immediate response was a loud snort of laughter. "Not that I know of!"

"Then what's going on?"

"I've been doing some thinking. About both you and James. Your brother came to me before the holidays. Started a conversation we probably should have had years, perhaps even decades, ago."

Justin rubbed a hand down his face. If this was Jackson's attempt at some sort of reconciliation after all these years, he was totally unprepared for it.

"It made me realize how much I missed of you boys growing up. You especially."

Whoa. He definitely hadn't seen that coming. "I don't know what to say."

"Then I'll just do the talking for a bit." He took a deep breath as if to steady himself. "I know I should have tried harder to contact you. But your mother was a…a difficult woman. The time to cast blame or bad-mouth anyone is long gone. But she loved to remind me how much trouble you were."

"I remember."

"Only, you really weren't. I think you were a convenient way to prove to me that I was insufficient, that there was something I couldn't handle. I'm convinced she took you with her that night just to drive that point home. I couldn't handle you. So she left and took you with her."

Justin tried to process all he was being told. Given what he knew of his mother, it wasn't a terribly farfetched theory. But the idea that he'd simply been a pawn in his mother's argument stung more than he would have liked.

"That still doesn't explain why you chose to let her get away with it. Why you didn't make any kind of attempt to have some sort of contact, or even a relationship."

"I have no excuse, I'm afraid. Except that maybe on some level, I let her convince me of it too."

Jackson looked away then, studied a Bruins banner he had hanging on the wall to his left. "I know I should have tried harder to track you down. But she moved around so often. Support payments went direct to her bank account. And as the years grew longer, the prospect seemed more and more futile. But I'm trying now, if it's not too late."

A week ago, Justin would have told his father precisely that it was too late. But a lot had changed since then.

He'd met Carli Tynan.

Justin braced himself against the cold wind as he stood outside Carli's door on the footstep. He'd gone over various ways he might approach the conversation countless times in his head. But for the life of him, he still had no idea where he would start once she opened the door. He'd called earlier to tell her he would be stopping by. To say she was shocked would be an understatement. It had been

unclear whether that was pleasant shock or the opposite.
He supposed he was about to find out.

Taking a deep breath, he rang the doorbell, then waited.
It opened within seconds and Carli stepped aside to let
him. The apartment was just as festive as he remembered;
Christmas decorations still adorned every wall and corner.
Hard to believe that had only been a few short days ago.

"I'm surprised you're still in town." She looked different, tired. Dark smudges framed her eyes; her skin appeared paler. When she turned and walked to the sofa,
there was unmistakably less of a spring in her step.

He had done that to her; he couldn't deny it. And he
wanted to kick himself for his behavior. Well, it was the
reason he was here.

"I decided to delay my return flight."

"I see. Can I get you anything? Coffee or something?"

This felt so wrong. Just a couple of days ago they'd spent
the night sleeping in each other's arms in front of a cozy
fireplace as a turbulent snowstorm raged outside. Now
they were addressing each other as strangers.

"No, thank you."

She motioned to the loveseat he stood next to. "Have
a seat."

He took off his coat and sat, trying once again to come
up with the right words to say. He should have tried harder
to make her understand at the store. Instead, he'd run.

Something he deeply regretted now.

He had to tell her that. But when he tried, they both
started talking at the same time, awkwardly speaking over
each other.

Justin ran a hand through his hair. "Please, go ahead."

"I was just wondering why you delayed your flight."

"Or why I'm here, for that matter?"

"That thought had crossed my mind, as well." She

pulled her feet under her and positioned herself into a ball on the couch. "I imagine it has to do with the Cape store?"

"In part."

"I don't understand."

"I was actually just hoping to try to clear the air between the two of us."

"I see."

"I should have had the courtesy of listening to you that day, Carli."

Her gaze shifted downward, and she hugged her knees.

"I mentioned something to you the first day I arrived. When I made the mistake of judging you, do you remember that?"

"I think so, something about how it had nothing to do with me and everything to do with Jackson."

Bingo.

He should have known she was sharp enough to recall exactly what he was referring to. She was one of a kind. What a fool he was, to have had a chance with someone like her and to have blown it the way he had.

"And apparently, I didn't learn my lesson the first time I messed up."

Women like Carli didn't come along twice in one lifetime. His mishandling of it all was just one more thing in a long line of missteps he was going to have to live with. He got the distinct impression it might be the biggest. He had only himself to blame.

To spare her the effort of summoning a response, he stood and grabbed his coat. "I should leave. Thanks for giving me a minute."

Carli jumped up too. "Wait, before you go." She walked over to the oak angled desk under the corner window and pulled out a sketch pad. Tearing off the top sheet, she handed it to him. "I just finished it."

It took Justin a moment to realize what he was looking at. Then he remembered the framed sketch he had seen mounted along her parents' hallway.

She had drawn *him*. The piece of paper had one large portrait of him as an adult in the center and then another drawn smaller in the corner. The smaller one portrayed him as a boy. She had clearly based it on the newspaper captioned photo Mr. Freider had given him back at the Cape.

The resemblance in both was amazing, detailed and nuanced.

But more than merely replicating his physical features, the charcoal portrait seemed to capture his aura, right down to his soul. Only someone who had looked beneath the surface to his very core could have been able to draw him the way she had. The effect rendered him speechless.

"Do you like it?" she asked in a nervous and hesitant voice. How could she possibly be insecure with talent like that?

"It's the nicest thing anyone's ever given me. Or done for me, actually."

Yeah, he thought as he stared at the picture. He had definitely blown it.

CHAPTER THIRTEEN

CARLI HAD FULLY intended to give Justin the sketch since the moment she'd started it after the heartfelt conversation with her mother. It just hadn't occurred to her that he would be there in person to accept it. She'd expected to have to mail it to him at some point. When they were both somehow past the fateful events of the last week.

She figured that would have put the ball squarely in his court. He'd beaten her to the punch, however, when he'd surprised her with a phone call earlier this afternoon.

"I planned on rolling it and packaging it for you," she told him. "But since you're here, it's yours to take."

He blew out a deep breath. "I don't know what to say. Except I thought you said you had stopped sketching?" His gaze never left the paper he held in his hands.

"Yeah. I had. But I was inspired." She wasn't going to tell him just how inspired she'd been. The sketch had taken hours, and she'd been working nearly nonstop. In fact, she'd been tidying up furiously after receiving Justin's call that he was coming by.

It had been shocking enough to discover he was still in town. But to have him actually want to visit her apartment was a whole other level of altered reality. She wasn't entirely sure she wasn't dreaming this whole thing up at this very moment.

"I can't help but feel honored," he admitted, and a silly rush of girlish pleasure shot clear through her toes. "Can I ask you something?"

"Sure."

"Why did you ever stop in the first place? You have an amazing gift for it."

She had a hunch the question may have been coming. This was the risk she'd known she was taking when she picked up the charcoal pencil.

"Let me guess, it's a long story."

"Actually, it's not. It's quite an old, regular story, in fact."

He quirked an eyebrow in question.

"It's hard to put your heart into a drawing unless you feel a true joy in doing so. I'd lost that for a while. Now it seems to be back."

Justin's eyes flicked over her face. "I must say I'm honored."

She wanted to tell him there was so much behind her rendering of his image. His face was the first thing she saw when she closed her eyes before going to sleep. Those hazel eyes of his haunted her dreams and even her waking moment. But what purpose would it serve? Some things were better left unsaid.

She followed Justin as he made his way to the door. Suddenly, he pivoted on his heel. Carli's heart thud against her chest. He couldn't leave just yet.

"I almost forgot. I emailed you a document with detailing some ideas. For the Cape store. Please take a look when you get a chance."

Just a request to look at a file. "Oh, I'll be sure to do that."

Without another word, he opened the door and left.

Carli stared helplessly outside her window as she

watched Justin walk briskly down the street, the sketch tucked under his arm. She felt torn and helpless. But what was there to do? They'd made their peace as best as could be expected.

So why did she feel like a boulder was sitting on her rib cage?

Just to give herself something to do, she flipped open her tablet and called up the email program. As he'd said, Justin's email sat toward the top. Clicking it open, she began to read.

It didn't take much time to come to a decision. She couldn't let Justin fly to Seattle and walk out of her life. She didn't even bother to grab her coat.

"Justin wait!"

Justin was almost afraid to turn around. What if he was simply imagining her voice? It was very likely he wanted to see her so badly that his mind was playing tricks on him. But when he turned around, there she was. Without a coat.

"Carli?"

He quickly went over to her; she was shivering. "You're freezing. And I don't even have a scarf to offer this time."

She laughed at that even as she rubbed her upper arms with her hands in an effort to get warm.

Justin didn't think about right or wrong at that moment. He simply went to her and put his arms around her shoulders, pulled her close.

"What are you doing out here? It's about twenty degrees."

Her teeth chattered as she answered him. "I think it's less than that."

He pulled her closer.

"I wanted to tell you I looked at the email," she said against the base of his neck.

"Okay. You could have simply typed a reply."

She shook her head. "No, that would not have worked."

"It wouldn't have?"

"No way. We clearly have to discuss all your suggestions in person."

A heady feeling of warmth began to spread through his chest. "I see."

With her in his embrace, he inhaled the scent of coconut shampoo and that soft subtle scent of hers that he'd grown so fond of. God, he'd missed it.

"There's no other way," she said, snuggled tight up against him. "You're going to have to have dinner with me."

"Is that so?" he asked, unable to stop himself from dropping a hint of a kiss to the top of her head.

"Uh-huh. You're just lucky my mother passed on her lasagna recipe to all her girls."

She had no idea. Justin hadn't realized he could be so lucky. Lifting her chin with his finger, he decided he needed to show her with a kiss.

How in the world had he been talked into this? Justin adjusted the scratchy fake beard and groaned as he looked in the mirror in his new room at the Sailor's Inn. The answer stood next to him. Carli Tynan could probably get him to do anything with that sweet smile of hers.

Also, she'd reminded him of all the times he'd uttered the words "I'll make it up to you, somehow" since he'd met her. But this was hardly playing fair.

She stepped up to him and placed the velvet red hat atop his head. "You know, for someone who insists he's not really that into Christmas, you make a pretty good Santa Claus."

"If you say so." The goose-down pillow that was supposed to be his fake stomach threatened to drop once more, and he tightened the belt that held it up. Carli had informed him this morning that the actor who usually played Santa at the Westerson snowman competition had backed out due to a nasty case of the flu. She thought Justin would be the perfect replacement as he was the stranger in town and therefore less likely to be recognized by the older children.

Frankly, he didn't think he was going to be able to fool anybody. For one thing, every time he tried to yell "Ho-ho-ho!" he sounded utterly ridiculous. Which was exactly how he felt.

"You'll do fine," Carli reassured him. "You just have to walk around the tree farm commenting on all the contestant snowmen and hand out a few toys along the way. Hammond's was very sweet to donate those, by the way. Not to mention the matching donation to Toys for Tykes."

He shrugged. "I'm surprised there wasn't any kind of donation program to that charity up until now."

"There wasn't one until you started it." She gave him a peck on the cheek.

"Uh-uh." He grabbed her gently by the waist, pulling her up against his length. "You're gonna have to do better than that. Seeing as you're the only reason I'm dressed in this ridiculous costume and about to make a complete fool of myself."

Taking him up on his challenge, Carli hooked her arms around his neck and brought his mouth down to hers.

"How's that?" she asked with a breathless sigh when he finally managed to pull away.

"I'd say it'll do. For now."

The truth was he'd never be able to get enough of her. They'd been spending most of the days together since that fateful morning he'd stopped by her apartment. To think he had almost simply emailed her then left town. Taking the chance to go see her had been the best decision he'd ever made.

Unlike the decision to agree to this whole Santa thing. That was a totally different story. Carli noted the time on her cell phone. "We should make our way down. It's officially about to start. We'll have to sneak you out the inn's receiving door in the back of the building."

"Just tell me I don't have to ride in a sled."

The tree farm was bustling with activity when they arrived. Justin hoisted the toy bag over his shoulder and was immediately surrounded by a slew of youngsters.

"Santa's here!"

Despite himself, Justin had to admit this was somewhat fun. The cheers and laughter from the children as he handed out toys buoyed his spirits. Or maybe that was just the effect of Carli's infectious laugh as she walked by his side. He even attempted a lame "Ho-ho-ho" once or twice. Eventually, the onslaught of children approaching them slowed to a steady trickle, with a single child here and there. Good thing. His bag of toys was nearly empty.

"Aunt Carli!" Ray's exuberant voice rang behind them, and they both turned around as the boy ran up.

"Ray!" Carli bent and embraced her nephew. "Would you like to say hello to Santa?"

Ray's response was a knowing giggle. "That's not Santa! That's Justin!"

Carli gave a frantic look around and put her gloved finger to Ray's mouth. Luckily, no other kids were near them at the moment.

"Shh, you don't want to spoil it for the other kids."

"Okay."

"But how did you know?" Carli asked the child as Justin crouched to give him a fist bump.

Ray shrugged as if it should be obvious. "Prolly 'cause his eyes. But mostly 'cause I know him. He's my friend."

"I see."

"And he's your boyfriend!" Ray added, nearly shouting this time as he clearly thought this was a hilarious thing to say.

Justin's eyes met Carli's over Ray's head. A surge of emotion shot through him. Her nose had gone a deep cherry-red in the cold. She wore a fuzzy elf's hat on top of her head with a small bell at the end. Her ears were adorned with the same snowman earrings she'd worn the night of her office party. The whole look was meant to appear whimsical and fun in the spirit of Christmas.

He didn't think any woman had ever looked more strikingly beautiful.

"You're right," Carli answered her nephew. "He is my boyfriend."

EPILOGUE

One year later

JUSTIN SCANNED THE large and ever-growing crowd in front of him. All of Westerson appeared to be here. He'd been an official resident for just under a year now, and it never ceased to amaze him the degree of loyalty the people of this town had for each other.

How he'd managed to snare one of their own as his fiancée he would never fully grasp. But he knew better than to ever take it for granted.

The object of his thoughts approached him from the side of the dais. "It's time to cut the ribbon," Carli prompted.

Mr. Freider came to stand next to her. He would be the one doing the actual cutting. After having managed the store for over two decades, and how hard the man had worked to bring the new version to fruition, he more than deserved the honor.

James and Noelle stood ready behind them near the podium. They'd flown in two days ago for the grand opening of the new and improved Hammond's Toys Cape store. A project that had been a year in the making.

"Ready?" he asked her.

"I think so. Funny, I know everyone here quite well. But I'm still nervous to speak in front of all these people."

"You'll do great," he assured her.

Carli leaned into the microphone and cleared her throat. "Thank you everyone for coming," she began. "We are so excited to unveil the new Hammond's Toys Cape store. Although the name has not changed, a lot inside the store has. For those of you who haven't had a chance to read the write-up in the *Westerson Eagle* or haven't otherwise heard, Hammond's now is so much more than a toy store. It's been expanded to include a teen center, an arts and crafts area, which will offer weekly lessons, as well as a state-of-the-art arcade. And so much more in the way of seasonal activities depending on the time of year." She gave him a smile that shot pleasure through his chest, then took a deep breath. "I can't tell you how proud it makes me to tell you that all this was the brainchild of my fiancé, Justin Hammond." She held her hand out toward him.

Justin's turned to the audience and took a mock bow. "That was the easy part," he yelled toward the crowd. As was the financing. Justin had found willing investors in a relatively short period of time once he explained his vision. The store was such a central point of the town, it only made sense to have it offer more reasons for the customers to visit and more for them to do once they got there. All those new attractions Carli mentioned would not only bring in their own revenue, they'd increase traffic to the actual toy store—resulting in higher sales.

Carli continued. "And now, without further delay, we would like to welcome you to the new Hammond's."

Cheers and raucous clapping erupted before she even finished the sentence. Once the applause died down, the five of them watched as Mr. Freider handled the comically large scissors to cut the wide red ribbon. Two newly hired employees dressed as elves pulled the double doors open to let the still cheering crowd into the renovated store.

His brother came to give him an enthusiastic handshake. "Well, done, man."

"Thanks." It was taking a while, but they were slowly starting to get to know each other. Bonding over the two women in their lives played no small role in their growing relationship.

"I can't tell you how much Noelle appreciates Carli's gesture," James told him, his gaze traveling to where the two ladies stood chatting by the doors. "She's really looking forward to being a bridesmaid."

What was one more? Justin thought. At this rate they were going to have the largest bridal party ever heard of. Not that he was complaining. Carli Tynan deserved to have the wedding she wanted, down to every detail. "I'm glad they're growing so close."

Right on cue, the two women shared a laugh at something Carli had said. Justin and James went to join them.

"You did great," he told her as James and Noelle entered the store.

"I'm glad that part's over," she replied. "Now we can finally start planning for the other big event."

"Oh? I'm not exactly sure what you might be referring to. There's a lot happening," he teased, and gave her a playful tap on the tip of the nose. She meant the wedding, of course.

"Very funny."

Justin pulled her to him and gave her a deep, lingering kiss. Something told him planning their nuptials was going to take just as much time and effort as opening the new store. That's what happened when you had a family as large as the Tynans and everyone possessed input they had to share.

He wouldn't have it any other way.

The easiest decision by far had been picking the date.

Twelve months from now, Justin would be walking his Christmas bride down the aisle.

He could hardly wait.

* * * * *

CHRISTMAS BRIDE
FOR THE BOSS

KATE HARDY

To Gay, my much-loved stepmum,
who's the living proof that stepmothers are
AWESOME

CHAPTER ONE

'ALL RIGHT, MISS FIRTH. You have ten minutes to convince me why I should invest in your company.' Jamie Wallis leaned back in his chair, unsmiling, and looked at her.

Sophie caught her breath.

This was it.

The next ten minutes could change her entire life.

She needed to be more professional now than she'd ever been. And she really needed to ignore the fact that Jamie Wallis was one of the most beautiful men she'd ever met. The photographs she'd seen didn't do him justice. And Eva hadn't warned her that you could practically drown in his dark eyes.

Focus, she told herself. Because everyone's counting on you to get his backing. And you don't do relationships any more. Not since Joe. You finally learned your lesson: focus on your business.

'Thank you,' she said. 'I'm assuming you've gone through the accounts I sent you, so you'll already know our company's bottom line is solid.'

He inclined his head, still unsmiling. 'So why exactly are you asking me to invest in your company?'

She took a deep breath. 'Because as well as you owning several resorts, your company offers specialist holidays to travellers, so Plans & Planes—being a travel agency and event planning service—fits in very well with your business. Especially as we're introducing a new service which merges both sides of our company—something you don't offer at the moment.'

'Which is?' he asked.

'A planning service for people who want to get married abroad. We can organise everything from the wedding ceremony and reception through to the honeymoon, plus accommodation for the guests, and we'll deal with all the paperwork.' It had been her brainchild and she'd been so looking forward to developing the new service.

Until Eva had dropped her bombshell.

'And your approach to me has nothing to do with the fact that your former partner is my late wife's cousin?'

Sophie had expected that question and worked out her answer in advance. 'Eva suggested you as a potential investor, I admit. But I researched your company before I decided to approach you. I'm not looking for nepotism. I'm looking for someone who sees a good investment that fits in with their own business plans.'

'I see.' He steepled his fingers. 'What about the fact that Eva's leaving the company? How do I know that everything at Plans & Planes isn't going to take a massive nosedive without Eva at the helm?'

It was a fair question and Sophie wasn't going to take it personally. 'The impact of Eva's departure on the business is mainly financial.' The impact on her was another matter: Eva was Sophie's best friend as well as her business partner and she'd miss Eva hugely. 'Eva's deputy, Mara, has worked for us for the last three years and she's ready to step into Eva's shoes on the travel agency side,' she explained. 'Mara has the experience, the knowledge and the capability to take that part of the company forward. I'm staying to manage the event planning side and the new weddings abroad service, so there's continuity of management.'

He made a couple of notes. 'If the business is flourishing, why do you need an investor?'

'Because, as I'm sure you're aware, Eva is moving to New York with her fiancé.' Aidan had been headhunted by a top New York advertising agency and the opportunity was too good to turn down. 'So she needs me to buy out her half of the business.'

'And you have no savings you can use to buy her out, Miss Firth?'

She had, until two months ago. She took a deep breath. 'No.'

'Why?'

Telling him the truth would make it sound as if she was trying to manipulate him. Plus it was between Sophie, her brother and her sister-in-law. She wasn't going to break their confidence. 'Personal reasons,' she said.

'Won't your bank give you a loan?'

She winced inwardly, knowing how bad her answer was going to sound, but she wasn't going to lie. 'No.'

He raised an eyebrow. 'Because your financial management isn't good enough?'

'There's nothing wrong with my financial management,' she said patiently. 'The business is doing well.'

'Then why don't you have savings, Miss Firth?'

'Personal reasons,' she repeated.

'That, Miss Firth, is tantamount to telling an insurance company that you're a businesswoman. It's too vague. They'll need to know precisely what business you're in so they can assess the risk.'

'I'm not asking you to insure me, Mr Wallis. I'm asking you to invest in the business.'

He gave her a cool, assessing look. 'Miss Firth, if you want me to invest in your company, you can't hide behind "personal reasons".'

Maybe she could tell him some of it. Broad brush rather than details. 'All right,' she said reluctantly. 'Since you ask, I lent my savings to someone I love very much.'

'Then surely you can ask that person to return the money, now you need it for yourself?'

'No.'

He frowned. 'Why not?'

Because the money had been spent, and her brother and sister-in-law were already under enough pressure. This was their fourth attempt at IVF, and she didn't want to make it any harder for them than it already was. 'I can't explain more without breaking a confidence.'

'So you'd rather see your business go under?'

'Of course not. We have four staff and a roster of reliable temps, and I want them to have job security.'

He shrugged. 'Then ask for the money back so you can buy out Eva's share of the business.'

They were at stalemate. Or maybe there was another way round this. 'Do you have siblings, Mr Wallis?' she asked, already knowing that he did but not knowing how close he was to them; not every family was as close as hers.

He inclined his head. 'Two.'

'If they needed you, would you hesitate to help?' she asked.

'Of course not.'

Just what she'd hoped he'd say. 'Then I can safely

say you would've made the same decision I did, in those circumstances,' she said.

'Given that I don't know the circum—'

His mobile phone shrilled, cutting him off mid-word. He glanced at the screen, as if about to hit the button to decline the call, then frowned.

'I apologise, Miss Firth. I'm afraid I need to take this.'

From the expression on his face, this was definitely a private call, Sophie thought. 'Shall I wait…?' She indicated the reception area outside his office.

He looked grateful. 'Thank you.'

Sophie left Jamie's office, sat down on one of the chairs and closed her eyes.

The bank had already said no. It was pretty clear that Jamie Wallis, her plan B, was going to turn her down. So now she needed to work out a plan C.

Crowdsourcing? No. It'd make her look as if the business had run out of money. Which it hadn't.

Offering shares in the business to the rest of the team? But Mara was about to get married and the other three were saving up the deposit for a flat. None of them had any spare money, much less the ability to raise a loan to buy out part of Eva's share in Plans & Planes.

And Jamie's suggestion of asking Matt and Angie to return the money was completely out of the question. Her brother and sister-in-law had been eligible for one free cycle of IVF treatment; it hadn't worked and they'd already used up all their own savings and taken out a loan to pay for the next two cycles, which had also failed.

OK, so there were no guarantees that the fourth cycle would be the lucky one, and if it had been purely a business decision Sophie probably would have decided that the risk was too great. But this wasn't a business decision. How could she possibly have stood by and watched their hearts break when she could do something to help? So she hadn't hesitated on offering to fund another cycle of treatment. She'd said it was a loan that Matt and Angie could repay whenever, but she'd always intended to quietly forget about the money. If the IVF worked and they had the baby they so desperately wanted, it would be the best repayment she could ask for.

'So let me get this straight,' Jamie said, scowling at the phone. 'You're telling me that Cindy broke her leg skiing yesterday, so she won't be able to walk, let alone work, for at least another two months. And you can't offer me a temporary replacement for her because the nanny who took over while she was on holiday is already on another assignment, and everyone else on your books is already either on an assignment and can't possibly be moved, or has gone down with a virus.'

'I'm afraid so, Mr Wallis. I know it sounds like a feeble excuse, but it's quite a nasty virus. It takes a couple of weeks to get over it. I'm so sorry,' Felicity, the agency manager, said.

'Effectively you're leaving me in the lurch.' Was there anyone in his staff he could ask to switch roles temporarily? He could hardly ask one of the resort team to move to London for two months, especially with Christmas coming up. There was nobody suitable in his London team, either. Those with children already had enough on their plates and he couldn't expect them to neglect their own children for Sienna. The ones without children didn't have the relevant experience. Short of asking his mother to help—and he knew from first-hand experience that his mother preferred to parent at a distance—Jamie knew he was stuck.

'I wish it wasn't the case, but I'm afraid the situation's completely out of my hands, Mr Wallis,' Felicity said.

He could try another agency, but he still wouldn't be able to guarantee having a new temporary nanny in place by the end of today—or that she'd be able to stay until Cindy was back at work. He didn't want to dump his daughter on a string of women she didn't know. Sienna needed continuity.

'How soon do you think you'll be able to get me a nanny to replace Cindy until her leg's healed?' he asked.

'I really don't know, Mr Wallis. It depends how quickly my staff recover. It might be a week, or it might be a fortnight.'

Although Jamie really wanted to shout at Felicity in utter frustration, he knew that would be counter-productive. Fran had always said you caught more flies with honey. His late wife had always been more patient with people than he had; he found it hard to be charming in the face of sheer incompetence. 'This is going to be very difficult for me,' he said, resisting the urge to twist the guilt by reminding Felicity that he was a single father and didn't have anyone to take up the slack. 'But could you please call me as soon as someone's available?'

'Of course, Mr Wallis. Thank you for being so understanding.'

He forbore to comment, not trusting himself to stay polite.

And now he had a problem. A big one. An unspecified time—anything between a few days and a couple of months—without a nanny, and even when someone became available it might not be for the whole period that Cindy was away. He was in the middle of setting up a new resort, so he simply couldn't take the best part of the next few weeks off work to look after Sienna. He'd trusted the agency to deal with any situation like this, and they'd let him down. Badly.

What the hell was he going to do?

It was rare that he found himself in a situation where he wasn't in complete control, and he hated the feeling of being helpless.

Sophie Firth was sitting in the reception area outside his office. Right now, they were both in a mess. She needed someone to invest in her business quickly so she could afford to buy out her partner; and he needed a nanny for the next few weeks.

He could maybe help her—especially as Eva was his late wife's cousin and he ought to support his family—but right now he needed to focus on sorting out his immediate problem. He was going to have to turn her down.

He took a deep breath and went out to the reception area. 'Miss Firth, I'm sorry to have kept you waiting.'

'That's fine,' she said.

He raked a hand through his hair. 'I'm sorry—I can't help you right at this minute. Something's cropped up and I need to deal with it.'

Just as Sophie had expected. She needed Plan C. Disappointment still flooded through her. He wasn't even going to be honest and say he wasn't interested.

Something's cropped up.

And to think he'd called *her* on being vague.

Then again, there was something akin to despera-
tion in his eyes—as if something had happened and
he didn't have a clue how to deal with it. From the research she'd done on his company, she knew he was
a shrewd businessman; his company had grown from
strength to strength in the last few years, and even the
death of his wife hadn't affected the business. What
could have happened to throw him like this?

Before she could stop herself, the words came out.
'Are you all right?'

He looked at her in shock. 'How do you mean?'

'You look,' she said, 'as if someone just dropped
something on you from a great height.'

'You could say that.' He sighed. 'It's my problem. I
have to deal with it.'

But he sounded as if he didn't have the faintest clue
where to start.

This was none of her business. She had enough of
a problem herself. She should just walk away. Instead,
she found herself asking, 'Can I get you a cup of tea
or something?'

She cringed even as the words came out. It was his
office, not hers. What she was saying was totally inappropriate.

But he smiled at her. The first real smile she'd seen
from him. And it made her knees weak.

'That's kind,' he said.

'And inappropriate. Sorry.'

He shook his head. 'That's kind,' he repeated. 'But
at the moment tea isn't going to help.' He looked at her.
'Given your business, you must know people in lots of
different career areas. I don't suppose you know any
nannies, do you?'

'Nannies?'

'That call just now was from the agency which supplies the nanny who looks after my daughter. Cindy—our nanny—broke her leg last week when she was on a skiing trip. And the agency has nobody available to stand in for her right now.'

So he needed childcare help?

Maybe she could turn this into a win-win situation.

'So I need someone to invest in Plans & Planes, and you need a nanny.'

He looked at her. 'Yes.'

'Maybe,' she said carefully, 'there's a solution that will work for us both. A business solution.'

'You know a nanny?'

'Not *exactly*.' She took a deep breath. 'What type of hours are we talking about?'

'Sienna's at nursery school five days a week, nine to four-thirty.'

Long hours for a little one, she thought. 'So your nanny takes her to nursery school, picks her up, and that's it?'

'And works evenings and weekends.'

So when did Jamie Wallis spend time with his daughter? she wondered.

More to the point, it made her own half-formed plan unworkable. Time management was one of her best skills, but even she couldn't cram an extra twenty-four hours into a day. 'Can that be negotiable?' she asked.

'How?'

What was the worst he could do? Say no. Which was pretty much what she thought he'd say anyway. She had nothing to lose—and potentially a lot to gain. And she wasn't afraid of hard work.

'I could be your temporary nanny,' she said, 'and you could invest in my business.'

He stared at her. 'You're a qualified nanny?'

'Not a qualified nanny,' she said. 'But my parents' next-door neighbours own a nursery school, and during sixth form I had a part-time job there—Wednesday afternoons, when I didn't have lessons, and two hours after school on the other weekdays. So I have experience of working with under-fives. Even if it was ten years ago. Plus I have a four-year-old niece and a two-year-old nephew, and I'm a very hands-on aunt.'

'Define "hands-on".'

'I see them every week. I babysit, so I do everything from playing to craft stuff and singing. I do bathtime, bedtime stories and the park.' She looked at him. 'I sometimes have to work with children as part of an event, so I—and all my staff—have an up-to-date Disclosure and Barring Service check certificate. And I'm happy to give you Anna's details so she can give you a reference from my time at the nursery school.'

A quid pro quo.

Sophie Firth wasn't a qualified nanny, but she was the next best thing.

'So you'd give up your job for the next two months?' he asked.

'No. That's why I asked about compromise,' she said. 'My business partner is leaving in six weeks' time. We need to reallocate all her work and recruit a new member of staff. Plus I already have a full diary. I can reallocate some of my work, and do the rest while Siena is at nursery school and at weekends.'

So he'd be with Sienna twenty-four-seven. Just

the two of them. His throat went dry at the idea. He couldn't do it. 'I need a nanny and weekends,' he said.

'I can do one day. Two halves, if that works better for you. But I need experienced staff, and recruitment takes time.'

This was starting to sound workable. 'I could lend you a couple of my staff to take off some of the pressure. Ones with experience in the travel industry and who've worked with—well, not events in the way you run them, but promotions. There must be a fair crossover in the skill sets involved.'

'There is,' she agreed.

'So if I lend you some staff, you'll do the full weekend?'

'Two half days or one full,' she repeated.

'I'm in the middle of negotiating a new resort. I can't take time off work right now.' That wasn't the only reason, but he wasn't discussing the rest of it with a total stranger. Even if she was potentially sorting out his huge headache.

'You said you had siblings. Can't they pitch in and help?'

'They live too far away.'

'What about your parents?'

Absolutely not. His parents had never been hands-on when he and his sisters had been tiny. They'd always been focused on the business. Until the next generation was old enough to have their lives organised—and that was one of the reasons why his sisters had moved to Cumbria and Cornwall respectively. Gwen Wallis had tried to run their lives in the same way she ran her business. Not wanting to explain that, he shook his head.

'I apologise if I've just trampled on a sore spot,' she said softly. 'That wasn't my intention.'

It sounded as if she thought his parents were elderly and frail, or had passed away. That wasn't the case but it was too complicated to put into words. 'It's fine,' he said. 'So you do weekends?'

'Two half days or one full,' she repeated.

He wasn't sure whether to be more exasperated or admiring. She wasn't budging. Then again, she was already making a big compromise—giving up a large chunk of her working week and meaning that she'd be running two jobs at the same time.

Admiring, he decided. Sophie Firth had a good work ethic—and she'd thought on her feet to come up with a solution that would benefit them both.

This was crisis management. *Good* crisis management. She'd seen the problem, come up with a solution and seen where the gaps were. It was the best proof she could have given him that she was good at her job, and investing in her business would be a sound decision on his part.

'Obviously I need to check out your references with the nursery school,' he said.

'And talk to Eva—you know her, and she's known me since our first day at university. She can give you a personal reference.' She took out her phone and handed it to him. 'Just so you can be sure I'm not calling her while you're otherwise occupied and priming her on what to say.'

He really liked how quick she was. The way she thought. If it wasn't for the fact that she was fighting for the survival of her own business, he'd be tempted to offer her a job as a project manager on his team.

'All right. If your references check out, you've got a deal.'

* * *

She'd done it. Sophie knew that Anna and Eva would give her a good reference.

But her conscience couldn't quite leave it there.

'Two caveats,' she said.

'Which are?'

'Firstly, you'll be strictly a sleeping partner in Plans & Planes, and you don't interfere in the way I run things.'

He raised an eyebrow. 'What if I can see where you can make improvements to the business?'

'You can make suggestions, but you don't interfere,' she said. 'Though that's not the deal-breaker.'

He looked intrigued. 'What is?'

'Your daughter gets the final say.'

He frowned. 'How do you mean?'

'She meets me. We spend some time together. And then you ask her—and *not* in front of me—if she'd like me to look after her while her nanny gets better. If she says no, then it's a no.'

He nodded. 'That's fair. And it also tells me you're the right person for the job, because you're putting her needs first.'

But why wasn't *he*? Sophie wondered. Yes, he had a business to run—but it was much bigger than hers. He could delegate a lot of his work. Why didn't he take the time off to look after his daughter?

Given that she'd already made a gaffe about his parents, this wasn't something she could ask directly. She'd need to be tactful.

'Okay. I'll talk to Eva and your parents' neighbour. Can you give me the numbers?' he asked.

He didn't know Eva's number? Well, maybe Fran—as Eva's cousin—would have been the one to stay in

touch. 'You're probably best to call her at Plans &
Planes.' She gave him the office number. 'Failing that,
this is her mobile.'

He wrote the numbers down as she dictated them.
'Thank you.'

Anna Harris confirmed everything Sophie had told
him.

'She worked for me during sixth form—two hours at
the end of the school day, plus Wednesday afternoons.
The kids loved her. I did try to persuade her to do her
degree in early years education, but her heart was set
on doing English.' Anna paused. 'I thought she was
running her own business?'

'She is. She's, um, doing me a favour,' Jamie admitted.

'Ah. Typical Sophie. Of course you're right to check
her out, but I have no hesitation in recommending her.'

'Thank you,' Jamie said.

It almost felt superfluous to check her out with Eva
as well, but he wanted to be sure. For Sienna's sake.
Because he did love his daughter, even if he kept himself at a distance. He wanted the best for her.

Only, the best meant *not* him.

He dialled Eva's number.

'Good morning. Plans & Planes, Mara speaking,'
the woman on the other end of the phone said, sounding cheerful and welcoming.

Mara was Eva's second in command, according to
Sophie. If her business acumen was as good as her
phone manner, it boded well for the company, he
thought. 'Good morning. May I speak to Eva?' Jamie
asked.

'May I ask who's calling?'

'Jamie Wallis.'

'Oh!' For a second, Mara sounded flustered. Clearly she not only knew who he was, she also knew how important he could be to the future of the firm—and that Sophie was meant to be schmoozing him right now. 'I'll just put you through, Mr Wallis,' she said.

Eva answered, seconds later.

'How are you, Eva?' he asked.

'Fine, thanks, Jamie. And you?'

'Fine, fine.'

'Um, aren't you in a meeting with Sophie right now?' She sounded worried.

'Loo break,' he fibbed. Because explaining their deal would take too much time.

'Oh. Right.'

'Eva. Look, I know I haven't seen you for a while—'

'That's OK,' she cut in. 'Everyone understands.'

He mentally filled in the rest of it: how difficult things must have been since Fran died, and how it's harder to stay in touch with people who aren't in the immediate family circle. It was true, but he was guiltily aware that he often hid behind his circumstances.

'Thank you. I just wanted to ask you a couple of things,' he said. 'Would you mind?'

'Of course,' she said.

'You've known Sophie how long?'

'Eleven years. Since we met on the first day at university.'

'And you've been in business together for five years.'

'We'd still be in business together for the next fifty years, if Aidan hadn't been headhunted,' Eva said. 'But it's just not doable to run my half of the business from a different continent and a very different time zone, and it's not fair of me to dump all the work on Sophie and still expect to mop up half the profits.'

Good points, he thought. 'So you'd say Sophie was reliable and trustworthy?'

'Absolutely.' Eva's voice was firm with conviction.

And now the crunch question. 'And she's good with kids?'

'Yes. She babysits her niece and nephew all the time. Why?'

'Idle curiosity,' he fibbed.

But there was one little thing that was bothering him. He knew he was being a bit underhand, but he consoled himself that this was the quickest way to get the last bit of information he wanted. And wasn't all meant to be fair in love, war and business? 'And I've worked out for myself that she's kind-hearted. It was nice of her, wasn't it, to help her family with the money?' It was an educated guess; Sophie had only said she'd lent the money to someone she loved, but she'd also asked if he would help his siblings if they needed it. Which made him pretty sure she'd lent the money to one of her siblings.

'Yes, but that's Sophie all over—always thinking of others before herself,' Eva said. 'I really hope the IVF works for Matt and Angie this time.'

So he'd guessed right. She'd lent the money to one of her siblings and their partner. For a very personal reason: an expensive course of IVF treatment. And she'd refused to break their confidence by telling him what she'd done. Then again, if she *had* told him the truth, it would've looked as if she was trying to tug at his heartstrings and manipulate him. He liked the fact that she hadn't done that.

'Let's hope so,' he said. 'Thanks, Eva. Good luck in New York.'

'Thanks.' She paused. 'Jamie, I know I'm only an in-law, and not even a close one because I was Fran's cousin, but you're still family. Don't be a stranger.'

'Thanks.' Guilt flooded through him. He had been a stranger. Especially to Fran's family. Because how could he expect them to be rally round him, when he was the one responsible for all their pain—the one who was responsible for his wife's death? It would be like sprinkling salt over a wound. He couldn't do it. 'I'll talk to you soon,' he said, knowing it was a polite fiction and also knowing that Eva was well aware of the fact, but what else could he do?

Jamie walked back into the room and returned Sophie's phone. 'Thank you for your patience, Miss Firth. We have a deal.'

Yes. The business was safe, Eva would get the money she needed, and her staff had job security again. Mentally, Sophie punched the air. 'Thank you,' she said, trying to keep her voice businesslike.

'Though, actually, I probably didn't need to make those calls. I'm a reasonable judge of character.'

That's what she'd thought about herself. Dan and Joe had proved that to be a lie. She couldn't have got it any more wrong if she'd tried. 'I'm happier that you checked me out properly,' she said.

'OK. Do you drive?' he asked.

'Yes.'

'That makes life easier. I have a car that Cindy uses, so I'll put you on the insurance. Perhaps you could let my PA have a copy of your driving licence and let her know all the information that the insurer would need.'

'Sure. I have my licence with me.'

'Good. So are you able to meet Sienna this afternoon?'

If Sophie wanted to save her business, she didn't have much choice. She'd just have to move her meetings. 'What time do you want me to meet you at the nursery school?'

'It's probably better if I pick you up from your office and take you with me,' he said. 'Perhaps I could pick you up at half-past three, to give me time to brief you?'

'All right.'

'Thank you, Miss Firth. Or may I call you Sophie?'

'That rather depends on whether you expect me to curtsey and call you "sir",' she said dryly.

He smiled. 'Jamie will do.'

'Sophie.' She held out her hand. 'So, to recap, if Sienna likes me, then my side of the deal is that I'll be your temporary nanny until Cindy can come back to work. Your side is that you'll buy out Eva's share of my business, and lend me two staff while I'm nannying for you, to help with the transition.'

'Deal,' he said, and shook her outstretched hand.

Her skin actually tingled where he touched her. Which was so inappropriate—if this worked out, technically he would be her part-time employer and her part-time business partner. She couldn't afford to react to him like that. Worse still, he'd quickly masked an expression of surprise, so she had the feeling that he'd felt exactly the same.

This had the potential of being a complete and utter disaster. Especially with her track record in relationships, and in any case Jamie Wallis was a single father who really didn't have time for a relationship.

Maybe she should call off the deal.

But she didn't have a plan C and she needed him to buy out Eva's share of the firm. So she'd just have to ignore every bit of attraction she felt towards him and keep this strictly professional.

'One thing I should have asked you,' he said. 'Given that this means you'll be juggling your workload and it's going to take up more time in your day, will it be a problem with your partner?'

'I don't have a partner,' she said. 'And, just to make it clear, I'm not looking for one.' She knew that not all men were the same—her stepfather and her brothers were all wonderful—but she always seemed to pick Mr Wrong. Three years of dating Dan, and thinking that he was going to ask her to marry him when instead he'd dropped a bombshell; and then Joe, who'd lied to her from the outset and she'd felt disgusting and grubby when she'd learned the truth.

She wasn't going to put herself through all that again, falling in love with someone who would let her down and break her heart. After Joe, she'd promised herself that she'd keep all her relationships either business or strictly platonic. 'So I'll see you at half-past three,' she said. 'You have my mobile phone number in your file. If you could text me in the next couple of minutes, so I have your number, we can keep each other posted if anything crops up.'

'All right,' he said.

'And I'll see your PA with my driving licence on my way out.'

'Thank you, Miss F—Sophie,' he corrected himself. 'See you at half-past three.'

It looked as if he had a new nanny and a new business partner, Jamie thought as Sophie left his office.

A bossy one who liked to run things her own way; but he thought part of that might be bluster. The fact she'd said that Sienna should make the final decision told him that she'd be fair and listen.

Sophie Firth intrigued him. She was the first woman to intrigue him since Fran. If he was honest with himself, she was the first woman to attract him since Fran—with those sincere brown eyes and a warmth that drew him—but he pushed the thought away. It would be too complicated to have any kind of relationship with her outside a purely professional one.

Plus, after what he'd done, he didn't deserve one.

This was going to be strictly business.

'So Jamie actually said yes?' Eva asked.

Sophie lifted both hands in a 'whoa there' sign. 'It all hinges on whether Sienna likes me.'

'Sienna?'

'He's got a nanny crisis. The deal is, if Sienna likes me, I'll be her temporary nanny until her real nanny's broken leg has healed. And in return he'll buy you out.'

Eva frowned. 'So what about Plans & Planes? Are you hiring a temp to replace you?'

'No. I'm borrowing two members of his team to help with the workload,' Sophie said. 'I'll be here when Sienna's at nursery, and I can catch up with paperwork in the evening.'

'Well, that explains why he asked me about you and kids when he called. I thought he just wanted to double-check that you were a safe bet in business,' Eva said thoughtfully.

'What did you tell him?' Sophie asked.

'That I've known you since our first day at uni, and if Aidan hadn't been headhunted we'd still be business partners when we're really old, and you have a niece and nephew that you see all the time,' Eva said.

Sophie relaxed. 'OK. Well, you certainly helped. I just have to hope that Sienna likes me—or I'll have to start dreaming up a plan C.'

'But you're going to be working stupid hours, if you're being a nanny on top of what you do here,' Eva said, looking worried.

Sophie shrugged. 'It's not for ever, just for a couple of months, maybe. I'll manage.'

She hoped.

'So, to save me putting my foot in it, what actually happened to your cousin?' she asked.

'They were on holiday, two years ago, and Fran fell ill,' Eva said. 'She died before they could fly her home. It was so sad. She was only thirty-three.'

'And that means Sienna was only two when it happened, so she'll only know her mum through photos and videos. Poor little mite,' Sophie said.

'Jamie was devastated. I'm not sure he's really recovered. Today was the first time I'd really spoken to him since the funeral,' Eva said.

'Didn't his family rally round?'

'One of his sisters lives in Cornwall and I think the other lives in Cumbria,' Eva said.

No wonder he'd said they were too far away.

'And he said his parents can't help, either,' Sophie said. 'So I'm guessing they're either too frail or they've passed away.'

'Oh, they could help, all right,' Eva said, 'but his mum would take over. Fran said Gwen was really overbearing and forever trying to organise their lives for them. The epitome of a difficult mother-in-law.'

'Ouch.' That might explain why Jamie's sisters had

moved so far away from London, Sophie thought. And why Jamie seemed to keep himself at an emotional distance.

'Fran's mum is lovely, but Fran looked so much like her, I think it just brings back what he's lost every time Jamie sees her,' Eva said. 'Plus they live in Norfolk, so they're a bit too far away for him to be able to ask them for help.'

'Poor man,' Sophie said. Now she was beginning to see what made Jamie Wallis tick. And he had an even better excuse than she did for avoiding relationships: he was still a grieving widower, whereas she'd simply lost trust in her own judgement of people.

When Jamie left his office at half-past two, his PA raised an eyebrow as he passed her desk. 'Is everything all right?'

'Nanny crisis. I'm getting the potential temp to meet me at the nursery school,' he explained.

Her face softened. 'And how is Sienna?'

'Fine. And hopefully she'll get on with the temp.' If he kept referring to Sophie as 'the temp', hopefully that was how he'd come to see her. And he was absolutely not going to think about her caramel hair and how it would be lit with gold in the sunshine. For pity's sake. He didn't have *time* to think like that about anyone.

He called in at his house to pick up the file Cindy had left for the temporary nanny while she was on holiday, showing Sienna's routine, then drove to Plans & Planes. Sophie's office was very different from his own; the downstairs acted as the shop front for the travel agency, but when Mara showed him upstairs, where the event management side was based, he could see that the office was completely open plan, with two small rooms that he assumed were for client meetings.

Eva, who was sitting at one of the desks, came over and greeted him with a hug. 'You're a lifesaver, Jamie. Thanks.'

'Hopefully, Sophie's going to be a lifesaver for me, too,' he said.

'That all depends on whether Sienna likes me. It's the deal breaker,' Sophie reminded him as she joined them.

'Ready to go?' he asked.

'Ready.'

He handed her the file when she got into the car. 'Cindy put this together for when she was away. It's Sienna's routine plus a list of answers to the kind of questions she'd expect someone to ask.'

'That's useful. Thank you. I'll read it on the way to nursery school, if that's all right with you,' she said. 'And maybe you can answer any further questions I might have?'

'Sure.' He liked the fact that she was so businesslike.

Sophie's misgivings increased as she skim-read the file. 'Let me get this clear. You expect the nanny to get Sienna up in the mornings, then help her get her bathed and dressed and breakfasted?'

'And help her clean her teeth, then drop her at nursery school,' he finished.

'Why don't you take your daughter to nursery school yourself?'

'Because I have a business to run. I need to be in the office quite a while before she needs to be at nursery school.'

Sophie knew Jamie was a single father, but from

what she could see the work-life balance just wasn't there. When did he get to spend quality time with his daughter? According to this file, he didn't even eat with her in the evenings. There was a menu of what looked like typical nursery food, which clearly she would be expected to cook. Did Sophie eat on her own, or with the nanny? Sophie's heart sank.

Fran had died two years ago, so surely Jamie should be smothering his daughter in cotton wool rather than using his work to avoid the little girl? It sounded more and more as if he was a cold workaholic who put his business first, second and third.

Sophie could remember what it felt like to be the daughter of a workaholic, one who'd missed every school performance and every parents' evening because he was always too busy. Her father had never had the chance to put things right because he'd died of a heart attack when she was ten. She was so aware of all the things they'd missed out on; even though her mother had remarried six years later and Sophie loved her stepfather dearly, she still missed her father and wished they'd had the chance to share things.

Maybe, she thought, she could change things for Sienna so the little girl didn't grow up with that same hole in her life, that same sense of loneliness and wondering secretly if something was wrong with her because her dad didn't spend time with her the way her friends' dads did. And, even if seeing Sienna reminded him of what he'd lost, at least Jamie still had his daughter.

Jamie Wallis didn't just need a nanny, he needed someone who could help him fix his relationship with his little girl.

And Sophie thought she might just be the one to do that.

CHAPTER TWO

WHEN JAMIE PULLED up in the nursery school car park, Sophie asked, 'Should I stay here in the car? Because then it won't confuse anyone.'

'In case Sienna decides she doesn't want you to look after her? Good point.' He nodded. 'I'll be as quick as I can.'

He climbed out of the car, went over to the gate and spoke into the intercom, and then disappeared through the gate, shutting it behind him.

Sophie read through Cindy's file again while she was waiting for him to return with Sienna. The more she read, the more sure she was that things needed to change. Jamie was a workaholic, the way her own father had been, and he wasn't seeing anywhere near enough of his daughter—which wasn't good for either of them.

A movement caught her eye and she looked up. She saw a little girl walking nicely down the path next to Jamie; obviously this must be Sienna. She was a pretty child, with a mop of curly blonde hair and her father's dark eyes.

She climbed out of the car and waited until Jamie and Sienna had reached her before crouching down so she was on the little girl's level. 'Hello. I'm Sophie,' she said. 'And you're Sienna, yes?'

The little girl nodded shyly.

'Sophie's going to spend the rest of the afternoon with us,' Jamie said, 'so you can get to know her a bit better and decide if you want her to look after you until Cindy's leg is mended.'

Again, there was a shy nod.

Better start as I mean to go on, Sophie thought. 'Would you like me to help you into the car seat?' she asked Sienna.

The little girl gave another nod, and Sophie's heart squeezed. Maybe Sienna was just a bit shy, particularly as Sophie was a stranger. She really hoped that Sienna wouldn't be this quiet once she'd got to know her; one of the joys of being an aunt was having a niece and nephew who chattered nineteen to the dozen to her and burst into song at the least provocation.

She opened the rear door, helped Sienna get into the car, buckled her into the car seat and double checked it before climbing in next to her and buckling up her own seat belt.

'So what did you do today at nursery school?' Sophie asked.

'Painting,' Sienna said, her voice little more than a whisper.

'That's nice.' Sophie had always enjoyed the painting activities when she'd worked at Anna's nursery school. 'Did you bring any of your paintings home with you?'

Sienna shook her head.

Maybe the nursery school staff had kept the paintings for assessment purposes. Sophie tried another tack. 'Did the teachers read you any stories today?'

'Ye—es.' But Sienna wasn't forthcoming about what the story was, or what her favourite book was, the way Sophie's niece Hattie would be.

Then again, a car wasn't the easiest place to have a conversation with a small child. Sophie let the conversation lapse until they were back at Jamie's house. Then she helped Sienna out of the car, and waited for Jamie to unlock the front door.

'I'll give you a quick guided tour,' Jamie said. 'Obviously this is the hallway.' He took her through the downstairs, room by room. 'Living room, dining room, playroom, my office, downstairs cloakroom, kitchen.'

The house was beautiful, a large Edwardian villa with polished wooden floors, pale walls and windows that let in plenty of light; but it felt more like a show-house than a home. There were no pieces of artwork from nursery school held to the fridge by magnets or pinned to a cork board in the kitchen; there were no family photographs anywhere, either. And Sophie had never seen such a tidy playroom in her life. It made her wonder if Sienna was even allowed to touch her toys, or maybe there was a strict rule about only playing with one thing at a time.

This definitely wasn't a normal home. Even though her own father had put his job first, last and in between, her mother had made sure to give all three children her time and affection.

Then again, Sienna didn't have a mother to balance out her father's drive for work.

'I'll make us a drink,' Jamie said when they reached the kitchen. 'Coffee or tea?'

'Coffee would be lovely, thanks. Just milk, no sugar.'

'Would you prefer a cappuccino or a latte?'

'As long as it's coffee, I really don't mind. Whatever's easy,' she said.

'Fair enough.' He made two mugs of coffee via a very posh coffee machine and poured milk into a plastic beaker of milk for Sienna. 'I'll be in my office if you need me,' he said.

Obviously she and Sienna needed to spend time together so they could get to know each other, but this felt almost like an excuse for him to avoid the little girl. Or maybe she was being unfair to Jamie.

'Shall we go into the playroom?' she asked Sienna.

The little girl nodded.

In the playroom, Sienna agreed to do some drawing and colouring together. Sophie couldn't help noticing how the little girl coloured very carefully, making sure she stayed within the lines, and used pastel colours. So different from her exuberant niece Hattie, who always picked the brightest colours and wasn't in the slightest bit concerned if she coloured over the lines. The little girl reminded Sophie of herself as a child, desperate for her father's approval and never quite getting it.

'How about a story?' she asked.

Again, Sienna was quietly acquiescent.

'What's your favourite story that Daddy reads to you?' Sophie asked.

'Cindy always reads my bedtime story,' Sienna said.

'OK.' Sophie's sister-in-law Mandy had been very eloquent about the benefits of having a male role model reading to children, so her brother Will always read to Hattie and Sam at night. Maybe if she told Jamie, he might consider reading to Sienna. But, as her sole parent, why wasn't he doing that already?

Sophie read a couple of stories to Sienna, scooping the little girl onto her lap and persuading her to join in with some of the words. And when she made a tremendous pause before the last repetition of a refrain in one particular book, she was finally rewarded with a giggle from Sienna.

'What would you like for dinner tonight?' she asked when they'd finished the story.

'We always have chicken nuggets on Monday,' Sienna said.

Sophie remembered seeing the menu plan in Cindy's file. Just to check that her suspicions were correct, she asked, 'Does Daddy have chicken nuggets, too?'

'Daddy doesn't have dinner with me. He's usually still at work.'

'So Cindy has dinner with you?'

She nodded. 'In the kitchen.'

'Well, Daddy's home today, so he can eat with you and me. And we don't have to stick to eating chicken nuggets just because it's Monday. Let's go and see what's in the fridge, shall we?'

Just as Sophie had hoped, Jamie clearly had either asked the temporary nanny to do a grocery shop the previous week or he had his groceries delivered. The fridge was half-full of fruit and vegetables; there were a couple of chicken breasts and a packet of minced beef. There were also a couple of supermarket ready-prepared meals, which told her that Jamie didn't bother cooking for himself in the evening and just shoved something into the microwave to heat through.

'Do you like spaghetti Bolognese?' she asked.

Sienna nodded.

'Good. That's what we'll have for dinner tonight. Daddy, too. Cindy's file says you have dinner at six?'

'Yes.'

'Great. You can help me cook dinner.'

Little girl's eyes were round. 'Can I? Really?'

Sophie's suspicions deepened. 'Do you cook with Cindy?'

'No.'

'Not even cupcakes or cookies?'

Sienna grimaced. 'They're messy.'

So who was the neat freak? Cindy the nanny? Or was this an extreme reaction by Sienna, wanting to be super-neat and tidy so her father would approve of her? 'Mess is exactly what aprons are for. And vacuum cleaners,' Sophie said firmly. 'I make cupcakes with my niece Hattie all the time. She's the same age as you.'

Sienna looked shocked.

Oh, honestly. Sophie had to bite her tongue. Right at that moment she wanted to shake Jamie Wallis until his teeth rattled. The whole point about childhood was to have fun while you were growing up and learning about the world. And, yes, she could understand that not everyone was comfortable living in total chaos, but if Sienna made a mess she could also learn how to clear up again.

'We'll make cupcakes tomorrow afternoon,' she promised. 'With sprinkles.'

'Chocolate sprinkles?' Sophie asked hopefully.

'Absolutely yes.' She'd pick them up tomorrow, together with a few other things she enjoyed doing with Hattie and Sam. She smiled at Sienna. 'Right, I need you to do a very important job for me—can you show me where the pots and pans are?'

While she was directing Sienna to help her get the ingredients, she texted Jamie.

Dinner at six. You are eating with us in the kitchen. No arguments.

He ignored her text.

Well, fine. She wasn't daunted.

Just before she was going to serve up, she rang him. 'You have three minutes.'

'I'm in the middle of something.'

She didn't care. She'd already given him prior warning about when dinner would be ready. If he hadn't paid attention, that was his problem. 'I'm serving up now. Come and wash your hands for dinner.'

He hung up on her, and she wondered if she was going to have to go and drag him out of his study. But then she heard the door open and he strode into the kitchen.

Sienna beamed. 'Daddy, you're sitting here between me and Sophie. I laid the table. And I helped cook the bisgetti.'

'Spaghetti,' he corrected. 'Did you?' He gave Sophie a speaking look.

'She was a brilliant sous-chef, just like my niece Hattie,' she said.

Conversation during dinner was like pulling teeth. Jamie seemed to have no idea whatsoever how to talk to his daughter. Was he just hopeless with children in general, or was there something else going on here?

Sophie did the best she could to include both of them. Once they'd eaten, she said, 'It's bathtime, now, Sienna. Perhaps Daddy can do your bath and read you a bedtime story while I do the washing up.'

Bathtime.

Water.

Jamie had to dig his nails into his palms as a picture flashed into his head. Fran, her golden curls wet and plastered to her head. Her face so swollen and puffy, just like her throat had been inside, so no air could get through.

Fran, dead.

He'd avoided bathing his daughter ever since, leaving the job to Cindy. Sienna looked so much like Fran that he just couldn't handle seeing her with wet hair and getting those flashbacks, the dreams that had had him waking in tears for weeks after it had happened.

OK, so it had been two years and anyone would think he'd come to terms with it by now—he was over-reacting. But he couldn't bear it. He just couldn't.

And Sophie really expected him to do bathtime?

Jamie looked horrified. 'Cindy—' he began.

'—isn't here. And you have a special question to ask Sienna which needs to be with just the two of you together,' she reminded him.

Oh, God. There was no way round this. He was just going to have to face his demons.

'Let's choose a story,' he said, desperately hoping that maybe if he dragged his feet a bit, he'd either be able to think of an excuse or Sienna might decide she didn't want a bath after all.

But it didn't work out that way.

He had to go through with it.

He made the bath as shallow as he possibly could.

'Cindy puts more water in—and more bubbles,' Sienna said.

'Well, we haven't got time tonight,' he said, hating himself for lying to his little girl but not wanting her to know about the nightmares in his head.

'And she washes my hair.'

No. Just no. 'Not tonight,' he said. 'And we need to talk about Sophie. Would you like her to be your nanny until Cindy's leg is mended?'

To his relief, it headed his daughter off the subject of her bath and hairwash.

'I like Sophie. She's funny. And she does all the special voices in a story,' Sienna said. 'And she let me help her cook bisgetti. I was her sushi.'

He couldn't help smiling at that. 'Sous-chef.'

'Can she stay? Please?'

'Yes,' he said. Even though Sophie Firth was pushing him into doing things he normally avoided. Because the alternative meant taking time off and doing everything for Sienna himself until the agency sent a replacement—which could take a couple of weeks.

He hauled his daughter out of the bath and dried her swiftly, before helping her into her pyjamas. 'Story,' he said. 'And then I need to talk to Sophie.'

Jamie had gone absolutely white when Sophie had suggested that he did Sienna's bedtime routine. What was the problem? she wondered. She was starting to think that there was more to it than Jamie being a cold workaholic. But what? She could ask him straight out, but she had the feeling he'd avoid the question. If Sienna agreed to let her stay, then maybe she'd have enough time to find out exactly what was going on—and help.

She'd just finished the washing up when he came downstairs.

'Well, you were a hit,' he said. 'I asked her, and she says she'd like you to stay until Cindy comes back.'

Though she noticed he didn't look too pleased about it.

'So I'm looking at my new sleeping partner, then?' she asked.

His pupils dilated slightly and she realised how her words could've been interpreted; she felt a tide of colour surge into her face. 'I mean my business partner who invests but lets me get on with running things and doesn't interfere,' she clarified.

'Business partner. And you're my new temporary nanny.'

'Right. I'm glad. Sienna's a lovely little girl. I'm going to enjoy looking after her. So I guess your solicitors need to talk to mine about the buyout, assuming you agreed with the figures in my proposal.'

'Uh-huh.' He paused. 'Plus I need to give you the car keys. Hang on a sec.' He fished a set of keys out of a drawer and handed them to her. 'And the spare key for the front door. I was thinking you might find it more convenient to stay here overnight in future. Cindy's staying at her boyfriend's flat until her leg mends, so you can use her suite—or the guest suite, if you'd prefer.'

Staying overnight? That hadn't been mentioned before. It wasn't part of their agreement. And she wasn't giving him another excuse to avoid his daughter. 'Ah, no,' she said. 'You'll be getting Sienna up in the mornings. Though I'll be here before you have to leave for work.'

He blinked. 'But Cindy—'

'—does things slightly differently than I would.'

'She's a trained nanny.'

Meaning that she was supposed to follow Cindy's instructions? Sophie wanted to rip that ridiculous file into little pieces and jump up and down on it. 'Well, I'm not,' she reminded him. 'As I said, I'll be here before you have to leave for work.'

'Right. And once you've dropped Sienna off, your day is your own until nursery school pick-up. I'll give you the code word, and I'll give the nursery school manager your details so she knows who you are,' he said. 'Would you mind if I took a photo of you for their records?'

'Sure.' She had something similar in place with Hattie's nursery school.

He took a photograph of her on his phone. 'Thank you.'

'And you make sure you're home in time to eat with us in the evenings.'

'I have to w—' he began.

'Of course you have to work—I realise you have an empire to run.' She tried to keep the sarcasm out of her voice. 'But you're the boss, so you can choose where you work. It doesn't have to be in the office all the time. You have an Internet connection here.' She folded her arms and gave him a challenging look. 'So I want you here in time for dinner with us at six, and if you're late I'll make you eat cold, soggy, overcooked Brussels sprouts. And you won't be able to refuse because it'll be in front of Sienna.'

He looked utterly shocked. 'Oh, my God. Eva didn't tell me—'

'—that I was even bossier than your mother?' she finished.

His eyes widened. 'How do you know my mother's bossy?'

'What's sauce for the goose is most definitely sauce for the gander,' she said. 'You asked Eva about me— which meant I could ask Eva about you.'

'I think,' he said, 'maybe I should have tried a different agency for Cindy's temporary replacement.'

'Tough. You've already asked Sienna and she's made her decision.'

'I want you to go by Cindy's rules. Sienna needs structure and continuity.'

She needed love and laughter, too, Sophie thought, but didn't say it. 'Let's try just a couple of tiny, tiny changes,' she said. 'Humour me. Spaghetti was all right tonight, wasn't it?'

'Well, yes,' he admitted.

'Good. Is there anything you really don't like to eat?'

He said nothing, but she could guess what he was thinking and grinned. 'Don't worry. I won't make you eat chicken nuggets or fish fingers with shaped potato products, peas and tomato ketchup. Hattie and Sam eat what Will and Mandy eat, so Sienna can eat what we eat. Plus, if she's involved in making dinner, she's more likely to eat it without a fuss.'

He frowned. 'How do you know?'

'My sister-in-law Mandy is a health visitor. I guess chatting to her, plus working at Anna's nursery school, means I've picked up a few things along the way.'

'I see. And I'm guessing you'll be the first to see the new baby, too.'

She looked at him, eyes narrowed. 'What new baby?'

'I know about the IVF,' he said.

She blew out a breath. 'Eva blabbed.'

'I made an educated guess and she filled in the gaps. Which I admit was probably underhand of me—I kind of let her think that you'd told me everything. But I like the fact you didn't try to manipulate me with a sob story.'

Sophie wasn't sure whether to be cross or relieved. 'So now you know the circumstances, do you agree you would've done the same for your siblings?'

'Of course I would.' He paused. 'Do they live near?'

'We all live in London. Not in each other's pockets, but no more than half an hour's Tube journey away from each other—and that includes Mum and Dad.'

He looked slightly wistful, and she guessed that maybe he missed his sisters. But asking him might be a question too far.

'Well, I guess I'll see you tomorrow,' he said.

'Sure. Though I have a couple of questions first.'

He looked wary. 'Which are?'

'Do you have a housekeeper?' she asked.

'A cleaner who comes in twice a week,' he confirmed. 'She does the ironing but not the laundry.'

'So laundry's part of my duties?' she checked.

'I guess I can handle that until Cindy's back,' he said.

'Fine. What about your grocery shopping?'

'I order online, and Cindy picks up any top-up things during the week.'

'I'll do the same. Obviously I'll make sure I have receipts for everything,' she said. 'And I'll give you a list of what I need you to order.'

He frowned. 'Aren't you using Cindy's menu?'

'Not unless you want to eat chicken nuggets,' she said sweetly. 'I thought we could have sticky salmon tomorrow. My sister-in-law Mandy has a gorgeous recipe, and Hattie and Sam absolutely love it. I can pick up the ingredients on the way to nursery school tomorrow afternoon.'

'OK. Anything else?'

'That's it for now.' She smiled. 'Goodnight, new business partner.'

'Goodnight, new business partner and temporary nanny.'

Sophie closed the front door behind her and headed for the small car parked on the gravel outside the house. There was a child's safety seat in the back, as she'd expected, so she'd be ready to take Sienna to nursery school tomorrow. She sat behind the steering wheel and closed her eyes for a moment. If anyone had told her first thing this morning that her life was going to be turned upside down for the next couple of months, she would never have believed it.

Right at that moment, she felt slightly daunted.

Sienna was so like the little girl that she herself had once been, desperate to please her dad and trying to be the perfect daughter. And it was heartbreaking, seeing the distance between Sienna and Jamie. They were all each other had. OK, so maybe this was none of her business; but on the other hand how could she just stand by and let the situation get worse, when she knew first-hand the sort of damage it could do?

Why did Jamie avoid his daughter? Did he doubt his ability as a father? Or was Eva right and he was so wrapped up in his grief that he couldn't think of anything else?

She had two months with them, maybe.

Would that be enough time to fix things?

This morning, Jamie had expected to have a short business meeting with Sophie Firth and politely turn down the opportunity of investing in her company.

And then he'd met her.

She was bright and she thought on her feet. She stood by her convictions and she wasn't afraid to say no. She'd practically glowed when she'd spoken about the new direction for her business. He'd liked her energy and warmth.

Maybe his nanny crisis was the answer for both of them.

Except now he was in a really weird situation: she was his business partner and sort of his employee at the same time.

He remembered the way she'd blushed when she'd called him her sleeping partner and then obviously realised how the phrase could be taken. And it felt as if his temperature had just spiked along with his pulse rate.

Oh, for pity's sake. He couldn't be attracted to her. It would be way too complicated. OK. This was simply a physical response due to abstinence, he reminded himself. He was not interested in what might make Sophie Firth blush all over.

And he wasn't going to let himself think about the fact that she was single. Available. Because he didn't have time for a relationship. He didn't want a relationship. He didn't *deserve* a relationship, not after what had happened to Fran. And no way was he letting himself lose control and fall for someone.

All the same, he found it hard to concentrate on his work for the rest of the evening. It unsettled him to realise that he'd spent more time with Sienna today than he had in weeks. He felt bad about the way he was avoiding his daughter, but every time he saw her she reminded him so much of Fran. The older she got, the more she looked like her mother, and his guilt crucified him every time he looked at her.

It had been two years.

Would it ever get any easier?

The next morning, Jamie found himself slightly flummoxed by having to get Sienna up, dressed and breakfasted. And his heart squeezed when he saw how grateful his daughter looked just to be spending time with him.

He really was making a mess of things. If Fran was here, she'd flay him alive.

But he simply didn't know what else to do. With business, he knew where he was. Being a single parent... It was better for Sienna that her nanny, who knew what she was doing, could look after her.

Or so he'd told himself for the last two years.

When Sophie rang the doorbell, he was shocked by how pleased he was to see her. Particularly because he thought it was more than just because she was rescuing him from his own fatherly ineptitude. And that would be a really bad idea.

'I'll see you later,' he said, kissed Sienna's cheek, and covered his confusion by rushing off to work.

Sophie noticed how Sienna's smile dimmed once her father had gone. OK. Today she'd look at what was happening, and how she could make small changes to bring Sienna and Jamie back together. Gradually, so he didn't realise what was happening and dig his heels in—because she'd already worked out that he was stubborn. But there was definitely more to it than him focusing on his work.

She took Sienna to nursery school, then headed to work at her own office. She picked up a couple of things for Sienna during her lunch break, reassured Eva and the rest of the team that everything was absolutely fine, then left the office early enough to drop by supermarket before picking Sienna up from nursery school.

'Daddy says I have to sit in the back,' Sienna said,

her dark eyes wide with worry when she saw that Sophie had moved her car seat to the front passenger's seat.

'We're on my time, so we're on my rules,' Sophie reassured her with a smile. 'My niece Hattie always sits in the front with me if I pick her up on my own. And we sing on the way. Did you do any singing at school today?'

Sienna nodded.

'Good. Then you can teach me the song on the way home,' Sophie declared, and strapped the little girl safely into the seat.

Sienna was shy at first, and Sophie deliberately got some of the words wrong, to make the little girl laugh and relax. And by the time Sophie parked the car, Sienna was singing at the top of her voice.

Back at Jamie's house, they unloaded the shopping. 'And I bought this for you,' Sophie said, handing Sienna a package wrapped in sparkly paper with a sparkly ribbon.

'But it's not my birthday,' Sienna said, her dark eyes wide.

'It's a Tuesday present, and you're going to be using it in, ooh, about five minutes,' Sophie said, 'so open it.'

Sienna was thrilled to discover a pink apron with white spots. 'It's beautiful! Thank you!' She hugged Sophie, who hugged her right back.

'My pleasure, sweetheart,' Sophie said. 'Right. Shall we make cupcakes?'

Once the cakes were in the oven, she texted Jamie.

Home by six or cold soggy Brussels sprouts. Your choice.

As she'd half expected, he didn't reply. But she was quite prepared to go through with her threat.

She and Sienna made the sticky salmon together, and prepared the rice and green vegetables. Sophie was pleased that the little girl started to chatter a bit more to her, talking about what she'd had for lunch and what her favourite things were.

Again, the little girl laid the kitchen table for three. She'd just finished when they heard the crunch of car tyres on gravel.

'Daddy's home!' Sienna rushed to the door to greet him.

Jamie looked a bit shell-shocked at the greeting, but to Sophie's relief he hugged the little girl.

'Daddy, the big hand on the clock is nearly at the top and the little hand is at six, so that means you have to wash your hands for dinner,' Sienna said, and Sophie had to hide a smile.

She clearly didn't hide it well enough, judging from the speaking look Jamie gave her. 'We've been practising telling the time,' she said. 'Sienna's very good. Maybe we can play "What's the Time, Mr Wolf?" after dinner.'

Was that panic she saw in his eyes?

But what was so scary about playing with a child? Especially when that child was his own daughter?

Deciding now wasn't the right time to tackle it, she served dinner. Jamie was careful to include Sienna in his compliments. But when the little girl was bringing a cupcake over to the table for her father, she tripped over her own feet and dropped the plate, which smashed on the tiles.

Sienna's mouth opened wide in shock, and then she burst into tears.

On instinct, Sophie scooped her up and held her close. 'It's OK, sweetie. It was an accident, and it's easily cleaned up.'

'But I made that one specially for Daddy,' Sienna sobbed. 'It had extra sprinkles.'

'We can put extra sprinkles on another one in a minute. Now, I want you to sit and cuddle Daddy for me so I know you're not going to cut yourself, and I'll clear up all the broken bits, OK?' Sophie asked.

Sienna's lower lip wobbled. 'I broke the plate.'

'It's all right. I promise it doesn't matter,' Sophie said, and glared at Jamie over the top of Sienna's head. Just when was he going to step in and reassure his daughter?

'It's fine, Sienna,' he said. And he did at least hold her while Sophie was clearing up, though he looked uncomfortable.

Sophie helped the little girl to add more sprinkles to another cupcake, and Jamie was suitably complimentary. But Sophie's temper was simmering just below boiling point. She agreed to do bathtime if he did the bedtime story, though she had to stop herself banging the pots and pans around while he read Sienna a story.

When she heard him come downstairs, she went into the hallway. 'Can we have a word? Your office?'

'Sure.'

She closed the door behind them. 'I'm keeping my voice low so Sienna doesn't hear me and start worrying. But I'm not your employee, so I don't have to be careful what I say in front of you, and I'm telling you now that I'd like to shake you until your teeth rattle.'

He winced. 'I'm sorry.'

'It's not me you should be apologising to, it's your daughter. Every child makes a mistake or drops things or breaks things. It's part of how they learn. It's not as if she *deliberately* threw that plate against a wall.'

He rubbed a hand across his eyes. 'I know.'

'She needed reassurance. From you, not me.' She put her hands on her hips and glared at him. 'And, for your information, I know first-hand what I'm talking about.' And even though she knew it was unfair to take out her frustration at her father's behaviour on Jamie, she could see that he was making exactly the same mistake—and that wasn't fair on Sienna. I'm speaking as someone who grew up desperate for her dad's attention, but he was always so busy at work that he didn't have time for his kids. I wanted to make sure I was the perfect daughter—I was his only daughter, so in my view I had to be better than Matt and Will, but I never felt as if I was good enough for him. He never made time for me. Is that how you want Sienna to grow up?'

'No. Of course not.' He looked shocked.

'I don't think you're a monster,' she said.

'No?' he asked dryly. 'Doesn't sound like it.'

'I think you're so caught up in your grief that you're forgetting you're not the only one who's hurting. And the people around you tiptoe round you instead of calling you on it.'

'Whereas you don't tiptoe.'

'Not any more, I don't.' She had, once. The people-pleasing from her early days had spilled into her teens and her early twenties. But her experiences with Dan and Joe had changed all that. She'd tried to be the perfect girlfriend, and she'd failed just as badly as when she'd tried to be the perfect daughter. And she'd got her heart broken twice in the process. 'I'm twenty-nine. Old enough and wise enough to call it as I see it.'

* * *

Jamie looked at her. There was something in her expression that said the tiptoeing round people wasn't just because of her dad—but now wasn't the right time to ask her.

'I'll make more effort,' he said.

'Good. Because she's a lovely little girl.'

Guilt squeezed round his heart like a vice. Except he wasn't sure he had a heart any more. Just a block of ice.

So he focused on business to push the emotion away, the way he always did, to put himself back in control of the situation.

'By the way, I asked my HR team to draw up a shortlist of the people in our team with experience in promotions as well as travel. They came up with a shortlist, and we have six people who'd be interested in the secondment. Perhaps you'd like to interview them tomorrow.'

She looked momentarily startled by his change of topic, but then nodded. 'Thank you, I will. Do they all work at your office?'

'Yes.'

'Then it makes sense for me to come over to your office rather than call them all over to mine.'

He liked the way she thought. Economy of time. 'I'll make sure we keep a meeting room free for you tomorrow. Would half an hour each be enough?'

'If I can see their CVs beforehand, yes.'

'I'll email them over to you. And, Sophie? I *am* sorry about what happened tonight. I don't mean to be...' His throat closed on the words. *A bad father*. He knew he'd let Fran down and he was letting Sienna down. But he didn't know how to be any different.

She shrugged. 'Tomorrow's another day. Being

a parent isn't easy. Draw a line under today and try again.'

Given her fierceness earlier, he was surprised that she was being so kind. And the way she'd phrased it... 'Are you sure you're not secretly a trained nanny?'

She smiled, then, and he was shocked to feel awareness pulsing through him. Sophie Firth had a beautiful mouth, and he actually found himself wondering what it would be like to kiss her.

Oh, for pity's sake.

This wasn't fair on either of them. He was really going to have to keep himself in check.

'I'm just an ordinary woman,' she said.

No, he thought, you're much more than that. And I can't let myself notice.

He needed to put a barrier between them; yet at the same time he found himself wanting to be with her. Learning what made her tick. Which was crazy. He couldn't do that.

'I'd better let you get on. I'll see you tomorrow,' he said.

'OK.'

She'd just got to the door when he said her name. She turned around and looked at him. And either his feelings were written all over his face or she'd picked it up in his voice, because she walked right back over to him.

'I think,' he said, 'I need help. With Sienna. Fixing all the stuff that...' He dragged in a breath. *All the stuff he was getting so badly wrong.* 'I don't have the right to ask you. We hardly know each other.'

'But I grew up with a workaholic dad. I can see things from Sienna's point of view—and from yours. So I'm the obvious person to ask,' she said.

His thoughts exactly.

'Plus I'm not your employee. So I'm not going to tiptoe round you or be scared to tell you what I think.'

Could he?

Should he?

But her dark, dark eyes weren't full of pity. They were full of warmth. Of kindness. Of understanding. Part of him desperately wanted her help; part of him wanted to keep his distance and his self-control.

Though he knew he had to do the right thing, for his daughter's sake. Even if it cost him personally.

'Help me, Sophie,' he said softly. 'Please.'

She reached over his desk and squeezed his hands briefly. Again, it wasn't pity in her face but fellow feeling; and again, he felt that completely inappropriate leap of his libido.

'Yes,' she said.

CHAPTER THREE

THE NEXT MORNING, after dropping Sienna at nursery school, Sophie drove to Jamie's office rather than her own. He'd clearly briefed Karen, the head of his HR department, who showed her to the interview room and brought her coffee and a jug of water.

All the candidates on the shortlist were good and would fit in well with her team, but by the end of the interviews Sophie had two definite choices. She just needed to run them by Jamie first. She texted him.

Can I talk to you for five minutes re interviews?

He called her back immediately. 'Sure. Do you have time for lunch?'

'You actually take a lunch break?' she asked.

'Usually it's a sandwich at my desk,' he admitted. 'But it's probably a better idea to be away from the building if you want to discuss the interviews.'

'OK.'

'You don't usually have a lunch break, either, do you?' he asked.

'Busted. Same as you,' she admitted.

'Meet you in the lobby in five minutes,' he said.

She thanked Karen for her help, promised to give

her a final answer in an hour's time, and went to meet
Jamie in the lobby.

'There's a nice café round the corner,' he said.

'That sounds good.'

She let him shepherd her out to the café, where they
ordered coffee and sandwiches, and found a quiet corner table.

'So how did it go?' he asked.

'They were all good candidates. But two of them
stood out for me. I just wanted to run them by you to
see what you thought.' She passed him the files.

'Good choice. That's who I would've picked,' he
said.

'So it's a two-month secondment?'

'If that gives you enough time.'

'Just about. Thanks. Though we need to sort out
salary payments and what have you.'

'Karen can advise you on the details,' he said.

'So that's number one ticked off the list,' she said.
'Now for number two.'

'Number two?'

'What we discussed last night.'

When he'd asked her to help him.

When he'd finally admitted that he was struggling
to be a dad and hated that he was getting it so wrong.
Jamie hadn't told her yet just why he found it so hard,
but he would. In a few days. The more time he spent
with her, the more he found himself trusting her. Eva
was right about Sophie being utterly reliable.

But there was more to her than that. Something that
he couldn't let himself think about. So he'd have to
keep it strictly business, for his daughter's sake.

'Firstly,' she said, 'I think we need to rejig your routine so you always eat dinner with Sienna.'

'What if something really big crops up at the office—something that only I can deal with?' he asked.

'Something that big won't happen every month, let alone every day,' she said. 'OK. If there's a major crisis, then you call in advance and you explain it to her at her level.'

So he'd be eating dinner with Sienna every night. Seeing Fran's face in hers, and feeling the guilt twist in his gut. But he knew Sophie was right. For Sienna's sake, he needed to do this.

'Secondly,' she said, 'you need to do the bedtime story every night, because it's good for children to have a male role model as well as a female one when it comes to reading.'

'That sounds like something your sister-in-law would say,' he said.

'Got it in one,' she informed him cheerfully.

And how strange that the twinkle in her eye made his heart feel as if it had done a flip. Apart from the fact that that was anatomically impossible, it was totally inappropriate. Sophie was his business partner and temporary nanny. He shouldn't blur the boundaries and make this personal.

'Thirdly, from what I can make out, Sienna gets looked after by the nanny at weekends.'

'Yes.' He flapped a dismissive hand. 'Because I have to work.'

'Not every single hour of every single day, you don't. You need to learn to delegate,' she said. 'If you're going to build a bond with Sienna, you need to spend time with her—and that means doing things with her at weekends.'

He went cold. Getting really involved. Getting close to someone else he could lose with no warning. And he was like his own parents; he wasn't a natural at dealing with children. He didn't know how to relate to them. Plus he loathed all the tears, tantrums and screaming that seemed to go hand in hand with the playground. 'Please don't suggest I should take her to one of those play places.'

'Play places?' She looked baffled.

'You know the sort I mean—the ones kids get invited to for birthday parties. The places with a ball pit and slides and what feels like wall-to-wall screaming.' He'd always hated them and had persuaded Fran to take Sienna to them while he escaped gratefully to the office.

Sophie grinned. 'They're not *that* bad.'

'Yes, they are,' he said feelingly.

She looked at him, her dark eyes widening. 'Hang on. Are you telling me that Sienna never goes to birthday parties?'

'Of course she does.'

She folded her arms. 'But?'

'Fran used to take her. Cindy takes her now,' he admitted.

'OK. Well, doing things with her that you hate probably isn't the best idea. Scratch the play places, but there are other things you can do. You could start with the park on a Sunday morning—even if you just go for a walk and talk about what you see there, which dogs she likes and that sort of thing. Though Hattie and Sam love the swings and the slide, and if you time it right the play area in the park isn't usually that crowded.'

'Right.' He didn't believe a word of it.

'And it's Bonfire Night this weekend,' she said. 'I

did a bit of research last night, and there are a few firework displays scheduled around here on Saturday night, including one at a local infants' school. I'll email you the details.'

'Bonfire Night.' Fran had loved fireworks. They'd had fireworks at their wedding. And Jamie had avoided them ever since Fran's death. Fireworks were the last thing he wanted to see.

'It'll be fun,' Sophie said.

No, it wouldn't. It would be hell.

'The school display is probably your best bet. It'll be small, they usually have quieter fireworks so the younger ones aren't scared by loud bangs, and there will be stalls with hot dogs and hot chocolate and glowies.'

'Glowies?' he asked, mystified.

She smiled. 'Necklaces, wands, tiaras and glowsticks. Kids of Sienna's age absolutely love them.'

'How do you know all this stuff?'

'Because I went to a firework display with Hattie last year. And it's worth giving in and buying everything on the stall that she likes, because there's no chance of losing Sienna for even a second in the crowd if she's lit up like a firework herself.'

'Got you,' he said. And maybe she had a point. Maybe it was time he faced his demons once and for all. Fireworks and Fran and guilt. 'All right.' He paused. 'Are you busy on Saturday night?'

'I'm supposed to be catching up with work. Though I guess I can move things round,' she said carefully.

It would be unfair of him to ask her, especially as he knew she was the kind of person who put herself out to help people and would find it hard to say no. But he couldn't face doing this all on his own. Being the single dad, seeing the pity and sympathy in people's eyes—pity he didn't want, and sympathy he didn't deserve. 'Would you come with us?' he asked. 'Please?'

'OK,' she said. Just as he'd known she would.

'I know I'm taking time out of things you'd want to do for your own business,' he said. 'And maybe I can help a bit with that.' Remembering what she'd insisted on as part of their agreement, he added swiftly, 'Not interfering. More like being a sounding board.' As she was kind of acting for him, where Sierra was concerned.

'A sounding board,' she said.

'Someone to bounce ideas off. Someone to listen. And you could even delegate some stuff to me.' He paused. 'Tell me about the Weddings Abroad thing.' Where business was concerned, he felt much more at home, He knew what he was doing. There were no emotions to mess things up.

'It came out of the event management,' she said. 'We plan all kinds of events, from corporate to personal—product launches, conferences, birthday parties and weddings. One of my brides was in tears, a fortnight before her wedding, because there were so many family arguments and everyone was being difficult and refusing to agree on anything. She said to me she wished she and her partner had decided to elope to Cuba instead, and actually asked me if I could cancel everything and arrange it.'

He smiled, guessing that she would've risen to the challenge. 'Did you?'

'No. I brokered a few agreements instead—a few compromises, so the bride got her happy day and the ones who were being difficult agreed to put their differences aside and be polite to each other for the wedding and the reception.'

Typical Sophie, he was beginning to realise. Fixing things quietly and sensibly, without a fuss.

Was that what she was doing with him and Sienna?

'But it made me think. Some people have difficult families, and others are maybe missing loved ones and would find it hard to have a traditional wedding in England without them. Having a wedding abroad would solve all those problems. So I looked into it, and found out what paperwork you need in each of a dozen different countries, how much time you need to allow for arrangements, and who to contact. Between us, Eva and I have the admin, the venues, cakes, flowers and dresses sorted.' She lifted a shoulder. 'It's just a shame that Eva's not going to be here to help launch the new service.'

'And you arrange the honeymoon as well?'

'And the hen night and stag night, if that's what my clients want.'

While she was talking about the project, Sophie was really glowing, Jamie thought. She was clearly one of these people who liked being able to wave a magic wand for people and make things better.

She was already making a difference to himself and Sienna—something he hadn't expected and was incredibly grateful for, even if at the same time it made him a bit antsy.

She glanced at her watch. 'Sorry. I tend to get a bit carried away when I talk about my pet project.'

'That's OK.' He'd enjoyed seeing her all animated. Though he couldn't help wondering why she was single. She was beautiful, she was nice, and she had an enormous heart. Why hadn't someone snapped her up years ago?

'I guess we ought to be getting back,' she said. 'But one last thing before we go—Cindy.'

'What about her?'

'If I were her,' she said carefully, 'I'd be worried sick about Sienna.'

'I've already spoken to Cindy. She knows Sienna's in good hands, her job is still there when she's ready to come back to it, and I'm still paying her full salary so she's not struggling financially.'

'That isn't the same as seeing Sienna for herself,' Sophie said. 'And I've been thinking about this from Sienna's point of view. Please don't think I'm trying to trample on a sore spot, but her mum didn't come back from a holiday. And now her long-term nanny hasn't come back from a holiday. I think she needs to see Cindy for herself, so she knows it really is a broken leg and you're not trying to break bad news to her gently.'

That had never occurred to him, and it felt like a punch in the stomach. 'I…' He blew out a breath. 'Yes. You're right.'

'So would you mind talking to Cindy and asking her to call me, so I can arrange to take Sienna over to see her?'

How could he possibly say no to that? 'Sure.'

'Good.' She smiled at him. 'I'll see you this evening. We have fajitas for dinner tonight.'

He frowned. 'Fajitas. Are you sure Sienna—?'

'Yes. I won't make them overly spicy. They're one of Hattie's favourites, and she'll love them,' Sophie reassured him. 'I'll walk back to the office with you because I need to talk to Karen. Thank you for lunch.'

'Pleasure.' And, to his surprise, he found it was. He

hadn't just been polite. It was the first time since Fran had died that he'd had lunch on his own with a woman who wasn't related to him or doing business with him. This wasn't officially a date—but it wasn't entirely a business meeting, either.

And that evening, when Jamie went home, it actually felt like coming home. He found himself looking forward to Sienna running to greet him, to the scent of home-made food—to the sheer warmth of the place, something that had been missing for far too long. At the same time, it threw him; it made him feel less in control.

He washed his hands under Sienna's directions, then walked hand in hand with her into the kitchen, where Sophie was busy at the stove. 'What can I do to help?'

'Sit and enjoy,' Sophie said, putting the serving dishes in the middle of the table.

Without a word to Sophie, he helped Sienna load her tortilla with lightly spiced chicken, peppers, onion, salsa and guacamole. Sophie's smile said she'd noticed and approved.

It had been a long, long time since he'd found himself enjoying a family meal—and it was all thanks to Sophie. So, he thought, was the sparkle in his daughter's eyes.

Maybe he could do this.

Maybe he could be a dad.

Maybe he could be the family his daughter deserved.

'So how was your day?' he asked Sienna, and was treated to a blow-by-blow account of her day at nursery and helping Sophie mix the spices for the chicken. It shocked him a little, because he'd never heard so many words from her in one go.

'And we're going to see Cindy on Saturday,' Sienna finished, beaming. 'We're going to make her a special card and a cake.'

Clearly Cindy had returned Sophie's call. 'That sounds good,' he said.

When they'd finished dinner, Sophie said, 'Bathtime now, Sienna.'

Dread coursed through him. Sophie had let him off the previous evening. Was she going to make him do bathtime tonight?

'And Daddy will need to wash your hair,' Sophie added.

He felt sick. But, short of telling her the truth about how he felt and why, he had no choice but to get on with it.

'Remember to put a facecloth over your eyes, Sienna, so you don't get any shampoo in them,' Sophie said.

He hadn't even considered that. What kind of rubbish father did that make him?

Gritting his teeth and trying not to let his tension show, for Sienna's sake, he took his daughter up to the bathroom. He ran a shallow bath—though at least tonight she didn't call him on it. Rinse, lather, rinse, lather, he told himself. And he managed it—thankfully because Sienna had a facecloth over her eyes she couldn't see the pain in his face when he looked at her wet curls. But he managed to dry her off, comb out the tangles and dry her hair. And when he'd finished the bedtime story, she wrapped her arms round his neck.

'Love you, Daddy.'

'Love you, too.' And he hoped she couldn't hear the crack in his voice.

* * *

'Thank you,' he said to Sophie when he'd settled Sienna to bed and come downstairs again.

'Just doing my job,' she said.

'Since you won't let me pay you for looking after her,' he said softly, 'you're doing me a favour rather than it being a job.'

'It's not about the money,' she said, flapping a dismissive hand. 'It's a quid pro quo. You need help; so do I. We're simply helping each other out.'

'All I've done is set the legal wheels in motion to buy out Eva's share.'

'And lent me two members of staff.'

'Karen tells me you're insisting on paying them, so that doesn't count.'

'It's fine,' she said.

'Actually, it's not. I feel as if I'm taking unfair advantage of you,' he countered.

She gave a hollow laugh. 'Trust me, you're not.'

That laugh alerted him. 'Sounds like experience talking.'

She looked away. 'It doesn't matter.'

'I think it does,' he said softly. 'Come and sit down. Talk to me.'

She shook her head. 'It's the proverbial hill of beans that doesn't matter.'

'*Casablanca*,' he said.

'Yes. Not that it was a Rick and Ilsa thing in my case,' she added dryly. 'Let's just say where business is concerned, I'm a good judge of character—but where my love life's concerned, I'm not so good.'

So who had taken advantage of her? he wondered. Whatever had happened had clearly hurt her deeply.

But she was already gathering her belongings. 'I'll see you tomorrow.'

'See you tomorrow,' he echoed.

And how strange that the light seemed to dim when she closed the door behind her.

The rest of the week followed a similar pattern for Sophie: picking up Sienna, dropping her at nursery, cramming in as much work as she could before nursery pick-up, then making dinner for the three of them. Jamie was clearly getting more used to the bedtime routine, doing bathtime and story time with a bit less reluctance, and Sophie loved the fact that he and Sienna were getting closer.

On Saturday morning, she'd agreed that Jamie could spend the morning in the office while she and Sienna went to see Cindy. They made a cake first thing and decorated it with pink sugar hearts, butterflies and sparkly sprinkles. Sienna had made a get well soon card, the night before, and Sophie had helped her to write the words inside.

Cindy buzzed them in through the intercom, and Sienna practically ran inside to hug the woman sitting in the chair with a cast on her leg and crutches propped up beside her. 'Cindy!'

'Oh, sweetie, I've missed you!' Cindy said, holding the little girl tightly.

'I missed you, too. Daddy said you broke your leg.'

'I fell over on my skis,' Cindy explained, 'and it's going to take a few weeks for my leg to get better. That's why the doctor put the big plaster on it.' She gestured to her cast.

'Sophie's looking after me until your leg's better,' Sienna said. 'And we made you a cake.'

Cindy blinked in surprise. 'You did cooking?'

'Me and Sophie cook tea every night, and Daddy eats it all up, every little bit.'

Cindy raised an eyebrow at Sophie. 'Really?'

'Really,' Sophie confirmed with a smile. 'Nice to meet you at last, Cindy.'

'And you, Sophie.' Cindy shook her hand.

'When you rang, you said there was a park nearby,' Sophie said. 'Maybe I could push you there in your wheelchair, so you can get some fresh air and Sienna can run around and go on the slide, and work up an appetite for a slice of that cake.' And it also meant she'd be able to talk to Cindy privately without Sienna overhearing.

'Sounds good,' Cindy said, clearly guessing exactly what Sophie meant.

'I made you a card, too,' Sienna said, shoving it into Cindy's hand.

'It's beautiful,' Cindy said when she opened it. 'A rainbow and a dog. That's lovely. And your writing's very neat.'

'Sophie helped me,' Sienna confided in a loud whisper. 'Sophie's really kind.'

Cindy gave Sophie an appraising look, and nodded. 'That's good. Shall we go to the park? You can help Sophie push my chair.'

'Yay!' Sienna said.

Once they were at the park and seated where they could see Sienna playing on the slide and the swings, Cindy turned to Sophie. 'I can already see the change in her. You're good for her. And I'm so glad you brought her over to see me. I was worrying about her having a string of temps.'

'Jamie was pretty insistent that he wanted continuity,' Sophie said. 'The agency let him down. Apparently everyone on their books was either already on an assignment or had gone down with that virus that's doing the rounds. Jamie was pretty angry about it.'

'So how do you know Mr Wallis, exactly?' Cindy asked.

'I co-own a business with Fran's cousin, Eva. Eva's fiancé has been headhunted, so she needs me to buy her out. I needed someone to invest, and Jamie needed a nanny,' Sophie explained. 'Although I'm not a qualified nanny, I had a part-time job in our neighbour's nursery school during sixth form. I have a niece who's the same age as Sienna and a nephew two years younger, and I'm a very hands-on aunt. Plus my sister-in-law's a health visitor, so I can ask her anything I need to. So this a kind of quid pro quo. I'm looking after Sienna, and Jamie's buying into my company.'

'I see,' Cindy said.

'I have to say, you're not what I was expecting,' Sophie said. 'Not after reading that file.'

Cindy groaned. 'The rules.'

'Which I'm guessing are Jamie's rather than yours.'

'I just wrote Sienna's routine down.' Cindy sighed. 'It's not what I want it to be. It just kind of evolved, and Mr Wallis is a bit set in his ways. But from the sound of things you're not sticking to it.'

'No, I'm not,' Sophie agreed. 'I guess the difference is I'm not actually working for him, so I can call things as I see them without any worry that I'm going to lose my job.'

'It's not so much losing my job I worry about,' Cindy said, 'as not being able to look after Sienna any more. I've looked after her since she was a baby.'

And she clearly loved the little girl dearly, Sophie

thought. 'So you knew her mum, then. What was Fran like?'

'Lovely—a real dynamo, but she always made time for Sienna. Mr Wallis was different when she was around. He wasn't quite so much of a workaholic because she could always get him to stop and smell the roses.'

'Hang on. He still makes you call him Mr Wallis after four years?' Sophie checked.

'Fran was the one I saw most of,' Cindy said, 'and Mr Wallis was always more formal with me. Though don't get me wrong. I have a lot of respect for him, He's a fair employer and he lets me take my holiday to suit me.' She gestured to her leg. 'And he's still paying me, even though I can't work.'

Money isn't everything, Sophie thought. 'Just he's totally buttoned up.'

'Losing your wife at such a young age is hard.'

'But it doesn't give you a good excuse to avoid your daughter and make your nanny look after her all the time,' Sophie said quietly.

'I think,' Cindy said, 'it's because Sienna's the spitting image of her mum and he finds it hard to cope. Every time he sees Sienna it must remind him of Fran and what he's lost, and he kind of buries himself in work to help him cope. Plus Fran once let it slip that he was pretty much brought up by nannies as well, in a house where children were meant to be seen and not heard.'

'So I'm also guessing he doesn't see much of Fran's family?'

'They live in Norfolk.'

'That's only a couple of hours' drive away. If he didn't want to make a weekend of it, he could still let her see her grandparents for the day.' She paused. 'Are you in contact with them?'

Cindy looked wary. 'Why?'

'Don't worry, I'm not going to march over to Jamie and blab,' Sophie said. 'My dad was a workaholic who died young, so I kind of know what it's like to be in Sienna's shoes. And I think she needs her extended family.'

'Agreed,' Cindy said.

'So I was thinking, sending them bits of Sienna's artwork and the odd photograph might be a way of starting to bridge the gap.'

'We're there already,' Cindy said. 'On my phone, I have addresses, phone numbers and email addresses— which I could accidentally copy to you while I update the grandmas on what's happening with Sienna.'

'Accidentally sounds perfect,' Sophie said with a smile. 'And that means they'll know to expect contact from me, too.'

'So you've actually got him eating dinner with Sienna?'

'And doing the bedtime story. He's done bathtime for the last three nights, too.'

'You,' Cindy said with a grin, 'are either a genius or you own a real magic wand.'

Sophie smiled. 'I'm just bossier than his mother.'

Cindy laughed. 'Now that I don't believe. When you send Mrs Wallis photos and artwork, be prepared for a tide of advice and a bit of criticism in return.' She looked at Sophie. 'Though if you've achieved dinner, bath and bedtime story in a week, you might just be a match for her.'

'I'll keep you posted with how things go,' Sophie said. 'And we're going to a firework display tonight.'

'Just you and Sienna?'

'No. All three of us.'

'You definitely have a magic wand,' Cindy said. She smiled. 'Next you'll be telling me you've got him to do messy stuff.'

'That,' Sophie said, 'is an excellent idea. We'll start with glitter, I think.'

Cindy's smile widened. 'Now I know Sienna's in good hands.'

'She is,' Sophie promised.

That evening, they walked to the firework display at the local infants' school. Sienna was all wide-eyed and excited. 'We're seeing real fireworks, Daddy?'

'Yes, we are.' He masked his expression of pain almost instantly, but Sophie had seen it. What was so bad about fireworks? But now wasn't the time or the place to ask.

They wandered round the stalls together, each holding one of Sienna's hands. At the stall selling glow-sticks, necklaces and wands, he bought one of everything for his daughter.

'You and Sophie need to have a necklace, too,' she insisted.

'These are on me,' Sophie said with a grin. She cracked the stick and curved it round, fixing it with the connector at the back of Jamie's neck.

'It's pink, just like mine!' Sienna said in delight.

He cracked the stick of Sophie's necklace and sorted out her connector, and Sophie was very aware of the way her skin tingled when his fingertips brushed against her. 'Yellow. You look as if your halo's slipped,' he murmured in her ear, and the tingle spread down her spine.

In another life...

But they were strictly business associates, she reminded herself.

'We need to take pictures to send to Cindy.' And to the grandmothers, she thought. Jamie duly crouched down to be on Sienna's level, and Sophie took a couple of shots on her camera.

'We need a picture with you, too,' Sienna said.

She crouched down on the other side of Sienna to take a photograph of the three of them together. And just for a moment they looked like a family...

But that wasn't part of the deal.

And even if she was in the market for a relationship—which she wasn't—Jamie Wallis wasn't Mr Right. It was way too complicated.

As if Jamie, too, was slightly discomfited by that picture, he shepherded them over to the food stalls and distracted Sienna with hot chocolate and a hot dog. And when the firework display started, he actually lifted Sienna onto his shoulders so she could see the display better.

Sophie could hear the oohs and ahhs of people around them as the fireworks burst into the sky; it was a magical display, but there was something even more magical going on right next to her, with Jamie finally starting to act like a father instead of a reserved guardian.

Sienna chatted all the way home, still holding both their hands, clearly thrilled about the fireworks.

'Will you stay for a coffee or a glass of wine?' Jamie asked.

'Coffee, please,' Sophie said, 'as I'm driving. Do you want me to make the coffee while you get Sienna into bed?'

'That'd be good. Thanks.'

Once she'd made the coffee, Sophie could hear him reading the bedtime story. His resonant and slightly posh voice reminded her of a Shakespearean actor she'd had a crush on for years. Sienna was clearly enjoying every second of it because Sophie could hear delighted giggles.

How much this house had changed in the last week.

Though they still had a long way to go.

She'd just sent the photo of Jamie and Sienna to Cindy when Jamie came into the living room. 'Thank you,' he said. 'Tonight was a lot easier than I thought it was going to be, because of you.'

'What was so difficult about going to a fireworks display?' she asked.

'Fran loved fireworks,' he said simply.

And she'd brought up all the memories. Brought back all the loss. Guilt flooded through her. 'I'm sorry. I wouldn't have pushed you to go if I'd known.'

'For Sienna's sake, I'm glad you did. Plus it was time I faced it. I can't keep depriving her of all the things Fran loved, just because it's hard for me.'

It amazed Sophie that he had such insight—but she was glad for Sienna's sake that he could see it.

He raised his cup of coffee at her. 'And thank you for this, too.'

'No problem.'

'So I was wondering…how did you and Eva start the business?'

'Event planning and travel agencies aren't so far apart,' she said. 'I'd worked for an events company during the university holidays and they offered me a job when I graduated; it was the same for Eva with the travel agency side. And then I think we both got to the point where we realised we were stuck and we had next to no chance of getting promoted unless we moved to a different company. We were talking one night and realised how much the two businesses had in common. We'd both saved money, planning to buy a flat, but we put the money into the business instead. And I'm glad we did.' She paused. 'What about you?'

He lifted one shoulder in a half-shrug. 'My family's in the hotel trade, so it was always on the cards that I'd either work for them or set up on my own in a similar line of business. I was working for my parents when a former stately home came up for sale. There was a lot of land with it, including a wood, and it was the perfect place to develop as a resort offering activity holidays. I'd inherited money from my grandparents, so Fran and I talked about it and decided we'd go for it. We bought the property and got planning permission to build log cabins in the grounds. We built a pool and developed cycle trails and nature trails through the woods, and there's a lake where people can go fishing. And from there we developed a couple more.'

'I've stayed at one of your resorts,' Sophie said. 'We went for a hen weekend.'

'Not your cup of tea?' he asked.

'Going for a long walk in the woods in torrential rain is maybe not the most fun thing I've ever done,' she said. 'But I did appreciate your spa area afterwards.'

'I'm glad.' He smiled. 'That was Fran's idea. She said not everyone liked doing outdoor stuff and we needed something for rainy days as well, so we've got a roster of tutors and we run specialist creative courses—everything from photography and art to creative writing and crafts, cake decorating and pottery. And we listen to what our guests suggest, too. If there's a trend in their comments, that's something we know we need to add or change.'

'Again, not so far away from what we do at Plans & Planes,' Sophie said. 'So how many resorts do you have now?'

'Four in England, one in Italy, one in the South of France where we offer a short course in perfume-making—that was one of Fran's last ideas. And we were thinking of developing one in the Caribbean, but...' He tailed off and shook his head. 'Not after Fran died. I couldn't bear to go back.'

She could see the pain in his eyes. 'I'm sorry,' she said. 'I shouldn't have asked. This must be difficult for you.'

He grimaced. 'I'm being maudlin. I'll shut up.'

'Maybe,' she said, 'talking about her will help.'

'Nothing helps,' he said, and she could see the lone-liness in his face.

How could she just let him sit there and suffer?

So she walked over to the sofa, sat down beside him and wrapped her arms round him.

She knew the hug was a mistake as soon as she'd done it. She could smell the citrusy scent of his shower gel and feel the steady thud of his heart against her. And this surge of sheer attraction, tempting her to jam her mouth over his and let him lose himself in her, for-get his pain for a while...

This was insane.

It had to stop.

Now.

She dropped her hands pulled away. 'Sorry. I over-stepped the boundaries. I just thought you could do with a hug.'

'I did. Thank you,' he said.

Though she noticed that his pupils were huge. And she had a nasty feeling that her own were in a similar state. She couldn't even put it down to low lighting because she'd left the overhead light on. 'I, um, I'd better get going.'

'Thank you for today,' he said. 'For everything you've done. I appreciate it.'

'No problem. I'll see you Monday.'

Panic skittered across his face. 'Sophie, I know it's pushy of me to ask, but… I don't have a clue what to do with Sienna tomorrow. There's only so much storytelling and colouring we can do in a day.'

'You could always do something messy,' she suggested.

'Messy?'

'Glitter. Glue. Paint.'

He looked horrified.

She frowned. 'Didn't you do that sort of thing as a kid?'

'No. My mother didn't like mess.'

And you either followed in your parents' footsteps or you rebelled. From what she'd read in Cindy's file, clearly Jamie had chosen to walk the same path as his mother.

Her thoughts must have shown on her face, because he said, 'There's nothing wrong with liking a tidy house.' She could even hear the slight defensiveness in his tone.

'And there's nothing wrong with a bit of mess, either,' she said. 'It doesn't take that long to clear up.' She'd call into the shops on the way here tomorrow, to get the art supplies she knew he didn't have. 'I'll see you tomorrow at eleven.'

And she left without finishing her coffee, and before she did anything really crazy—like sliding her arms round his neck and kissing him stupid.

Jamie hadn't felt this mixed up in a long time. Since Sophie had put her arms round him like that, it felt as if part of him had been locked away and the key was rusty but starting to turn in the lock.

How close he'd been to leaning forward and kissing her. Finding out if that perfect Cupid's bow of a mouth tasted as sweet as it looked. If she'd kept her arms round him for one more second, he knew he would've wrapped his own arms round her in return and kissed her until they were both dizzy.

It was just as well she'd pulled away.

He didn't want to feel, to lay himself open to risking the devastation of losing someone close again, the way he'd lost Fran. Plus his guilt told him he didn't deserve that kind of closeness.

But part of him longed to see the daylight again. To see the world in full colour.

And when Sophie Firth had wrapped her arms around him, the world had felt bright again. Real. Warm. *Living.*

He was going to have to be really, really careful. Take cold showers. Mentally tattoo a note on his hand to keep his distance. For all their sakes.

CHAPTER FOUR

ON SUNDAY MORNING, Sophie visited a nearby toyshop to buy art supplies, then drove to Jamie's house.

'Sunday morning is art morning in my niece Hattie's house,' she announced to Sienna. 'So I thought we could do the same. I brought us some paint, paper, brushes and stuff.'

The little girl looked thrilled. 'Really?'

'Really. I thought we could make firework pictures. I used to do this when I worked at the nursery school, and it's really fun.' She smiled at Jamie. 'While Sienna and I set up the playroom, your job is to fish some cardboard tubes out of the recycling bin, Jamie.'

'But won't they be—well, all messy?' he asked.

Not as messy as what she planned to make him do, she thought, hiding a smile. 'It's the recycling bin,' she reminded him. 'They're clean when they go in and so are the tins and plastic.'

She shepherded Sienna into the playroom, fished a large square of plastic sheeting out of her bag and spread it over the table to protect it, then got Sienna to put on a long-sleeved apron. 'Now it doesn't matter if we get a bit messy—that's what aprons are for,' she said. She put a large sheet of paper on the table in front of Sienna. 'Would you like to choose two colours of paint?'

'Pink,' Sienna said immediately—just as Sophie's niece would have done, and Sophie had to hide her grin. 'And yellow.'

Sophie squeezed pink and yellow paint from the bottles onto paper plates.

'And now for the clever bit,' she said when Jamie returned with the cardboard tubes. 'Where are the scissors, Sienna?'

'In the drawer.' Sienna gestured to the cupboard where her toys and colouring pencils were kept.

'Thank you.' Sophie retrieved the scissors, made cuts halfway down the first tube, spaced a centimetre apart, then spread the fronds out to make a kind of fan. 'So what we do now is dip the cardboard in the paint, press it on the paper and lift it up again.'

Sienna followed her directions. 'Oh—it looks just like the fireworks in the sky last night!'

'I think Daddy should do some, too,' Sophie said, unable to resist.

'Ah—no. I need to get some work done,' he said.

'You can spare us ten minutes.' No way was she letting him wriggle out of this. 'Would you like to use the same paint, Jamie, or a different colour?'

'The same paint's fine,' he said, giving her a speaking look, but to her relief he knelt down by Sienna's table and duly made some firework patterns on another piece of paper.

'And we can use different sized fans to make different sized fireworks,' she said, cutting some more of the cardboard rolls.

Sienna was delighted, and even more thrilled when Sophie produced glitter from the bag.

'This is how we make the picture sparkle,' Sophie said. Out of the corner of her eye, she could see Jamie flinching at the idea of glitter everywhere. She managed to get his attention, then mouthed, 'That's what a vacuum cleaner's for.'

And to his credit he made more pictures with Sienna, chatting to her about her favourite fireworks from last night and even sprinkling glitter on top of the paint with her. Sophie didn't say a word, but she was thrilled that he wasn't using his normal excuse of work to rush away. He was actually spending quality time with this daughter.

They went from making firework pictures to painting with brushes, and Jamie delighted Sienna by painting the outline of a cat for her to paint in. 'I didn't know you could draw kitties, Daddy!'

He looked as if he'd just surprised himself, too. Sophie sat back on her haunches, watching them with a smile. It was lovely to see Jamie really interacting with Sienna, the way her brother always had with Hattie and Sam, especially as she knew from talking to Cindy that he was way out of his comfort zone with messy play. And when Sienna—with paint and glitter on her hands—leaned across the table, saying, 'I love you, Daddy,' and left paint and glitter smeared all over his white shirt, Sophie held her breath. Would this be his breaking point? A man who liked order and control would find this particularly hard to deal with.

But, instead of being snippy about the mess she'd made of his shirt, he simply said, 'I love you, too, Sienna,' and kissed her.

And right at that moment, Sophie thought, I could love you, too...

She shook herself.

That wasn't going to happen.

She was rubbish at relationships, and Jamie's life was already complicated enough without adding her into the mix.

'I need to go,' she said when Sienna had had her fill of painting. 'I'll clear up all the art stuff first.'

'Don't worry about it. I'll clear up,' Jamie said, surprising her. 'Stay for lunch. Even if it is only going to be cheese on toast.'

She blinked. 'You're offering to cook for me?'

'I can cook,' he said.

She thought back to the supermarket ready meals she'd seen in the fridge. 'I'm not sure I believe you.'

'Here's the deal,' he said. 'If I burn lunch, I clear up. If I don't, you clear up.' He mouthed, 'And you clean the paint out of my shirt.'

'Deal,' she said. 'Sienna and I will lay the table while you make the cheese on toast.'

And it was perfect.

'Now do you believe me?' he asked with a grin.

She raised an eyebrow. 'Strictly speaking, cheese on toast isn't actually cooking. It's just putting bread and cheese under the grill.'

'It still counts,' he insisted. 'Doesn't it, Sienna?'

The little girl nodded. 'But only if I make it with you next time.'

'I think you might have a negotiator in the making there,' Sophie said.

After lunch, she cleared away. 'I need to go now,' she said with a smile. 'But it's a nice day. Maybe you could both go to the park.' When panic skittered across Jamie's face, she said, 'Sienna, do you want to go upstairs and find a nice warm jumper?' Once the little girl was out of earshot, she said to Jamie, 'It'll be fine. You've got this.'

'How do you know I can do it?'

'Because I do,' she said. 'This is like dropping you into a pool full of cetapods and expecting you to swim. You won't know if the cetapods are whales or sharks until you swim up to them. But when you do, you'll realise they're all whales.'

'What if they turn out to be sharks?' he asked.

'Then you call me, and I'll come and fish you out before the sharks eat you. Now go and change your shirt so I can get the paint out of that one.'

'Bossy,' he said, but he did what she'd asked.

Even though Sophie was supposed to be working at home, she spent most of the afternoon thinking about Jamie and wondering how he was coping. But when he didn't call, she knew he didn't need her.

Which was meant to be a good thing.

Though it left her feeling slightly melancholy—and then cross with herself for being so ridiculous. Jamie Wallis was off limits. And the unexpected feelings she'd started having towards him were simply because she was spending so much time with him. Propinquity. She knew he thought of her solely as Sienna's temporary nanny and his business partner.

'So don't even start to begin hoping that things might be different,' she told herself sharply. 'Because they're not. You keep it professional. No emotions.'

In the park, Jamie couldn't stop thinking about Sophie. What was it she'd said? Go for a walk, talk about what you see, ask Sienna about her favourite dogs.

It was the first time he'd ever taken Sienna to the park on his own; before Fran's death, they'd gone as a family, and afterwards he'd left it to Cindy, because trying to pretend that everything was normal had just been unbearable.

But this… Since Sophie had pushed him out of his comfort zone this morning, he was going to give this a try. He walked round the park with Sienna, holding her hand and letting her chat to him. And then, when he could see that the play area wasn't too crowded and hear that the shrieking was at bearable level, he pushed her on the swings and even went down the big slide with her. He smiled nicely at the other families in the play area and tried to ignore the ache of missing Fran.

And then he felt a flood of guilt when he realised that the figure next to him in his head wasn't Fran: she was Sophie. Which wasn't anywhere near their arrangement. He needed to forget the idea of this right now, because he wasn't going to get a second chance to mess up.

But the thought wouldn't quite shift.

Whenever his skin had accidentally made contact with hers, he'd noticed a faint blush on her cheeks, or her pupils had grown larger. He had a feeling that she was just as aware of him as he was of her.

What if…?

A tingle ran down his spine and he shook himself mentally. No. It had to stay strictly business between them. And he needed to get his self-control back. Fast.

On Monday morning, when Sophie walked into the kitchen, she handed Jamie's clean but unironed shirt back to him. 'It was washable paint. Easy-peasy.'

'Thank you,' he said, and his slightly shamefaced expression told her that he knew he'd made an idiot of himself over the messiness issue.

'So how were the sharks?' she asked.

'You were right. They were whales,' he told her.

She smiled. 'Good. Now go to work. Sienna and I have stuff to do.'

Funny how easily she'd slipped into a routine. It felt second nature to take Sienna to nursery school before she went to the office, then to pick her up and cook dinner together, to read together and sing and play.

This felt like being part of a family.

Like the life she'd expected to have with Daniel, until he'd dropped his bombshell. Like the life she'd thought to build with Joe—until she'd learned the truth about him. So what was to say this would be third time lucky? With her track record, it'd be third time unlucky. And there was Sienna to consider. The little girl had had more than enough upheaval in her short life. She didn't need the prospect of more heartbreak.

This was temporary, Sophie reminded herself. And she loved her job. She was happy concentrating on her career and looking forward to going ahead with the new strand to the business, organising weddings abroad.

But, as every day passed, she found herself growing closer and closer to both Sienna and her father. Even though she tried to keep a tiny bit of distance in there, particularly with Jamie, it felt as if it was melting away by the second.

And when on Friday evening he was struggling to come up with ideas of things to do with Sienna at the weekend, how could she refuse to help him?

'The aquarium's always a hit with Hattie and Sam,' she said. 'They love watching the fish and going through the tunnel to see the sharks. Oh, and the penguins. They're Hattie's favourite.'

'Would you come with us tomorrow afternoon?' he asked.

She ought to say no. Keep the distance between them. But he needed her help and she couldn't just turn away. That wasn't who she was. Besides, she could always get up a couple of hours early to catch up with her own work. Thanks to Jamie lending her two really talented members of his team, everything was going just fine at Plans & Planes. 'Sure. Provided I get to look at the jellyfish and the sea horses—they're my favourites.'

'Deal,' he said. 'And I'm paying for your ticket, as I asked you to join us.'

'Only if I buy us dinner. And that's non-negotiable.'

'All right. Thank you,' he said.

'I'll meet you at the front door—say two o'clock?'

'That'd be perfect,' he said.

Outside the aquarium, Sienna greeted Sophie with a squeal and a hug. Jamie's greeting was rather more restrained, but even so his smile made Sophie's heart feel as if it had just done a backward somersault.

She was really going to have to keep a tight rein on herself. He's off limits, she reminded herself. But it felt as if part of her was standing there with her fingers stuck in her ears, saying, 'La-la-la—I can't hear you.'

Jamie had already printed out their tickets at home, to save them having to queue up, and they headed for the penguin zone. He'd clearly read up about the creatures, because he said to Sienna, 'These ones are called Gentoo penguins. And their black and white colouring is camouflage for them.'

'What's camoo…?' Sienna frowned.

'Camouflage,' he repeated carefully. 'It means a special colouring so they look like their surroundings.'

'But water's blue, Daddy. Why aren't they blue, too?'

He smiled. 'It's all to do with how light looks under water. The water looks black and the sunlight looks white. So the camouflage means the penguins look like water and sunlight to any big killer whales that might come along and want to eat them.'

Sienna shivered. 'I don't like whales. I like penguins.'

'There aren't any killer whales here,' Sophie promised her. 'But not all whales eat penguins. Some whales just eat fish, like the minke whales.'

'What's a minke whale?' Sienna asked.

'A very pretty black and white whale. I went to Iceland last summer and I saw minke whales playing in the sea, and they're beautiful.' Sophie grabbed her phone and scrolled through it until she found a photograph. 'Look. I was at the front of the boat and I saw one jump all the way out of the sea and I took his picture—isn't he beautiful?'

Sophie stared at the picture, her eyes round with amazement. 'He jumped all the way out of the sea?'

'Right in front of my eyes. It was amazing,' Sophie confirmed.

'Iceland. Would that have been a research trip for your Weddings Abroad project?' Jamie asked, looking interested.

She nodded. 'I saw half a dozen brides while I was out there. Apparently it's very popular to have the wedding ceremony one day, then go out to do photographs the next day, either on one of the black sand beaches or at one of the waterfalls. Can you imagine how amazing it is to have rainbows in your wedding photos?'

'I like rainbows,' Sienna said.

'They're my favourite, too,' Sophie said. 'Rainbows and the Northern Lights. Though obviously you don't see the Northern Lights in the summer, because you've got the midnight sun. And that's beautiful, too.'

'Are you going to get married, like Cindy and Jack are?' Sienna asked.

She'd thought so. Twice. And how very wrong she'd been. 'Maybe one day,' she said.

'Cindy said I could be her bridesmaid. Can I be your bridesmaid, too?'

'We'll see, sweetie,' Sophie said gently. 'That might be a long time in the future.'

Jamie saw a flicker of sadness in Sophie's eyes. That, plus what she'd said to him a while back about not having good judgement where her love life was concerned, made him sure that someone had let her down very badly. And that brief moment of sadness made him want to give her a hug.

Then again, that probably wasn't a good idea. When she'd given him a hug, it had made all sorts of feelings start bubbling up—feelings he couldn't afford to have. In his experience, love meant loss—something he never wanted to risk again. And he was going to have to make a real effort not to let himself be drawn to her.

She'd sounded wistful when she'd talked about rainbows in wedding photos. Was that what she'd wanted? But it would hardly be tactful to ask. And he needed to head his daughter off before *she* asked. 'Hey, Sienna, do you know what penguins' wings are called?' he asked.

'They don't have wings. Penguins can't fly,' Sienna said.

'Ah, but they do have wings,' he said with a smile.

'Instead of using them to fly, they use their wings to help them swim.'

Swim. He pushed thoughts of Fran away. Nobody was swimming here apart from the creatures who lived in the water. And there wasn't any coral that he could see.

'I know—flippers!' Sienna said.

'That's right.'

They watched the penguins sliding down the ice on their bellies and dive into the water.

'They're so clever, Daddy,' Sienna said, her nose practically pressed against the glass as she watched them.

'They certainly are. Did you know that Gentoo penguins make their nests out of pebbles rather than sticks?'

'I didn't know that, either,' Sophie said. 'I'll remember to tell Hattie that.'

They headed through the shark tunnel, and Sienna was fascinated by the sight of the sharks swimming beneath their feet.

'Did you know some sharks can lose thirty thousand teeth in their lifetime?' Sophie asked.

And Jamie thought, Sophie's full of the kind of facts that children liked. He'd just bet her niece and nephew adored her. He could already see the bond she'd formed with his daughter, and how Sienna looked up to her.

It would be all too easy to fall in love with a woman like Sophie. A woman who'd walked unexpectedly into his life, who was supposed to be his business associate, but who had somehow managed to make him start to feel all the things he'd blocked off since Fran's death. He'd smiled more in the two short weeks he'd known her than he had in the previous two years. And that made him feel antsy. What would happen next? Where did they go from here? It was full of unknowns.

The next stop was the octopus.

'Did you know they have three hearts as well as eight arms?' he asked.

'And they're related to a creature you can see in the garden, especially when it's been a rainy day,' Sophie added. 'Can you guess, Sienna?'

The little girl shook her head. 'Worms?'

'Nearly,' Sophie said, ruffling her hair. 'How about a clue? The creature normally has a spiral shell.'

'Oh—a snail!' Sienna said, smiling.

And funny how her smile made his heart squeeze. Not just because it was so like Fran's, but because she looked happy. And seeing his daughter happy was the best feeling in the world.

They paused in the rock pool area, so Sienna could stroke a starfish and touch an anemone.

'The nennomy looks like a flower,' she said.

The mispronunciation charmed him. 'It's an anemone,' he said. 'Say it after me.' He broke it down into syllables, and Sienna copied him. And then she went back to her original pronunciation. 'The nennomy!'

He smiled, not wanting to spoil her fun by lecturing her. 'It's pretty.'

The area was really crowded, and somehow he ended up sliding his arm round Sophie's shoulders. She turned to glance at him, her dark eyes wide and with a slight flush on her cheeks. Right at that moment, he really, really wanted to kiss her. The thought shocked him deeply; he hadn't felt like that about anyone since Fran.

No way was he going to kiss her in the middle of the crowd, especially with Sienna in front of them. But he had to admit that it was getting more difficult to keep a professional distance between them; and his arm was still round her shoulders when they left the rock pool area. He had to force himself to put a more appropriate distance between them. But then his hand bumped against hers, their fingers tangled together, and for the life of him he couldn't pull away, even though he knew it would be the sensible thing to do.

He gave her a sidelong glance. From the expression on her face, she was feeling the same way: torn between attraction and trying to be professional. Not wanting to take the risk, and yet wanting it at the same time.

Sienna was walking in front of them and clearly hadn't noticed a thing, luckily.

Could they do this?

Should they do this?

He didn't know the answer, but he couldn't stop holding Sophie's hand. And she didn't pull away.

Once they'd seen the displays that Sophie had said were her favourites, the seahorses and the jellyfish, they went to the gift shop.

'What was your favourite animal here, Sienna?' Jamie asked.

His daughter's face was all lit up as she said, 'The penguins!'

'Shall we see if we can find a new bedtime story about penguins?' he asked.

'Yes, please!' Sienna looked thrilled. Jamie glanced at Sophie and the warmth and approval in her eyes made him feel hot all over.

While he and Sienna browsed the bookshelves—and picked up a soft, cuddly penguin at the same time—Sophie found a small penguin wearing a red hat with a white bobble and a loop to hang it from a Christmas tree.

'It's a bit early yet—I never put my Christmas tree up until the first of December,' she said, 'but I'm going to buy you this now so you can put it on your tree when you decorate it, Sienna.'

The little girl was delighted. 'Thank you! Though I'm too little to decorate the tree.'

Jamie saw the surprise that Sophie quickly masked. Clearly her family had different rules from his. When he had been growing up, his mother had always decorated the tree on her own, and Jamie and his sisters had never been involved. His mother liked the tree to look professional, with everything matching and all the baubles spaced the perfect distance apart. He'd ended up doing the same, and even Fran hadn't been able to persuade him out of the habit.

Sophie clearly realised she might have made a gaffe and distracted the little girl. 'Can you help me find a nice present for my niece Hattie and my nephew Sam? Hattie's the same age as you, and her little brother Sam's two. What do you think they might like?'

Sophie helped her to find a soft shark for Sam and a colouring book and pencils for Hattie.

'Perfect choices,' Sophie said. Though Jamie noticed that she still bought the Christmas tree ornament. Given that Cindy wouldn't be back by the first of December, he had a feeling that Sophie intended to make some changes to his routine there, too.

They had dinner together at a restaurant on the south bank, a family-friendly place with a nice children's menu. Sienna chose a quesadilla and a smoothie followed by churros, he and Sophie both opted for a chicken enchilada, and they ordered a bowl of sweet potato fries to share.

When they reached for the fries at the same time and their fingers touched, Jamie felt a frisson of desire all the way down his spine; and he noticed again that Sophie had a slight flush on her cheeks.

It was getting harder and harder to ignore.

Maybe they needed to talk about it. Set out some ground rules. Get things back under control.

'Come back with us and have a glass of wine with me?' he asked when they went to the tube station.

She looked slightly wary.

'You're not driving. Just one glass of wine. No strings,' he said. 'And I'll call you a cab home.'

She paused for so long that he thought she was going to refuse. But then she nodded. 'OK.'

Sienna chattered happily about penguins all the way home.

'I'll put Sienna to bed if you don't mind opening the wine,' Jamie suggested. 'There's a bottle in the fridge.'

Once he'd read the new penguin story to her—twice—he could see Sienna's eyes drooping. 'Time for sleep, now,' he said.

'Love you, Daddy.'

His heart contracted sharply. For the last two years, he'd been wrapped in his grief and had kept his daughter at a distance. And now he realised how much he'd allowed himself to miss out on. He felt a surge of guilt because he'd let his daughter miss out on it, too. 'Love you, too, Sienna.' He kissed her goodnight. 'Sleep tight.'

When he went downstairs, Sophie was sitting on one end of the sofa, with two glasses and the opened bottle of wine on the coffee table.

'Thanks for today,' he said.

'I enjoyed it, too. I always love going there with my niece and nephew.'

He poured them both a glass of wine and sat next to her. 'So are we going to talk about the elephant in the room?'

'That we ended up holding hands in the aquarium?' She blew out a breath. 'I apologise. It was a mistake.'

Which was the right answer. Now they could go back to being professional and pretending it hadn't happened.

Except his mouth had other ideas. 'Was it?'

'If things were different, then maybe not.' She looked away. 'But you have Sienna to think about and you don't need any complications.'

All true. All perfectly valid excuses. Part of him wanted to take them—but a bigger part of him didn't. And if they took this slowly, carefully he could keep his feelings under control.

'Sienna didn't notice anything today. And Sienna doesn't need to know anything right now,' he said. 'This could be just you and me. When she's asleep, or maybe...' He gave her a wry smile. 'I can't believe I'm about to ask you out on a lunch date. I don't even *have* lunch breaks.'

'Exactly. It's too complicated.'

'We could try the simple version,' he suggested.

She shook her head.

But she'd more or less admitted that she felt the same attraction that he did. That in other circumstances she'd consider seeing him. So what was holding her back? 'Why not?'

She sighed. 'It's not you, it's me. I have hopeless judgement in men.'

'So you picked the wrong man. It happens.'

'I spent three years of my life with Dan,' Sophie said. 'How rubbish does that make me?'

'It makes you nice,' he said, 'because you see the best in everyone.' She'd seen something in a man who kept himself safe inside a layer of ice and excuses. And she'd not only seen the best in him, she'd dragged it out, too. He'd resented her for it at times, but he was beginning to see the benefits.

And for Sienna's sake he'd always be grateful to Sophie for that.

'More like a naive idiot, where my love life is concerned,' she said.

He reached over and took her hand, squeezing it briefly and letting it go again to let her know he was on her side. 'You're very far from being an idiot. Is Dan the one who took advantage of you?'

'The first one.' She took a sip of wine. 'I met him in my last year at university—at a party—and I really thought he was the one. We moved in together after we graduated, and I thought we were happy. We were both working slightly mad hours, because I was trying to build my career in event management, and he was training to become an accountant so he was working and studying at the same time. He'd done an economics degree but that didn't exempt him from many exams, so he had to keep going away on some residential course or other.' She grimaced.

'It never even occurred to me that he'd cheat on me while he was away, but it turned out he had a different girl on every course he went on. I didn't often join him at work social events, because they tended to clash with events I was managing—but when I did go to a party with his work friends, I always had this faint suspicion that people were avoiding me. I thought it was just because I wasn't in the same business world and they were being a tiny bit snooty about it, but it turned out to be because they all knew what he was doing and were too embarrassed to talk to me.'

'Which is his fault, not yours.'

'But why didn't I put all the pieces together?' she asked. 'We'd been together for three years when he said he wanted to talk to me. He'd organised dinner out somewhere really flashy. I was so sure he was going to ask me to marry him, because it was actually our third anniversary that night.'

Jamie didn't like where this was going. He had a feeling this was where her heart had been broken. And what kind of lowlife would've done that to a woman like Sophie? It'd be like kicking a puppy or snatching sweeties from a small child.

'Instead, he told me he'd had a fling with someone. A junior in his office. She was pregnant. He said he wasn't in love with her and he didn't want to be with her, but obviously he had to pay child support for the baby.'

It sounded to Jamie as if Dan was the sort who'd try to weasel out of paying child support, too.

'And then he said he'd decided to fight her for custody and he asked me if I'd help him look after the baby.'

He blinked, not quite sure what he was hearing. 'What?'

She looked away. 'I know. How could I have spent three years of my life with someone who was that mean-spirited? The worst thing was, he was shocked when I said no. He thought I was being unreasonable.'

'Hang on.' Jamie could barely process this. 'This is

the man who had a fling, wanted to fight the woman for custody so he wouldn't have to pay her anything, and expected you to look after the baby he'd had with someone else—and he said *you* were being unreasonable?'

She grimaced. 'We had a massive fight. He said I was being selfish. And that's when it came out about all the rest of the women he'd cheated on me with. I just walked out of the restaurant and called Eva. She met me at my flat with her car, and we moved all my stuff to her place. She reminded me to call the bank and put a freeze on our joint account so he couldn't just empty all the money into another account, and then I got my name taken off the rent. It was pretty toxic for a while, but I did the right thing. If I'd forgiven him and stayed, I know he would've cheated on me again within the next month.'

'What happened to the baby?' Jamie asked.

'Apparently he's living happily with his mum and her parents. Dan didn't get very far with his custody case—and I don't think he even sees the baby.'

'He sounds like the worst kind of guy,' Jamie said, 'but not all men are like that.'

'I know,' she said softly. 'I have two brothers and a stepdad who are fabulous, and Eva's fiancé Aidan is lovely.'

'But?'

She sighed. 'Dan wasn't my worst mistake—just the first one.'

He waited, knowing that if he gave her enough space she'd eventually talk.

She took another sip of wine. 'I met Joe in a coffee shop. He sent a choc-chip muffin over to me via the waitress, and then we got chatting and he asked me out. I thought he was a nice guy. It took me six months to work out that we never saw each other at weekends, I'd never been to his place, he never stayed at my place overnight and we only went out to small places around where I lived. I thought it was because he was busy at work, and so was I.' She grimaced. 'How stupid was I not to realise that he was avoiding places where he might see people he knew? And he never invited me back to his place because he wasn't the single man I thought he was. He was married.' She closed her eyes briefly and shook her head. 'Worse still, it turned out that his wife was pregnant. She had terrible morning sickness—and, instead of supporting her, like any decent guy would, he was having an affair. With me. This time, I was the other woman. And I really hated that. I've been there. I know how horrible it feels to be the one cheated on. But I was the other woman, Jamie. I let him cheat on her with me.'

'It wasn't your fault.'

'Of course it was. I agreed to go out with him.'

'It's perfectly reasonable to assume that if someone asks you out, they're not involved with anyone else,' Jamie said gently. 'You really weren't the bad guy here.'

'That's not how it feels.'

'If you'd had any idea that he wasn't single, you wouldn't even have accepted the choc-chip muffin,' he said. 'You have integrity.'

'Thank you.' She blew out a breath. 'But after Dan and Joe, I just can't trust my judgement where my love life is concerned.'

'So, what? You're giving up and spending the rest of your life alone?'

She looked at him. 'You make it sound as if I'm a coward.'

'You're afraid to trust your judgement again.'

'I'm not a coward, Jamie. I just don't want to make any more mistakes. I made two pretty bad ones.'

'Everyone makes mistakes,' he said. 'You just try to learn from them. And yours were different mistakes.'

'At root, they were the same. Trusting people I shouldn't have trusted.'

'People who took advantage of your kindness. Which I guess I'm doing, too.'

She shook her head, grimacing. 'That's different. It's for Sienna. And you're not telling me lies.'

No, but he also wasn't telling her the whole truth about Fran's death. Because he didn't want her to dislike him as much as he disliked himself.

But there was one thing he could do. Something she'd done for him, too.

He took the glass from her and placed it on the coffee table. 'Last week, I was maudlin and hating myself and I really needed a hug. You did that for me and it made me feel a whole lot better. This week, I think it's my turn to give you a hug.'

And he wrapped his arms round her, holding her close.

Mistake.

Big mistake.

Because he could smell the vanilla scent of her shower gel and feel the warmth of her skin. And it made him want to push past another boundary and kiss her. To feel how soft her mouth would be against his, how sweet.

No matter how much he told himself that it would be kissing her better, he knew he was being selfish. Putting his own needs before hers. Because Sophie was vulnerable. She'd done nothing wrong—and yet she blamed herself for being duped by a serial cheater and then a selfish charmer who'd broken his marriage vows.

Could he really say that he was a better man than Joe or Dan? He wasn't a cheat or a liar—but he had been responsible for Fran's death. And he'd let his guilt and the pain get in the way of doing what he should've concentrated on, looking after his little girl.

So in his own way he was probably worse.

Sophie could do so much better than him.

Instead of giving in to the urge to kiss her, he let her go. Stroked her face. 'Don't ever change, Sophie. You're kind and you're lovely.'

'A naive, stupid sucker,' she corrected.

'Better to be naive and believe the best of people than be cynical and bitter and think everyone's just out for themselves,' he countered.

'Maybe.' She shook herself. 'I'd better go.'

She'd barely touched her wine, he noticed.

'I'll call you a cab.'

'It's fine. I can get the Tube.'

'I promised I'd call you a cab.'

'If I stayed and had a glass of wine with you. Which I didn't. I'm sorry I wasted your wine.'

He squeezed her hand briefly. 'Don't apologise. It's my fault for pushing you to talk when you didn't want to.'

'I kind of did that to you,' she admitted.

'Yeah. But you were right,' he said. 'Talking helped.'

She didn't look as if it had helped her much, though. She looked as if she regretted what she'd told him. And he really didn't know how to fix it.

'I'll see you on Monday,' she said. 'Call me if you need anything.'

'You, too,' he said. 'And I'm sorry if I made you feel bad. That wasn't my intention.'

'I know. It's just hard to forgive myself for being such a pushover.'

There were things it was harder to forgive yourself for, but he didn't want to go into that. 'Don't change who you are,' he said. 'Have a good Sunday.'

'You, too.'

And he let her go. Before he did something really stupid. Like kissing her.

CHAPTER FIVE

JAMIE ENDED THE call and sighed. He felt a bit guilty that he needed to ask Sophie for her help yet again; then again, this was part of their deal. Had Cindy not broken her leg, it wouldn't have been an issue because she would've been looking after Sienna anyway.

However, had Cindy not broken her leg, he wouldn't have got to know Sophie this well in the first place. He might not even have invested in Plans & Planes.

But he really, really liked the woman he was getting to know.

He called her. 'Good morning. Are you super-busy right now?'

'Why?'

'Because there's a problem I need to sort out at work—and it's not something I can delegate,' he explained.

'So you want me to look after Sienna?'

'Please,' he said. 'Just for a couple of hours. And, because I don't want to take complete advantage of you, I'll cook dinner for you tonight.'

'Cheese on toast again?' she teased.

'No. Name it and I'll cook it.' Even as he said the words, he knew he was giving her the chance to challenge him and suggest something outrageous.

'Chicken parmigiana,' she said. 'I'll email you the link to a recipe. I already know you've got all the ingredients in the fridge and the cupboard. And you can bake some jacket potatoes and steam some vegetables to go with them.'

He knew she was testing him and expecting him to say no; she'd clearly already worked out for herself that it was quite a while since he'd bothered cooking anything properly. 'All right—and thank you. See you at half-past two?'

'Sure.'

At half-past two, Sophie arrived with a DVD and a bag full of ingredients. 'This is what rainy Sunday afternoons are for,' she said to Sienna. 'We're going to make dessert and some cookies, and then we'll watch a movie.'

'Yay!' Sienna looked thrilled.

'Thank you for coming,' Jamie said. 'I feel a bit guilty for asking you.'

'It's fine. It's what we agreed,' she reminded him. 'Go and do your work.'

While Jamie was stuck at his computer, he could smell something gorgeous. Vanilla? Chocolate? If he sneaked into the kitchen, would they let him steal a cookie?

Just as he was considering it, there was a quiet knock on his study door, then a louder knock. 'Come in,' he said.

The door opened and Sienna came in, carrying a plate containing a single choc-chip cookie; Sophie followed her, carrying a mug of coffee.

'You made the cookie?' he asked, though he already knew the answer because there was still a smear of flour across his daughter's nose and she was wear-

ing the pink apron with white spots that Sophie had
bought her.

'I made it specially for you,' Sienna said proudly.

'It smells absolutely scrumptious.'

She looked worried, as if not sure whether that was a
good thing or a bad; clearly she hadn't come across the
word before. 'That means "delicious" and I can't wait
to try it,' he said with a smile. 'Thank you, Sienna.'

He took a mouthful. The cookie was still warm and
it tasted even better than it smelled: buttery and choco-
laty with a hint of vanilla.

'Is it all right?' Sienna asked, still looking worried.

'It's the best cookie I've ever had in my whole life,'
he said. 'Thank you, darling. Can I have another one,
please?'

She beamed. 'Yes! As long as you promise to eat
your dinner.'

He wasn't sure whether that was Cindy's influence
or Sophie's, and had to hide a grin. 'I promise.'

She brought him another cookie. 'We're going to
watch a movie now, all about a princess.'

'Sounds good,' he said. 'Have fun.'

She smiled again, waved him a shy goodbye, and
trotted off with Sophie.

Even though Jamie was concentrating on his file,
he could hear the faint sound of music in the background—clearly something from the movie. Then he
heard Sophie singing along with the music; she had
a really good voice. He heard Sienna's higher voice
joining in with part of the chorus, and then he heard
Sophie say, 'Let's rewind the movie a bit and sing it
again together.'

He couldn't resist tiptoeing out to the hall and peek-
ing into the living room.

Sienna and Sophie weren't just singing, they were dancing in front of the television and clearly having a wonderful time. And they didn't look anything like temporary nanny and her charge: they looked like a family.

This was the sort of thing Fran would've done with Sienna. The sort of thing *he* should've done, in Fran's absence, instead of letting his own childhood get in the way. Gwen Wallis had been a great believer in children being seen and not heard, and he'd followed in his mother's footsteps. But, since Sophie had come into his life, Jamie had discovered that actually he liked the sound of hearing his little girl giggling and singing.

Once Cindy came back, there would definitely be some changes made to their routine—changes he knew Cindy had tried to implement before, but he'd been too wrapped up in his grief and his guilt to let her make them.

Guilt still froze him, but he knew it was time to think about moving on. It was time to make Sienna's world a better place: starting with cooking dinner for them all tonight.

And Sophie? Last night, she'd made it very clear she wasn't looking for a relationship. He could understand why; she'd dated a couple of men who'd treated her badly and had made her think it was her fault, when in reality it had been their problem rather than hers. Maybe he could help her see that it wasn't her fault— and that maybe it was worth dating again. And that maybe it would be worth dating him...

He shook himself. They'd known each other a fortnight, that was all. This was all happening much too soon. Then again, she was the first person who'd really got through to him since Fran. Her warmth and her openness were irresistible, and he hadn't been able to help responding to her, even though his head was telling him that he shouldn't give in to the crazy impulses—that would lead to falling in love and losing control of his emotions.

Sophie Firth was special.

Jamie went back to his office and finished sorting things out, then cooked dinner. Just as Sophie had promised, all the ingredients were in the fridge. Funny, cooking dinner for them made him feel as if he was really part of a family. He was horribly aware he'd always left the cooking to Fran because she'd enjoyed it and he wasn't bothered either way; he'd been happy to deal with the household chores that she hated instead. But this… This was very different.

Was this the second chance he'd wanted deep down but had thought was unobtainable?

Was Sophie the one who could redeem him?

He shook himself. Once she knew the truth about Fran's death, she'd back off. It was pointless even trying. Better to keep things strictly professional.

He went into the living room. 'OK. Dinner's ready in five minutes. Come and wash your hands.'

Despite his resolutions, the warmth in Sophie's smile curled deep inside him, melting another layer of ice from round his heart.

'This is scrumshuss, Daddy,' Sienna said after her first taste, clearly wanting to use her newly learned word.

'It's good,' Sophie added with a smile. 'OK. I believe you now. You can cook.'

But when she retrieved dessert from the freezer, he realised she'd more than outdone him.

'Are those *penguins*?' he asked.

'Banana penguins,' she confirmed with a grin. 'I thought after yesterday these would be perfect. It's really easy to make them—you just dip the banana in melted chocolate, make the feet and beak out of dried apricots, and use marshmallows and chocolate chips for the eyes.'

'We maked the penguins before we maked the cookies,' Sienna said gleefully.

So that must've been what some of the giggling was about. He didn't have the heart to correct his daughter's grammar. 'I'm impressed.'

'Not my idea,' Sophie admitted with a smile. 'I don't think it was even my sister-in-law's, actually. I think she got it from the Internet.'

'They're great,' he said. He would never have thought of them in a million years.

The banana penguins were a total hit, and Sienna chattered about them all the way through bathtime—and even though he still insisted on shallow baths, he could manage bathtimes now without flashbacks.

Jamie read three stories to Sienna, then headed downstairs to join Sophie.

'I feel bad about you doing the washing up,' he said, noticing that she'd put everything away neatly as well.

'Hey. You cooked. In my book, that lets you off dishwashing duty,' she said with a smile.

'Can I get you a glass of wine or a coffee?'

'Thanks, but I need to be going,' she said. 'This is Hattie's favourite film of all time and I promised to take it back tonight.'

'OK. Thanks again for today,' he said.

'My pleasure.'

'Seriously—you saved my bacon and you make Sienna happy. It's good to see her laughing.'

'She'd be like this with Cindy.' Sophie paused and looked him straight in the eye. 'And with her grand-parents.'

Not his own parents. He couldn't imagine them dancing or singing. 'Fran's parents live quite a way away.'

'And you have guest rooms,' she pointed out. 'They could stay for the weekend. Or midweek. Whatever works for you all.'

'I...' He sighed. He knew she saw right through him and she'd counter any excuse she made. 'You're right. It's an excuse. But every time I look at Fran's mother, I see Fran.'

'And it hurts? I get that,' she said. 'But there has to be a point where the good memories start to take over. When you start to remember Fran with smiles instead of tears. Would she have wanted you and Sienna to be miserable for the rest of your lives?'

'No,' he admitted.

'Then think about it. Sienna needs more than just you and Cindy in her life,' she said gently. 'And, take it from me, it's lovely to see your parents playing with the generation below yours, singing the same songs you remember them singing to you and telling the same terrible jokes.'

'What if you don't remember your parents singing to you and telling you jokes?' The words came out be-fore he could stop them.

She reached up to stroke his face. 'That's when you get to teach them how to do it. How to loosen up and have fun.'

Even Fran hadn't been able to make him loosen up totally, so Jamie knew he didn't have a chance in hell of making his parents loosen up. Even now, despite heading towards the age when they really ought to retire and enjoy their lives, they were still focused on work and the business, and he was really glad he'd struck out on his own rather than agreeing to take over from them—because he was pretty sure neither of them intended to retire. 'Maybe,' he said, trying to be diplomatic.

But her hand was still against his face. His skin tingled where she touched him. How could he resist twisting his head slightly so he could press a kiss into her palm?

Her dark eyes widened—with shock or desire? he wondered.

He wanted to kiss her properly.

But it was too soon. Instead, he took her hand and folded her fingers over the place where he'd kissed her. 'Goodnight, Sophie. See you tomorrow,' he said.

'Tomorrow,' she said. Was it his imagination, or was her voice slightly husky?

Sophie was glad she was driving, because it meant she had to concentrate on the way to her brother and sister-in-law's instead of letting herself dream about Jamie Wallis and brooding over the way he'd kissed her palm. She managed to sidestep all mentions of Jamie when she was sitting in their living room, drinking tea and enjoying their company. But all too soon she was back in her flat and the pictures in her head wouldn't go away.

What would it be like if Jamie kissed her properly? Kissed her like a lover?

She shivered. This was a bad idea. He was vulnerable; he was still hurting over his wife's death to the point where he had trouble spending time with anyone who reminded him of Fran. And even though she knew that Jamie wouldn't lie to her and cheat on her, the way Dan and Joe had, she still thought anything more than a professional relationship between them would be a disaster.

The problem was, when he'd kissed her palm, she'd almost stepped forward and kissed his mouth.

Jamie Wallis was gorgeous with a capital G.

And she really would have to keep reminding herself that he was off limits.

Over the next few days Sophie and Sienna started making things to prepare for Christmas. An advent calendar with pockets for little gifts, which Sophie planned to pick up at the same time that her sister-in-law bought gifts for her own advent calendars for Hattie and Sam; home-made decorations for the Christmas tree, painting yogurt pots with metallic paint and sprinkling glitter on them and making a hanging loop from a tinsel pipe cleaner; and a home-made photo frame made from macaroni stuck onto cardboard and covered with spray paint.

Jamie discovered 'stained glass windows' on various windows around the house, made from black sugar paper with shapes cut out and coloured tissue paper stuck over the gaps to create the 'stained glass'. And there was a painting of a Christmas tree made out of handprints, and an angel with wings made out of handprints—all things that he knew Fran would've enjoyed doing with their daughter. Things he wouldn't even know how to start doing.

And every day his daughter came more and more out of her shell, laughing and smiling and responding to Sophie's warmth.

He really wasn't sure whether he was more charmed

or terrified by it. But everything in his house felt different. *Better*.

How could Sophie have changed everything so much in three short weeks?

And where did they go from here?

On Saturday afternoon, Sophie and Jamie took Sienna to the Natural History Museum.

'I can remember coming here with my parents when I was tiny,' Sophie said. 'My brothers were dinosaur-mad. They loved it here. Whenever Mum asked us where we wanted to go for an afternoon out, Matt and Will always wanted to come here.'

'What about you?' he asked.

'Oh, me, too. My favourite was the triceratops because of its frilly neck. And we all nagged and nagged to go to Lyme Regis on holiday, in case we found a dinosaur on the beach.'

'Did you really find a dinosaur?' Sienna asked, her eyes wide.

'No, but we did find some fossils.' She smiled. 'I still have the first ammonite I ever found.'

'What's a nammo…?' Sienna stumbled over the name.

'An ammonite was a sea creature with a spiral shell, a bit like a snail's shell but bigger,' Sophie explained. 'I can show you one here.'

They wandered round the exhibition together, and Sophie came out with a stream of terrible dinosaur jokes. 'Sienna, what do you call a sleeping dinosaur?'

'I don't know,' Sienna said, playing along.

'A Stego-snorus!' Sophie told her with a grin.

And when they got to the scary animatronic Tyrannosaurus Rex and Sienna started to look worried,

Sophie squeezed her hand. 'Which dinosaur had to wear glasses?'

'I don't know.'

'Is Daddy going to guess?'

'Nope,' Jamie said.

'You're going to groan,' she warned. 'Wait for it… The Tyrannosaurus Specs!'

But she saved her most terrible one until last. 'Where does a Triceratops sit?' When Sienna shook her head, Sophie grinned. 'On its Tricera-bottom!'

The joke had Sienna giggling like mad, and even Jamie couldn't help smiling.

'You can blame my mum for those,' she said with a grin. 'She's the one who taught me them.'

Jamie couldn't remember his mother—or his father—ever telling a joke, much less the sort that a child would appreciate. He pushed the thought away. He didn't have to be like his parents. He was pretty sure that his sisters weren't like their parents—even though he hadn't seen either of his sisters for months, using the excuse that they lived just too far away. But Sophie had shown him that all he had to do was to be himself.

In one of the exhibition rooms, they found themselves in a queue where they were slightly squished together, just as it had been last week; and it felt natural to Jamie to slide his arm round Sophie's shoulder and hold her close, protecting her from the squash. She didn't pull away, and even when the queue thinned out again her fingers ended up curling round his.

Maybe this was the way forward. Baby steps negotiated quietly, instead of big declarations.

When Sienna had had her fill of the museum, they found a family-friendly restaurant. 'It's my turn to pay, so don't argue,' he informed Sophie outside the restaurant.

'OK. Thank you.'

And it really felt like a family meal out. He noticed the way Sophie was with his daughter, encouraging her and drawing her out, and Sienna responded to Sophie's warmth. He was aware that it was the same for him, too; part of him was flustered by his growing feelings for her, but part of him wanted more. Much more.

Back at the house, she made coffee while he settled Sienna in bed, and was curled up on a corner of the sofa, doing something on her phone, when he came downstairs.

'Hey.' He sat next to her and took her hand.

She looked wary. 'I thought we agreed last week that this would be a bad idea.'

'It is,' he said. 'But I can't stop thinking about you. And I've got a feeling it might be the same for you.' Because otherwise why had they ended up holding hands in the museum, earlier that day?

She blew out a breath. 'I'm rubbish at relationships, and you're vulnerable.'

Both statements were true; but both things could be changed. 'So maybe we should just muddle through this together and see how it works out,' he said. 'Humour me.'

'Humour you, how?' she asked.

'Like this,' he said, and leaned over to brush his mouth against hers. Just once. Not demanding, not threatening, just letting her know how he felt. Leaving the next move to her.

Sophie couldn't remember the last time someone had kissed her properly.

She certainly couldn't remember the last time someone had made her knees feel weak in two seconds flat.

And that kiss, even though it had been sweet and gentle and had left the next move up to her, had made every nerve-end in her lips tingle.

'We can't do this,' she said, resting her palm against his face.

Big mistake. Now her hand was tingling as much as her mouth. And she wanted to slide her hand into his hair and draw his face down to hers. Kiss him back.

'This is a really bad idea,' he said, his voice deep and husky and sexy as hell.

His mouth was saying one thing, but his eyes were saying something different. Tempting her to kiss him back, to hold him.

She wasn't sure which of them moved first, but then somehow she was sitting on his lap, his arms were wrapped round her, her hands were in his hair and his mouth was jammed against hers.

When Jamie broke the kiss, Sophie couldn't speak. All her words, her protests, her common sense had been driven clean out of her head.

'This is insane,' she said at last.

'Absolutely,' he agreed, and ran the pad of his thumb along her lower lip.

The next thing she knew, her lips had parted and he was kissing her again. As if he was trying to be sensible but he just couldn't resist her.

Which was how it felt when she kissed him back. He was irresistible.

'You… I… This is all too complicated,' she said.

He stroked her hair. 'Or maybe it's simple. Maybe it's just about you and me.'

'What about Sienna? What about Plans & Planes? What about…?' Her words dried up as he caught her lower lip gently between his teeth.

And then she stopped thinking and kissed him again.

'Sienna doesn't need to know about this until we're ready to tell her,' he said when she broke the kiss. 'And we're both sensible enough to keep business and personal separate. Whatever this thing is between us, it has nothing to do with business.'

'Agreed.'

'I don't know where this is going. I don't know what I can offer you. Part of me is scared because I'm used to being in control of my thoughts and my feelings,' he admitted. 'But I like the way you make me feel. And I don't want that to stop.'

Sophie had thought everything was simple with Joe and with Dan—and it had turned out to be nastily complicated. So maybe Jamie was right about this thing between them and this was the complete opposite: it looked complicated at first glance, but at heart it was simple.

'So we take this day by day,' she said. 'No promises.'

'Sounds good to me.' He kissed her again. 'And nobody else needs to know, until we've worked out what we're doing.'

'Agreed.'

'I haven't felt like this in a very long time,' he said softly.

'Me neither.'

'So we'll take it slowly,' he said, and gently set her back off his lap and on the sofa next to him.

Kissing. Holding hands. Sort-of dating.

'I feel like a teenager,' she confessed.

'Me, too.' He gave her a wry smile. 'Until Cindy's back at work, I can't date you the way I'd like to. I can't take you dancing, or out to dinner, or any of the more traditional things.'

'That's OK. I've been enjoying what we do with Sienna.' She gave him a sidelong glance. 'And we can do dancing here.'

'Is that an offer of a slow dance, or what you were doing with her in front of that movie?'

She groaned. 'Don't tell me you saw that?'

'Yup,' he said with a smile. 'You both looked happy. As if you were having fun.'

'We were. Next time, you ought to join us,' she said.

'Maybe I will. The next rainy Sunday afternoon.' He stole another kiss. 'And when it's a rainy Sunday night and Sienna's asleep, then it's just you and me dancing. To something slow and sweet.'

'I'll hold you to that,' she said. She kissed him again, then stood up. 'And I need to go.' While she still could.

On Sunday morning, Jamie had a project meeting, so Sophie picked Sienna up and took her to the park to meet up with her sister-in-law, niece and nephew.

'This is my niece Hattie, who's the same age as you, and her little brother Sam,' Sophie introduced them. 'And this is their mum, Mandy.'

'Hello,' Sienna said shyly.

'Let's go on the swings,' Hattie said, taking her hand.

Sienna glanced at Sophie for direction, and Sophie smiled and inclined her head.

Hattie immediately started chatting to her, and Sophie followed with Mandy and Sam.

'She clearly adores you,' Mandy said, 'and from the look on her face it's obvious you adore her.'

'She's a lovely little girl,' Sophie said.

'Even so. Be careful,' Mandy warned.

'I know. He's off limits. My business partner.' Sophie had explained the situation to Mandy just after she'd agreed to be Sienna's temporary nanny. 'And he's vulnerable. He was widowed really young, remember.'

'From what you've told me over the last couple of weeks,' Mandy said thoughtfully, 'it sounds to me as if you're falling in love with both him and Sienna.'

Sophie had a nasty feeling that her sister-in-law was right, but shook her head. 'I've learned my lesson after Dan and Joe. I'm not going to lose my heart to anyone ever again.'

'Just be careful, that's all,' Mandy said. 'I don't want to see you hurt again.'

'I promise,' Sophie said, crossing her fingers surreptitiously behind her back. She certainly wasn't going to tell Mandy about the hand-holding yesterday and the kissing last night.

The little girls insisted on going on every single piece of equipment in the park, from the swings to the see-saw to the slides and the bouncy chickens on enormous springs. Sophie took pictures on her phone of the little girls on the slide together, and another one of herself and Sienna at the top of the big slide, holding hands and ready to zoom down to the bottom.

And when they were finally done and Sam was starting to get just a little bit grizzly, they went to the café at the edge of the park for brunch.

'Pancakes and milkshake for me, please,' Hattie said before they'd even looked at the menu.

'And me, please,' Sienna added.

'Pancakes!' Sam beamed at them.

'Pancakes all round, I think,' Mandy said with a smile. 'Sophie, a cappuccino for you?'

'Yes, please.' Sophie stood up and patted her shoulder. 'I'll go and sort it all out if you don't mind staying here with the children.'

The café had colour-in menus, and the girls had just finished colouring them in neatly, while Sam scribbled exuberantly over his, when their drinks and a stack of pancakes arrived.

'I think the girls have just found their new best friend,' Mandy said quietly to Sophie. 'If Jamie's OK with it, maybe Sienna would like to come and play over at our place next weekend.'

'I'll check with him and let you know, but I can't see a problem,' Sophie said. 'It's nice that they get on so well.'

After a second round of milkshakes and coffee, they headed for home.

Sienna was quiet, and Sophie assumed she'd tired herself out at the park and had fallen asleep in the car. But when she glanced at the little girl, she realised that Sienna was crying silently.

'Sweetie, what's wrong?' she asked.

'I wish I had a mummy like Hattie does,' Sienna said, sniffing.

'Oh, darling. I know it's been hard for you.' And then Sophie realised she hadn't even seen a photograph of Fran in the house. She was going to have to tackle Jamie about this, even if it meant wrecking the fragile beginnings of what was happening between them. She could tell Sienna until she was blue in the face that her mother had loved her dearly, but without physical proof—photographs and videos—the little girl's doubts would remain. 'But your dad loves you very, very much.' And he was going to get a lot better at showing it, if Sophie had anything to do with it.

When they got back to the house, Sienna's tears had dried, but the evidence was still there in the puffiness of her eyes.

'What happened?' Jamie mouthed over the top of his daughter's head.

'Tell you later,' she mouthed back.

'So where did you go this morning?' Jamie asked.

'We went to the park and then we had pancakes,' Sienna said. 'I made a new friend. Her name's Hattie. She's the same age as me and her favourite colour's pink, too.'

He raised an eyebrow at Sophie. 'You took her to meet your family?'

'I usually spend some of the weekend with my family,' she corrected, 'and meeting them at the park meant I got to see them as well as spend time with Sienna. The girls had a great time.' She took her phone out of her bag and showed him the photographs. 'I'm going to print some of these out when I get home, Sienna, so you can stick them on your fridge with magnets.'

'Come and tell me about the park and your pancakes,' Jamie said. 'And then I'll read you a story.'

Sienna obligingly told him about every single piece of equipment she'd been on, but he was only halfway through the story when she fell asleep on him.

Gently, he stood up, still cradling her, then set her back on the sofa and tucked a blanket round her. Then he pointed to the kitchen.

Sophie nodded and followed him.

'So what happened?' he asked, keeping his voice quiet.

Sophie blew out a breath. 'I'm so sorry, Jamie. I feel horrible that she got so upset. She saw Mandy and Hattie being close, like any other mum and daughter, and it made her miss Fran.' She bit her lip. 'She said on the way home that she wished she had a mummy.'

Jamie went white.

'Look, I don't want to make things worse, but there isn't a single picture of Fran in your house,' she said.

'Because it hurts to look at them,' he said.

'I get that,' she said softly, 'but not having anything at all is hurting Sienna. Right now, I think she needs to know that her mum loved her. Or am I missing something here? Was Fran maybe not the maternal type?'

He shook his head. 'Fran loved her. Loved her more than anything.'

'Then Sienna needs to know that, Jamie. Even if it hurts you to see the pictures, she needs to see them so she can see that love for herself. She needs to see pictures of her and her mum together—video, too, if you've got it.'

'I...' He sounded as if the words had just choked him.

'Would it help you if I went through the photos with you and picked some out?' And she really hoped he realised that she was trying to be supportive rather than pushy.

He swallowed hard. 'Maybe.'

'Did Fran have a baby book?'

He nodded. 'I put it away in a box, along with the wedding photos.'

'Sienna needs to see it,' Sophie said gently. 'She's really careful with things, so she won't damage it. But she needs to know it exists and her mum loved her.'

'Come into the office,' he said.

He switched on his computer and they went through the files of photographs together.

'She's so like Sienna,' Sophie said. Those same blonde curls and sweet smile.

He nodded. 'That's why I...'

She mentally filled in the rest. Why he'd found it so hard to be with his daughter, because she was a constant reminder of what he'd lost. And Sophie had pushed him and pushed him and pushed him.

'Fran's very beautiful,' Sophie said.

'And she was nice. Funny. Sweet. She made me a better man,' he said. 'And when we had Sienna, I thought life couldn't get any better. I was so happy. Our little family... It wasn't like I remember things being when I was a small child. It was different.'

A close, loving family like her own, Sophie thought, rather than the cold, old-fashioned family Cindy had confided to her about.

He dragged in a breath. 'Two weeks before we went to the Caribbean, Fran told me she was pregnant. Six weeks. Sienna was going to have a little brother or sister.'

So he hadn't just lost his wife. He'd lost a child as well. No wonder he was still hurting for the might-have-beens. She wrapped her arms round him. 'That's hard. I'm so sorry.'

'Every time I look at Sienna, I see what might have been. And I hate myself for it.'

'But you can't live in the past, or in what might have been,' she said softly. 'Live in the here and now. Look at what you have. Sienna's the sweetest, sweetest little girl. And she loves you dearly.'

'How can she, when I hardly spend time with her?'

'She loves you,' Sophie repeated. 'And you love her.'

'Of course I do. She's part of me. And I'm letting her down.'

'Things are changing,' she said. 'You're spending more time with her now and it's going to get easier every day. And then you'll get to the point where you see what you have now, instead of what you lost. You're making good memories together. The fireworks and the dinosaurs and the painting and the stories.'

'Uh-huh.'

He didn't look convinced, and her heart bled for him. She held him more tightly, just for a second. 'It's going to be OK, Jamie. Really, it is. Now let's find some photographs of Sienna with Fran and print them out. Maybe you can make a collage together and put them in a frame in her room.'

His eyes were wet, as if he'd been blinking back tears. 'I should've done that before.'

'I don't think you were in the right place to do it before,' she said gently. 'But you are now. And it's going to be OK. I promise.'

CHAPTER SIX

On Monday morning, Sienna was bright and chirpy. 'Come and see what Daddy and me makes,' she said, tugging at Sophie's hand.

Up in Sienna's bedroom, there was a new frame on the wall; either Jamie had recycled it from somewhere or he'd managed to find a craft place still open when Sienna had woken yesterday after her nap.

And the frame was filled with a collage of photos of Sienna with Fran.

'My mummy's in heaven but Daddy says she still loves me, even though I can't see her,' Sienna said, 'and he says every time I look up and see the stars twinkling it's to show me she's smiling down at me.'

Sophie had to blink back a rush of tears. 'Yes, he's right.'

'So I do have a mummy like Hattie.'

'You do, darling.' Sophie couldn't help hugging her.

Later that night, when Jamie came downstairs after reading Sienna's bedtime story, she hugged him.

'What was that for?' he asked.

'What you did for Sienna. Even though I know it must've been like sprinkling salt in your wounds.'

'It was,' he admitted. 'But for her sake I should've done it a long while ago.'

'You've done it now. And that's a really good thing.'

He stole a kiss. 'Thanks to you.'

She stroked his face. 'Hey. I didn't do much.'

'Yes, you did. You gave me the strength to face something I found really tough,' he said, 'and I appreciate it. I know I ought to let you go, but come and sit with me for a while?'

'OK.'

He led her over to the sofa in the living room, then drew her onto his lap. 'So how's it going with Plans & Planes?'

'Good. Georgia and Lily have both settled in really well, and Georgia's been excellent at dealing with the events side.' She smiled at him. 'This isn't really the appropriate place to say this, but I'd really like to poach both of them permanently.'

'I have a half-stake in the business,' he said, 'so if moving staff around between the two businesses means an increase in productivity, that's fine.'

'I haven't asked them yet,' she warned.

'I'll talk to Karen and prime her that you're going to ask—and if they want to move across permanently, it's fine.'

'Thanks.'

'You're really going to miss Eva, aren't you?' he asked.

'She's been my best friend for eleven years—a huge part of my life,' Sophie said. 'But we can do video calls, and still send each other texts and emails. And I have work to keep me busy.'

'Two jobs, at the moment,' he said, looking faintly guilty.

'Two half-jobs,' she corrected. 'And I know we were

talking about Plans & Planes, but I'm going to switch hats. It's December next week.'

Jamie groaned. 'I have a nasty feeling I know what's coming next. You want to do the tree.'

'Yup.'

He sighed. 'I'd kind of noticed the home-made ornaments appearing on all the windowsills.'

'It was a bit of a hint. Kids love helping to decorate the tree.' Then a nasty thought hit her. 'Or do you have a problem with Christmas?'

'No more than any other day of the year,' he said.

But he seemed reluctant and she couldn't work out why. 'Didn't you used to decorate the tree with your parents?'

'No,' he said shortly.

More of that ridiculously Victorian 'children should be seen and not heard' business? she wondered. 'OK. Maybe it's time to start making some new traditions with Sienna,' she said carefully.

'You're not going to give in until I agree, are you?' he asked wryly.

'That would be a no.'

He rolled his eyes, though she noticed that he was smiling—so he couldn't be too put out by her suggestion. 'OK. I'll finish early on Friday and pick her up from nursery and choose a tree.'

'A real tree, not an artificial one.'

'A real tree.' He paused. 'Would you come with us?'

She grinned. 'I'd love to.'

'You're one of these people who really loves Christmas, aren't you?'

'Yes. It's the best day of the year.' She frowned. 'Don't you?'

'It's just another day. And the holidays are way too commercial.'

'Christmas is what you make it,' she said firmly. 'In my family, we give each other token presents and spoil the children. Sam's getting a train set this year— Will and Mandy have bought a massive wooden track, and the rest of us have bought trains or accessories. We're doing the same with Hattie's doll's house. And I'm pretty sure all of us are going to be on the floor, playing with them. And then there will be the board games, and someone will decide to change the rules, and there will be forfeits involved—probably involving cake and chocolate.'

He said nothing, not being drawn on what Christmas was usually like for him and Sienna. She guessed that since Fran's death it had been a very, very quiet affair.

'You could,' she said quietly, 'come and join us if you want to. There's plenty of room and my mum always cooks way too much food.'

'You're inviting us for Christmas?' He looked shocked. 'But won't your parents mind?'

She shrugged. 'The way Mum sees it, the more, the merrier.'

'I...' He blinked, as if he couldn't quite take it in.

'You don't have to say yes right now. Think about it.'

'How would you introduce us?'

She smiled. 'My family already knows about you both.'

His eyes widened. 'Do they know...?'

'About you and me? No. They just know you bought Eva's share of the business and I'm helping you out on the nanny front. And obviously Mandy, Hattie and Sam have met Sienna.'

'Uh-huh.' He seemed to relax.

'You and me—that's just between us. Because it's still very early days,' she said. 'As far as everyone else is concerned, you and I are business associates and are sort of getting to know each other as friends.'

'Friends.' He stole a kiss.

'And I'm going with you to choose the tree on Friday simply as your friend.'

Friends. He thought about it. They *were* becoming friends. He liked Sophie a lot, as well as being attracted to her.

But friendship plus attraction added up to a very different sum. One that scared him. Could he trust her with his battered heart? Could he relinquish control and let himself love her?

She kissed him back. 'I need to go. But I'll see you tomorrow. Have a think about Christmas. No pressure—I won't say a word to Sienna.'

On Friday afternoon, Jamie and Sophie took Sienna to the garden centre to choose a Christmas tree together. Sienna and Sophie made a beeline for the tree decorations, and Jamie didn't get a chance to say that he already had decorations, because Sienna was oohing and ahhing over the most glittery things. Even though the things that she picked out made him wince inwardly at their garishness, there was no way he could say no. Particularly as Sophie took the basket and insisted on paying.

Sophie suggested they put the tree in the living room, the furthest distance from the radiators and the fire. 'Because then it won't dry out,' she said.

And then they proceeded to decorate the tree together.

It was so different from the tree he usually had, with

its matching colour scheme and the baubles a regulation distance apart and sober white lights. Sophie had bought gaudy coloured lights that flashed in different patterns, and Sienna was thrilled by them. Jamie gritted his teeth and looped the lights around the branches, starting from the top.

The elegant glass baubles he normally used were replaced by a mixture of Sienna's painted yoghurt pots and the glittery decorations she'd found at the garden centre, plus the penguin with the Christmas hat they'd bought at the aquarium.

It looked terrible. A complete mess. Every sinew in his body screamed to put some sort of order to it.

But his daughter was smiling. So he didn't say a word.

'We need to put the star at the top, Daddy.' Sienna produced a cardboard star that she'd painted gold and then sprinkled golden glitter on it.

There was a gold ribbon secured to the back of the star so he could tie it to the tree.

'That's perfect, Daddy. It's the Bethlehem star.' Sienna beamed and sang 'Twinkle, Twinkle Little Star'.

Jamie had the biggest lump in his throat and he couldn't say a word.

'Sienna, can you stand in front of the tree and sing that for me again, please, sweetie?' Sophie asked.

Sienna obliged, scrunching her hands up and opening them wide to the word 'twinkle'.

'That's the song Bethany asked me to sing in the Christmas concert,' she said.

'Because you sing it so beautifully,' Sophie added.

'Sophie's making me angel wings for the concert,' Sienna said, doing a little happy wiggle. 'And a halo.'

Couldn't she just buy a proper costume in a shop?

Jamie wondered. But he glanced at Sophie before he said it, and clearly she'd guessed what he was thinking because she gave the tiniest shake of her head to warn him to shut up.

'That's lovely, darling,' he said instead.

'And now I want a picture of you both in front of the tree,' Sophie said, 'for Cindy.'

'I want you in the picture, too, Sophie,' Sienna said.

'Let's have one with you and Daddy, and then one with all three of us,' Sophie suggested.

'Yay!' Sienna said with a smile.

Sophie took a few shots on her phone, then said to Sienna, 'Do you want to help me send this picture of you and Daddy to Cindy?'

'And to the grannies,' Sienna added.

Grannies? What was going on? Jamie gave Sophie a suspicious look.

'Later,' she mouthed.

He waited until after Sienna's bedtime story to tackle Sophie. 'Right. Explain about the grannies.'

She sighed. 'It's nothing so terrible. I just send her grandmothers photos of Sienna and bits of her artwork.'

'Both of them?'

'Both of them,' she confirmed.

He narrowed his eyes at her. 'That's not in your remit.'

'You didn't say I couldn't,' she pointed out.

'How did you get their details?'

She mimed a zip across her mouth. 'I'm taking the Fifth on that one.'

He scoffed. 'You can't, because you're not American and we don't have a constitution.'

'In that case, I'm not telling you, because then there can't be any comebacks,' she said. She narrowed her eyes at him. 'And there *mustn't* be any comebacks, Jamie.'

He was pretty sure that Cindy must have given her the information. 'I can't believe—'

'Stop being so prissy,' Sophie cut in. 'Sienna's their granddaughter. All grandparents love getting their grandkids' artwork and sticking it on the fridge. And, for your information, they loved the pictures I sent them of you two with the dinosaurs last week.'

'Hang on. This is my mother you're talking about, too?' he checked, not quite believing it.

'Yup. Granny Gwen and Granny Rose.'

'And my mother hasn't given you a list of detailed instructions about Sienna?'

'No,' Sophie said. 'Well, she tried. Then I explained to her I'm not actually your employee.' The corner of her mouth twitched. 'And that actually I'm bossier than she is.'

He rolled his eyes. 'Hardly.'

'Oh, but I am. Look at that tree. It's there—even though you hate it,' she said, 'and you're quivering and desperate to make everything all neat and regulated and subtle.'

'Well—yes,' he admitted.

'Which isn't what Christmas is all about, Jamie. Christmas is about having fun, about singing carols and pop songs, about having chocolate for breakfast and the dog having his share of Christmas dinner and then spending the afternoon farting in the living room because he's scoffed too much turkey. It's about games for the whole family, and tinsel, and really terrible cracker jokes, and paper hats.'

Jamie just looked at her, unable to think of a way to counteract anything she said.

'Oh, though I do have one regulation for next week-end,' she said with a smile. 'You're taking Sienna to see Father Christmas.'

'Right.' This was the first he'd heard of it.

She gave him the cheekiest grin. 'I've booked it and paid for it—I've got a time slot and everything. So that will soothe your soul about sticking to regulations.'

'Now you're mocking me.'

She walked over to him and kissed him lightly. 'I am. Because you're being pompous and you deserve to be mocked for that.'

And the touch of her mouth did more to silence him than anything she'd said.

Her phone beeped to signal an incoming text. She glanced at the screen, grinned, and handed the phone to him. 'Righty. Read this.'

The sender turned out to be his mother.

Oh, how sweet!

Gwen followed it up with a second message.

Twinkle, Twinkle. That was Jamie's favourite song at that age.

Jamie stared at the words, open-mouthed. 'Are you sure we're not in a parallel universe? How would she even know that? I don't remember my parents ever coming to school concerts when I was small. They were always working.' Just like he was, he thought with a twinge of guilt.

'But I bet they had a video camera—right from when they were really new on the market and hideously expensive,' Sienna said. 'And my guess is your dad taught your nanny how to use it and got her to film you and your sisters at all the things he and your mum didn't manage to get to.'

Now he thought about it, Jamie could remember their nanny using an expensive camera. But even so. 'My mother...' He blew out a breath. 'That text can't possibly be from her.' It didn't sound like her. Fond. Warm. Loving. Soft. That wasn't his mother at all.

'It is. Call her and talk to her, if you like. And, while you're at it, ask her to come to the nursery school Christmas concert. I bet you she'll say yes.'

He shook his head. 'She'll be too busy at work.'

'Ask her,' Sophie said again.

Another message came in. He looked at the screen. 'You've got a text from Rose.' Fran's mother.

'Read it to me,' she said.

There was a lump in his throat making him croak as he read the words. 'It says, "She looks just like my Frannie. Thank you, Sophie." And there are three kisses.'

'I know you think you have to do this all on your own, with the support of a nanny—but you don't,' she said softly. 'It's coming up to Christmas. Give everyone a chance, Jamie.'

He scowled at her. 'I suppose you're going to suggest now I have everyone here for Christmas.'

'That's an even more brilliant idea than coming to spend Christmas with my family,' she said. 'Let me know the guest list and I'll send the invites out for you tomorrow.'

'Hang on. This is going way too fast for me, Sophie,' he said, panic flooding through him at the idea.

'OK. I'll back off. Maybe not a big gathering at your house this year. But you still need to invite both the grannies to the nursery school Christmas concert.

And Cindy. *And* me, even though I'll be officially not needed by then.'

Jamie rather thought he'd still be needing her. But he didn't know how to tell her. So instead he said, 'My turn to be bossy. Come and have lunch with me on Wednesday.'

'Since when do you have a lunch break?'

'You had lunch with me when we talked about a temporary transfer for Georgia and Lily,' he pointed out.

'So this is a business lunch?'

'Personal,' he said.

She smiled, and butterflies started dancing in her stomach. 'I still think this is a bad idea. But OK. It's a…'

'It's a date,' he said softly. He drew her hand up to his mouth and pressed a kiss in the palm. 'You and me. I'll pick you up from your office. You can tell everyone it's business, if you like. But I'm telling you now there will be hand-holding involved. And I intend to make sure there's some mistletoe around.'

'Like this?' She sketched some in the air with her fingertip.

What else could he do but kiss her?

And she was gratifyingly flushed by the time he broke the kiss. 'Well, Ms Firth.'

'Well, Mr Wallis.' Her voice was gratifyingly husky, too.

'Oh, and while I remember—I can't come over to look after Sienna tomorrow.'

He frowned. 'Why not?'

'I have a small problem. To be more accurate, a small four-footed and waggy-tailed problem,' she said.

He blinked. 'You have a dog?' Yet she'd never mentioned a pet before.

'Just for tomorrow,' she explained. 'I'm puppy-sitting for my friend so she can do her Christmas shopping—so if you need me to look after Sienna you're going to have to bring her to my place.' She paused. 'You can work there, if you like. My kitchen table functions very well as a desk.'

It sounded seriously domestic. Something that should have had him running for cover. But the idea was too irresistible to turn down. 'OK.'

'And Mandy was asking if Sienna can come for lunch and play with Hattie on Sunday afternoon.'

Given that Sophie was being so accommodating, he thought that he really ought to do the same. 'Sure.'

'Great.' She stole another kiss. 'Right. We both have work to do. See you tomorrow.'

'Tomorrow.' And he was really looking forward to it.

On Saturday, at Sophie's flat, Jamie felt as if he'd just stepped into a hug. The place was warm and comfortable, and she had photographs everywhere. The mantelpiece was full of graduation and wedding photographs, plus pictures of children he assumed were Hattie and Sam, and a picture of her and Eva at the Eiffel Tower. There were hand-drawn cards on the mantelpiece, and childish artwork held to the outside of her fridge with magnets.

Sophie Firth was clearly much loved. And he could see why.

'Meet Archie,' she said.

The liver and white springer spaniel wriggled in her

arms, clearly desperate to get down and start bouncing about.

'Are you ready for this, Sienna? He's very lively. And very lovely,' she said with a smile.

'Yay!' Sienna said.

Sophie knelt on the floor and let the pup down. He bounced about, his tail a wagging blur and his soft paws scrabbling everywhere, then leapt onto Sienna's lap and proceeded to wash her face with his tongue, much to her joy.

'I love him!' Sienna said.

'He'll calm down in a minute. Libby, my friend who owns him, says he does tricks. Shall we see if he'll do them for us?'

Sienna nodded and cuddled the puppy.

'Coffee?' Sophie said to Jamie.

'I'll make it.'

She shook her head. 'Get yourself settled at the table. I don't have a posh coffee maker like yours, but I promise it's decent coffee.'

She made coffee for them and poured a glass of milk for Sienna; although Jamie was officially supposed to be working at his laptop, he couldn't help watching Sophie as she showed Sienna how to get Archie to sit and hold up one paw for treats.

It wasn't that maybe he could fall in love with Sophie Firth.

He already had.

That innate warmth and kindness, the sweetness of her mouth—she was adorable. Even when she was being bossy, it wasn't like the way his mother took over things; she had a way of making it feel as if you'd been the one to make the suggestion in the first place.

And there was a strong bond between Sophie and his daughter.

For the first time in two years, he could see the future—and he liked what he saw. A future full of laughter and love and real happiness.

He knew he didn't deserve it.

But for Sienna's sake—and Sophie's—he'd work for it.

Sophie and Sienna took the pup out for a walk, once Sophie had finished her milk. 'We can only take him out for a little while,' Sophie explained, 'because he's still a baby. Libby says it's five minutes' walk for each month of the pup's age, so that's fifteen minutes of walking and I'll have to carry him after that.'

'Will you come with us, Daddy?' Sienna asked.

He was supposed to be working.

But the sun was shining. How could he resist his daughter's entreaties—or the big amber eyes of the spaniel? 'Sure,' he said. And Sophie's smile made him feel warm all over.

In the end, he was the one who ended up carrying the pup—who'd curled up and gone to sleep next to the park bench while Sienna was playing on the swings—and Sophie held Sienna's hand as the little girl skipped back to Sophie's flat.

Sophie made toasted cheese and ham sandwiches for lunch, and Archie had a tiny piece of ham along with his kibble, sitting nicely and putting his paw up to ask for a treat.

How could Jamie be anything but charmed?

Even when the pup had a couple of accidents on the kitchen floor by the back door, Sophie was good-natured about it. 'He's just a baby. And my kitchen floor isn't carpet. All I need is a mop and some disinfectant. The floor'll dry quickly enough.'

Later in the afternoon, when Sienna had talked Jamie into watching a princess movie in the living room with them, the pup was quiet and Jamie assumed he'd fallen asleep next to Sophie's feet. But then Sophie went into the kitchen to make a drink and came back looking absolutely horrified.

'What's the matter?' he asked.

'You know all those memes where they say silence is golden—unless you have a pup, in which case silence is really, really suspicious?'

No, he didn't. He wasn't quite sure what a meme was, but the whole thing about a quiet pup being suspicious sounded like a warning. 'What's he done?'

'Your shoe,' Sophie said, looking guilty, and handed it to him. 'He's chewed it. Um, quite badly.'

Both ends of the lace had been bitten off to the point where it was unusable, and the pup had chewed all round the inner edge of the shoe. The tongue beneath the laces was particularly badly savaged. No way was he going to be able to repair them.

'I should've kept a closer eye on him,' she said, biting her lip.

'Hey—I was here, too,' he said. 'I thought he was asleep. It isn't your fault.'

'Are you going to be able to drive home?'

'If you can lend me a lace to keep me going,' he said. 'But I don't think I'll be wearing those shoes again after that.'

'I'll replace them.'

He shook his head. 'It's fine. And it's a good lesson to learn: never leave shoes around within a puppy's reach.'

Sophie carried the dog over to a cupboard in the living room and searched one-handed in a drawer. 'I don't have any laces,' she said. 'But I think I can do something with elastic bands.'

'Thanks,' he said.

When the film ended, he said, 'We need to go home now, Sienna.'

The little girl shook her head. 'I want to stay with Sophie and Archie.'

'Not today,' he said. 'We can maybe come and visit another time.'

'But Archie won't be here.' Her lower lip wobbled.

'Maybe we can go and see him together at my friend Libby's house, another day,' Sophie suggested.

'Can we, Daddy?' Sienna asked. 'Please?'

'Yes, darling. But we need to let Sophie get on.'

'Bye, Sophie.' The little girl hugged her. 'Thank you for having me. Love you.'

Sophie hugged her back. 'It was a pleasure and I love you, too.'

Archie, not to be outdone, licked Sienna's face.

'And I love you, too, Archie.' Sienna kissed the pup's nose.

'I'll see you tomorrow afternoon, just after lunch, and we'll go and play with Hattie,' Sophie said. 'I'll just fix Daddy's shoe before you go.'

She did something complicated with the elastic bands, and to his surprise they actually held his shoe on his foot.

'I really am sorry about the shoes,' she said.

'It's fine. It's not as if they were brand new.' He smiled at her. 'See you tomorrow. And thank you for today. It's been great.' It shocked him how much he'd enjoyed it. Even though Sophie's flat was tiny, it was warm and welcoming and he'd felt completely at home.

This was all going way too fast. Scarily so.

But he didn't think he wanted to stop it.

CHAPTER SEVEN

SOPHIE WAS HALFWAY to Mandy's house with Sienna in the car seat on Sunday when her phone rang. She switched it through to the hands-free system on the car. 'Hello?'

'Soph, it's Mandy. Sorry, I meant to ring you earlier. Sam's gone down with a rotten cold and he's running a temperature.'

'Ah. So we need to reschedule the play date?' Sophie asked.

'Sort of,' Mandy said. 'Will's going to look after Sam for me. I thought maybe we could take the girls swimming instead.'

'Hang on a tick. Would you like to go swimming, Sienna?' Sophie asked.

'I've never been swimming,' the little girl said.

Sophie glanced at her in surprise. Given that Jamie owned several resorts, all of which had a pool… Surely he'd visited them with Sienna and let her enjoy the children's activities?

'Sienna's the same size as Hattie and she's got two costumes, so Sienna can borrow one,' Mandy said. 'And you can borrow a costume from me, Sophie. We've got spare swimming towels and spare armbands, too. Would you like to go swimming, Sienna?'

'Yes, please!' Sienna said, and it was settled.

At Mandy's house, they moved Sienna's car seat to the back and fixed Hattie's next to it, and the two little girls chattered all the way to the sports centre.

But Sienna clung to Sophie's hand on the way from the changing rooms to the pool, clearly nervous.

'It'll be fine, Sienna,' Sophie reassured her. 'We're going in the little pool, and it isn't very deep. I promise I won't let you go under the water. We're just going to sit and play.'

It took a little while for Sienna to relax, but once she'd overcome her initial nervousness of the water she started copying Hattie, the two little girls had a wonderful time in the pool.

'This is the perfect Sunday afternoon,' Mandy said with a smile, and Sophie had to agree.

Jamie glanced at his watch. It was nearly four in the afternoon and it was starting to get dark. Plus it had been raining steadily for the last hour, so they couldn't have been at the park. Surely Sophie should have brought Sienna back by now?

Feeling twitchy, he was about to call Sophie's mobile phone when he heard the sound of car tyres on gravel.

Sienna rushed to find him as soon as the front door opened. 'Daddy, Daddy, guess what? Me and Hattie went swimming!'

It felt as if his blood was roaring through his ears. *Swimming.*

Fran had died, swimming. She'd died in the ocean and he hadn't been with her. Guilt slammed into him. And the woman he'd been considering bringing into his life, into Fran's place, *had taken his daughter swimming.*

She'd really overstepped the mark—and so had he.

He wasn't going to yell at her in front of Sienna. But he couldn't just let this go.

'Darling, can you go upstairs and draw me a picture?' he asked once he'd greeted his daughter with a kiss.

'Yes, Daddy.' Sienna beamed at him and skipped up the stairs.

'Kitchen. Now,' he mouthed at Sophie.

She frowned, but followed him in there.

'Close the door,' he said, his voice clipped.

Her frown deepened. 'Jamie? What's going on?'

'I need to talk to you and I don't want Sienna to hear any of this,' he said, keeping his voice low.

She closed the door. 'I don't understand. What's the problem?'

'You took Sienna swimming.'

'Because Sam had a rotten cold and Mandy didn't want Sienna to pick it up. She called me when I was about halfway to their house and suggested we could go swimming instead. Sienna said she'd love to go when we asked her, so Mandy lent us both costumes and towels plus some armbands for Sienna.'

'You took Sienna swimming,' he repeated.

'Which is a perfectly normal thing to do with a small child,' Sophie protested. 'The pool's not far from Mandy's house, there are lifeguards, and actually there's a very shallow pool especially for little ones, so she wasn't in any danger of teenagers splashing her or bumping into her by accident.'

She really wasn't listening. Did he have to tell her in words of one syllable? 'I don't want her swimming, and you had no right to take her without asking.'

'You left her in my charge,' she reminded him. 'You

were in a meeting, so I didn't get the chance to ask your permission. And I don't see why swimming is such a big problem for you. It's a life skill Sienna's going to need when she's older and she'll have swimming lessons at junior school, so it's a good idea to start getting her used to the water now.'

He clenched his teeth. 'Fran died because she went swimming.'

Sophie stared at him as his words sank in, her face paling with shock. 'Fran *drowned*? Oh, my God. I'm so sorry, Jamie. I had no idea. I thought she died because she fell ill while you were abroad.'

'She didn't drown,' Jamie corrected. 'She went diving and got scratched on a coral reef. It turned out she was allergic to the coral sting—she went into anaphylactic shock. The diver with her called for help and started bringing her back to shore, but the allergic reaction made her face and throat swell up, she couldn't breathe and her heart stopped. She was dead by the time the medics got to them.'

'I'm so sorry. I didn't know.' Sophie blew out a breath. 'Why didn't you tell me?'

'It's not exactly the kind of thing that comes up in conversation.'

'But you could have made sure the information was in Cindy's file. What if the real temporary nanny had taken Sienna swimming?'

'Swimming isn't on the list of activities Sienna does. The real temporary nanny,' he pointed out, 'would have stuck to the rules.' Whereas Sophie had well and truly broken them.

'Jamie, I don't know what to say. I'm sorry. But what are you going to do when Sienna goes to school? Tell her teacher that she's the only child in the class who's not allowed to go swimming?'

'Yes,' he said.

The expression of anguish in her eyes turned to anger. 'That's not reasonable, and you know it. What happened to Fran was desperately tragic, and I'm sorry for your loss and Sienna's, but there aren't any coral reefs in English indoor swimming pools. And what if when Sienna's older and she's messing about with a group of friends, and one of them thinks it'd be funny to throw her into an outdoor pool? If she can't swim and it's a deep pool, what then? You're prepared to let her drown?'

'Her friends will be too sensible to throw her in a pool.'

She rolled her eyes. 'Jamie, you were a teenager yourself once. A student. You know how sometimes things get out of hand. Nobody means any harm, but things happen. Isn't it better that she knows how to get out of trouble?'

'My daughter doesn't swim. End of,' he said curtly. He couldn't tolerate the idea.

'But—'

'No buts,' he cut in.

'You're not being fair to her.'

'I don't care. She doesn't swim.'

Sophie blew out a breath. 'So, what? You're never going to take her to the seaside, either?'

'Correct.' How could he let her anywhere near the sea, the thing that had killed her mother? Why couldn't Sophie understand that he was trying to protect his little girl? 'That's one of the reasons we don't go to Norfolk. Do you know where Fran's parents live? In a village right next to the North Sea.' It was way, way too dangerous.

'Why?' she asked, shaking her head in apparent confusion. 'Why are you going to deprive Sienna of the sheer joy of paddling at the edge of the sea on a hot summer's day, when you know she'll be perfectly safe because you're holding your hand? Why won't you let her build a sandcastle, put seaweed flags and shells on the towers, and fill up the moat with sea water? Why won't you let her look for foss—?' She broke off. 'Hang on. I told you about my childhood, about me and my brothers wanting to find a dinosaur on the beach at Lyme Regis. You could've said something then.'

'Sienna was with us.'

'Later, then,' she said. 'Why didn't you tell me?'

'Because it was all my fault!' The words came out slightly louder than he'd intended, and she flinched.

But she didn't back down.

She didn't stop asking questions, either.

'Why was it your fault, Jamie?'

'Because it should've been me,' he said. 'We were in the Caribbean, looking at a potential new resort. The place looked fine and we planned to try out the activities on offer. I was meant to go out diving around the coral reef, but I'd eaten something that disagreed with me and was ill that morning, so she went out instead. And she died.' He clenched his teeth. 'None of us knew she was allergic to coral. If I hadn't been ill I would've been the one who was stung, not her. It would've been painful, maybe. But Fran would still be alive.'

Sophie had assumed that Fran had died from some kind of tropical disease—but now she knew Fran's death had been caused by an allergic reaction to a coral sting, and

Jamie blamed himself because she'd taken his place on the diving trip when he'd been too sick to go.

Now she understood why he was being so unreasonable about her taking Sienna swimming. And why he'd backed away from his daughter, not just because she reminded him of what he'd lost, but she reminded him of his guilt.

Guilt he shouldn't been carrying in the first place, because it hadn't been his fault at all.

'You might have been allergic to the coral, too,' she pointed out.

'I'm not.'

'It's not your fault that Fran died.'

He gave her a look of sheer contempt. 'Of course it is. If I'd gone on the diving trip instead of her, she wouldn't have been scratched by the coral and she wouldn't have died.'

'You'd eaten something that disagreed with you,' she reminded. 'In that situation, when you're being sick or you've got an upset stomach, you can't even walk round a resort, let alone anything else. You need to rest and stay close to a bathroom and drink plenty of water. Diving was completely out of the question.'

'It's my fault,' he repeated stubbornly.

'No. But I tell you what *is* your fault,' she said. 'Sienna and Rose. You're backing away from them because every time you see them they remind you of Fran, and you feel the loss and the guilt all over again.' She lifted her chin. 'For their sake, you have to break the cycle and get past it. Don't let it ruin Sienna's life any more than it has already. Find a counsellor who can help you.'

'It has nothing to do with you,' he said.

'Actually, as I'm her temporary nanny, it has everything to do with me,' she said.

No, it didn't. He couldn't handle this. What the hell had he been thinking? He was better off as he'd been before he'd met Sophie. Alone. *Safe.*

He knew what he needed to do now. 'That's easily sorted.' He stared at her. 'I'll call the agency tomorrow morning and ask them to send someone. You've been here a month. At least some of their staff must've recovered from that virus by now.'

'What?' She looked at him in disbelief. 'You can't sack me. You're not my boss.'

'I believe the phrase you used is "a business partner who doesn't interfere".' He folded his arms and glared at her. 'I'm not interfering in Plans & Planes, and you're not interfering with my life any more.'

'Don't be so ridiculous. I'm not interfering.' She shook her head, trying to clear it. 'I'm trying to understand what the hell's going on in your head.'

'You don't need to. Now, I'd like my car key and front door key back, please.' He held out his hand.

'You don't mean this.' He couldn't mean this. She could just about handle the fact that he wanted to keep the relationship between the two of them strictly business—all along she'd expected this to be third time unlucky—but he *couldn't* take it out on Sienna. Not like this. 'The deal is that I'm looking after Sienna until Cindy's leg is healed.'

He lifted a shoulder. 'I've changed my mind. I'd like you to go. Now.'

'Then do I at least get to say goodbye to Sienna?'

'I don't think that's appropriate.'

What? Sophie could understand why he was upset—

her actions had inadvertently brought back his loss and grief—but this was totally unreasonable. 'That's not fair. She's lost enough in her life.'

He gave her another of those witheringly cold looks. 'You should've thought about that before you took her swimming.'

'Oh, for pity's sake! *I didn't know how Fran died,*' she reminded him through clenched teeth.

'Even if you had, would it have made a difference?'

'Yes. Of course it would. I would've discussed it with you.'

His expression said that he didn't believe her. 'My keys.'

Right now he wasn't being reasonable; the more she argued with him, the more entrenched he was becoming. So maybe it was better to give a little ground now and try to talk about it again when he'd calmed down. She rummaged in her bag and took out the keys. 'Please don't do this, Jamie. It's not fair on any of us.'

'Thank you for your help over the last month,' he said coolly.

Help? It wasn't just helping him out over a childcare crisis. It had started out that way, yes—but they'd grown close over the last few weeks. He'd been trying to persuade her to date him. They'd kissed. Held each other.

And now he was ending it.

Ending everything.

'Tell Sienna if she ever needs anything, I'm here,' she said.

'That won't be necessary,' Jamie said, and his expression was practically Arctic.

Maybe tomorrow, when he'd calmed down a bit,

she could try talking to him again. But for now she concentrated on putting one foot in front of the other, and walked out of the kitchen. Out of his house. Out of his life.

Jamie watched the door close behind Sophie. He couldn't believe how quickly and how badly the row had escalated.

Why did he feel that this was somehow his fault? Because it wasn't. Sophie had taken Sienna swimming without asking him. How could Sophie not see that she was massively in the wrong?

He damped down the hurt and anger and frustration, not wanting Sienna to see it, and went to check on her.

'Where's Sophie?' she asked, looking up from her drawing.

'She had to go.'

'But she didn't come and kiss me goodbye.' Sienna's bottom lip wobbled.

'She had to go to a meeting,' Jamie fibbed, hating himself for lying but wanting to save his daughter from any more hurt.

'Oh. Well, I'll give her my picture tomorrow,' she said.

Sophie wasn't going to be there tomorrow. Not that he was going to tell Sienna that right now. And guilt squeezed him even harder when he saw what she'd drawn: a swimming pool, with two little girls who were clearly herself and Hattie, and two women who were clearly Sophie and Hattie's mum.

Sienna had obviously loved her afternoon at the swimming pool.

And he hated himself that little bit more.

* * *

'But why isn't Sophie taking me to nursery school?' Sienna wailed the next morning when Jamie broke the news to her. 'I need to give her my picture!'

'Sophie can't look after you any more,' Jamie said. 'I'm sorry.'

'Is that because she's in heaven with Mummy?'

The question cut him to the quick. Was that really the first thing his daughter thought of when someone was no longer around? Sophie had suggested it but he hadn't really believed her. Now he was beginning to think that Sophie might've been right. 'No, she's not in heaven, darling. She's just busy at work. She was only helping out as long as she could until Cindy's better.'

Sienna was crying. 'I love Sophie.'

So do I, Jamie thought, but she put you at risk and I can't handle that. And I can't handle feeling things that I can't control, either. 'I'm going to take you to nursery school this morning. You'll have a new nanny this afternoon who'll look after you until Cindy's leg is mended.'

And Ellen turned out to be everything he wanted in a nanny. Middle-aged, no-nonsense, and she stuck to the rules in the file.

Though he did keep two things from Sophie's regime. He ate dinner with Sienna, even though Ellen kept to the nursery menus rather than the kind of food Sophie had let Sienna help her cook. And he made sure that he was the one to read Sienna a bedtime story. Tough, since the swimming incident, Ellen was the one who did bathtimes and hair-washing.

'Right,' Eva said on Wednesday morning, perching on the edge of Sophie's desk. 'Ignore all your calls. We need to talk. What's happened?'

'It doesn't matter,' Sophie said, looking away.

Eva raised her eyebrows. 'On Monday, you looked as if you'd cried yourself to sleep the previous night, then cried all through your shower that morning.'

She had.

'Yesterday, you looked twice as bad. Today, you look worse still. So something's obviously up, Soph. And, yes, I know I'm going away soon, but I'm still your best friend and I'll always be here for you. So *talk* to me.'

'Sorry.' Sophie scrubbed at her eyes. 'Give me a tick and I'll sort out my make-up a bit better.'

Eva reached across the desk and hugged her. 'I'd much rather you talked to me.'

'All right.' Sophie blew out a breath. 'Jamie sacked me.'

Eva stared at her in obvious disbelief. 'What?'

'As Sienna's nanny.'

'Why?'

'I took her swimming.' Sophie bit her lip. 'I thought you said Fran died from an unexpected illness.'

'She did,' Eva said.

'Jamie told me she went diving and had a massive allergic reaction to a scratch on coral,' Sophie said. 'He went bananas when he realised I'd taken Sienna swimming.'

'Oh, my God. I had no idea that's what her illness was. I just assumed…' Eva spread her hands, looking upset. 'Well. It didn't feel right to ask for details. We all just assumed it was some tropical disease that didn't have a cure.' Eva hugged Sophie again. 'He'll calm down and apologise.'

'It doesn't matter about an apology. I just want him to calm down and for things to be back to how they were.' Sophie squeezed her eyes shut. 'He's not answering any of my calls, Eva.'

'He's got a Y chromosome,' Eva reminded her. 'It means he doesn't always think things through.'

'I miss Sienna.'

Eva gave her a narrow look. 'And you miss Jamie. It wasn't just business, was it?'

'You know my track record in men. I always pick Mr Wrong.' Sophie sighed heavily. 'I screwed up yet again.'

'Jamie's a nice guy. He's fair—well, most of the time he's fair,' Eva amended. 'Just give him a chance to calm down. Then he'll realise he's been a total idiot. He won't know how to fix things, being a guy, but give him a few more days and then try calling him again, act as if nothing's happened, and…'

Sophie shook her head. 'It's over, Eva. I blew it.'

Eva hugged her again. 'I'll talk to him.'

'No. I don't want to be the pathetic woman who doesn't know when to stop and drags everyone else into the break-up,' Sophie said. 'I just have to chalk this down to experience.' And she was never, ever going to let herself lose her heart to anyone again.

Order. That was what Jamie liked. What Ellen was making sure he had.

So why did it feel so wrong? he wondered.

No more home-made Christmas decorations; but he hadn't removed the tree that he'd decorated with Sienna and Sophie, hideously garish and tacky though it was.

No more Sienna trotting into his office to interrupt him, with flour smeared across her face and in her hair, carrying a cookie or a cupcake she'd baked especially for him and looking so pleased with herself.

No more chaos or dancing or singing.

And it got worse on Saturday when he and Sienna queued up to see Santa at the grotto in a nearby department store. There was tinnily annoying Christmas music, teenagers capering about dressed as elves, children in the queue getting fretful because the wait to see Santa was getting too much for them...

If Sophie had been with them, it would've been different. She would've got the kids around them singing along with the Christmas songs and doing the traditional actions. She would've revelled in the spirit of things; whereas Jamie felt distinctly Scrooge-like and had to bite his tongue to stop himself saying, 'Bah, humbug!'

He missed Sophie.

Irrationally and stupidly, he missed her. He missed the warmth of her smile, the laughter in her eyes, the way she made a room feel like home just by walking into it.

And he didn't have a clue what to say to his daughter to get them through the interminable wait to see Santa. Sophie would probably have spun some story about the elves in Santa's workshop to distract the little girl. But he didn't have the words. He wouldn't even know where to start. And Sienna was just clinging to his hand, white-faced, looking as if she wanted to be a million miles away.

He could do with being a million miles away from all this nonsense, too.

He'd even suggested that morning that maybe they should skip the visit, but Sienna had been stubborn about it. 'Sophie said we were going to see Santa.'

So Santa it was.

And his own Christmas spirit had more than deserted him, Jamie thought grimly.

Finally they were at the head of the queue, and Santa gave a jolly laugh as they walked in. 'Good morning, young lady. And what's your name?'

'Sienna,' she said shyly.

'That's a lovely name. And you've come out all the way to see me today?'

She nodded.

'I'm very pleased. Have you been a good girl?'

'Yes,' she whispered.

'I know you wrote to me to tell me, but I always like to hear children tell me. So what would you like for Christmas, Sienna?' he asked.

She took a deep breath. 'I want Sophie to be my new mummy.'

'Well, sweetheart, that's a bit tricky, because the presents I give are all wrapped up, and I can't wrap a person up,' Santa said gently.

'Daddy had a big fight with Sophie and she went away,' Sienna said.

Jamie wanted the earth to open up and swallow him.

'I love Sophie, and she loves me.' Sienna's bottom lip began to wobble and a tear rolled down her cheek. 'I want her to be my mummy. My mummy's in heaven but Sophie isn't. And I love Sophie.'

Jamie dropped to his knees beside her and put his arms round her. 'Don't cry, darling. And I don't think Santa has time to talk about this right now.'

'Oh, Santa *always* has time,' Santa corrected, giving him a speaking look, and Jamie felt about two centimetres tall. 'Tell me about Sophie, Sienna.'

'She came to look after me when Cindy, my nanny, broke her leg. Sophie's lovely. I love Sophie. My grannies love Sophie.' Sophie swallowed a sob. '*Everybody* loves Sophie.'

'Does Daddy love Sophie?' Santa asked gently.

'I don't know. But I think Sophie loves Daddy.'

How? Jamie wondered. How could Sophie possibly love him, when it was his fault that Sienna's mother was dead, he was a rubbish father, and he'd pushed Sophie away without letting her have a say?

'I think,' Santa said, 'you and Daddy need to talk. And sometimes it's hard to say the right words, so I'm going to give you a very special teddy bear to help you. A black and white teddy bear.'

'Like a penguin?' Sienna asked.

He smiled. 'Just like a penguin. What you do is sit with Daddy and you tell the teddy bear what you want to say to Daddy. And then things will work out. I can't give you a mummy for Christmas, sweetheart, but that bear will help you.'

'Thank you.' Sienna accepted the wrapped present gratefully. 'Thank you, Santa.'

'Merry Christmas,' he said.

'Merry Christmas,' Jamie said. 'And thank you.'

Sienna clutched the bear tightly as they left Santa's grotto.

'Would you like to go for a milkshake?' he asked.

She shook her head.

He had a pretty good idea what his daughter wanted to do instead. 'Let's go home and talk to the bear,' he said. 'Though maybe we should get him a Christmas hat first.' Because that was what he was pretty sure Sophie would've suggested.

They bought the Christmas hat for the bear and headed back to their house. Ellen was there, waiting for them; she smiled and was kind, but she just wasn't

Sophie. And the house wasn't home without Sophie, either.

They ate lunch, though Sienna didn't eat much, pushing her food around on the plate because she was clearly too upset to eat. Then, finally, they sat down with the bear. Jamie knew that this was going to test him to his limits; and he also knew that, whatever happened, he was not going to let his little girl down.

'Why did Daddy fight with Sophie, Bear?' Sienna asked.

'Because sometimes Daddy gets things wrong, and Daddy needs to learn to listen,' he said.

Sienna looked thoughtful. 'Does Daddy love Sophie like I do, Bear?'

He owed her honesty. 'Yes, I do.'

She turned to him, the bear temporarily forgotten. 'So can Sophie be my mummy?'

That was the key question. The one he couldn't answer without Sophie.

'It's not just up to me, darling,' he said. 'I need to talk to Sophie. And you know sometimes when you have a fight with a friend, it takes a little while to make things up?'

She nodded solemnly.

'I promise I'll try to make things up with her. But it might take a while.' He paused. 'Would you like to draw a picture of your bear?'

'For Sophie?'

He nodded. If need be, he could always photograph it on his phone and text it to Sophie—or maybe ask Eva to play postman for him, if Sophie was ignoring him.

When Sienna was settled, he took his phone, ready to text Sophie.

Where did he start?

They'd both been in the wrong. But saying that was maybe not the most tactful opening.

In the end, he sent the simplest message he could think of.

Please can we talk?

If she ignored him or said no, he'd have to try a different approach. But the most important thing right now was re-establishing contact.

There was no answer. She might be busy, he told himself. Her phone might be stuffed in her handbag, in a different room, and she might not have heard it signal an incoming message or seen the text.

Or she might do what he'd done when she'd tried to call him earlier in the week and just ignore the message.

He hoped, for all their sakes, her silence was just because she was busy.

'Ellen, would you mind looking after Sienna for a few minutes for me, please?' he asked.

'Of course I will, Mr Wallis,' she said.

'Are you going to see Sophie?' Sienna asked hopefully.

'Not yet,' he said. 'I need to wait for her to answer my text first.'

She looked deflated. 'You're going to work.'

No, but he didn't want to burden her with where he was going. 'Yes,' he fibbed. 'I'll be as quick as I can.'

He grabbed his coat and headed to the florist round the corner to buy flowers, then walked to the cemetery.

Suitably, it was raining.

He took out the old flowers from the vase on Fran's

grave and put the new ones in their place. 'Hi,' he said. 'I miss you.'

And of course she didn't answer. She couldn't answer.

'I'm sorry,' he said. 'I let you down. If I hadn't eaten that stupid fish curry, I wouldn't have been ill and it would've been me scratching myself on the coral reef, not you. You would still have been here to see our daughter grow up.'

And he'd let her down there, too. He swallowed hard.

'I've made a real mess of it, Fran. I've been a coward and an idiot, and I've hurt Sienna. I've hurt your mum. I've behaved like *my* mum.'

The rain came down a little bit harder.

'I want to make it right,' he said. 'With Sophie, I was getting there. She showed me how to be a proper dad to Sienna. How to be human again instead of a block of ice.' He sighed. 'Except I overreacted and I pushed her away.'

And he didn't know if she was going to give him a second chance. He didn't deserve one, not for his own sake. But surely Sienna deserved a chance?

'I love you,' he said to Fran, 'and I always will. But Sienna's growing up and she really needs a mum. And I need someone to—well, manage me, I guess. Someone I can love, the way I love you. Because love doesn't just fit in a little box. It expands.' He dragged in a breath. 'I want to be a family again. And it feels right with Sophie. It doesn't mean I don't love you any more. And I'll never forget you. I'll remember you every time I hear our daughter laugh. And I want to hear Sienna laugh a lot, Fran. I don't want her to grow up like I did, a kid who was seen but never heard. I want her to have a normal childhood. To feel loved. So I'm going to ask Sophie to forgive me, and I'll do whatever it takes to persuade her to give me a second chance—to marry me and be a family with me. I hope you can understand that.'

And maybe he was just being fanciful: but right at that moment the rain stopped, and a ray of sunlight caught the droplets of rain on the flowers he'd put in the vase in front of Fran's grave.

Was it Fran giving him a push and telling him that life had to go on, and she wanted him to find happiness?

He hoped so.

It certainly made his heart feel lighter.

He rested his hand on her grave. 'I love you, Fran. I'm sorry we didn't get the chance to grow old together. But I've met someone who's taught me to love again, someone who's taught me to reconnect with our daughter. And I hope we're going to have a happy life.' He swallowed hard. 'I just need to get her to forgive me, first.'

Just.

Funny how he could negotiate difficult contracts and do megabuck deals without turning a hair. But this emotional minefield… He just need to hope that Sophie would talk to him and give him the chance he'd been too stupid to give her.

CHAPTER EIGHT

Please can we talk?

SOPHIE STARED AT the screen. Given that Jamie had ignored her phone calls last week and had made it very clear that he didn't want anything to do with her, this was the last thing she'd expected—to the point where she'd left her phone in her handbag and hadn't bothered checking it, so the message had been sitting there unread for a couple of hours.

What did he want to talk to her about?

The fact he'd started with the word 'please' was a good thing; it sounded as if he really was prepared to discuss things instead of going off at the deep end. And she'd been so miserable without him and Sophie in her life. Even throwing herself into work hadn't helped much; she was too aware of how much she missed them.

OK.

Monday, half-past twelve?

That question mark made all the difference: it meant this was a suggestion, not a demand.

Fine. Suggest somewhere neutral?

The café opposite your office? Or do you know somewhere better?

Café's fine. See you at twelve-thirty.

See you then.

Sophie found it really hard to concentrate at work on Monday.

'You're twitchy,' Eva said.

'Because I'm meeting Jamie at lunchtime,' Sophie admitted. 'He wants to talk.'

Eva smiled. 'See? Told you so. All he needed was some time to calm down.'

'Maybe. But I have absolutely no idea what he wants to talk about.'

'He's probably working out how to apologise because he knows he's in the wrong,' Eva said. 'Do you want me to come with you?'

'I love you dearly for offering,' Sophie said, 'but it's fine.'

'Where are you meeting him?'

'At the café across the road from here.'

'Then text me if you need me and I'll be straight over,' Eva said.

'I will.' Sophie hugged her. 'Thank you.'

She walked into the café at twenty-nine minutes past twelve. Jamie was already there, and was sitting at a table where she could see him easily from the door. He raised a hand as she scanned the room. That tiny hint of vulnerability in his smile melted her heart.

But he probably wanted to discuss business, she

warned herself. This wasn't going to be personal. Maybe he wanted her to talk to the new nanny about some of the things she'd done with Sienna. So she wasn't going to let herself remember how it had felt when he'd held her hand and kissed her. That was in the past and it was staying there.

She walked over to him. 'Hello, Jamie.'

'Thank you for coming, Sophie,' he said. 'Can I get you some coffee?'

'Thank you. That'd be nice.'

He gestured to the chair opposite his. 'Please sit down. I'll be back in a minute.'

Her nervousness increased as she waited. He'd still given her absolutely no idea what he wanted to talk to her about, and she couldn't tell a thing about his mood from his polite formality.

He returned bearing a mug of coffee just the way she liked it.

'Thank you,' she said.

'I'm glad you agreed to meet me.'

'Uh-huh.' She'd already decided to let him do most of the talking, so she waited to hear what he had to say.

'First of all,' he said, 'I owe you a massive apology—I went off at the deep end, last week, and I shouldn't have taken out my worries on you.'

She narrowed her eyes at him. 'Or sacked me, when you weren't technically my boss.'

'Or asked you to leave,' he said, 'when you'd done so much to make Sienna's life better—and mine.' He sighed. 'I'm an idiot.'

'I'd kind of already worked that one out for myself.' Her resolve to let him do all the talking vanished in a rush of curiosity. 'But what made you see it?'

'Would you believe, a stuffed panda?'

Sophie stared at him, not understanding. 'A stuffed panda? How?'

'I took Sienna to see Santa. He asked what she wanted for Christmas,' Jamie explained. 'And he said he couldn't do what she wanted, but he gave her a bear and said if she used it to talk to me I might be able to sort things out.'

That was amazing psychology on Santa's part, she thought. 'What did she ask for?'

He winced. 'There's no way to prepare you for this, so I'll tell you straight. Sienna wanted you to be her mummy.'

Sophie stared at him, completely floored by what he'd just told her. 'I don't know what to say.'

He lifted a shoulder in a resigned half-shrug. 'You don't have to say anything.'

'What did you say?' she asked.

'To Santa or the bear?'

'Both.'

'Thank you to Santa. And to the bear...' He raked a hand through his hair. 'That was one of the toughest conversations I've ever had. I said that it wasn't just up to me. That I needed to talk to you. And sometimes when you have a fight with a friend it takes a little while to make things up.'

'Good answer,' she said. 'You didn't make any promises you can't keep and you were honest with Sienna.' Though had she just compounded her past mistakes? Was this like Joe and Dan all over again and Jamie only wanted her for what she could do for him, not for herself? 'Is that why you're talking to me now?'

'For her sake? Partly,' he admitted. 'But also for mine. I've been doing a lot of thinking, the last few days. The house doesn't feel right without you.'

'In other words, you don't like your new temp nanny?' she asked wryly.

'Ellen's lovely and she's going to stay with us until Cindy's back,' he said. 'It's not that at all. It's *you*. I miss you.'

Could she trust him? Did he mean it? She'd been here before.

Though Jamie wasn't Dan or Joe. It wasn't fair to judge him by her past mistakes.

'The last month, things have been different,' he said. 'You made me look at my life and I didn't like what I saw. And then I panicked when I found you'd taken Sienna swimming.' He took a deep breath. 'I'll be honest with you. Feelings make me twitchy. I like being in control. Emotions—well, I was panicking and refusing to admit things to myself, and I guess I used the swimming as an excuse to push you away. Which was unfair of me and wrong.'

And it had hurt her deeply.

'I like the person I am when I'm with you,' he said, 'and I want to keep being that person. I want you back in my life, Sophie, but not as Sienna's nanny and not just as my business partner.'

She didn't quite dare to hope. 'So what are you saying?'

'I know I messed up, and I know you've been hurt before—but I'd never cheat on you like Dan and Joe did, and I won't ever lie to you like they did.' He looked earnestly at her. 'Just as you've shown me that I can be a better person, I want to show you that you can trust me.'

'How do I know you won't go off at the deep end again, the next time I do or say something you don't like and I can't read your mind?' she asked.

'Because,' he said, 'you've taught me to talk. You and the bear that Santa gave Sienna. Plus you were right about the counselling. I talked to a friend who trained as a GP, and he recommended someone who happens to have a cancellation this week. So I'm going for the first session tomorrow.' His eyes narrowed for a moment. 'That Santa isn't related to you, by any chance, is he?'

'No. I have no idea who that particular Santa was, but I've arranged having a Santa at events before now, so I know the kind of training they do,' she explained. 'They're taught how to deal with it when small children ask them to make a terminally ill person better or bring someone back from heaven.'

'Or ask them if someone will be their mummy,' he added, wincing.

She nodded. 'And the way your Santa handled the situation sounds perfect.' Particularly as it had made Jamie sit down with his daughter and really communicate with her.

'So will you give me a chance to make it up to you and see how this thing works out between us?' he asked.

'No promises to Sienna,' she warned. Just in case it went wrong again.

'No promises,' he agreed. 'I just want to spend time with you. And I don't mean for Sienna's sake. For me, too. Dating you properly as well as spending family time with her.'

Dating you properly. A thrill went down her spine at the idea. 'OK. And it might be nice to meet your new nanny.'

He gave her a wry smile. 'Why do I get the feeling that you're going to tell her to ignore that file?'

'More than that, I'm going to rip that file into little pieces and jump up and down on it,' she said. 'And then I might put all the pieces in a puddle and jump up and down on them all over again.'

'I've kind of got the message,' he said.

'Good.'

'Will you come and have dinner with us tonight?'

'If you're cooking,' she said.

He nodded. 'Chicken parmigiana?'

'And banana penguins. You'll need Sienna's help for that.'

'Sounds good,' he said.

Then, to her shock, he leaned across the table and kissed her. His mouth was warm and sweet, and every nerve-end in her lips tingled.

'That wasn't part of the deal,' she said.

'It's how you're supposed to seal a deal,' he said.

'That's not how we sealed the deal about me being your temporary nanny and you buying out Eva.'

'And that was my mistake,' he said, and kissed her again. 'See you tonight. Six o'clock. And if you're late I'll serve you cold, congealed Brussels sprouts.'

She grinned. 'Sounds as if you're listening and learning.'

'I am.' His eyes were full of warmth. Full of promise.

And Sophie allowed herself just a tiny glimmer of hope for the future.

That evening, Sophie stood on Jamie's doorstep, clutching a bottle of wine and some chocolate Christmas tree decorations. How ridiculous to feel nervous. Jamie had asked her here, and she knew Sienna would be pleased to see her. All the same, she took a deep breath before she pressed the doorbell.

A few seconds later, the front door opened and Sienna rushed to greet her with a hug and a squeal. 'Sophie!'

'Hello, sweetheart.' She hugged the little girl. 'These are for you, to go on the tree.' If Jamie hadn't removed all the gaudy decorations and replaced them with subtle, tasteful, soulless ones.

'Thank you!'

'And this is for you,' she said, handing the wine to Jamie.

'Thank you.'

She laughed. 'You do know you've got chocolate smeared over your face, right?' And it was incredibly endearing, because it meant his attention had been completely on Sienna and making the banana penguins together, and he hadn't been thinking about mess.

He looked shocked. 'I have?'

'Uh-huh.' On impulse, she rubbed the smear away with her thumb.

His pupils widened, and she felt an answering lick of desire.

Had Sienna not been there, he might have greeted her very differently indeed. With a kiss, like the one he'd left her with in the café...

'Come in,' he said, and Sophie was gratified to hear the huskiness in his voice.

Dinner was fabulous. 'No sprouts,' he said with a grin. And she was really pleased to discover that he'd left the tree exactly as they'd decorated it together.

'Can I read your bedtime story tonight, Sienna?' she asked when she'd helped the little girl add the chocolate decorations to the tree.

'Yes, please,' Sienna said with a smile.

Sophie noticed that the black and white bear had pride of place on Sienna's pillow. The bear that had helped her break the final barriers with her father.

'Did Daddy ask you?' Sienna asked, when they were alone.

Sophie could guess exactly what Sienna was talking about. Would she be her new mummy? But it wasn't something she could answer yet. She and Jamie still needed to sort things out between them.

'He told me about Santa and how he talked to you and your lovely bear, here,' Sophie said. 'And you know when you have a big fight with someone, sometimes it takes a little while to make it up?'

Sienna nodded solemnly.

'That's where we are right now. Your dad and I still need to talk a bit more and finish making up. But one thing that won't ever change,' she promised, 'is me being part of your life. I'll always be there.'

Sienna hugged her. 'I love you.'

'I love you, too.' She read the story and kissed the little girl goodnight, before heading back downstairs to Jamie.

'Will you stay and have a glass of wine with me?' he asked.

'Yes, but there's something I need to do first,' she said.

He laughed. 'I'm way ahead of you. Come with me.' He ushered her into the kitchen, opened the file that was lying on the kitchen table and ripped up the first page, then offered her the next page. 'Your turn.'

Between them they ripped up the entire contents of the file.

'There aren't any puddles tonight,' Jamie said, 'but I can improvise, if you like.'

'Just knowing all those rules are gone is enough,' she said with a smile.

He poured them both a glass of wine. 'Come and sit with me.'

And she discovered that he really did mean sitting with him, when he scooped her off the sofa and settled her on his lap.

'This,' he said softly. 'This is what's been missing from my life. You, close to me. And thank you for giving me a second chance. I'm not going to mess it up.' He stole a kiss. 'I'm tempted to ask you to stay tonight, but I know it's too soon.'

'It is,' she agreed.

'Will you let me take you to dinner on Wednesday— just the two of us?' he asked.

'You mean on a proper date?'

'A proper date,' he confirmed. 'Ellen will babysit.'

'I'd like that,' she said.

'Good.' He stole another kiss. 'So how's work going?'

'OK. We've got Eva's leaving do on Thursday, and we're all going to miss her horribly.' She stroked his face. 'You?'

'We're closing the deal on the next resort,' he said. 'It's a former manor house in the Cotswolds, and we're going to run some specialist cookery courses.'

'Sounds good,' she said. 'And I guess you can showcase local foods to go with it.'

'And we always feature work by local artists, which we sell without taking commission,' he said. 'That way we help the local economy, too.'

And somehow they ended up talking business and bouncing ideas off each other.

'So much for "no interference",' he said wryly.

She smiled. 'Maybe we need to renegotiate that bit. Brainstorming with someone who isn't quite as involved as you are is really useful.'

'So when are you launching the Weddings Abroad service?'

'After Christmas,' she said. 'I've got slots booked at a few wedding fairs, and I'm working on pieces for wedding magazines and websites.'

'Let me know if you need to borrow any staff.'

'Thanks. I will.' She stole a kiss. 'And I'd better go. Good luck with the counselling tomorrow. Call me if you need to talk.'

'Thanks.' He stroked her face.

'And I'll see you on Wednesday.'

'I'll pick you up at seven—although I'm not actually eating with Sienna, I can still be with her when she has her dinner,' he said. 'And I think she'll be pleased that I'm going out somewhere with you.'

'Sienna *and* her bear,' Sophie said with a smile.

Jamie could barely concentrate all day on Wednesday. He'd managed to book a quiet table for two in a really romantic restaurant in Covent Garden; and when he called for Sophie at seven, he did a double-take.

He'd first met the efficient businesswoman in her navy suit. Then he'd seen the softer side of Sophie, wearing jeans and a sweater and happy to do messy things with a child or take her to the park. And now he was seeing another side of her, in a little black dress and high heels with her hair in a sophisticated updo and red lipstick that he itched to kiss off her.

'You look stunning,' he said.

She inclined her head. 'Thank you. You don't scrub up too badly yourself.'

He held her hand all the way there in the back of the taxi. They walked hand in hand around the marketplace and enjoyed the Christmas lights and decorations.

'We have to bring Sienna here,' Sophie said, 'to see this reindeer—she'll love it.'

And Jamie loved the fact that Sophie thought of his daughter, even though they were out on a date.

The restaurant was full of fairy lights, and he could see how much she liked the ambience. He did, too.

'It's my first date in a long time,' she said.

'Me, too,' he said. 'In fact, it's my first "first" date in more than a decade.'

'So what was your first date like with Fran?' she asked.

And he really appreciated the fact that Sophie didn't shy away from talking about his late wife. 'Typical student thing. We went to see this super-arty play. I don't think either of us worked out what was meant to be happening. And then this door on stage got stuck and the whole thing fell apart.' He smiled at the memory. 'We felt a bit guilty, but we sneaked out in the interval and went for a drink instead.'

'Sounds like fun. And I know the kind of play you mean.' She smiled. 'I've seen a few of those in my time, too.'

'I think I prefer the more commercial stuff,' he said.

'As a former English student, I ought to say I like the arty, impenetrable stuff best,' she said. 'But I agree with you. I like something with characters I can root for.'

'Maybe,' he said, 'we could go to the theatre.'

'I'd like that,' she said. 'But, as it's Christmas, I'd vote for the panto. With Sienna. And popcorn.'

'That sounds good, too.'

She reached over to squeeze his hand. 'You don't have to answer, but how did the counselling go yesterday?'

'It's early days,' he said. 'But I like the guy, he's easy to talk to, and he's given me a ton of homework to do before next week.'

'That sounds positive,' she said.

He nodded. 'It's not going to be an instant fix, but I want it to work so I'm going to put the effort in.' For her sake and Sienna's, as well as his own.

The rest of the evening went incredibly quickly, and Jamie was shocked by how late it was when he glanced at his watch. 'Sorry. That was really selfish of me, considering it's midweek and it's Eva's last day tomorrow.'

'It's fine,' Sophie said with a smile. 'I've really enjoyed tonight.'

And he really enjoyed taking her home and kissing her goodnight on the doorstep.

'Can you sneak off for a couple of hours on Friday lunchtime?' he asked. 'It's the nursery school concert and I know Sienna would love you to be there. Especially as you made her angel costume.'

'Did you ask the grannies?' she asked.

'Strictly speaking, we're only supposed to have two tickets per child for the concert,' he said. 'But I talked the nursery school manager into letting me have three extra tickets, in the circumstances.'

'The grannies and Cindy?' she asked.

'Absolutely.'

'Good. OK. I'll meet you there,' she said, and gave

him a lingering kiss. 'Goodnight, Jamie. And thank you for tonight.'

He waited for her to go indoors and close the door, then headed for the tube.

And his heart felt lighter than it had in years.

On Friday, Jamie waited in the nursery school reception area with Cindy and the grannies. As he expected, Sophie turned up dead on time. She kissed him warmly, hugged Cindy, and then turned to the grannies. 'Gwen and Rose. It's so lovely to meet you properly.'

'And you,' Rose said, hugging her. 'My niece Eva has told me so much about you, I feel I already know you.'

'Jamie tells me nothing,' Gwen said, 'but Sienna's said a lot.' She smiled, and hugged Sophie too.

No inquisition from my mother? Jamie thought, surprised. But it was a relief, too.

They found their seats and Jamie laced his fingers through Sophie's.

And the concert was magical.

Last year, he would've been wincing at the out of tune singing; this year, he found it charming. And, best of all, his little girl was standing on the stage in a white dress, with huge lacy angel wings trimmed in marabou and a headband with a marabou halo. Teamed with her golden curls, the effect was enough to make him have to blink back the tears.

Though he noticed there wasn't a dry eye in the house after 'Away in a Manger' and then 'Twinkle Twinkle'.

Christmas.

And this year was going to be a really, really special one.

After Sophie had gone back to work, Jamie's mother took him to one side. 'I'm not going to interfere,' she said.

He gave her an arch look. His mother was the epitome of interference.

She noticed, and flapped a hand dismissively. 'I know I've steamrollered you in the past, but I've learned from Sophie that there's a better way of managing you. I just wanted to make sure you know she's a keeper.'

He nodded. 'I know.'

'Good. Then I'll leave you to do something about it.'

Given that he knew Sienna had video calls with both of her grandmothers, he asked, 'I take it Sienna's told you what she wants?'

'She has,' Gwen agreed. 'And Rose and I think that child is wise beyond her years.'

'She is,' Rose said, coming over to them and clearly overhearing the last bit. 'Jamie, you're still a young man. Fran would understand. You're not replacing her—you're opening your life to someone new.'

'Because love doesn't just fit in a box. It grows,' he said.

The grannies looked at each other. 'He's learning,' Gwen said in a stage whisper.

Over the next few days, Jamie found his life changing even more. Somehow he'd agreed to spend Christmas Day with Sophie's parents, Boxing Day with his and New Year's Eve with Fran's.

And Sophie was as warm and sweet when she went out with him and Sienna on a family day as she was when it was just the two of them. Having her back in his life made him realise how much the last two years had been lived in shadows and monochrome. With Sophie, he had the sunshine back and full colour. And it felt *right*.

He thought again about Sienna's request. I want Sophie to be my mummy.

He wanted Sophie, too.

But he needed to show her how special she was to them. How it wasn't going to be like her last two relationships, because this one was for keeps.

In the end, he hatched a plan with Sienna, and invited Sophie over for dinner on Christmas Eve. He made a tagine that could simmer happily without needing any attention; it would take only minutes to steam some green vegetables and cook some couscous. And then he and Sienna spent the afternoon making special shortbread biscuits in the shape of Christmas trees, iced them with melted chocolate, and used sparkly pink sprinkles to spell out each letter of their message.

He just hoped he was doing the right thing.

In every business deal he'd done in the last ten years, he'd known exactly what he was doing. This was fraught with unknowns.

He just had to trust to the wisdom of Santa and the black and white bear.

'Merry Christmas,' Sophie said when Jamie opened the door to her.

'Merry Christmas.'

'I brought special Christmas chocolates,' she said, handing them to Sienna. 'Reindeers.'

'They're so pretty!' Sienna exclaimed.

Jamie kissed her. 'Come and sit down.'

But when she tried to walk into the kitchen, Jamie

ushered her into the dining room instead. 'The kitchen's out of bounds.'

'Because it's a secret,' Sienna said importantly.

Sienna suppressed a grin. Clearly the little girl had helped make dessert and wanted it to be all fanfares and excitement. 'OK.'

Jamie had laid the table in the dining room for the three of them, including crackers, and he'd poured sparkling apple juice for Sienna as well as champagne for Sophie and himself.

'That was fantastic,' Sophie said when she'd finished her tagine. 'I'll help you clear away.'

'No. You have to stay put,' he said.

'If you're sure.' She grinned. 'You make a beautiful waiter, and that little smear of sparkles on the end of your nose is the perfect touch.'

He stared at her, looking shocked. 'I've got sparkles on my face?'

Sienna giggled. 'Pink ones, Daddy. They've been there all afternoon.'

He groaned. 'Sienna, you could've told me.'

'But you always say I look cute with flour on my face,' she pointed out.

'And I think *you* look cute with sparkles on your face,' Sophie added with a grin.

He spread his hands. 'I give in. The sparkles can stay.'

It was a lovely warm family moment that made Sophie want the rest of her days to be like that. But maybe she was being greedy.

Once he'd cleared the table, he returned to announce, 'We have a very special pudding.'

Sienna looked anxious. 'What if we drop it, Daddy?'

'Do you think Sophie should come into the kitchen to see it, instead?' he asked.

She nodded.

'OK. But we don't want to spoil the surprise—Sophie, you have to close your eyes.'

'Don't worry. We'll hold your hand so you won't bump into anything,' Sienna promised.

How could she resist? Sophie closed her eyes and let them take her hands and lead her into the kitchen.

'Stand still and keep your eyes closed,' he said.

She could hear rustling, then a dismayed, 'Daddy, I smudged that one!'

'It's fine, she won't mind,' Jamie reassured Sienna.

'Ta-da!' Sienna said. 'You can open your eyes now.'

She did. And what she saw on the kitchen table was a row of Christmas-tree shaped biscuits, each with a letter made out of sparkly pink sprinkles.

And together they spelled out 'WILL YOU MARRY US?' The 'W' was smudged, as Sienna had said, but it didn't matter. The words blurred as Sophie's eyes filled with tears.

'Sophie?' Jamie asked. 'Are you all right?'

She swallowed hard. 'Yes, just a bit overwhelmed.'

'Will you marry me and make a family with us?' He dropped to one knee. 'The ring's temporary, because if you say yes I thought we could choose the ring together as a family. But for now...' He offered her a small cardboard box that looked as if it was home-made.

She opened it to discover a gold tinsel pipecleaner twisted into the shape of a ring, and felt a single tear spill over her lashes.

'You're crying!' Sienna looked horrified.

'They're happy tears,' Sophie explained, 'not sad ones. Yes, I'll marry you.'

Jamie slid the ring onto the ring finger of her left hand. 'Sorry, it's a little bit too big.'

'We can tweak it.' She twisted it slightly. 'See? Now it's the perfect fit.'

She dropped to her own knees so she was at the same height as Sienna, hugged the little girl and then kissed Jamie.

'So Santa brought me what I really wanted for Christmas after all, even though he said he only gives things you can wrap up,' Sienna said, beaming. 'I knew he would.'

'He brought me what I wanted, too,' Jamie said.

'And me,' Sophie said softly. 'It's going to be a happy, happy Christmas.'

EPILOGUE

Four months later

'I CAN'T BELIEVE that this is Plans & Planes' first wedding abroad—and it's yours!' Eva said, making a last adjustment to Sophie's veil.

'It made sense for our wedding to be the first,' Sophie said with a smile. 'Besides, Iceland's the only place where we're guaranteed a real rainbow in our wedding pictures.'

'And trust you to want a waterfall and rainbows in the background of your wedding pictures,' Eva said, laughing.

'I wanted to have a wedding with a difference,' Sophie said.

'And how.'

There was a knock on the door, and Mandy came in with the two youngest bridesmaids. 'We're done with the hair,' she said with a smile.

'And you two look very beautiful indeed,' Sophie said. Sienna and Hattie were wearing simple white dresses with a ballerina-length tulle skirt and red T-bar shoes. The girls each had a flower crown of red roses, which looked as good in Hattie's straight dark hair as it did in Sienna's mop of blonde curls.

'The rest of the flowers are waiting for you downstairs. A basket of red roses each for the girls, Eva's bouquet of cream roses, and your bouquet of red roses, Sophie,' Mandy said.

'Wonderful. And the corsages and buttonholes?' Sophie asked.

'They're all there, too.' Mandy smiled. 'What with you being a wedding planner and this being your trial run for the new service, everything's running like clockwork.'

'I sorted out all the paperwork early on, talked to the district commissioner and the pastor, and once that's done all the rest is simple. And if there's a brief hitch in the clockwork for any reason,' Sophie said, 'there are back-ups in place.'

'I have the briefcase with all the master plans,' Eva said.

'Which I'll take care of during the service and photographs,' Mandy promised. 'Matt and Angie are keeping an eye on Sam for me, so I can do anything you need me to.'

'Thanks. And I've primed Mum and Gwen to hang onto the capes for the four of us, just in case it gets chilly—even though it's late April,' Sophie said.

'Now, I've made sure Jamie isn't anywhere around to see you before the wedding,' Mandy said. 'I sent him to walk off to the church with Will.' Jamie had asked Sophie's oldest brother to be his best man. 'They're going to text me when they get there.' Her phone beeped and she glanced at the screen. 'And that was your dad to say that the wedding cars will be here in ten minutes.'

'Perfect,' Sophie said. 'And even the weather's being kind to us.' The sun was shining and, because the windows in the hotel were all floor-to-ceiling, the rooms were flooded with light.

'It's going to be a perfect day,' Sienna said. 'The day you marry my daddy and you become my mummy.'

Sophie had to blink back a tear. 'Absolutely, darling.'

Ten minutes later, the three bridesmaids and Sophie's mum were settled in one car, and Sophie went with her father in the other car. It was only a short drive to the church: a beautiful white wooden building with a square tower, a red roof and spire. There were arched windows on the side of the church and the tower, and the square red entrance door had a rose window above it and narrow rectangular windows beside it. From one side, the church was set against the rich green backdrop of the mountainside, counterpointed with the last snow of late spring; on the other, it was set against the rich turquoise of the sea and the dramatic basalt rocks.

'Ready?' Sophie's dad asked.

She nodded.

'For what it's worth, you've definitely picked the right one this time,' he said. 'We all like Jamie very much. And, most importantly, I think he'll make you happy.'

Sophie hugged her father. 'Thanks, Dad.'

The photographer took shots of them in the car and getting out, then in front of the church with the three bridesmaids.

And then it was time to walk down the aisle to Jamie, with the organist playing Bach's 'Jesu, Joy of Man's Desiring'.

Inside, the tiny church was full to bursting with their family and closest friends, crowded into the light wood pews. Everyone was smiling as she walked down the aisle on her father's arm, with Sienna and Hattie behind her and Eva bringing up the rear—but the smile she was focused on was Jamie's, and the way he mouthed 'I love you' as soon as Will had clearly nudged him to let him know that Sophie was walking towards him.

From this day forward...

Sophie took his breath away.

Jamie smiled as his bride walked towards him. Typically Sophie, she'd mixed traditional with a few quirks. She was wearing a simple white dress with an ankle-length tulle skirt, and high heeled red shoes to match the simple bouquet of red roses she carried. Eva's dress was similar but in red, and his daughter and Hattie both looked adorable carrying baskets of roses.

As she reached him at the altar, she mouthed, 'I love you, too.'

The ceremony was as simple and plain as the little church, full of light and love. And when the pastor finally pronounced them married and told Jamie he may kiss the bride, Jamie thoroughly enjoyed flipping Sophie's veil back and kissing her thoroughly.

The organist played Pachelbel's 'Canon' as they signed the register, then switched to Mendelssohn's 'Bridal March' as they walked back down the aisle.

'Well, Mrs Wallis. It's all official now,' Jamie whispered.

She smiled. 'It certainly is.'

The photographer took some group shots outside the church, and then most of the wedding party headed back to the hotel, while Jamie, Sophie, the bridesmaids and Mandy headed out to the Skógafoss waterfall for the final set of photographs.

On the way, it started to rain.

'Don't tell me—your contingency plans involve

umbrellas that just happen to match your bouquet?' Jamie teased.

'Funny you should say that,' Sophie teased back. 'Though the saying goes, if you don't like the weather in Iceland, you wait five minutes.'

And, just as they reached the waterfall, the sun came out.

'Perfect timing,' Jamie said.

When the wedding cars had parked, Sophie and Eva both swapped their high heels for flat red pumps so it would be easier to manage the rocky terrain.

'Look, Hattie—there are two rainbows!' Sienna said as they neared the waterfall, and gasped in amazement.

The photographer took the group photographs first, before the little girls got cold enough to need the capes Mandy had brought along. And then the bridesmaids and Mandy headed back to the hotel, leaving the new bride and groom to have the final shots taken.

'This is perfect,' Jamie said, and stole a kiss. 'You look incredible. And with that rainbow... I want one of you on your own, with the waterfall and rainbow behind you, so I can have a framed photo of you on my desk.'

'Great idea. I want one of you, too,' Sophie said.

They were careful not to get so close to the waterfall that Sophie's dress would be soaked by the spray, but the photographer took plenty of shots of her laughing and with her veil blown by the wind as well as more formal poses.

'That's perfect,' the photographer said after a final shot of them together. 'I'll have a file ready for viewing by the time you've eaten, and then I'll come back to do the photographs of the cake-cutting.'

'Thank you,' Jamie said, and shook his hand.

Back at the hotel, everyone was sitting around and talking when they walked in, and a cheer went up.

'I know, I know—you're all starving and we kept you waiting,' Jamie teased. 'But I promise the photographs will be worth it. We got our rainbows.'

He and Sophie stood by the doors to the banqueting suite and welcomed everyone and thanked them for making the trip to Iceland.

'Thank you so much for inviting us,' Rose said when she reached the head of the receiving line. 'I mean, we're not really family...'

'Oh, yes, you are,' Sophie said instantly. 'You're Sienna's grandparents, and that makes you my family.' She hugged the older woman. 'I'm not trying to replace Fran, but I hope you'll come to think of me as family, too.'

Once they'd eaten, Sophie's dad made the first speech. 'Thank you for coming, everyone. The wedding planner told me to keep this very short, and she's a stickler for time management, so short it is.'

Everyone laughed, knowing exactly who the wedding planner was.

'I'm thrilled everyone could make it here to Iceland,' he continued. 'Including my twin grandchildren-to-be.'

Everyone looked at Angie, who simply glowed and patted her bump. 'Thanks to Sophie,' she said.

'I'm hugely proud of my daughter Sophie,' he said. 'She's one of the kindest people I know. And she's going to make an amazing stepmum for my new granddaughter Sienna. I'd like to welcome Jamie and Sienna to the family, and I'd ask you all to raise your glasses to the new Mr and Mrs Wallis. The bride and groom.'

'The bride and groom,' everyone echoed, and clapped as Sophie's father sat down again.

'I too am on a warning from the wedding planner about talking too much,' Jamie said, making everyone laugh. 'I'd like to thank Barney and Jane for welcoming Sienna and me so warmly,' Jamie said. 'And to my parents and Fran's for taking Sophie to their hearts as much as Sienna and I have. I'm thrilled to have married the most gorgeous woman in the world, I'm glad you're all here to share our special day, and I'd like to say a special thank you to Will for being my best man, and to Eva, Sienna and Hattie for being such fabulous bridesmaids. Please raise your glasses to the best man and the bridesmaids—Will, Eva, Sienna and Hattie.'

'Will, Eva, Sienna and Hattie,' everyone chorused.

'I honestly don't know why everyone's so scared of the wedding planner,' Sophie said with a grin. 'All I said was don't rattle on because we want to have cake and dancing. But I'd like to thank everyone for sharing today with us, especially because it meant travelling all this way. And to Aidan's boss for headhunting him—without that, I might never have met Jamie properly.' She smiled. 'And a special thank you to my lovely bridesmaids, all our parents—and I'm including you in that, Rose and Geoffrey—and to Jamie, who let me tear up his ridiculous rule book.'

Everyone laughed, and then Will stood up. 'I'm not scared of the wedding planner at all.' He spread his hands. 'I have video evidence of her singing nursery rhymes to her teddies, seriously out of key, and I'm not afraid to use it.'

'Bring it on,' Sophie called, laughing.

'And because I'm not scared of the wedding planner, we're going to break her timetable and break tradition. Instead of the best man making the speech, it's going to be the youngest bridesmaid.' Will went over to Sienna and lifted her onto her chair, standing by her so she could keep her balance.

'I'm not scared of the wedding planner,' Sienna said. 'Because she's my mummy now and I love her.'

There were audible gulps, and several people had to reach for tissues.

'And me and my best friend Hattie have really pretty dresses,' Sienna continued, undeterred. 'And we saw two rainbows *this* big by the waterfall!' She stretched her arms out wide.

Will whispered in her ear, and she said, 'Oops. Thank you, everyone, for coming. Sophie makes my daddy and me smile again, and I'm glad she's my mummy now. That's all.'

Everyone cheered.

'Well done, kiddo,' Will said, hugging her, then set Sienna back on the floor.

'That's it for the speeches,' Jamie said. 'Cake and dancing, as promised.'

'But because we're getting married in Iceland,' Sophie said, 'we wanted to take one of the Icelandic traditions—the *kransekaka*—so the cake-cutting is going to be a little bit different. How it works is that we cut the first piece, then all the guests come up and break off a piece to eat and make a wish for us.'

She and Jamie posed with a knife in the tiered rings of the conical-shaped cake while the photographer took a few shots, then actually cut the first piece. And everyone came up to break off a piece of cake and wish them every happiness for the future.

Once the cake was done, the singer of the band—who'd been playing quiet guitar and piano music throughout the wedding breakfast—came to the front of the stage. 'We're Ástrós, and my name's Astrid,' she said. 'We'd like to invite the bride and groom to the floor for the first dance. And we also have guest vocalists—don't we, girls?'

Sienna and Hattie, holding hands, skipped over to the stage.

Jamie looked at Sophie. 'Did you know about this?'

She shook her head. 'Did you?'

He shook his head.

'Mandy,' they said together.

The guitarist played the introduction, and then the girls launched into a slightly off-key version of 'Somewhere Over the Rainbow'. They were a little quiet to start with, and forgot some of the words, but Astrid helped them out and their voices grew stronger and stronger.

'This is the perfect start to our married life,' Jamie said, holding Sophie close and swaying to the music with her.

'A long and happy life,' Sophie said.

'Filled,' Jamie added, 'with rainbows.'

* * * * *

LET'S TALK
Romance

For exclusive extracts, competitions
and special offers, find us online:

 facebook.com/millsandboon

 @MillsandBoon

 @MillsandBoonUK

Get in touch on 01413 063232

For all the latest titles coming soon, visit
millsandboon.co.uk/nextmonth

MILLS & BOON

THE HEART OF ROMANCE

A ROMANCE FOR EVERY READER

MODERN

Prepare to be swept off your feet by sophisticated, sexy and seductive heroes, in some of the world's most glamourous and romantic locations, where power and passion collide.

HISTORICAL

Escape with historical heroes from time gone by. Whether your passion is for wicked Regency Rakes, muscled Vikings or rugged Highlanders, awaken the romance of the past.

MEDICAL

Set your pulse racing with dedicated, delectable doctors in the high-pressure world of medicine, where emotions run high and passion, comfort and love are the best medicine.

True Love

Celebrate true love with tender stories of heartfelt romance, from the rush of falling in love to the joy a new baby can bring, and a focus on the emotional heart of a relationship.

Desire

Indulge in secrets and scandal, intense drama and plenty of sizzling hot action with powerful and passionate heroes who have it all: wealth, status, good looks…everything but the right woman.

HEROES

Experience all the excitement of a gripping thriller, with an intense romance at its heart. Resourceful, true-to-life women and strong, fearless men face danger and desire - a killer combination!

To see which titles are coming soon, please visit

millsandboon.co.uk/nextmonth

JOIN US ON SOCIAL MEDIA!

Stay up to date with our latest releases, author news and gossip, special offers and discounts, and all the behind-the-scenes action from Mills & Boon...

 @millsandboon

 @millsandboonuk

 facebook.com/millsandboon

 @millsandboonuk

It might just be true love...

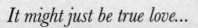

GET YOUR ROMANCE FIX!

Get the latest romance news, exclusive author interviews, story extracts and much more!

blog.millsandboon.co.uk

MILLS & BOON

MODERN

Power and Passion

Prepare to be swept off your feet by sophisticated, sexy and seductive heroes, in some of the world's most glamourous and romantic locations, where power and passion collide.

MILLS & BOON
True Love
Romance from the Heart

Celebrate true love with tender stories of heartfelt romance, from the rush of falling in love to the joy a new baby can bring, and a focus on the emotional heart of a relationship.

MILLS & BOON
MEDICAL
Pulse-Racing Passion

Set your pulse racing with dedicated, delectable doctors in the high-pressure world of medicine, where emotions run high and passion, comfort and love are the best medicine.

Eight Medical stories published every month, find them all

millsandboon.co.uk